2

W9-BMN-378

The
COWBOY
AND THE
Vampire

Clark Hays
Kathleen McFall

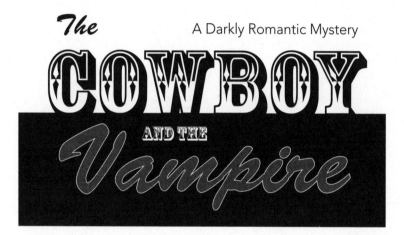

A Darkly Romantic Mystery

MIDNIGHT INK
WOODBURY, MINNESOTA

Second Edition
First Printing, 2010

First Edition of *The Cowboy and the Vampire* by Clark Hays and Kathleen McFall, published 1999, ISBN: 1-56718-451-0, 1 printing.

Book design and format by Donna Burch
Cover design by Kevin R. Brown
Cover art: © iStockphoto.com / Larysa Dodz, photo retouching by John Blumen
Editing by Connie Hill

Midnight Ink, an imprint of Llewellyn Worldwide Ltd.

Library of Congress Cataloging-in-Publication Data

Hays, Clark, 1966–
  The cowboy and the vampire : a darkly romantic mystery / by Clark Hays and Kathleen McFall. — 1st ed.
    p.   cm.
  ISBN 978-0-7387-2161-3
  1. Vampires—Fiction. I. McFall, Kathleen, 1960–   II. Title.
  PS3558.A864C69   2010
  813'.54—dc22   2010016094

Midnight Ink
A Division of Llewellyn Worldwide Ltd.
2143 Wooddale Drive
Woodbury, MN 55125-2989
www.midnightinkbooks.com

Printed in the United States of America

To Stephanie
for your unbounded enthusiasm,
and
to Rex,
a very good dog

THE CHARACTERS

TUCKER: A hard-luck cowboy from Wyoming whose love for Lizzie Vaughan draws him into a web of Vampiric intrigue. Never one to back down from a challenge, he's willing to see it through, even if that means going to New York City.

LIZZIE: Hot-shot reporter, unwilling Queen of the Vampires, and host to the ancient Vampiric legacy of the uncreation. An unsuspecting carrier of an extraordinary collection of Vampire genes leading back to Biblical times. Is she capable of living this destiny? Or will she be the manipulated pawn of a new Vampiric line?

JULIUS: Leader of one faction of Vampires and a shrewd strategist in the war between good and evil. Suave and debonair, he covets the power carried by Lizzie's blood and will do anything to make it his own. The uncreation is to be his destiny, and nothing will prevent him from achieving this vision.

ELITA: Julius' right-hand woman and lover. A beautiful, powerful, and ancient Vampire descended from Eden's serpent. She has the power to sexually attract any human, and she uses the power brilliantly. Lizzie's noble lineage, however, makes Elita seethe with jealousy, as does the love between Lizzie and Tucker.

LAZARUS: The only Vampire powerful enough to challenge Julius. Deeply reflective, he lives with his followers in isolation in New Mexico, a climate he remembers fondly from the Biblical days of his life before being resurrected from death. He has become flabby of late, overly fond of HoHos and reading the tabloids. But he is never one to be underestimated, a fact that Julius keeps in the forefront of his mind. Lazarus is determined to protect Lizzie and, through her, to safeguard the balance of good and evil.

DAD: Tucker's father and the voice of reason as events begin to take on supernatural aspects. He may regret ever leaving the ranch, but someone has to look out for his boy.

LENNY: Sole member of the LonePine militia and eccentric weapons specialist. He's been Tucker's friend for years. He's willing to help, even though he thinks Tucker has gone a bit nuts. Vampires? Who's Tuck trying to fool?

REX: Tucker's sensitive and loyal dog. From his perspective, Vampires smell bad, but seem to be good sandwich makers.

A secondary cast features Tucker's much-maligned horse SNORT, Lizzie's doomed cat FELIX, a host of evil Vampiric consorts, a doctor who once practiced with Hippocrates, servants who aren't what they seem, old lovers, alcoholic cowboys, cheerleaders, staff writers, and trespassing alpacas in cowboy country.

THE SETTINGS

LONEPINE, WYOMING: Bastion of the old West and site of Tucker's ranch: two hundred acres of prime Wyoming grassland on which there is one tree, some rocks, a water tank, and a single-wide trailer. It's a small town with typical small-town problems — like what to do besides drink beer and wonder about who's cheating on whom at the Sleep-O-Rama Motel.

MANHATTAN, NEW YORK CITY: Center of the American Vampire contingent and Lizzie's home. There are a million things to do in New York. Her current diversion is hiding from the undead in old churches, and looking for sources of blood without actually having to kill anyone.

THE LAZARUS COMPLEX, NEW MEXICO: Hidden in an ancient valley deep in the remote hills of New Mexico, Lazarus maintains a desert fortress bristling with high-tech weapons. He hopes it will be enough to protect Lizzie from Julius when he comes for her. As the Vampiric world moves toward civil war, one thing is certain: the very future of humanity depends on the strength of this lonely desert outpost.

PART ONE:
DEATH

"I CANNOT BELIEVE ONE person is worth this much trouble." She leaned forward and tapped her clove cigarette into the ashtray. Julius patted the back of her hand. The scented smoke irritated his sinuses, as she was well aware, but he smiled frigidly through the haze of it and through her pettiness.

"Elita, my dear, jealousy is so unbecoming."

"Julius, I have known you a great number of years, too many perhaps." He maintained his smile but it failed to reach his eyes. "And you know," she continued, "I have nothing but respect for your judgment." She paused long enough to measure the effects of her remarks, but no change was visible on his pale countenance. She shrugged her shoulders, a delicate motion. "Why not simply take her and be done with it? Why make such a fuss out of it?"

"Fuss? You have adapted well to the clichéd words of this era, my dear." His expression abruptly changed and, smooth as the velvet texture of his words, he leaned forward, drawing her close with a fierce stare. His voice reverberated with buried passion. "I wonder, Elita, how you can question me at all. You, of all people, should fathom the importance of blood. In her veins run two thousand years of royalty. The first family. And with it, the power of the uncreation. Our people will have their due, and I shall be the one who gives it to them. We will honor the past by seizing the future." He leaned back into his chair and luxuriantly sipped a cognac.

"This," he waved futilely, setting the cognac quietly on the table, "this centuries-old diaspora will end. The Adamites have had their chance. We have let them play their little games and live their little lives in the sun. We have hidden away from them as if they were to be feared." He paused, savoring the taste of his own words.

His voice dropped to a low, soft growl, a mesmerizing tone. "That is about to change. I caution you, lovely Elita, it would serve you to be on the winning side. I would miss you," he added, "should you take it upon yourself to make some misguided effort to turn back this tide."

He stopped her hand in midair as she moved her cigarette toward her lips. "My dear, I have seen the future and the future is Lizzie Vaughan. Are we clear on this?"

She nodded sullenly and stood. As she did, every man in the bar stopped to study her: the pale skin, the silky black hair falling to her shoulders, the cling of the dress to her narrow hips, the erotic strength flowing from her. Women turned too. Elita, aware of the eyes but heedless, ran her fingers through her hair, arranging it behind her ears to reveal her slender throat. Bending toward the table, she stubbed out her cigarette and brushed at imaginary lines in her dress as she straightened.

"Oh yes, we are clear. Far be it from me to stand in the way of your machinations. As if I could. Elizabeth Vaughan. What a tedious name. Now, if you'll excuse me."

He tilted his head in agreement, his dark lips forming a dismissive but appreciative smile. Elita turned and walked toward the door. Pausing by the bar, she laid her hand on the shoulder of a young man sitting alone. Leaning close to him, her lips brushing against his hair, she whispered in his ear. He nodded vigorously, gulped at his beer and slammed the glass down. Quickly he stood, marveling at this turn of extraordinary luck. With eyes mocking her young victim's adoration, she gently twined her arm around his waist. Smiling triumphantly over her shoulder at Julius, Elita disappeared into the night, hips swaying, her conquest in obedient tow.

ONE

Me, I like the sunrise. There ain't nothing on this earth that compares to seeing that first glow lighting up the sky, touching everything with golden fingers and dripping copper-red honey down the jagged slopes of the Teton Mountains into the timberline below. Sitting out on the porch with a steaming cup of coffee scorching my fingers through the enamel and Rex curled up tight at my feet, life seems close to perfect. There's a quietness in the air that always makes me think today is the day to make things right. No matter how hopeless it might have seemed when I bedded down the night before, morning always comes and with it the familiar sense that maybe I can fix an old mistake or two, lay a claim on a parcel of the future.

'Course, oftentimes the sunrise comes way too early and I keep my eyes screwed shut against it, wishing I could sleep right through, especially when the remnants of last night's whiskey are percolating around my bloodstream. Still, I can honestly say that I've seen more sunrises than I ain't, which is more than most folks can claim.

This morning, however, I wouldn't argue with folks calling me loco for being such an early riser. The high-beam lights from my truck was half-blinding me as I tried to herd my neighbor's funny-looking goats back through the hole in the fence, cussing and throwing rocks at them in hopes of getting them off my property. The fence wires have a mysterious habit of cutting themselves right next to my water tank, and them goats, known to some as alpacas, mistakenly think it's okay to come traipsing through to drink.

The first couple dozen times those damn alpacas trespassed, Rex rounded them up and sent them skittering home like the champion cow dog he is. Eventually, those goats took to spitting on him and so damaged his pride that he now refuses to even get out of the truck when they're around. Cow dogs are touchy about that sort of thing. This morning, he was sitting in the driver's side looking nonchalantly the other way like he was dreaming of a better place, the kind of place where dogs don't get spit on by goats.

All God's creatures must have a purpose and I suspect that holds true for alpacas, but I just can't tell what that might be. Best I can figure, their purpose in life is to act haughty and spit on whatever they can't shit on. But from my point of view, all that really matters is that they ain't cows, and cows was all that was intended to be raised out here. That's why Wyoming is called the Cowboy State and not the Alpacaboy State. Times are changing and you got to go where the money is, but the day Wyoming becomes known for its overpriced goats, well, that's the day I pack my bags.

After finally chasing them goats off, I set about splicing the wires together with numb fingers. Ever since George Harlan moved here from back East, it seemed I'd gotten pretty handy at fixing this particular stretch of fence. A hundred years ago, this sort of activity would have gotten Harlan shot. 'Course, a hundred years ago there wasn't alpacas in these parts, or big city folks looking to get away from it all. Back then, Wyoming was so far away they had to pay people to come here. Now we got movie stars strutting around with purple cowboy hats and pointy silver boots trying to blend in with the locals.

Cursing under my breath, I stapled the wire into the posts and threw the wire stretchers in the back of the truck, scooting Rex over from the driver's seat. I gave one last glare at them goats lined up at the fence glaring back at me. "For Chrissakes, Rex, this is your ranch too," I said and poured a cup of coffee out of the thermos. It was so bitter I nearly choked, and tossed it, steaming, onto the frosty ground. Rex ignored me all the way back to the trailer.

I stomped inside, pulling off my boots and tossing them in the corner, along with my coat. Rex slunk in and jumped up on the couch, curling up with a sigh. I hadn't had nothing to eat since the last time I ate, so was mighty disappointed to find the fridge woefully empty. Rex was still pretending to ignore me, but watched out of the corner of his eye as I pulled my boots back on. "I ain't gonna apologize," I said, "but you're more'n welcome to ride into town with me for breakfast." He jumped up and scrabbled past me on the linoleum, nosing the trailer door open. By the time I stepped outside into the struggling sunshine, Rex had already loaded up through the driver's window which I always leave open for him 'cept when it's miserably cold. He was setting behind the wheel yawning and wagging his little stump of a tail and I reminded him for the umpteenth time that I was driving and to scoot the hell over, which he did reluctantly.

We set out, rattling down the ruts that serve as my front drive, bumping our way over two hundred acres of prime Wyoming grassland. When I say grassland, I mean just that: land with grass on it. Perfect for grazing though, and for decoration there's a beautiful tree and some lovely rocks down in one corner right next to my galvanized steel water tank. That same well supplies the water to my single-wide trailer that makes up in charm what it lacks in size. One of these years I plan on building me and Rex a little cabin, or at least adding on to the trailer, but that sort of stuff is a long ways off. Right now, I'm just happy that me and the bank own such a lovely piece of property.

Holding the wheel steady with my knee, I turned out onto the highway and put a chew in. Along the way, I met a bunch of folks I knew well enough to swerve across the center asphalt line like I was going to hit them and then they'd throw their arms up as if to cover their faces from the coming accident. All in all, it was big fun on Highway 14 at seven in the morning, which says a lot about the entertainment prospects of living in LonePine.

LonePine, Wyoming, has a steady population of 438 people, except on the Fourth of July Rodeo and Outdoor Barbecue when folks come from as far away as the next county. Suddenly, there'll be several thousand people standing around in the sun, drinking beer and waiting until it's dark enough to go inside and drink beer. Not counting dirt roads, Highway 14 is the one major thorough-fare in LonePine connecting it to other, more exotic places like West Yellowstone, Montana, and Salt Lake City, Utah. Cruising the main strip takes a grand total of three minutes. There's a bank, a pharmacy, a dress store, and a post office on one side. On the other side is a Manny's Dollar Store, which doubles as the mall, a video store, and the Sagebrush Cafe. Most important to the local folk, 'cause they figure so largely in LonePine's social pursuits, are the Silver Dollar and The Watering Hole. These two bars are famous for near a hundred miles around and even this early in the day there were several trucks parked out front. If I happened to drive by around midnight, they'd still be there.

Conveniently located behind the Silver Dollar is the Sleep-O-Rama Motel, where most of LonePine's public affairs are tended to. LonePine was one of the first towns in Wyoming to institute a recycling program, only it wasn't for empty pop cans and such, it was more in the area of personal relationships. Due to the limited number of available mates, folks round here took to using other people's. Under this system, one man's wife might be another's girlfriend and one woman's husband might be another's boyfriend. For the sake of fairness, those who participate in this program switch off partners every couple of months or so and thereby prevent any sort of jealous altercations from developing. The system is not foolproof, however, and many a heated discussion has erupted in the parking lot behind the Sleep-O-Rama centered around just how married a given individual may be. It's usually resolved, after many beers, in a repledging of love at one of the two saloons. All in all, LonePine is just like any other sleepy, one-horse town in the wild, wild, dying West.

Although I was hungry for breakfast, I pulled into the post office first to check my mail that had been piling up for near a week. Before I even had a chance to open my box, Melissa Braver walked in and started talking at me. Owing to the generous nature of her natural assets and her willingness to display them to her fullest advantage, she was somewhat of a destination resort around these parts. Melissa and me had stepped out a few times back in the days, but lived through it and even remained friends against the odds.

"Tucker, where you been?" she asked. "I haven't seen you around."

"Been up on Widow Woman Creek trying to patch up the north end." I checked my box. "Bills, bills, overdue bills," I grumbled. "Hey, what's this?"

"What's what?" Melissa asked.

"It's a postcard from Lizzie." I held it up. It was a close-up photograph of Dorothy's ruby slippers, the heels clicked together, and "There's no place like home" written under them. Well now, maybe today would be better than I had thought.

"That your city girl?"

"Yeah."

"I don't know what she sees in a washed-up old cowhand like you," she said, a trace of what's-she-got-that-I-ain't in her voice.

I shook my head. "Me neither. Must be my rugged good looks and keen intellect."

"I think she's just naturally attracted to bullshit," Melissa said as she pulled a bunch of envelopes out of her mailbox. "Hey, look at this, I may already be a winner!"

I didn't want to read the postcard with Melissa standing right there watching me so I slipped it into my back pocket. "I'm gonna get some breakfast. See ya later."

"Next time she comes out, you bring her round, Tucker. Don't be stashing her up at your trailer. She'll get bored as hell up there."

"Like she won't in town. She's from New York City for Chrissakes. There's more people living in her goddamn apartment building than in all of LonePine together."

I left the post office and went on inside the Sagebrush Cafe, counting up the money in my pocket which, frankly, wasn't very much more than all the money I had in the world. It was still enough for biscuits and gravy and coffee and some scrambled eggs. The spare change I found in my jacket would cover a double order of hash browns. Hazel, a waitress at the Sagebrush since the American Revolution, or at least in the thirty-five years I'd been eating there, took my order. I had her bring round a cup of coffee first and then pulled out Lizzie's postcard. It might've been my imagination, but it seemed to smell like honey and oranges. Didn't say much, just that she missed me and thought maybe it was my turn to visit; and something about her latest assignment on Dracula. For the life of me, I will never understand city people. Hazel delivered a plate full of food, so I slipped the postcard back into my pocket and let my mind drift back a ways.

I met Lizzie about six months ago. She's a journalist from New York City, one of those intellectual types. I'd like to say it was her smarts that caused me to fall for her, but that would be a lie. I was first struck by how dang pretty she was, but I knew even then that behind them looks was a powerful mind capable of rankling me without even trying. She'd come out to do a story about cowboys and ended up in LonePine with a bunch of notebooks and a camera, looking sort of lost. The first time I seen her was at the Silver Dollar, all made up in a flannel shirt with the sleeves rolled up, skin-tight jeans with someone's name on the label, shiny, leather-fringed cowboy boots that looked like they pinched her feet, and a bandanna knotted around her neck. She looked like an extra from one of those fancy catalogs, a big city notion of country. Despite the fact that she was breathtaking to look at, my day had been pretty dismal, so I did my best to ignore her and took a stool at the far end of the bar for a nice, quiet beer.

She was setting with a broken-down old alcoholic, name of Vince McCready, who we all call "Reride," due to the number and extent of his rodeo injuries that grow in proportion to the number of times he's retold his story. It all dated back to one unfortunate incident he'd had with a milk cow that formed the whole of his rodeo experience, and was as close to cowboying as he'd ever get. She was making a real point of not noticing me not noticing her, which I noticed much to my chagrin, and it began to interfere with the enjoyment of my beer. I paid for it and left it sitting half full on the bar and strolled nonchalantly for the door. Reride saw me and grabbed hold of my arms.

"Tucker, I'd like you to meet Lizzie Vaughan. Lizzie, this here's Tucker, an old friend of mine. We go way back."

She stuck out her hand, smiling mischievously. I touched the brim of my hat.

"She's here from New York City, writing a story about cowboys."

"Pleasure, ma'am," I said. "I hope you find some."

Her eyes danced and there was a reply forming on her lips, but I went on outside before she could deliver it, leaving Reride sputtering in defense.

I didn't think about her at all until the next time I seen her, several days later at the Cooper Ranch. They hold a monthly jackpot roping so all the cowboys from around LonePine can put ten dollars apiece toward the jackpot that Mr. Cooper always wins. Ten dollars is more than a fair price to pay for the privilege of roping in his outdoor arena and drinking warm beer. Add to this the chance that somebody's sister-in-law will be visiting from out of town and what shapes up is four-star entertainment in metropolitan LonePine.

Since it's only a few miles from the trailer, I rode Snort down. Rex trailed along behind us, sniffing and pissing on every bush and post while I followed a routine Snort and I developed for ensuring maximum performance from him: flattery. It's a little something I picked up from dating. Horses are by nature a bit vain and Snort is by nature even more so and constantly needs his ego attended to. I guess it's not so much empty flattery as it is positive reinforcement. Seems fair that if I expect him to perform like the best horse on the planet he needs to know that he is the best horse on the planet. So that's exactly what I told him as we trailed along, bent forward over his neck whispering in his ear about how fast he is, how strong and smart, how handsome and how lucky I was to have such a fine horse. I could feel the pride swelling up in him with each word and even though he can't tell me what a wonderful, strong, and handsome rider I am, it's pretty damn clear that he trusts me right up to the end. It's there in his eyes and in every fiber of horse muscle underneath my legs keyed up and poised, waiting for my command.

There's a bond develops between a horse and rider that is stronger than just about any, with the possible exception of parent to child. It's different, though, because it's more like equals coming together to form one powerful thing which is sort of like the bond between the night sky and a shooting star. Without Snort, I don't think I would be who I am today. I suspect, however, that without me, Snort would probably be just as happy in somebody else's barn, so long as there was plenty of oats.

The field behind the Cooper Ranch was already full of trucks and trailers and horses and screaming kids and horse shit. Someone had the foresight to bring a big old grill; charcoal smoke filled the air and they was burning hamburgers and hot dogs for a dollar apiece. I guided Snort on through, nodding at folks I knew, which was everyone. Rex found a truck to crawl under and lay there panting in the shade. I didn't recognize the rig.

"Rex, get on outta there. Come on, go find Kenny's dog. Come on, Rex, find Lady. Find Lady."

"Is your dog LonePine's version of a matchmaker?"

I kneed Snort around and saw that it was that city girl Lizzie with her camera. "Stop that," I said, but my damn fool horse went all *National Geographic*. He started smiling and puffed up his chest and struck his most noble horse pose. I pulled my hat down over my eyes and dug my heels into his flank, but by that time she was bent over taking pictures of Rex who'd adopted his sensitive dog look. Then he rolled over on his back so she could scratch his belly. "For God's sake, quit with the pictures. Rex, come on." I yanked at the reins and Snort jerked his head back like he was about to pull a stubborn until I fixed him with a savage look.

"Lizzie," she said, "Lizzie Vaughan."

"Dammit, put that thing away."

"You're Tucker, right? How about an interview, Mr. Tucker?"

"Just Tucker. No mister. And no, thank you. Now if you'll excuse me, I got a roping to attend."

"Well, good luck, just Tucker. Maybe I'll get some nice shots of you roping."

I heard her talking nice to Rex, that little traitor, so I left him to her as Snort and I eased on into the holding pen beside the arena. Snort kept looking back over his shoulder to see if maybe she'd take some more pictures and I had to gently remind him with my bootheels to watch what he was doing.

There was probably forty people up in the stands or else leaning over the fence spitting tobacco juice out into the loose dirt of the arena. Forty people is a big turnout, what with haying season in full swing.

One of the Dryer boys, probably Junior by the crease in his hat, was backed up in the chute waiting his turn, so I pulled Snort to a stop so we could watch from outside. Junior give a nod and they turned the calf out. As soon as it cleared the chute, Junior put the spurs to his old nag and they jumped out after it. He spun his loop and galloped along and directly gave it a toss. By the time the calf hit the end of the rope, Junior had jumped down and was running up to it, holding his pigging string. He tossed the calf and grabbed three of its four legs and looped his string around them once, twice, and then with a half hitch he threw his hands clear to signal the judges he was done and to stop the clock. He got back up on his horse grinning because it was a good time. It wasn't no winning time, but it was good.

The crowd was hollering and he seen me and took off his hat to wave across, and I waved back and then pointed behind him at the calf. He looked around in time to see it struggle up to its feet, the pigging string coming loose. He slumped in the saddle and everybody groaned. I could hear his dad laughing from somewhere behind the stands.

After two beers and a burger, it was my turn in the chute. Snort was all keyed up and I knew I could come real close to Mr. Cooper's time, which was all anybody wanted. They dropped the gate and the calf darted out. Snort bunched up and exploded after him, and I had my loop built and it sailed out graceful as can be, floated above the calf's head, then settled down over him. The calf kept running forward—they ain't particularly bright—and hit the end of the rope, causing it to flip around. Snort immediately started backing up and dragging the calf along, bleating in distress.

I leaped out of the saddle, the pigging string clamped down hard between my teeth, feeling each second reverberate between me and Snort as they ticked by. I ran down the rope with one hand looped over, measuring the tension as I caught the calf by the neck and flank, dug a knee in and hoisted it up to flop it down sideways. The arena was dead quiet, everyone silently marking the seconds. I caught Snort's eyes, all chestnut concentration, and then disaster struck.

Faint from the distance came a sort of shriek. Snort and I both swung our heads in time to see Lizzie lose her balance after leaning too far over the fence and tumble, camera and all, into the arena. I caught Snort's eye again and there was panic there and bewilderment, and though I tried to calm him with a look, he fell all apart. Before I could get the string looped around my calf's legs, Snort stepped nervously forward, craning his neck to look at Lizzie sitting all sprawled out in the mud and wiping the cow shit off her camera. As the rope slacked limp, the calf got a foot down and lunged out of my grip, butting me in the nose, drawing twin streams of blood and a string of curses, quickly lost in the laughter from the stands.

Glaring at her now, as she stood up and dusted the filth off her ass, I threw my hat and sat down in the mud. She give me a little nervous kind of smile that rankled me deep and I swiped my sleeve across my face to mop up some of the blood and fought the urge to go over and give her what for.

Snort come back to his senses pretty quick, took one look at me and ducked his head in shame. He started shuffling his feet as I pulled my rope off the calf and coiled it, tying it to the saddle, all the while whispering to him things like, "I ought to sell you for glue, you worthless turd," but kept on petting him so it'd look to the spectators like I was trying to reassure him. "I'm walking you home, you understand me? You ain't even worth setting on, you walking sack of Alpo." To a horse, there was nothing worse than being walked.

I did too, walked him right out of the arena, through the parking lot and past her sitting on the fence with Rex down at her feet.

"How's the nose?" she asked, jumping down in my way.

"S'all right," I said, trying to step past.

She laid her hand on my arm and I pondered for a moment how someone so irritating could look so damn beautiful and how her hand could feel so warm plumb through my shirtsleeve. "If you'll pardon me..." I said.

"You looked good. Good form, I mean."

"Thanks, you too. Come on, Rex."

"Look, I'm sorry if I distracted you."

"Sorry don't buy the groceries," I said and turned sideways to move past her.

She run her hand down Snort's neck and he nuzzled up against her. "Your horse likes me."

"He ain't particular," I said.

"And you are?" she asked.

I just nodded and led Snort on by.

"How about that interview?" she called out.

"Naw, I think you done enough damage. Come on, Rex." I looked over my shoulder and seen that Rex wasn't moving. He was mesmerized complete. "Fine, stay."

He must've quickly found out she didn't have no food, because by the time Snort and I got to the road, Rex came slinking along behind, just out of yelling range. Once we got home, I didn't say nothing to either of them, just pulled Snort's saddle off and turned him out. I left Rex outside too, pointed grimly at the alpacas and shut the door. He looked hurt, but had enough sense not to whine. Which is more than I could say for myself, since my nose hurt like hell.

Three beers, two aspirin, and one hour later, my head had just about quit hurting. It didn't come as no surprise that I heard a rig turning up my road. Rex wasn't barking, and he barks at everyone, so I knew right off it was her. Despite my better judgment, I opened the door just as she was getting out of her rental with a six-pack of Coors in one hand and her camera in the other.

She held up the beer. "Hi. I brought a peace offering."

"Good, leave it on the porch," I said.

She smiled. "How's the nose?"

"Why? Want before and after pictures?"

"No, I came by for that interview."

"What interview?" I asked.

"I didn't know you raised alpacas," she interrupted, gesturing behind her.

"I don't. Them's my neighbors. And I don't give interviews neither, so get on."

"Look, if you don't give me some time, I'll just make one up and put your pictures along with it."

"You wouldn't."

"Probably not, but it sounded good." She peeked past me into the trailer. "How long has it been since a woman's been in here, anyway?"

"That really ain't none of your business. And that you can print." Rex was sitting on her foot, grinning like an idiot. "Another thing, you're ruining my dog."

"Come on. An hour, that's all I'm asking for. The beer's getting warm."

How'd she know I'd just drank my last one? "All right. One hour and that's it."

She asked me lots of stupid questions about being a cowboy. I guess I gave the right answers because before too very long when I leaned over and kissed her, she kissed me back. Then she spent the night. Not naked and under the covers as I'd hoped, but fully dressed and talking ninety miles an hour until we fell asleep on the couch. When the sun came up we was under a blanket all spooned up together.

We spent most of the next week together, during which time we drank a great deal of beer, ate microwave burritos, and spent every night together, though nothing much ever happened, which I must admit was something kind of new for me, but didn't feel too particularly strange. By the time she left for New York, we was both feeling kind of awkward. I sure didn't know what to say and if she did, she wasn't saying it. I told her I'd visit her soon, but not too very soon, since it was haying season and after that there was cows to trail back from summer pasture and then maybe between that and calving season I'd try to fly on out. I give her a hug and then stood in the Jackson airport watching her plane labor up over the mountains and felt what could only be described as, well, I just plain missed her.

She did come back though, and brought a copy of *Harrolds' Magazine* chock full of pictures of me, which was mildly embarrassing, considering how the story was called "The Last Cowboy." I got quite a ribbing about that 'round town, but that was okay, considering that she stayed well on two weeks. We got down to some serious rodeoing, mostly at night in my bedroom, and she taught me a great deal about riding rough-stock. By the time she left, she'd ended up grabbing my heart by the horns, wrestling it down, and slapping her brand on it. That was three months back and now I was starting to think maybe it was worth the price of a plane ticket to see what New York's all about.

TWO

I HATE MORNINGS. DETEST them. I have hated mornings since I was a kid. Back then I developed a technique for ignoring them, or at least for making them less abrupt, that I still use to this day, nearly twenty-five years later. Fixing on some unpleasant event from the day before, I visualize it in detail, find a phrase that best describes it, and then chant it over and over until all the meaning drops out. That allows me to kind of hypnotize myself first thing in the morning, right after I wake up, so that I can make the transition into daytime more smoothly. Today, the technique was not working particularly well, but it was delaying the inevitable rising from bed, searching for my cigarettes, and fumbling to make a cup of coffee to take into the shower with me.

The phrase, when I located it, was fairly straightforward. "I hate Vampires, I hate Vampires, I hate Vampires." My story was quickly turning into every journalist's nightmare of too much information and not enough angle. I should have taken the piece on windowsill gardening instead of this ridiculous assignment. Gardening might be boring, but at least I would have been done by now. If I had to interview one more child of the darkness, complete with silly clothes and fake fangs, I'd happily drive a stake into my own heart.

"I hate Vampires, I hate Vampires…" I suppose I shouldn't have been too surprised, in a city like New York, that there were countless freaks, more numerous than what some might call the normal population. Yet, these people believed so earnestly that they were Vampires, swishing about the city in capes and combat boots, drinking their own blood, then scurrying off to their day jobs at espresso shops or hair salons. "I hate Vampires." Felix hopped onto the bed beside me, meowed once, and rolled over on his back so I could scratch his belly. "What do you think about Vampires, little baby?" A loud purr was his only response. Bored even with my own thoughts, I stumbled into the kitchen and ground some coffee, filling the French press pot.

While the water boiled, I opened the window and crawled out onto the tiny fire escape for a smoke. When I had first looked at this place, the agent had called this a balcony. She had also called the one-bedroom apartment cozy. I called it tiny but had taken it anyway, figuring that it was by far the best I would get on my writer's salary, at least until I could get a book deal for something. My agent had told me that she would shop around the Last Cowboy idea, but I wasn't certain that I wanted to write about Tucker.

I was trying hard not to dip into the money Mother had left me, so I had taken this apartment temporarily, but as in most things, temporary turned into one year, then another, and now it was three. It wasn't so bad, I had plenty of money leftover for clothes and nights out, plus it was close to *Harrolds'* offices so I could walk to work any time, day or night. A perfect setup.

Two of the firemen across the street were reading the paper, sitting in lawn chairs on the station driveway. They smiled and waved. Strange alliances are formed in this city, I thought. Local

No. 24B Manhattan Firehouse was directly across the street from my apartment building and at least a dozen times a day the station wound up to respond to a variety of emergencies. The siren was always an earful, but mostly I didn't mind. The noise got me out of bed, my urban alarm clock, and the firemen were a worthy diversion as they hustled around with axes and hoses in their rubber clothes, or better yet, washed the fire engine in T-shirts and shorts. I liked to think that they watched out for me, making sure I could get into my building without too much hassle from the street warriors and dealers. Or maybe they just liked my ass. It was hard to tell, but I guessed it didn't matter much. Even if it was my ass and not the person attached to it, they still would probably come to its aid if anyone tried to hurt it.

The whistle of the teakettle interrupted my nicotine reveries. Stubbing the cigarette out, I returned to the kitchen where Felix was waiting patiently by his dish. I poured him some dry food and he rubbed against my leg in appreciation. With coffee in hand, I headed for the shower, setting the cup on the ledge and adjusting the water to just short of scalding. Most people sing in the shower. Not me. I do my best thinking there.

"I hate Vampires," I muttered again. This story was going to be the death of me. Not that the information was lacking. Quite the opposite. The research on Vampires had been routine, even interesting, and certainly productive. *Harrolds'* archives held first-class information on practically everything. Anything else I had gotten online or at the library's rare books stacks. Some of the material had just appeared each morning, dog-eared and underlined, on my desk—the efforts of an eager, or enchanted, underling seeking some brownie points, it seemed.

I had expected to be bored out of my mind, but had actually ended up somewhat intrigued. The mythical world of the Vampire was a far cry from the hordes of silly kids I had interviewed. Maybe that could be my angle, I thought, the difference between the Vampire myth in folk tales and literature, and the way that the current fad was so Hollywood, focusing only on the fangs and blood. In folklore, Vampires definitely did not spring up on cue wearing black capes and bearing fangs. Outside of Dracula, most historical characters fitting the Vampire bill were creations of frightened pre-literate societies, since these bloodthirsty Vampires could handily explain away contagious disease, overwhelming lust, inexplicable murders, and other kinds of mysterious but completely human phenomena. Still, I wondered, why the continuing fascination? What was it about the Vampire myth that kept its hold on humanity?

Tonight would be the last event I could possibly bear, a view I shared with my editor when he announced Ric had been assigned to take photos of the party. As if things weren't problematic already, working with Ric would be the icing on the cake. My thoughts wandered briefly to him and how we had so recently called it quits on our mild little romance. Actually in all fairness, I had called it quits. Not enough material for the long haul, I said at the time, as if I ever even wanted a long haul. Looking back, maybe I should have let him break up with me and I suppose it had been a little cold to do the deed by leaving a message on his phone. Oh well. Live and learn. None of that mattered anymore, now that there was Tucker. Thinking of him brought a smile and a delicious tingling to my body. Talk about opposites attracting. When this story is wrapped up, I thought, it's definitely time to pay him another visit.

Or should I? Maybe Tucker was better left as a precious memory—one not sullied by the unpleasantness of the inevitable breakup. Was I going to leave my job at the magazine to work on the weekly *LonePine Gazette*? And surely there was no place in Manhattan for Snort, and Rex would hate it, not to mention Tucker. But, despite all the obvious obstacles, and my strict rule of never staying with a man for more than three months, I wanted to see Tucker again and felt somehow we could figure anything out together. I wasn't sure why I was having a fling with a man more than two thousand miles away who lived in a trailer, unless I was in love, whatever that was. He certainly had said nothing about love or forever, thank goodness, but still, I could tell that he was feeling something. After this story I thought, I'll go back.

If this story is ever done. The invitation for tonight's affair had arrived two days ago, careful calligraphy on gold brocade paper promising "A Thoroughly Diverting Evening of Vampiric Delights." Whatever. Another chance for the uninspired undead to show off their pathetic nature. At least it was being held at the Weeber Gallery, a strike in the direction of respectable pretentiousness. Many an untalented artist had developed investment potential at the hands of Max Weeber.

The phone rang, but I sipped my coffee and enjoyed the shower. No one I knew would call me this early unless it was an emergency. A few minutes later it rang again. Cursing, I turned the water off and wrapped a towel around me, squeezing excess water out of my hair. I dripped over an indignant Felix as I lunged for the receiver.

"What?" I expected someone from the office.

Instead, a refined British voice replied. "Ms. Vaughan?"

"Yes."

"My master wished me to ascertain whether you would be attending our little gala tonight."

"Your master? What are you, a dog?"

"Yes, just so. Can we count on your attendance then?"

"I'll be there with bells on. Or should I say crosses?"

24

"Quite. Splendid then, I will inform the master. He will be most pleased."

"Listen, I thought Vampires slept during the day."

"Oh they do, Ms. Vaughan, they do." There was a click, and he hung up. Well, at least this party sounded like it might be a little classier than the mosh-pit spectacles I had been privy to for the last two weeks. I ruefully surveyed the red marks on the back of my hand. At the Spartacus club last week, a fat little man in a cape sank his plastic fangs in unexpectedly. I grinned at the memory of him hopping up and down and cursing in a most human way after I had stomped on his toes with my spike heel.

I read the paper, finished the pot of coffee, made another and drank most of it as I worked on the story. The phone rang again, but I checked the caller ID and saw that it was Ric. He didn't leave a message. I checked the clock and smiled. Since the party took place at night, there was no sense rushing into work. I thought about all the things I should have been doing. Going for a run, picking up my dry cleaning, following up on that phone call yesterday from a disgruntled assistant in the mayor's office, getting a new cleaning lady; the list was endless. Instead, I crawled back into bed to think a little more about Tucker and to read one of my Vampire research books, a piece written by some twentieth-century priest.

It was well after noon before I woke up. Felix watched me change into my office wear, a charcoal-gray tailored blazer with pinstripes, matching pants with cuffs, and a turquoise blouse. Just for old times' sake, I slipped on the cowboy boots, and checked the final result in the mirror. Not bad. The haircut from last week was a definite improvement. Shorter and sleeker. Mugging a bit for the mirror, I was satisfied that anyone I happened to run into would be impressed even before I opened my mouth. On the way out, I checked the mail, disappointed that there was nothing from

Tucker, but I never really figured him for the writing kind, and given his stubborn refusal to get a computer, the likelihood of an e-mail was zero.

At the office, things were in the usual state of turmoil, with Stan lumbering from desk to desk and making important editorial observations like "Where the hell is your story," and "You call this writing?" I waited until he returned to his office, knocked at the door, and he barked for me to come in.

"What do you want and how long is that damn Vampire story going to take?"

"I'll have it done by next Monday."

"Good, except I want to see a draft on Friday." He returned his attention to a folder on his desk, scowling. I waited quietly. "You're still here," he said at last, without looking up.

"Yeah, I just have one tiny question, more of a favor, really. I was hoping there was someone else who could take photos tonight..."

He cut me off with a wave of his hand. "Ric's the best we have, you are the best we have. Therefore, he goes."

"It's just that..."

"I don't want to be indelicate here, but you are the one who tumbled into the sack with him. You're a big girl. Deal with the consequences."

"But..."

"End of story."

"But, Stan..."

He scowled menacingly. "Listen, your last story about the cowboy was good, maybe the best this magazine has run in a while. But when it's all said and done, it ran in *my* magazine, therefore my decisions." He looked at his watch. "And shouldn't you be getting ready?"

I sulked over to Ric's desk and he looked up with wounded pride and a glimmer of hopefulness showing in his eyes. "Get it straight," I said before he could open his mouth, "I don't like this anymore than you, so just read the damn notes, we'll go to the party and you can take your pictures." I flagged down an intern and shoved some money in her hand. "Tuna on rye. Mayo, mustard, lettuce. No onions. And an iced tea." She looked at me blankly. "Go."

"Getting a little bit of an ego, aren't we?" he said, as the girl rushed out. I silenced him with a glare.

Later, I ate my sandwich while he leafed through the notes and the outline of the story. "You could play this role," he said at last.

"Me? A Vampire?"

"You've got some of the characteristics down pretty well already. What's it say in *Webster's?* A beautiful, unscrupulous woman who seduces and leads men to ruin."

I thought my response was pretty calm, given the thunder and lightning inside. "If I thought it would do any good to say I'm sorry, again, I would. But it won't, so let's just be grown up and get on with this assignment. It only lasted three months. We have to work together, so please try not to be petty."

"At least I would have the decency not to break up with someone by phone." He looked expectantly to me for sympathy. I had none to give out. I just smiled with complete insincerity to get myself out of this situation and took Ric's limp hand. God, I hated it when men acted in this insipid way. Ric brought my hand to his lips and kissed it.

"It's just, you're hard to get over," he mumbled.

I said nothing, knowing my silence was likely to be more effective than any words could be. It worked and Ric's mood changed quickly. Silence embarrasses men, makes them posture. Ric was true to his gender.

"I bet I can find another vamp tonight at our little party. Let's get this little blood-sucking show on the road, shall we?"

The Weeber Gallery looked innocuous from the outside. A young man was waiting at the door to inspect invitations. After showing him ours, he ushered us inside. It was a pleasant surprise to find the gallery well lit and crowded with an interesting mix of attractive people, not a single one of whom was wearing Gothic accessories or who appeared to be anything other than wealthy patrons of the arts gathered to view an exhibition. The pictures, granted, were disturbing. Huge canvases covering nearly the full height of the loft walls, dark and primal with looming shapes and hidden currents of erotic power. Other than that, it was sedate. No funeral fugues playing, no Halloween props serving as centerpieces with flickering candelabra and fake cobwebs, nothing at all to reveal the Vampire theme the invitation had promised.

No sooner had we entered than a young lady attached herself to Ric and diverted him away. I supposed that some might find her attractive in a breasty sort of Hollywood-starlet way. I was left to myself, wondering how long I would have to stay there, when a very distinguished older man approached. He was not particularly attractive, of average height, slim and fit, with jet black hair highlighted by just a touch of gray in his sideburns. His skin was smooth and pale and he wore an unremarkable gray suit that stood out only in its simplicity and impeccable cut. But as he introduced himself, his voice was low and powerful, like that of an animal, and his eyes burned fiercely.

"Good evening, Ms. Vaughan, I am Julius, your host and," he gestured behind us, "master of ceremonies, so to speak. I am glad you could make it."

"How could I say no?"

"How indeed?" He arched his eyebrow smugly.

"It's certainly not what I had expected."

"That could be interpreted a number of ways. I trust you are not disappointed."

"Not at all, pleasantly surprised, really."

"A glass of wine, then?"

"Please."

He snapped his fingers and a young man brought two glasses of Pinot Noir. "From my private reserve."

"It's wonderful. May I ask you a question or two?"

"Of course, if I may ask you a question or two as well."

"Me first. Where are the Vampires?"

"Why, Ms. Vaughan, you're talking to one."

"And all the others?" I looked over his shoulder at the genteel crowd.

"Also Vampires. Well, most of them. Some are Vampires by lineage only. They have yet to take the final step, the leap of faith, one might say."

"I guess after the people I have been interviewing for the last several weeks, this crowd seems tame in comparison. No fangs, or strange piercings, no blood swapping. What's behind it all?"

"The others you speak of are phonies, charlatans, wishful thinkers. Many of those you now see before you have been alive for hundreds, even thousands of years. But you doubt me, as you should. Now it is my turn. Tell me about your family, I am curious as to how a woman of your obvious good breeding came to be a reporter for such an insignificant magazine in this squalid city."

"I guess I'm important enough to be invited here. But that's beside the point. My life is not any of your business," I quickly answered, but felt a curious desire to tell him more about myself.

"Oh, but it is, it is." His voice was so mesmerizing, his hands so hot and soothing on my arm, that my words seemed to be physically coaxed out of me by his very presence.

"All right, here's the *Reader's Digest* condensed version. I never knew my father, he died in a hit and run accident a month before I was born. My mother never remarried. With the money from his insurance settlement, we lived quite comfortably. I was raised primarily in New York and Europe, Swiss finishing schools, French at the Sorbonne. Educated in a manner, my mother said, of which my father would have approved."

His eyes burned. "I'm sure he would have, had he been alive to see you."

"Did you know my father?"

"No. Not at all."

"Then why do you care?" And why was I telling a total stranger things about me that no one else knows?

"You interest me. I enjoy your ... writing skills. If you are to write of us, if you are to know us, then I would know you. Is there anything else you would like to tell me?"

"All I have left of my father is a faded picture, a large man with a kind face who my mother loved absolutely." Julius seemed to wince. "Now they are both gone and I am alone and spilling my guts to someone who thinks he is a Vampire. Isn't it funny how things turn out?"

"Hysterical." He patted my hand. "If only they could see you now. They would be so proud." His words sounded almost sincere, but there was mockery dancing just behind them. I pulled my arm free.

"Please excuse me for a moment." He slipped away, leaving me unsteady in the center of the room. I looked for Ric, but he was nowhere to be seen. Julius was talking in low tones to a beautiful woman with raven hair, his head bowed close to her ear. She nodded and disappeared through the throngs of people, who parted silently to allow her by. I was really starting to feel nauseated, and was cursing myself for revealing so much about myself.

He rejoined me, his approach a study in controlled power. "Now where were we? Oh, yes, you were telling me about your lovely mother and how she always handled things with such tact and grace."

I was embarrassed at the attraction he held over me, the force he exerted. My pulse was pounding in my ears, the blood felt dense, like tar pumping through my veins. "You knew my mother, then?"

He glanced at his watch. "We shall have to continue this at some other time, the festivities are about to begin. If you will excuse me." He pressed his lips close to my ear and whispered with a shocking savagery. "Do not move from this spot. I shall be back for you shortly." A thrill of fear ran down my spine and I stood rooted to the spot in spite of myself as he strode to the center of the room and clapped his hands. All heads swiveled to study him as the lights dimmed.

"May I have your attention, everyone. As you know, tonight is the annual Turning celebration, and we are honored to have a special guest." He looked in my direction and several of the guests whispered briefly, studying me. "For those of you expecting more pomp and circumstance, I fear you will be disappointed, but I am in no mood to prolong the ritual. Tonight, I am tired, and expediency will be the standard. Acolytes, present yourself." A group of almost twenty men and women of various ages stepped forward into the center of the room. What sort of charade was this?

Julius snapped his fingers and, on cue, twenty chains dropped from the shadows of the ceiling to hang six feet off the floor. "Your clothes." The group quickly shed their clothes, standing nude before the assembly, yet not at all uncomfortable. Instead, they stood relaxed; hands at their sides, completely exposed.

"Attendants, make them ready."

Twenty others stepped forward, men and women. They carried short lengths of rope with which they quickly fastened the hands of those standing nude above their heads, tying them tightly to the hooked ends of chain. The erotic image was startling, twenty naked people bound with their arms above their heads. And there appeared to be no unity of age or form. I could see several middle-aged women, their bodies softened by age, but still attractive; young men with knots of muscle and hairless chests; other women in the prime of beauty, with slim hips and full breasts; one very fat man, and another who must have been close to seventy, his flesh wrinkled and fitting loosely, but his eyes burning fiercely. Next to him, a teenage girl with a body like a teenage boy and pierced nipples couldn't hide the anticipation in her eyes. The incongruous body types, ages, and skin colors made the whole spectacle that much more lovely. My earlier sense of discomfort was rapidly being replaced by a sense of privilege, at what I quickly came to expect was an elaborate performance art piece. I only hoped Ric was not in the coatroom with Ms. Silicone U.S.A. and could actually get some shots of this. No matter what these people had planned, this already beat any other party or night club I had been to so far. My thoughts were clearing now that Julius had left, and a new angle on the story was forming in my mind, a very kinky story about fetishism and Vampires.

"Take your places," Julius intoned, sounding almost bored. The attendants stood beside them. "Knives." Twenty blades gleamed in the half light. I sucked my breath in, hoping this wouldn't be some sort of gross scarring ceremony. Everyone held their breath expectantly, waiting for Julius. He raised his hand. "Kill them," he said simply.

Twenty blades flashed out across twenty exposed throats, flesh parted, and a torrent of blood poured forth. Almost simultaneously, my knees gave out and I sank to the floor, barely stifling a scream. The bodies twisted, spasmed, and their eyes rolled back in their heads as hideous smiles swept across each face. I fought the urge to retch, watching in horrified fascination as their life's blood washed across their skin.

From his bloody vantage, Julius made eye contact with me, and smiled at my reaction, then drew a tiny blade from his vest. Two men were suddenly at my side, holding me up with grips of steel, forcing me to face the spectacle and not fall again. Although terrified, my eyes nevertheless were drawn to Julius who, with a delicate motion, pulled the knife across his own fingertips. Blood welled up from them and, never breaking our trancelike stare, he moved to the nearest body. One hand absently stroked the cold flesh, cupped the man's genitals, lightly touched his hair, and then he slowly inserted his own bleeding hand deep into the gaping wound in the man's throat. His hand lingered there for a few seconds, then he moved to the next body.

The process was repeated at each lifeless body. Man or woman, young or old, he let his hands move sensuously across their bodies, trailing blood with them. The process seemed to exhaust him, his face growing strained as he continued. Occasionally, he paused to lick a trail of crimson from some woman's breast or the inner thigh of a man, his tongue languidly following the rivulets. This seemed to bolster his sagging strength, at least momentarily.

After he touched the last man, Julius turned to the crowd, his face drawn and lips stained with blood. "We will welcome our new brethren to eternity as they awaken. For now, let the festivities con-

33

tinue." He wrapped a white cloth around his damaged fingers and crossed the floor toward me.

I struggled to break free and, to my surprise, the men let me go easily. I rushed toward the door, avoiding Julius. It was locked from the outside and I pounded on it futilely. Julius appeared next to me and quietly placed his hand on my shoulder.

"Are you afraid?" he asked.

I could only stare at him in disbelief.

"Would you like to leave?"

I nodded mutely.

"Come," he said, "let me see you to a taxi."

"Ric, where is Ric?" I whispered.

"Your friend? Not to worry, we escorted him home before the celebration began. His presence was not appropriate, especially given his advanced state of inebriation. Have no fear. He is in good hands."

As Julius drew a key from his vest pocket, he continued, his tone imparting a sense of calm in my mind, which was struggling to comprehend what I had just witnessed.

"Do not worry. You are precious to me in a way you do not yet understand. And do not fear for those whose death you have just witnessed. In a short time, they will awaken to a new world."

His voice kept me mesmerized inside a dark silence but under that blackness, my fear was rising. I struggled to maintain the silence as he opened the door and, taking my arm, escorted me into the night. The air was cool and clear, free from the smell of death, and I breathed deeply, gratefully. I kept moving, unsure of anything except my need to get away from this madman. I had to reach the police quickly.

"I shall be in touch, my sweet," he said, after hailing a cab. As I bent down to get in the cab, he pulled me back to him and kissed me on the lips. He tasted cold, like kissing copper. The kiss was short and then he bowed low, saying something I could not quite hear, something about a Queen. There was an edge of mockery in his voice. As I slid into the back seat, he directed the driver and paid him in advance. I could feel the power of his voice weakening its hold on me as we drove uptown. And then I began to scream.

NEW YORK CITY

SEPTEMBER 26, 12:14 A.M.

He stood in the doorway of the apartment. The darkness from without and within met in him and he wore it about his features like a cape and cowl. He cleared his throat and one of the men already standing inside turned toward him.

"She's not here, sir."

He sucked in a dry breath. "Your passion for so eloquently stating the obvious never ceases to amaze me."

The young man bowed his head. "Sorry, sir."

"It is not supplication I desire. I merely want to know where she is."

"Julius," a voice called from deeper inside.

"Yes, Elita, have you news?"

She stepped from the bedroom holding a note in one hand and a struggling cat in the other. Her emerald eyes blazed from the shadows and a pearl necklace looped around her throat glinted faintly, almost lost against the marble skin exposed there. "Perhaps. I found this in the bedroom, a note detailing the feeding procedure for this delicate creature," she said nodding at the cat, "named Felix."

"Hello, Felix," Julius said as he stroked the struggling cat's head. "It would appear the princess has fled the castle." He arched an eyebrow. "The question is where might a frightened young thing such as herself seek sanctuary?"

"Her friends, family?"

"We can rule out family since she has none." He smiled tightly. "But the male photographer seems an obvious choice. Elita, take two and see what you may find."

She smiled and stepped past, dropping the note to the carpet, but holding the cat tighter against her chest. "Poor thing must miss his owner," she said, stroking it softly. "I followed it home," she said to Julius. "May I keep it?"

He nodded and, in the silence of her departure, pointed a slender finger at one of the shadowy figures remaining. "Are you familiar with this type of machine?" He pointed imperiously to the darkened computer sitting impassively on the cluttered desk.

"Yes, of course," the young man responded.

"Then make it work on my behalf," Julius said, taking up a position behind the chair. His attendant turned it on and the screen flared to life, lighting the dark room with a pale indigo. Manipulating keys and mouse, the file manager was soon displayed. Inside, they found document titles and the two scanned them wordlessly until Julius tapped his finger to the screen.

"Correspondence. Let's take a look at that one, shall we?"

Letter after letter flashed across the screen, mostly pertaining to business.

"This is getting us nowhere." He dragged his finger down the screen, his fingertip making a dry, whispering sound.

"What exactly are we looking for, sir?"

"What we are looking for, my young acolyte, is a clue. A name. A destination. Wait, what's this?" His finger rested on a name. "Why, it seems she kept in contact with her little cowboy." He smiled. "Isn't that sweet. She has a hero." He snapped his fingers. "Desard."

An impossibly thin man with a crooked smile detached himself from the shadows to stand beside him.

"Yes, boss?"

"Find out where," he studied the screen, "LonePine, Wyoming is. When Elita finishes, I want you two to plan a little trip. Take as many as you like, but don't come back without Elizabeth Vaughan."

"Yes, boss." He slipped past into the hall.

"Desard," Julius called, "I don't want any loose ends."

Desard leaned back through the doorway. "How loose is loose, boss?"

"Use your discretion." Julius turned back to the computer, his mind already moving in a new direction. "Go back to the main files. That one, Vamp." He smiled a faint smile, a parody of happiness. "Let's see just how much our little princess thinks she knows."

THREE

It was just past dark before I realized I had wasted my whole day setting on my ass. I should've been up in the mountains watching the sunset and drinking a beer, all wore out from pounding fence posts, instead of setting on the couch drinking a beer, all wore out from watching reruns. Rex was curled up on the recliner, raising his head from time to time to make sure I wasn't going to do nothing productive. Other than getting up to change channels on account of the remote was broke, the odds were low. Mostly I just thought about how expensive it was going to be flying out to New York City, and how I didn't want to go to a stinking sprawl of a place like that anyway, but fair was fair.

Halfway through a twelve-pack of beer, and making pretty good time, I was letting my mind drift back on Lizzie and all the things I missed in particular, which was bringing a big, dumb grin to my face. All of a sudden, headlights swept across the trailer wall and Rex exploded out of his chair, barking like the devil himself was selling candy door to door. A car rattled across the cattle guard and the lights got brighter. I gave Rex a little kick with my stocking foot to turn his volume down. I figured it was Dad or, worse, Melissa Braver, come to see how lonesome I was. Admittedly, I was mighty lonesome, but it wasn't nothing either of them could help me with. I stood in the door with my shirt unbuttoned and my eyes shielded against the headlights. The car wasn't familiar.

About that time Rex quit his barking and stood wagging his little stump of a tail and whining. The headlights shut off and the door opened up and Lizzie stepped out. "Hey, cowboy," she said. You could've knocked me over with a feather.

"What the hell are you doing here?" I stammered and she walked on up natural as can be.

"Is this a bad time? I could come back later," she said, smiling. I just drew her into my arms and kissed her for all I was worth, and felt her pull herself tight against me. Standing there, we were able to say hello without words for better of ten minutes. Then we moved inside and continued saying hello, still without words, for better than two hours.

Later, she sat on the porch smoking. She was wearing nothing but one of my shirts with the sleeves rolled up and the tails tucked between her legs. Her bare skin glowed smooth like ivory in the porch light. Rubbing her hands together, she said, "It's sure getting cold out here." I said nothing 'cause I was still feeling warm all over from what had just transpired between us. She blew out a stream of smoke, and for an instant, a different kind of light surrounded her, like something from the past fondly remembered, making her look like an old-time photograph. She stubbed out her smoke, took my hand, and led me inside to the couch.

"I'm glad you're here," I said, wishing there were words that sounded better. I paused an instant before more words come to me. "But just exactly why are you here, and why the hell didn't you call?"

"I had to get away," she said, and shrugged as if that answered everything.

I waited for something else but she didn't say anything, so I said, "I suspect there's more to it than that."

She sighed and nodded in agreement but said only, "Seems like forever since I saw you last."

"At least three months," I said, which made her smile. "But that three months sure drug by. Couldn't hardly think about nothing but when I'd see you again."

"Is that right?" She arched her eyebrow "Thanks for letting me know how much you missed me. I figured you weren't much of a letter writer, but I didn't know your phone was broken."

"Disconnected, more like."

She arched her eyebrow.

"Well, not really. It's just, ahh, you know how the cowboy thing goes."

She laughed a deep, throaty laugh that made me warm all over. "No, I guess I don't. Why don't you tell me about it?"

I tried to think of something but couldn't. "Pretty damn boring, really. I'd much rather hear all about your exciting life in New York City."

Something dark passed over her like a shadow, only colder, and her response was cautious and forced. "A little too exciting, sometimes."

"Yeah? More exciting than usual? Must be, seeing as you up and left on such short notice. That ain't like you."

"Is it that obvious?" she asked and I nodded. "Remember that story I was working on? It just got a little weird."

She sounded serious, so I put a chew in. "What kind of weird?"

She shrugged. "I don't know. I'm overreacting. It's probably nothing. Some sick game that I don't understand."

I was quiet, figuring she'd spill when she was ready, as long as I didn't say nothing to stop the process. That's a little something I've learned through the years. Out here it's pretty damn easy to observe human behavior, since there's so few humans around. Not that small-town folks like myself are nosy, just interested. Besides, what else have we got to do? If I've learned anything, it's that folks love to share their secrets, but only when they're good and ready. 'Course, the quickest way to get them good and ready is to pretend like you ain't interested, and then be still and let nature take its course. Kinda like the cure for constipation, I suppose. Human behavior has a simple, biological equivalent, or so it's always seemed on those many nights I've spent ruminating with Rex under the stars, listening to Snort pass gas. I decided to just bide my time and let her do the talking.

We sat silently, watching Rex scratch, then lay his head against her thigh. In less than five minutes she was ready. "Okay, I think someone's after me." Bingo. One of Tucker's theorems of human behavior proved right before my eyes. I amaze myself sometimes "That's sort of why I came to see you," she continued. "I guess I wanted to get away for a while."

"'Cause you was scared?"

"A little, I guess. Mostly, I just needed to clear my head. Try to figure out if I'm imagining all this or not."

Honestly, I suppose I would have preferred some other kind of secret. That Lizzie might be in danger set the hair on the back of my neck up straight. I stood up to stoke the fire to give me something to do while I got my rising concern under control. "Tell me more," I said, rattling logs around with the poker.

She come stood next to me, brushing her fingers lightly against my temples, tracing the lines of my cheekbones. She let her hands come to rest around my neck. "Remember last time I was here, I told you that I loved you."

"Vaguely."

She arched her eyebrow. "I do love you. I'm certain of it now," she said.

I knew I should say something back, and that something should be I love you too. And I do love her, I do, which means it shouldn't be no harder to say them three words than any other three words in the English language, but for some reason when I tried to get them from my brain to my mouth they just sort of withered and blew off. There was a moment of silence that I hoped wasn't as awkward as it felt. She pressed her finger to my lips.

"Let's not talk right now. Wait until morning." She kissed me on the cheek, then lightly on the lips, and I felt my hands tremble as I circled them around her waist to kiss her back. I slipped my hand up her shirt, which was really my shirt, and cupped her breast, felt the nipple hardening against my calloused palm. Laying her down in front of the fire, I unbuttoned each button slowly, opening the shirt and falling in love again and again. She pulled my T-shirt off above my head, ran her nails down my back, and pressed against me. Her breath felt hot and ragged against my skin. Pushing me back, she looked straight into my eyes and I'd seen that look once before, from a bobcat in a trap. She whispered, "I love you, I love you," over and over again, like saying it once wasn't enough or even twenty times, sort of like she was chanting it.

The next morning she woke close and wouldn't hardly let go for me to start coffee. She kept one arm wrapped around my waist while I scrambled some eggs and I could feel her hair brushing across my neck and shoulders. There was some beans cooked off in the fridge so I warmed them too with some salsa and a few strips of bacon.

"Want toast?" I held up the bag and she ruefully shook her head at the sorry pieces visible therein. I shrugged my shoulders. "Didn't have much advance time to do no shopping."

I reached the bread back toward the fridge and she wrinkled up her nose. "Don't save it."

"Why not?"

"It's already bad and it won't get any better."

"It'll be fine for french toast later on." I set a plate full of food in front of her and took mine across the table. "Last night worked up a hunger," I said.

She smiled and poked at her plate, moving some eggs this way and that, and even going so far as to almost take a bite.

"All right, looks like it's time to talk," I said finally, my plate damn near polished and me trying hard not to be too obvious in eyeing hers.

"What do you mean?"

"You ain't hardly eaten a thing and you said even less."

"I don't eat breakfast. Ever." She sighed. "I need a smoke." She took her bag and opened the door, sitting in the doorway to light up. Snort wandered up to watch doleful from outside and Rex, engaged by her motion, thumped his stubby tail and lifted his head enough to watch, but decided instead to remain sprawled out in the patch of sunshine he'd claimed.

"Well?" I again prompted.

"Like I said, I just figured I should get away for a while." She blew a thin stream of smoke toward the sun.

"Well, you can't get much more away than LonePine."

"This is going to sound ridiculous, but hear me out." She paused. "You remember that Vampire story I wrote you about?" I nodded. "I went to this party, a Vampire party at an art gallery. A bunch of weirdos, but hey, a story is a story, or so I thought then.

Tucker, they killed twenty people. Right in front of me, in front of a hundred witnesses. But it was like these people were willing victims. They took off their own clothes and there was no one forcing them to go along with anything, they let themselves be tied up, seemed almost happy about it, then they offered up their throats to be slit. I thought it was a game, a joke but it wasn't. I saw them die, all of them. It wasn't fake blood, it wasn't an act. I almost passed out, it was so horrible. And no one said a thing, no one tried to stop the killing. They just kept drinking their wine and chatting like it was the commonest of events." She caught her breath on the last few words, talking fast, almost hysterically.

"Let me get this straight," I said. "You watched a bunch of Vampire weirdos murder twenty people, and then they let you just waltz out of there?"

"I," she shook her head, "I don't know, I just … it was as if they wanted me to see it, like it was done for me. I nearly fainted, but they held me up and made me watch. The host, Julius, kept looking right at me and smiling." She held a fresh cigarette. "Light this for me," she said and I took the matches from her trembling hand so I could oblige. "I ran for the door, right past the bodies all hanging dead, but it was locked. But then they just casually asked me if I wanted to leave, walked me out, and put me in a cab." She was silent a moment. "I called the police, of course, but when they called back later, they hadn't found anything. No bodies, no Vampires. Just a regular art gallery with regular art and no chains, no blood. The number Julius had given me on the invitation was disconnected. The police said his address was a cemetery."

"A cemetery? Is that a joke?"

"I don't know. I don't think so. The cops were not very happy, thought I had made the whole thing up. But I didn't, I swear."

"Who is Julius?"

"The one who invited me to the party in the first place."

"I already don't like him," I said, feeling a certain hardness come over me.

"He called, the next night. Said he wanted to see me. I told him that I didn't want to talk to him or see him or any of his strange friends again, ever. Later, I thought I saw someone outside my apartment. I just packed a bag and left. Didn't tell anyone but Ric and my landlady. She said she'd feed my cat."

"And then you came here."

"Don't get the wrong idea. It's not like I need someone to take care of me or anything like that," she snapped and then stood. Her jaw was set all hard, and she stared out at the mountains without saying a word. I could tell she was struggling to keep her defenses up, and doing a pretty good job of it.

"Well, you'll be safe enough here, I reckon."

"I don't need a protector, Tucker. I just had to get away for a while, get my thoughts in order, sort out fact from fantasy."

"I ain't arguing that." Plain to see this was new territory for her, this being scared. She stood without talking for a couple of minutes, the whole time Rex staring up at her. At last, something in her softened and she sat down beside me.

"I'm sorry I snapped. It's just that there's something about you and this place. I can't explain it."

"Might help to try."

"We are so different. Opposite worlds. I thought it was just some little fling, sex with a cowboy. The last cowboy. Something to brag about."

That hurt a little, and she must've seen it, 'cause she quickly went on. "But it turned into something else, something bigger. I don't quite know how to say it. I'm more me, or at least the me that I want to be, when I'm with you." She shook her head. "I know

46

this sounds crazy, maybe you can't understand—you've never been alone, without family. I've been completely alone since I was twenty, no mother, no father, no family, not even any friends. And honestly, I don't really like anyone very much." She shrugged, not so much pained at the admission as mildly embarrassed. "So, it's just been me. I thought I had it all figured out, thought I could take care of myself, make a name for myself. And I can do all those things." She was talking a mile a minute.

"Don't forget to breathe," I said quietly. She smiled a crooked smile.

"Now here I am, scared about all the weird things I saw at that party, but what's really weird is that I actually had some place, no, someone, I wanted to run to." She paused. "God, even the sound of my own voice is annoying."

"The only thing annoying about you is your stubbornness. I thought Snort was bad."

She laughed at that, poked me in the ribs and then got all serious again. "There's more and it's harder to say."

"I ain't going nowhere."

"It's hard because you've seen a side of me that no one else ever has. I bet you wouldn't even recognize me in New York."

I didn't answer, only because I didn't know what to say. I guessed that she had something big churning inside and thought it might be best for me not to steer her away from it by saying what might turn out to be the wrong thing.

"I've never done anything, not one thing, for anyone."

"Your life ain't over yet."

"How can a roughneck cowboy make me think like this? I was fine without you. Wasn't I?" And then she whispered, "This is a new concept for me, Tucker."

I sat for a minute, thinking, and spit into the pop can serving as a cuspidor. I set it down between us and despite the emotions clouding her eyes she managed a look of distaste at the chew juice.

"How long?" I asked.

"How long, what?"

"Are you staying?"

She looked out over the mountains, the snowcapped loneliness there, and sighed. "Hadn't really thought about it. A couple of weeks. A month. How long will you have me?"

"Hell, stay as long as you like," my mouth said, but all the while my mind was thinking just how long it had been since I'd had a woman underfoot and despite the severity of her situation, how it might interfere with this illustrious single life I'd been living. I had been thinking seriously about getting a satellite dish and now that was definitely off. Sure can't watch TV with a woman wanting to talk all the time. And what about Rex? He was used to being my significant other and now that would no longer be the case and he's awful sensitive. And I'd probably have to start buying groceries on a regular basis, and Good Lord my bathroom just wasn't big enough to keep all the things she'd want. A month, my Lord! In a month she'd be talking about babies and buying a house and . . .

"Are you sure?" she asked.

"Absolutely." A dark wind blew between us, and in that keening silence Rex sat up to regard us curiously, his head cocked to one side.

"How will you know when to go back?" I asked, finally breaking the silence.

"I'll get my head together soon enough. I'll call Ric in a week or so and see what's up."

That was probably the happiest week of my life, the happiest time of my life. Only thing that even came close was a shining and notable eight seconds of happiness when I had clung grimly to a disgruntled Brahma bull name of Boxcar at the LonePine Fourth of July rodeo. I was a high-school senior desperate to attract the attention of Missy Speck, a cheerleader and, as far as I could tell, the most beautiful girl in school. Although, with only eleven girls total in the class, it wasn't too wide a field.

On her account, I gave Boxcar the ride of my life, literally, since it was both my first and last professional rough-stock event. I was spurring him hard, digging my boots deep into his ribs and using that force to keep astride him. My free arm was whiplashing like a radio antenna and the crowd was roaring. I just knew that Missy had to be falling for me but good after a ride like this. The buzzer blew and everyone was on their feet stamping and clapping and spilling their beer, so I took off my hat and waved at the stands. As I started my dismount, my hand got all tangled in the rope and Boxcar, sensing eminent disaster, pulled right as I leaned left. I slipped down underneath him and he proceeded to tango on my face with such vigor that it pushed my nose way over to one side and dang near ripped my ear off. The rodeo clown pulled me free, left me lying in the mud and blood and bullshit listening to the sirens of the ambulance as it pulled into the arena thinking ain't that just the way it goes, from eight seconds of glory to waiting for a ride to the hospital.

Missy never came to see me in the hospital. I don't know why I even thought she would. The sad fact was the only visitors I had was Mom and Dad who brought me some Louis L'Amour books I'd already read a half-dozen times, a jug of orange juice, and a hopeful wish that Boxcar had stomped out my desire to be a rodeo cowboy, which, in fact, he had. Laid up there for three days, I got to thinking about how love was a doomed endeavor at best and how the price you pay for happiness is dear, even for just eight seconds' worth. I couldn't help but wonder what the cost of a week's worth of pure happiness with Lizzie would be. Seems it would have to be mighty dear.

That price began with a phone call. We had spent the last hour dancing close to country songs on the radio. She was laughing and when commercials come on we'd just hold tight and whisper wordless things back and forth. Eventually she set me down beside Rex and announced she was calling Ric to see how things were back in New York.

Now, by all rights I had no reason to begrudge Lizzie's friendship with Ric, but there was a certain glint come to her eyes when she talked about him and a nervous motion in her fingers that let me know they'd tried and failed. I'm man enough to admit that I was just a scrap jealous when she finally set about to calling him because I didn't know how quits they really was. Not being the jealous kind by nature, I wasn't real sure how I should be acting, so I settled on sullen with a speck of furious, and sat on the couch pretending to read *Western Horseman* and pretending not to listen. There was a heat flushing the back of my neck and my hands was clenched so tight my magazine was squeaking.

"Tucker."

"Hmmm?"

"Don't be jealous."

"What's that?" I choked out. "Jealous? I'm not jealous."

"He's just a friend."

"I'm not jealous," I said, my voice cracking. "'Sides," I muttered under my breath, "it's your life."

She punched the number in, listened for a minute, then hung up. "It's like his phone is picking up but he's not there. Listen." She held the phone to my ear and called again. It rang once, then there was a whistling emptiness that sounded cold and far away and a

50

wet click that was unlike a connection being made or unmade. I handed it back to her.

"That ain't right."

"Ain't isn't a word," she said, cradling the phone.

"Maybe not in New York."

"I'm going to try the office." She dialed in a new number. "Hi, Ric Castlin's desk, please. What? Ric Castlin." She put her hand over the receiver and said aside, "That's weird, the receptionist…" then made a gesture with her hand as someone took the line. "Mr. Meyers? This is Lizzie Vaughan, I was just trying to get hold of Ric…What?" She paled. "Oh my God." She turned to look at me, her eyes wide in disbelief. "He's dead."

There was more conversation, but her voice had grown cold, the words clipped and betraying no sense of what she might, be feeling. I held her hand and she avoided my eyes, stumbling over her words. After she hung up she sat looking blankly at the wall, silent tears streaming down her face, tears that were strangely out of place, as if falling from her eyes for the first time. When she did finally speak, it was with a quiet, detached tone that was mighty unnerving. "I didn't even cry when my mother died, why am I crying now?"

"Maybe you're crying for her too," I said softly. She looked at me quizzically, and just like that, the tears stopped.

"Ric committed suicide, slit his wrists. His boss asked if Ric had been acting weird." She shook her head.

"He would never," she said, "there was no reason."

"I'm sorry," I said, "truly. I know you were close." I put my arm around her, and she let me. Drawn by that, Rex come up too and did his best at comforting her. She petted him with trembling hands and he watched her with those big, serious eyes of his. I took her into the bedroom and we spent the night like that, me holding her and her holding Rex, who curled up in her arms, both of us waiting for her to sleep.

I couldn't help but think how she reminded me of an unbroke horse, one that needed gentling down. In my experience, they're generally anxious to come right up and take a lump of sugar and get petted, but instinct and stubborn pride keep spooking them so that they don't stay put for very long. That was two things we both had plenty of, instinct and stubborn pride, but there was something deep that was keeping me close with my hand out, and something that kept bringing her back to it. I usually don't have the patience for breaking horses. Dad has always said it was 'cause they tended to break me.

The next morning, more to get her mind off things than for any other reason, we decided to ride up to Widow Woman Creek and stay a few days. We borrowed a horse from Melissa, a bay name of Dakota, who Snort was more than a little sweet on. I packed us up a bag of food, a couple bottles of wine, and we set out that morning with Rex running ziggedy-zag and forth and back between us until by late afternoon we arrived at the cabin. Rex was plumb wore out and dragging along fifty yards behind with his head low. Lizzie got down stiff, walking gingerly on account of her tender behind, and I brushed the horses down and turned them out into the little corral. We set on the fence holding hands while they rolled around in the cool grass kicking their legs in the air.

Way back before me, Dad built this cabin up on Widow Woman Creek. It was where him and Mom first started. Wasn't much, but it was snug and real pretty. Set back into a stand of aspen that opened onto a beaver pond. The front porch looked all the way down onto LonePine, which was barely worth the look, and then on past to Campman Plains and right up into the mountains. Besides the view there was many other benefits such as no electricity and an antique wood stove that was both hard to keep a fire going in and also filled the cabin up with smoke. Outside the door was an old-fashioned pump that froze up and busted every fall, and inside was a rough-cut pine bed which was comfortable enough but still managed to fill my ass with slivers every time I slept on it. There's nothing like roughing it.

I spread our bedrolls out on the bed as Lizzie stood on the porch and watched the sunset, dipping cheese spread out of the jar with little crackers. "Dad built this place back in, hell, a long damn time ago," I said as I walked past and tossed first my saddle and then hers over the split-pole corral built right off the cabin wall.

"It's beautiful," she said. "Did you grow up here?"

"No. By the time they moved up here, Mom was four months pregnant with my brother. About fifteen minutes after the first snow fell she packed up all her stuff and moved back to town. Told Dad he was welcome to come with her if he wanted."

"Not entirely unreasonable."

"Guess not." I poured some dog food onto the ground. Rex sniffed at it and then cast a mournful look at the saddlebags with our food.

"I didn't know you had a brother."

"I don't. Not no more."

"I'm sorry," she said.

"Don't be." I pulled out a bottle of wine and screwed the cap off, to which she wrinkled up her nose. "I know this is probably not what you're used to, but it's all they had at the Gas 'N' Get."

We sat on the porch and sipped wine out of enamel coffee cups and watched the night come across the valley like a shroud pulled over the land. The sky come alive with stars and coyotes set to calling back and forth. Night birds whooshed through the darkness and now and again a fish would jump and break the surface with a distant splash. I built a fire and woodsmoke trailed between us and some even escaped out the chimney, but soon enough the crackle and warmth of a fire filled the cabin, making it downright cheerful. We passed several hours talking about nothing in particular and telling jokes and watching Rex be adorable until she got a look in her eyes that corresponded to a feeling I had in my heart and I took the cup from her hand and set it on the porch railing. Back inside, she stood by the stove as I undressed her there in the faint glow and shadow, mesmerized by the rise and fall of her breasts and her eyes burning like the embers in the fire. She pulled at me, at my shoulders, and then with her arms around my neck, pressed into me like we was just one body. I wrapped her up tight and laid her back onto the bed, onto the bedrolls still smelling of sunshine and of the horses where they'd been lashed. We made love under the first layer of coarse blankets quietly and slowly, both scared of this powerful thing between us, but neither of us backing down or hiding at all, just staring deep into each other and holding on so fiercely that it seemed there was nothing left in this broken-down old world but me and her and what was felt between us.

That and pine splinters in our private parts. And Rex, who'd crept up to the foot of the bed, and who I kept kicking at but he refused to budge until I at last grew tired of fighting him and he stretched out proper across the bottom blankets, trapping my feet.

"I CANNOT BELIEVE THIS place," Desard said, peering over the steering wheel of the rented Lexus as the headlights washed over the deserted main street. Rain was falling hard, running down the pavement.

Elita slid down in her seat and shook her head. "I haven't seen this much desolation since the black plague." She pointed. "Pull in there." The open sign of the Sagebrush Cafe flickered feebly in the darkness. "I want coffee."

They entered, Elita at the front with her elegant stride, followed by Desard, and behind him, two nondescript men with nervous eyes and pale skin. Strangers in expensive clothes with narrowed eyes. "Four, please," Elita said as Hazel looked up from the counter, her mouth hanging open. Well-dressed strangers in LonePine were surprising enough, more so after sundown.

"Uh, smoking or non?"

Elita blew a thin stream of clove-scented smoke in her direction and smiled. "Smoking."

Hazel ushered them to a booth. "This all right?"

"Of course it is, uh …" Desard leaned close to read her nametag. "Hazel. Of course it is. And we don't need those," he said, tugging at the menus under her arm.

"Nothing to eat?" Hazel asked.

"Just coffee," Elita answered as she paused to let one of her silent companions into the booth. "Four coffees."

Desard raised his hand. "And Hazel, make mine a decaf, would you? Otherwise I'll be up all night."

Elita stifled a laugh.

"I'll have to start a fresh pot," said Hazel, tucking her pad back into her apron.

"Quite all right," Desard said, shouldering out of his leather jacket to reveal a wiry frame nearly swallowed by a billowing silk shirt.

Hazel brought back four cups, filled three and returned shortly with Desard's decaf. After she left, Elita took a sip of the bitter brew, grimaced, and rolled her eyes.

Desard turned in the booth to stare from the window at the empty street and darkened buildings behind them. "I have died and gone to hell," he said to no one in particular.

A brief silence ensued until Elita looked narrowly at their silent companions. "Aren't you two the life of the party."

"Sorry, Miss Elita," one said, at last, "it's just that . . ." He shrugged and looked for support to his companion in silence, who continued to stare intently into his cup.

"Do you find me so uninteresting?" She rested her chin on the back of her hand.

"No. Nothing like that."

"They're shy," Desard mimicked in a falsetto, turning back around to rejoin the attempted conversation. "New recruits, my dear."

Elita meticulously stacked five sugar packets atop one another and pinched a corner between two carefully lacquered nails, peeling the ends away. She dumped the contents into her coffee and stirred, her spoon clinking against the sides of the cup—the only sound in the otherwise deserted diner. "So, how old are you?"

"I'm, uh seventy," one said.

"And you?" Her gaze rested on the quieter of the two near mutes.

"Eighty-eight."

"Why, you're just children."

"Told you so," Desard said.

"Tell me, I'm just dying to know. Why did Julius turn you? You obviously must have some redeeming qualities. Did you spend time in jail? Kill someone, perhaps? Rape? Telemarketing scam? Oh, never mind, I'm sure Julius had his reasons." She bit her bottom lip gently "I do love younger men."

Desard rolled his eyes and his thin shoulders shook with mirthless laughter. "It's so good to know that there are eternals in life, such as your insatiability. May I make a suggestion? Instead of catering to it just now, perhaps we should turn our attention toward finding our charge and getting out of the Middle Ages as quickly as possible." He swept his hand at the window and the emptiness behind it.

"So practical, Desard. Always so practical." She sat her empty cup down and regarded it impatiently for thirty seconds. "And practical is so boring. Oh, very well, let's put our heads together and . . ." She looked up, "What's this?"

A group of three cowboys entered, obviously suffering from the influence of alcohol. They stopped in the doorway, shaking rain from their hats. At the sight of Elita, they bumped together and stared openmouthed at her slender legs crossed at the knee, the creamy skin revealed by her sleeveless shirt, and the ruby glow of her pursed lips.

"Goddamn," one of them whispered, "look at her." They stumbled their way to a table across the room, arguing about who had to sit inside, thereby losing the view.

"What are the odds that one of those gentlemen knows our mysterious Tucker?" Elita asked.

"In this town, judging by the limited amount of available women," he flashed an eye toward Hazel, "chances are they're all related to him," Desard responded.

The tip of her tongue traced around the edge of her lips and she stood, sniffing across at the still-riveted cowboys. "Oh, I adore those hats."

"Yippi-Ki-Yay," Desard whispered under his breath as Elita walked over to the other table.

FOUR

NEXT MORNING, I WOKE at sunrise and sat in the door watching the sun come up with one eye and watching Lizzie sleep with the other. Pretty soon I got bored of thinking about how peaceful she looked and how beautiful and all that sort of thing so I put on some coffee as loudly as possible and a pot of oatmeal and laid some bread down to toast on the stove top. Eventually, between the noise and the smell of food, she opened her eyes and it was amazing to me how someone who looked like an angel asleep could wake so damn cranky, but after a cup of coffee and a smoke she was almost human. I just kept smiling and didn't let on that half the day was already wasted, although I might have mentioned it in the most offhand way, to which she reminded me that we were here to relax and to forget about the bad things happening around her.

After breakfast, I generously invited her to take a splash with me in the creek, which I cautioned might be cool but should feel quite invigorating. I went first, and as it turned out it was so invigorating that my testicles damn near shrank away to nothing, but I didn't let on or holler out and told her it was just fine and to come on in, which she did with a jump and quickly found out the lie. She let out a blood-curdling shriek and sprinted buck naked for the house, narrowly missing Dad's truck as he clattered up over the hill. If she was embarrassed she chose not to show it, just kept on running until she hit the cabin and slammed the door closed behind her.

Dad got out and hitched up his pants. "Bet that water's cold."

I pulled on my pants and boots and nodded my head. "Yep. What the hell are you doing up here?"

"Tucker, hate to be the bearer of bad news, but your trailer burned down."

"What? Are you sure?"

"I think I know what a burnt trailer looks like."

"Everything?" I asked, and he nodded.

We walked to the cabin and found Lizzie inside, fully dressed, wrapped in a blanket and sitting by the fire holding a cup of tea. She looked at me hard. "You said it wasn't cold. Jump in, you said. Invigorating, you said."

"Tucker always did have a strange sense of humor," Dad said, pouring himself a cup of coffee from the pot as I pulled on a flannel shirt.

"I wonder who I got that from?" I asked.

"Tucker's trailer burned down," Dad repeated to Lizzie.

"What?" Lizzie asked.

"Am I that hard to understand? It burned down. Ain't nothing left. Coffee's a tad bitter."

"That's the only coffee I got. Did Roy come out?" Roy was the fire chief in LonePine. He was also the brand inspector, justice of the peace, and sold vitamins mail order. Dad nodded a confirmation.

"What'd he say?" I asked.

"He said it looked like your trailer burned down."

Lizzie snorted.

"Well I guessed that much." Then I looked back at Dad. "Did he say what caused it?"

"Probably the wiring. I never did trust that wiring."

"Dad, for Chrissakes, you put that in."

"I know, and I never did trust it." He put his cup down. "I gotta head back down."

"I hate to belabor the obvious, but all my clothes?" Lizzie asked.

"Gone." He stopped at the door. "But if it means anything, you look fine without 'em." She blushed.

"I reckon we'll stay up here another night," I called after him. "Head back down tomorrow. Maybe run over to Jackson and get Lizzie some stuff. Can we stay with you?"

"I guess."

"You guess? Where else would we stay?"

"At the Sleep-O-Rama, I reckon."

"You told me I could stay with you any time I wanted."

"Yeah, well, that was before you didn't have no place to stay."

I started to say something else, but he raised his hand. "Forget it. Stay with me. What's family for?" He climbed in his truck and hollered through the window "If I ain't home, I'll leave the door unlocked."

We watched him pull out of sight. "I'm really sorry," I said.

"They're just clothes. I can get more."

"Well, if it means anything, you look better in Wranglers and one of my shirts than that drugstore cowgirl getup you had last time."

"I'm learning. I am sorry about your trailer, though."

"Just a trailer. I can get another."

"I don't suppose you have insurance?"

I rolled my eyes. "C'mon, let's go for a ride."

We walked down to the corral and I filled up a bucket of oats and handed it to her. She looked at it and back at me. "I told you already I don't eat breakfast."

"It's for the horses," I said, leaning on the fence and giving a whistle. "Get on in there and catch 'em."

One of the simplest pleasures in life I know is watching horses come in for goodies. Even though they know they're about to get ridden, it seems the call of the oats cannot be resisted. Even Snort, wiser than most horses I know, is still an absolute fool when it comes to the stuff. With Lizzie, as usual, he first played hard to get, rolling his eyes and stamping his feet and skittering this way and that, but by the third whistle he come galloping up to the fence in a cloud of frosty breath and appetite with Dakota close behind him. He thrust his head into the bucket so hard it almost fell out of Lizzie's hands, but she grabbed on strong and propped it on her knee, laughing.

"Easy, Snort, let Dakota in too," she said, pushing on his fore-head. He stepped back slobbering and chomping, and oats fell out of his lips as Dakota took a turn.

It was a peaceful sight watching that scene, especially after the run of bad luck we'd been having.

"Don't forget, you're supposed to be catching 'em," I said, slipping her some twine over the fence.

"What am I supposed to do with this?"

"Catch 'em around the neck."

She looped one piece over Dakota and passed her to me, then caught Snort and set the bucket down. He jerked his head up and back and the twine slipped free. Disappointment clouded her face as he backed up a step, but I caught his eye and shook my head. He was so ashamed that he had caused Lizzie any sort of discomfort that he stepped back up, still dangling the string around his neck to let her fasten it around him.

"What a good boy," she said, stroking his neck, and he lifted his head over her to grin broadly at me. I gave him a nod of approval.

I cinched the saddles on and she groaned as her sore ass hit the leather. We rode hard into the mountains, into the rough country where just being a tree was a struggle. It was cold up high. We were in thick jackets and leaned heavy on the warmth of the horses and the heat they gave off. Maybe it was the thin mountain air or the hunger I'd worked up from the ride, or maybe it was just that she looked so damn beautiful and vulnerable perched up on top of Dakota and looking solemnly out across the bony backs of the mountain peaks, but whatever it was I nudged Snort up close and took Lizzie's hand. She smiled and looked out into the emptiness below.

"My God, it's beautiful up here," she said. "All this granite and solitude." She swept her free hand about us. "Reminds me of the church I used to go to with my mother. The Church of the Holy Trinity. It was where my father's funeral was. I still go there. It's so quiet, so serene. It makes me feel like now, like I'm up high somewhere looking down."

Her words trailed off and it was then, listening to her, that those words which I'd found so hard to say before came right to me, and I realized they had been there all along. It hadn't been in my brain, but instead had been laying low in my heart, and now they come out of their own volition. "Listen, Lizzie. Look at me a minute, you need to know something. I love you."

"I know," she said. She sat silent in the saddle and looked down below. Finally she twisted around in the saddle. "What does that mean to you?"

That threw me for a loop. I hadn't never really thought about it that much. I always figured that love was just love, easy enough to recognize as such and what else needed to be said? I tried to figure out just what it did mean. "I dunno. A longing, I suspect. A longing that don't never stop, even after you get what you want."

"Like maybe the way you love this place?" she said.

"Yeah, though I reckon I've taken it for granted. But if I ever had to leave, I'd still love it."

"That's the way you feel for me?"

"Yeah." That didn't seem like quite enough so I added, "Now that I have you here, I can't imagine you ever leaving, but when you do, I still, I don't know…"

"Finish it," she demanded.

"It's just that I don't think I'd ever get tired of being with you."

I took her hand and squeezed it and she squeezed back, and even though we was both wearing gloves it was like I could feel her heart beating all the way through. There wasn't much else to say, so I nudged Snort around and started back, heard her do the same to Dakota. We rode in silence, other than an occasional "watch out for that rock" or "mind that branch." Occasionally, I'd twist around to look at her, just marveling at the sight of her in that oversized jacket with her hair down and blowing in the wind, all full of the setting sun and looking like something from the movies.

That night we spent in the cabin talked out from not saying nothing all afternoon. It got colder and a wind come up, bringing storm clouds full of lightning and grumbling thunder. "Looks like rain," I said as the first deluge hit like someone was standing outside throwing buckets of water at the window. Lightning lit up the dark and flashed in her eyes, revealing a love like I hadn't never believed in before but now seemed so natural. She smiled and, though it disappeared quick into the shadows, I knew she was seeing the same thing as I was. Even in the dark I could feel that smile. It was like her whole body was smiling and it got deep inside me and grew longer and harder and warmer as I pulled her close and felt the softness of her pressing into my chest, traced the curve of her hips and left my hands resting on either side of her waist. Her breath was sweet and she ran her fingers through what was left of my thinning hair, twining it this way and that.

In the roar of it, in the flash and crackle, we got lost a little ourselves. We made love, the two of us come together and hanging like the last leaf on a tree in the darkness. It was a love of no little sadness, a love that has to do with longing and the realization that it is not better to be alone, not stronger, nor freer, just more alone. That in fact we did need someone, desperately, daily, to make life even worth living at all. And that everything up to this point had been worthless, and between the two of us there had been a whole mess of worthless living. Afterwards, exhausted, I fought the urge to sleep as it is a well-known fact that women like to talk afterwards. "Goddamn," I said at last.

"What?" she asked sweetly.

"Nothing … just goddamn." And then I must have dozed off.

Rex sensed them first. I hadn't been asleep for all that very long when he got up agitated and stood by the door growling, his hackles up. Lizzie stirred and mumbled as he let out a bark.

"What is it, Tucker?"

"Probably nothing. Coyotes, I reckon. Rex, come lay down." His growls got deeper and he started to bark. "All right, all right. I'm up. Go on out there if you want." I held the door open with one hand. Rain was striking so hard it bounced and the air was thick with it. Rex decided he didn't want out so bad after all but backed up instead, barking furiously. Lizzie sat up and clutched the blanket around her.

"I can't see nothing," I said, peering out, then saw something dark slip sideways from shadow to deeper shadow down by the corral. I banged the door shut. "There's something out there."

"What?" Her eyes were wide and dark.

"Can't tell. By the way Rex is acting it could be a bear." Sounded reassuring, but there wasn't no bear as tall and skinny as what I thought I'd seen moving. 'Course, in that downpour, it could've been an elephant dancing a jig and I wouldn't have seen it clear. "Set tight. I better go take a look."

I pulled on some pants, stuck my feet down into my boots without socks and pulled on my battered old Stetson. Then I shouldered on a jacket and rummaged around in the saddlebags until I found my Colt python, a .357 with rosewood handles.

Lizzie watched wide-eyed from the bed as I checked the cylinder to see if it was loaded. "Think that's necessary?"

"Couldn't hurt," I said, slipping it into my waistband.

"Be careful."

I nodded. "C'mon, Rex." Reluctantly, he entered the downpour before me, hackles high and casting his head about. It was raining so hard I couldn't see two foot in front of me, just followed Rex and tried to keep my balance in the mud. The wind was howling, pushing the trees sideways and eventually we stopped and stood, me looking at him and him looking nervously back at me.

"What is it?" I hollered at him, his unease settling down into me enough to warrant pulling the pistol out and thumbing the hammer back. We slipped and staggered our way down toward the creek so I could check on the horses. Lightning flashed through the darkness and a shadow broke away from the fence.

"What the hell?" I broke into a run with Rex howling beside me. I couldn't see nothing of Snort or Dakota, though I could barely make out my own hand in front of me. I unlatched the gate and stepped through, whistling for Snort, the wind carrying it away before it even left my lips. Rain was streaming down my face and I was cursing it, the darkness, and Snort for not answering, when I tripped over something hard like a log and went sprawling down to my knees.

Another flash of lightning tore across the sky and, with its brief illumination, I found myself looking right into the wide-open eye of Snort, laid out stiff and dead. It was his foreleg I'd fell over and his neck was dark and open where something had savaged the flesh away.

By the time thunder cracked behind the lightning, I was already up and running for the cabin, screaming at the top of my lungs for Lizzie to for God's sake lock the door, and then there was this man standing before me where a moment before had been only rain. He was soaked through, but smiling a cold and toothy smile. Rex lunged insane at him and I never even hesitated, just fired point blank into his chest, twice and twice again. The muzzle blast lit up his thin face and he staggered and went down to one knee, his bony hand spread across the wounds as I lunged past. Then he reached out before I was past and clamped his hand around my arm, spinning me back as easily as a child. He was still smiling and my mouth was hanging slack at the sight of this man with four holes through him now standing. He hit me so hard it took a second or two for me to realize how hurt I was and that blood was streaming from my nose and eyes and I was falling backwards. I lay in the mud, ears ringing, vaguely aware that there was more people around me and also that I had lost the pistol and that Rex was yelping in pain.

"Get her," a woman said, "and finish him. And someone, shut that dog up."

I groaned involuntary as I was stood up. "You heard her," the one I'd shot whispered in my ear. "End of the line, Tex." His grip was like iron and his breath coppery and dry. "Nothing personal." Behind him I saw lights flare up from inside the cabin and muffled shouts.

"Reckon not," I mumbled as I fished my folding knife out of my jacket pocket and opened it with numb fingers. He caught a hold of my neck with both hands and started to choke the very life out of me when I jammed the knife blade into him just above his belt, all three and a half inches of it, and yanked it plumb up to his breastbone. He squealed and punched me in the stomach so hard I felt ribs give way and flew backwards like a skipping stone, all arms and legs and losing consciousness. I stopped rolling at the edge of the creek and struggled up to my feet, took a step forward and fell again, this time sliding into the water and gone with one last, desperate call for Lizzie.

It was Rex that saved me. The creek must have carried me down a ways and might've kept me there until I was drowned or frozen or both. I come to with the sunrise on a little washout, Rex curled up on top of me trying to keep me warm, and mostly failing on account of he was so cold himself and shivering so hard I could feel his bones rattling into me. What I meant to say was thanks for saving my life, but what come out was, "Fer Chrissakes, you're gonna shake me to death," and I pushed him off. Judging by the tracks in the wet sand, he'd tugged me up out of the water and it hadn't been easy. He licked at my face, happy I was alive and at the probability he would get a warm place to sleep and something to eat soon.

My ribs hurt something fierce and my head wasn't right on account of my nose being busted. Clawing at the frozen mud, I managed to stand unsteadily. I could see my breath and Rex's too as he cowered beneath me, bearing silent testimony to what had passed the night before. The sun come up over the mountains and in that orange and once-welcome light, I trembled and cried like a child. Eventually, there just wasn't nothing left in me except a numb and terrible rage. I found a branch thick as my arm and leaning on it hobbled up out of the mud and ice and toward the cabin. Past the corral and the frost-lined bodies of Snort and Dakota, I could see the cabin, its door hanging open.

I feared her dead. Laid out like the horses had been, her beautiful eyes open and an empty and accusing shine to them. But the cabin was empty, deserted and cold. The fire had long since gone out and its warmth was replaced by a sense of catastrophe, of a dark and terrible wrong made real. The chairs were overturned, clothes and supplies scattered across the floor, the mirror broken. I fell to my knees in the doorway and begged God she was all right, that somehow she had escaped into the woods and was hiding, cold but unharmed, and so I called for her until my throat was ragged and my ribs screamed out for me to stop. Then I thought of the man, the one I'd shot who hadn't died, and I knew she was gone and that I had failed her. She had come to me seeking safety, and I had failed her. Rex crawled his head into my lap and whined, giving voice to his own sense of failure, and I petted him like he was Lizzie and everything was all right.

"We gotta go, Rex. We gotta help her," I said at last. I pulled a blanket over my shoulders and hobbled out into the morning and the warm sun. It was going to be a hell of a walk. I saw the Colt glittering dully in the mud, cleaned and reloaded it, and stuck it in my pants, even though I was unconvinced it would do any good. The day I could no longer have faith in my Colt was a day I never seen coming.

I stood by the corral and looked out over the rails where Snort lay, looking soft and sleepy in the sun, but dead just the same. We may not have always seen eye to eye, but there wasn't no better horse I knowed of, and now he was dead and it too was my fault. There was a gaunt look to him as most of his blood had poured out of his ripped throat and washed away with the rain. Dakota's too. I sat down and held Snort's head in my lap. His hair was dried and stiff, like the flesh beneath. I told him how sorry I was and how I hoped he was in a better place where it was always sunny and the mountains was made out of rolled oats. And how, with any luck, maybe Dakota was there too and maybe they'd give Snort his balls back at the door and he could spend all eternity raising kids and eating and I promised I'd come visit soon as I was able and he could even ride me for a while. Plus, I took back all the bad things I'd ever said to him and all the times I'd threatened him with the Alpo factory. Then I told him I wished I could bury him, but seeing as how he was already dead and how fond he'd been of Lizzie, I figured I'd better see about her, but that I would come back in time to bury him proper. Lastly I swore a solemn oath to avenge him. Then I said goodbye.

The way back was not easy. I'm not accustomed to walking in the first place, and especially not with cracked ribs, a busted head, and almost frostbit. The plus side was that, being as mad as I was, it was easy enough to forget about the pain, except for the two or three times I near blacked out and had to kneel in the road until it passed.

By nightfall, I was limping down the drive to Dad's house with my head down and barely able to lift my feet. In that condition it took me a minute to realize that Rex was growling that awful growl again and casting his head from side to side and that Dad's door was standing wide open.

"Dad?" There was a sinking feeling in my heart and stomach. I pulled the Colt free of my pants, although it felt small and useless in my hand.

"Dad?" I stepped through, dropping the blanket off my shoulders. The inside was turned upside down, like the cabin had been, only worse. Dishes broke, clothes scattered, the John Wayne poster lying torn on the floor. I flipped on the light, set my jaw, and held the pistol out in front of me. There was the remains of a fire glowing in the fireplace, which led me to believe that Dad had been here recent and made me fear for him the more.

"Didn't learn your lesson the first time, Tex?" I couldn't see nothing and then he was standing beside me and plucking the gun out of my hand as easy as picking cotton. Then he sent me spinning across the floor with one careless jerk of his arm and into the kitchen wall where I crashed with a groan. "I thought I'd killed you. Oh well, I love loose ends."

"Here we go again," I said. He was standing over me like a pale and stunted oak tree.

"Shouldn't have cut me, Tex," he said, "that hurt."

"Real sorry 'bout that, you ugly son of a bitch."

"You will be," he said, "because I can make this last all night." He lifted me to my feet with one hand and held me suspended.

"Where's Lizzie?" I choked out.

"She's no longer your concern, cowboy," he said, and I knew that meant she was still alive.

"Where's Dad?"

"Your father? We'll find him soon enough." Any sort of relief I might have felt quickly disappeared as he tossed me over the kitchen table. Landing on the counter with a crash, I balanced momentarily there on the edge before falling to the floor, tangled up with a toaster and the coffee pot. "Time to see some blood, Tex." He squatted down over me with a leer. I kicked feebly at him as he reached out toward me.

There was a ratcheting sound of well-machined metal on metal, then a flash and a roar, and his grin disappeared in a mist of teeth and rotten flesh turned to vapor. Surprise and pain filled his eyes and he spun around to face Dad, who was leaning through the doorway trying to decide if he should shoot again as he steadied his .454 against the frame. The .454 Casull is the largest handgun in the world, next to which Dirty Harry's magnum ain't much more than a pop-gun. As such, it ain't particularly easy on the shooter, which is why Dad was hoping maybe one shot was enough. But already my jawless friend was gathering himself to jump and I hollered, "For God's sake, Dad, shoot him again, shoot him again!"

Dad grimaced and squeezed off another round that caught Pale and Ugly right below his breast pocket and knocked him up against the fridge looking down at a hole in his chest big enough to see right through to a picture of a six-point elk Dad had cut out of a hunting magazine and scotch-taped on the wall. That dead son of a bitch still wasn't dead though, only sorely inconvenienced and mighty pissed.

During the ruckus, I crabbed out of the kitchen and was now hunched down near the fire. I grabbed hold of a log end burned down to a point of glowing embers, and as he stood there dripping slime and wordless invectives, I thrust it as hard as I could into the hole that Dad had shot through him.

He clawed at the air and rolled his eyes and squealed a horrible squeal, and then the fire seemed to catch inside him and he went up with a whoosh and a roar like last year's Christmas tree, and there was nothing left but ashes and an awful smell of burnt toast.

"Goddamn," Dad said as he massaged his shooting wrist, "those city folks sure take their own sweet time a-dying."

THE PLANE LURCHED VIOLENTLY as it sped down the runway, as if uncomfortable with its cargo. Elita grimaced in spite of herself, checking her watch. "We are running half an hour behind schedule." Neither of her companions spoke. She drummed her finger on the armrest. "I said," she raised her voice, "we are running half an hour late."

"We'll make it," one of them said.

"We'd better," she said icily, turning to stare out the window at the darkness rushing by. "I am not particularly anxious to welcome in the dawn from ten thousand feet." She slipped a pack of cigarettes from her breast pocket. "God, I hate flying." She lit up a cigarette and clove smoke filled the cabin. "It seems I have forgotten your name. Again."

"David, Miss Elita. I am David."

"David, I want you to know that I hold you personally responsible for our delay."

"We should make it to LaGuardia by five, and Julius will be waiting. The sun won't be up for another hour. It will be fine, Miss Elita. Don't worry."

She swung her head around. "Make no mistake, I do not worry. I have not lived for three thousand years by worrying. I am a realist. We are late. Much later, and the sun will come up and we shall be stuck in our coffins inside the plane until night returns, during which time we are at the mercy of the unknown, including," she pointed a slender finger at Lizzie slumped in the back seat, handcuffs tight around her wrists, "our Queen." Her sarcasm chilled the air.

"But at least we have her," David said. "Julius will be pleased."

"His little helpers have done well." Either they missed the mockery of her tone or thought it best to ignore it.

They sat in silence as the minutes ticked by with the rushing of night air against the plane's thin hull. Eventually, the two men reached into a stainless steel container between them and withdrew plastic pouches of blood held at body temperature. The bags looked like individually packaged juices made for children's school lunch boxes. They used their teeth to puncture them and fed, slurping greedily. The crimson liquid spilled out, trickling over their lips. Across the way Elita could feel the surge of life flaring inside them and was momentarily tempted herself.

David raised a fresh bag and offered it to her. She smiled thinly and arched an eyebrow. "No, thanks, I'm trying to cut down on between-meal snacks." Her mind turned to Desard, gratefully blocking out the gluttony displayed before her. She had been unwilling to leave him behind in such unfamiliar territory, but he had insisted. Julius had said he wanted no loose ends, but she suspected Desard wished to even the score with the cowboy, making him suffer if he somehow was miraculously still alive. Chances were slim, but they had found neither his body nor any sign of that wretched dog.

Desard had been turned in the early part of the seventeenth century, not by Julius but by his long-time rival Lazarus. It had taken very little for Elita to tempt him away into the camp of Julius. In all honesty, she had seduced him almost as much for herself as for her master. There was an immediate attraction, but still she toyed with him for nearly a century, playing hard to get and keeping him at arm's length. When it seemed he could stand it no longer, she had given in to him, taken him as a lover. Theirs had been a brief but tempestuous relationship. After a mere forty years of sensual, blood-drenched passion, they had found one another incompatible for continued intimacy.

They remained very close, however, and leaving him in such a fashion unsettled her. He was prone to overzealousness and had such an utter lack of respect for Adamites. In one sense, of course, she wholeheartedly agreed with him. It is, after all, quite challenging to respect a food source. She continually cautioned Desard that this particular food source had brains, albeit limited, and well-sharpened stakes. Although they were frail, Elita had been forced to conclude over the centuries that an occasional Adamite or two had been extremely cunning and vicious. Luckily, she thought, by and large they tended to focus it on one another.

"She's coming to," David said. Lizzie, Queen-to-be, stirred in her chair, still unconscious, but straining against her manacles.

Elita stood up, stubbing her cigarette out in the ashtray. She crossed to the agitated woman and stooped down. Taking Lizzie's face in her hand, she bent close enough to smell the sweet scent of fear and distress still caked to her skin. As she watched the pulse flicker in Lizzie's neck, Elita felt the hunger seize her and brushed her lips lightly across the exposed softness of her captive's throat. Her lips grazed almost imperceptibly against the skin and she fought the urge to rip her open and drain the life from her, ending the games forever. Her entire body echoed this desire, her cells responding in kind, unwinding and reaching out in unison for the life pulse of Lizzie. Julius' stern face swam into view, loomed in her mind, and fearful of his wrath, she reached inside and found the strength to kill the hunger, to turn it off. Pulling back, she looked upon Lizzie's face. So soft, so delicate. So fresh. Her hand lingered on Lizzie's cheek for an instant, and the life in it transferred warmth to her icy hand. "Prepare another syringe," she said, turning.

David retrieved a black leather case from his suit coat. He pushed Lizzie's sleeve up and, though satiated from the packaged blood, still gazed longingly at the vein in the crook of her aim as he slid the syringe in. Soon this will not be a problem, Elita thought, watching. Soon, she will no longer be a temptation, but a temptress instead.

FIVE

It was like being a kid again and believing Dad could keep the monsters under the bed from getting me as I slept. Only this time the monsters were real, and instead of leaving the closet light on, he had his Casull in his lap to keep them from coming through the windows and ripping my throat out.

'Course, when I come to around noon, he was sprawled out in the recliner snoring like a chainsaw, with Rex curled up at his feet and drooling a puddle out in front of both of them. I give Dad's chair a nudge with my foot and he woke up with a start, cocking back the hammer.

"Easy, old man," I said, punching up the pillows so I could lean on one arm. "I thought you was supposed to be watching over me."

He put the pistol down, stood up and then give Rex a nudge. "Damn mutt, you were supposed to keep me awake." Rex stared wide-eyed up at Dad for a second, then come over to see if I was okay. After sniffing around my face while I pushed feebly at him, he decided I was okay and curled back up.

"Look at my house," Dad said, standing up to stretch, still mumbling excuses as to how he came to be sleeping when he was supposed to be guarding me. He started picking up broken things and straightening this and that, pausing only long enough to complain about how sore his shooting wrist was, rubbing it now and again. From the vantage point of the couch, I watched him mutter and mumble his way into the kitchen where he fished the coffee-pot out of the mess and blew Vampire ash off it before plugging it in "Least this still works," he yelled to me, and brewed up a pot.

When it finished brewing, he poured two cups and pulled a bottle of whiskey from the cupboard. With a steady hand he poured a stiff dollop into each cup. "I can't believe how much trouble kids can be," he said, handing me the cup. "Tell me one more time."

"Vampires, Dad. Vampires," I snapped. "Blood sucking, God-damn, got-Lizzie Vampires."

"I just can't believe it," he said.

"Can you believe that son of a bitch was standing there with a hole through him big enough to pack a lunch in?"

"Only 'cause I seen it."

"I'd already shot that bastard four times up in the mountains. Stabbed him, too."

He sat quiet for a minute. "Always told you that Colt was too small," he said at last.

I swung my feet out of bed and winced at the discovery of pain. "I gotta find Lizzie. I gotta go to New York." The room got a little fuzzy and he laid his hand on my shoulder, gently laying me back down.

"We gotta fix you up first, boy. Can't fight no Vampires all busted up. I'm gonna call the vet."

Doc Near has been practicing veterinarian medicine in the greater LonePine area at least since I was born. I know this to be true because he delivered me. Since the nearest hospital is close to a hundred miles away and the M.D. only comes up from Jackson on Wednesdays and Fridays, Doc Near is accustomed to treating a variety of human ailments and conditions on top of his animal doctoring. Him and Dad go way back, so when Dad made the call to Doc Near's receptionist saying it was an emergency, she said she'd send him right over.

Within fifteen minutes he come rattling up the road and parked his old blue truck down by the barn, no doubt expecting some sick cow or birthing mare to tend. Dad went out on the porch and waved him up to the house. While we waited, he pulled a box of powdered sugar donuts out of the cupboard and set them out on the table along with another cup of coffee fortified with a splash of whiskey.

"C'mon in," he hollered when he heard boots on the porch.

Doc Near pushed the door open and stood there in his one-armed coveralls, which made me suspect he'd been preg testing over at the Dryers' place, and also made me hope he'd washed up proper. There was sixty-odd years of living lining his face—every wrinkle and crease was like the rings in a tree trunk, bearing testimony to the hard winters and long summers he'd spent outside with his arm stuck up a cow or down a horse.

His eyes lit right up when he saw them donuts. "Howdy, old man. What's the emergency? Can I have some of them donuts?"

"Help yourself," Dad said, "and that's the emergency." He pointed at me.

Doc took a look at me setting bruised and uncertain on the edge of the bed. "Damn, Tucker. How'd you get so banged up?"

"That's a long story," I said.

There didn't seem to be much for him to do other than poke and prod around the painful parts and shake his head whenever I grunted. He set my ribs tight with gauze and cleaned up the scrapes I had around my neck and on my face where I'd been punched. He went out to his truck and come back with a handful of painkillers for doping up racehorses. Each one was about the size of a new potato and he said to gnaw off an aspirin-sized chunk whenever I got to hurting, so I went ahead and took a double dose. Right away, I got to feeling better and by the time I had told him my story, the pain seemed bearable. Down deep inside, though, lay a terrible fear and longing for Lizzie, quiet and despairing like a wounded bear holed up in the brush.

By the time I finished up telling about Dad shooting the Vampire, Doc was staring at me with his mouth hanging open. "That's some story," he said. "Are you sure you didn't fall on your head?"

"He's dead serious," Dad said, and Doc swiveled around to face him to see whether we was just pulling his leg, but Dad nodded solemnly. "I wouldn't have believed it neither, but I shot that son of a bitch and he just stood there looking surprised and not thinking at all about dying."

"Know anything about Vampires?" I asked.

"Tucker, for Chrissakes, I'm a veterinarian," he said, but that didn't seem to matter much once he started talking.

After fifteen minutes, about the only thing I learned for sure was that Doc Near could put away the donuts. All he had to say was really no different than anyone who had been single for twenty years and had a weakness for late-night television. He said Vampires are real strong. I already knew that. Vampires are real hard to kill, he said, which I had also learned. Vampires drink blood, he said, and although I hadn't found that out specifically, Snort's death seemed ample evidence of that theory. Other'n that, all he knew was that Vampires come from Transylvania, they're sort of a cross between dead and alive, which was why folks call them undead, and they can't stand sunlight, crosses, or holy water. "You got lucky," he said at last.

"I don't feel particularly lucky."

"Think about it. You tangled with one of them mythic creatures of the night and whipped his ass."

"Yeah, maybe so, but they still got Lizzie. And there's a whole lot of them I gotta get through to find her."

"What the hell do they want with her?"

"I don't know."

"Guess we'll find out soon enough," Dad said. He pulled a box of ammo out of his gun case, tossed it up on the bed with the Casull, and pulled a beat-up suitcase out of the closet by its rope handle.

"We ain't about to find out anything, 'cause you ain't going with me to New York."

"I sure as hell am." He drew his shoulders up high and stuck out his chest in what Mom used to call his John Wayne pose. Used to piss him off, but me and my brother liked to hear her teasing him that way. Ain't no one else in the world could've got by with it.

"Someone's got to watch your back, boy. Be damned if I'm gonna sit on my ass and twiddle my thumbs while you get yourself in trouble."

"Rex'll watch my back." He thumped the stump of his tail at the mention of his name. "Besides, I need you here in case she tries to call or something."

"You know," Doc Near said, cutting off our debate, "it probably wasn't the shooting that killed him. It was the log you stuck through him. Or the fire. The next time may not be so easy. You think about that?"

"If that's so, even the .454 won't be enough. You're gonna need something special," Dad said.

"How the hell am I supposed to kill them, then?" Then it hit me and I snapped my fingers. "I'm gonna drive up to Lenny's. If there's anybody can help me out now, it's him."

IN THE CHILL OF the early morning, in a darkness that gave little evidence the sun would ever rise again, the Lear jet taxied to a stop outside an isolated terminal building. Wordlessly, the pilot emerged from the cockpit, negotiated stoically through the seated passengers and opened the hatch, extending the stairs.

"Quickly," Elita snapped, "we haven't much time. David, you and your friend put her in the coffin by the back hatch. The ground crew will meet you there and escort our little Queen to the hearse. Make certain you leave the casket open a bit Remember, she's not undead yet. It would be a shame for her to expire by such pedestrian means as suffocation before Julius has an opportunity to turn her. I'll join you outside."

She took the stairs cautiously, scenting the predawn air like a panther. Satisfied, she walked briskly to the back of the jet, heels clicking across the tarmac. In all black, she was dressed in the manner of a mourner, a silk scarf around her throat and thin gloves past the elbow. She was aware throughout of Julius' presence, watching. Always watching. A baggage handler popped the back hatch and rolled a metal stand to the door. David and his companion wrestled a deeply lacquered coffin out of the plane and set it onto the stand. It was light in their powerful hands but unwieldy, and a corner of the hatchway ripped a long scratch down the center.

"Imbeciles," she snapped, rearranging the weighty bulk as easily as she might her hair. "Come, quickly" She studied the horizon for light. Pulling the scarf tighter, she ignored the famine in her stomach and soul, accompanying the lackeys as they rolled the coffin toward the hearse.

Julius was indeed waiting, demurely leaning against the hearse. He was dressed casually in tan linen pants and a soft leather bomber jacket. Calm as usual, his features were drawn and she wondered if he ate at all anymore or instead chose to suffer the hunger silently, using the pain to fuel his grandiose schemes. He embraced her lightly, kissed her coolly on the cheek. His gaze fell on the coffin. "I trust all went well?"

"We have her, if that's what you mean." She smiled weakly, while inside she raged at Wyoming, her hunger, Julius, the Queen, and cowboys in general.

"Where is Desard?"

"He chose to stay behind and take care of any …"

"Loose ends?" Julius interjected. "So loyal. So obedient."

"He'd make a fine dog," Elita said sarcastically.

"Charming as usual at the end of a long night. Let's take a look, shall we?"

"Here?" she asked, arching her eyebrow. "With all these people around?"

He waved his hand around. "Why, it's practically deserted. And who would dare question the newly bereaved?" He flipped the lid open, and stood frozen at the sight revealed. Lizzie lay on a satin pillow, her cascading hair framing her pale face. Still drugged, she rested peacefully, innocent as a child and breathing shallowly. "Quite lovely, even beautiful, I'd say. That certainly makes my task more pleasant. It's a pity, however, that she had to be brought against her will. I had hoped the party would whet her natural appetite for blood and create a willing participant." He stroked her cheek absently, ran his fingers through her hair. Leaning over, he pressed his lips to her forehead. "Now I shall appeal to her intellectual side, since the physical failed so abysmally. I certainly would not want history to write that I had not properly seduced the catalyst of our greatest act since Genesis."

"The uncreation," said Elita dutifully, knowing just when to chime in with the proper words for the conversation they had shared so many, many times before. She knew that it was likely to end sooner, and thus she was likely to get home sooner, if she simply helped him cycle through his enthusiasm, rather than try to divert him.

"Yes, yes," responded Julius, nearly in a whisper. "She will give me the power to reverse creation." Abruptly, he shut the coffin lid. "Job well done, Elita. Well done."

"Thank you, Julius," she said, hoping her jealousy was undetectable, "but can we continue this reunion later tonight?" She looked at her watch. "The sun is so very damaging to my complexion."

He smiled tightly. "Gentlemen, bring her along." Elita tried her best to ignore the rumbling in her veins.

SIX

Five miles outside of LonePine runs historic Highway 26. In LonePine, historic means that at one time in history it was paved. Now all that remains are asphalt patches, turning the road into a rubbled mess so that driving it makes me feel like an ant in a go-kart on the back of an alligator. After rattling along on it for twenty minutes, my teeth were almost shook loose and I turned off onto a comfortable set of ruts angling up behind a rock formation hidden by trees. Setting on a post halfway up was a video camera that marked the beginning of Lenny's property. Although the camera looks mighty sinister, I know for a fact he pulled it out of a dumpster behind a Gas 'N' Get in Salt Lake City, and it ain't connected to nothing. First appearances count for something, I suppose. I drove on past, up behind the rocks and trees into a clearing that Lenny called his bunker. To me, it's always looked more like a double-wide trailer.

Lenny has been a friend of mine since third grade when we used to take bullets apart and make little bombs out of the gunpowder. He's the founder and sole member of the LonePine Militia, except on every other Saturday when they meet out at the firing range and Lenny brings the beer. Most of LonePine tends to feel a whole lot safer knowing that he's holed up in his bunker with all them weapons, because we know they won't fall into the hands of the Russians or bored high school kids wanting to play tough. Lenny's trailer, I mean bunker, is fortified with unpainted aluminum siding and bales of straw stacked up to the windows. He lives in there with his wife June, who, for reasons unclear to the outside world, puts up with his curious ways. Must have something to do with love.

Their yard is a cluttered graveyard of snowmobiles, cars, and motorcycles in various stages of what he likes to call repair, but really means not running at all. Out front, for security reasons, he keeps a mean-spirited poodle that thinks it's a Rottweiler. There's also a German Shepherd laying about, but I ain't never seen him move, which means he's either dead or an ambush.

Lenny thinks the government is out to get him. Accordingly, he won't get a phone, figuring they'd just tap it. He also won't watch TV because the government beams out what he calls subliminal messages, telling us what to do. Most folks call the same thing advertising. He also won't pay taxes so as not to lend support to shady activities, but no one has noticed yet since he don't have a job. Instead, he supports his simple way of living by fixing things. There ain't much he can't fix, from a calculator on up to a jumbo jet. Folks round LonePine bring him all their busted stuff and directly he'll bring it back better'n new. One time he fixed old Mrs. Johnson's toaster so damn well that it started making perfect toast in about four seconds, but she ended up throwing it out the window when she got that month's power bill.

I killed the truck out in front of the trailer and cautioned Rex to stay in or else run the risk of facing the poodle, who chose that

moment to spring out from under the porch, yapping and slobbering. Like a trained assassin, she managed to pee on all four tires
in under thirty seconds. "Lenny, call your dog off," I hollered. "It's
me, Tucker."

The door cracked open. "How do I know it's really you?" he
called.

"Fer Chrissakes, Lenny, who would impersonate me?"

"Government agents. It'd be a perfect cover. Who'd suspect?
You're famous now," he said, "all that crap about the last cowboy
and all."

"Look at these boots," I said, hoisting my foot out the truck
window. The once-gray duct tape was tattered and brown and one
loose flap hung down like a ribbon. "You can't fake boots like these.
I probably borrowed the tape from you. Now call off your dog."

"All right, all right." He opened the door and stood there in his
camouflage pants with no shirt on. He looked a little like a Vampire himself, with his long black hair and pale skin from working
all the time indoors. "Commando, sit."

Commando crawled back under the trailer, but I could sense
her highly trained eyes still on me as I got out and walked to the
front door.

"Sorry Tucker, but ever since them government types come to
town two nights back, I been in a state of red alert."

"What government types?" I asked as I went inside. Their trailer
is real cozy in spite of the discount gun store look. There was rifles
and pistols and loose bullets and knives laying all over everything
and all kind of electronic stuff that I couldn't even begin to de-
scribe.

June was sitting at the kitchen table reading a well-worn book
by Carlos Castaneda. She smiled up at me. "Hi, Tucker," she said,
and then, noting my bandages, added, "what happened to you?"

"Got into a little scrap."

"Coffee?"

"I guess another couldn't hurt." She poured me a cup and set it down across from her, scooting a box full of ammunition and a pair of brass knuckles out of the way.

"What government types?" I asked again, sitting down.

Lenny drew up another chair. "There was four of them. Real secretive. Got a room at the Sleep-O-Rama but stayed inside all day. Told Hazel they was astronomers come to study stars. And now Terry Gleason turned up missing." He leaned in close like the room might be bugged. "June thinks she seen one of them black helicopters last night," he whispered. She nodded in agreement.

"They wasn't government spooks," I said. "They was Vampires. That's why they never left the hotel in the daytime."

They both just looked at me, Lenny frozen in mid-sip. When he finally broke the silence, he sounded a little irritated. "This is serious stuff, Tucker. Don't joke around."

I shook my head. "I'm serious as the day is long."

June squinted her eyes. "Tucker, Vampires aren't real."

"They're real enough to bust my ribs."

Lenny took a long hard look at me. "Are you out of your mind?"

"I wish I was. I know it sounds crazy and if I was listening to me, I would probably be thinking it was straitjacket time, but it was Vampires that done this to me."

Lenny set his coffee cup down and fiddled with the handle while June ripped the back off a book of matches and used it to mark her place in the book. They listened as I give them my story, "They come up to Widow Woman Creek and kidnapped Lizzie. You remember Lizzie?"

After a pause, Lenny nodded. "City girl, wrote that story 'bout you."

"Right. She was working on a new story about Vampires and how they was just pretend. Then she seen 'em kill some people and so she took off for out here. They come after her. I shot one of them four times and he just laughed at me."

"What with?" Lenny interrupted.

"My .357."

"You can't kill no Vampire with a .357."

"Lenny, I wasn't exactly planning on hunting Vampires."

"Were you shooting hollow points or jacketed?"

"Shit, I don't know. Cheap. They was cheap bullets I bought at the Dollar Store."

He nodded. "All right, all right, sorry. Keep going."

After I filled them in on the details, they stared open-mouthed. I half expected them to say I was out of my mind, and coming from those two, it would have meant a lot. June spoke first. "What do you suppose they want with Lizzie?"

I shrugged my shoulders. "Reckon it's because she seen them murder those people."

Lenny scratched absently at his leg. Directly he stood up and walked to the window "Vampires? Damn. You sure they weren't some kind of government supersoldiers, you know, like experimental cyborgs? They have the technology."

"They was Vampires, no doubt about it."

"Damn, Tucker, what do you aim to do?"

I nodded for a refill and smiled up at June in thanks. She opened up a box of graham crackers and we all took one. "They come out from New York City and I aim to go after them. But I'm thinking I need an edge. Maybe you could come up with something for me?" I asked hopefully. "Something that'll kill 'em."

"How long do I have?"

"I gotta leave in the morning. Got a flight booked out of Jackson."

"In the morning? Jesus H. Christ, I can't get nothing ready in one day. A couple of weeks maybe. Have to do some research, get plans drawn up, do some test shooting..."

"Listen, I ain't got two weeks. If there's any hope of getting Lizzie out of this alive I got to be in New York City by this time tomorrow."

JULIUS SAT IN FRONT of the fire and contemplated the flames through the amber swirls of his cognac. Something was disturbing his concentration, a sensation not wholly unpleasant, but relatively new. There was a factor outside of his reach, a wild card, and it hinged on the disappearance of Desard. He reached slowly for a soft cord suspended from the ceiling, hanging behind his chair. He pulled on it gently, almost as an afterthought. Somewhere in the recesses of the mansion a bell chimed imperceptibly. Within seconds there was a knock on the door and Jenkins, his servant for more than fifty years, entered.

"Sir?"

"Jenkins, please ask Elita to stop in for a little chat."

"Right away, sir." He closed the door and Julius stood to toss another log into the fire, stirring it briefly with the poker. Sparks flickered and were drawn up the chimney as he settled back into his chair. Elita entered, without knocking.

"You called?" she asked.

It is said that with time, one grows used to anything, that anything becomes tediously familiar. Not so, he reflected, with Elita. For untold centuries the sight of her never failed to stir him.

"Any word from Desard?" she asked, feigning indifference.

"None, I'm afraid."

"How unfortunate," she said lightly, but heavy emotions curdled her words. "I suppose we should fear the worst?"

"I can't imagine what could have happened."

"I can. The cowboy. He wasn't dead. He hurt Desard and Desard lost his temper. Our little cowboy must have guessed what he was up against."

"Is he that resourceful?"

"Would our Queen have given her heart to a simpleton?"

"Love knows no such distinction, I fear."

Elita crouched before the fire, taking in the heat. "Perhaps he will come for her."

"If he does," Julius said slowly, "we will eliminate him. What sort of threat can a lone farmer pose?"

"Cowboy. And it would appear Desard presumed the same."

Julius was thoughtful. Then he laughed. "A cowboy. How absolutely preposterous. If he comes, we will take care of him. Perhaps it will even provide a bit of entertainment."

SEVEN

When I woke, everything was fuzzy, and I had no idea where I was. My eyelids felt like someone had pasted them together, and cobwebs and old cotton candy had replaced my brain. My body was oddly heavy, as if the earth was pulling me toward its center, and I couldn't move my arms or legs. Had there been an accident? Where was I and who had brought me here? Breathe in, breathe out, breathe in, breathe out. Panic and hysteria hit at once as flashes of memory flew through my mind, engulfing me and threatening to take complete control. My breathing was labored and my head ached. Were those voices? Sounded like it, faint and mixed in with footsteps. Feigning sleep, I listened and tried not to scream. A doorknob turned, the footsteps entered the room, more than one pair. And the smell? Something familiar, sweet. Cloves, from a cigarette.

As if on cue, I felt the warmth of light breath close to my ears and a stream of sweet-smelling smoke was blown directly into my face.

"So, our little angel still sleeps," said the throaty voice of a woman.

"Yes, madam," came the courtly response. This one was a man.

"Or perhaps she just pretends. No matter. When she chooses to communicate, let me know right away. I would speak with her first, before anyone."

"I am sorry, madam. Master Julius has left strict instructions. No one is to speak with her unless he is present."

"And you?"

"I may communicate only about her need for sustenance or functional necessities."

"She is comfortable?"

"Of course. I will see to everything she needs."

"You'd better. Julius will have your head if she wants for anything."

"Yes, madam."

"Jenkins, I want you to come to my chambers tomorrow night, before the turning. I think it's time you and I had a chat."

"As you wish, madam."

I heard one pair of footsteps leave the room, waited for the smell of cloves to thin, and tried to figure out which one of them had left. When I was sure that the man and I were alone, I opened my eyes a sliver and watched him moving about. He was small and perfectly groomed, wearing a black suit. His hair was gray and thinning, and he moved with effort. The night spilled into the room as he threw open the heavy drapes.

Watching him move about, the fog of my mind began to clear and, with a rush, it all came back in a tumbling blur. The cabin, Tucker and Rex going out into the rain, the gleam of Tucker's gun, distant shots and faint shouts, hands roughly pulling me from bed, but then nothing else. A wave of nausea threatened as the memories crystallized. Tucker, Tucker. What could have happened to him? I knew it couldn't be good.

A fire was lit in a massive stone fireplace, crackling, the only source of light. The orange glow gradually illuminated the room as my eyesight grew accustomed to the dimness. It was a small room, densely furnished in Gothic style with period tables, chairs, foot cushions, shelves of books, candelabra, and dark, heavy drapes framing the narrow windows from floor to ceiling. Ornate wood trimmed the angles, polished to a high gloss. I skimmed the paintings on the walls, closely spaced and elaborately framed. The centerpiece was a dominating painting above the fireplace, a huge oil of a woman wearing a sheer blue gown. She looked familiar, but it took a few minutes to realize why. Oh God, she looked like me.

Panic surged anew, and I struggled to keep it at bay. I concentrated on my breathing, taking deep breaths, until I could master my own voice.

"Where am I?" I said as forcefully as I could muster to the man's back. He turned, startled by my voice.

"Are you hungry?"

"Am I hungry?" I echoed incredulously. Why would he ask such a thing at a time like this?

"Are you hungry?" he repeated.

Suddenly, it seemed like such a pertinent question, as my stomach growled impatiently. "Yes, I suppose I am."

"I will attend to it immediately. Should I select something for you, or do you have a preference?"

"I would like a filet mignon, medium rare, a glass of Pinot Noir, preferably from the Pacific Northwest, two Dungeness crab legs, new red potatoes, boiled please, and a chocolate mousse with whipped cream," I demanded.

"Yes, madam. As you wish." He moved toward the door.

I should be petrified or screaming, but instead a shaky sort of calm was descending. Like a fresh coat of paint over my fear.

"Wait," I called to the old man as his hand reached for the door. "I would like to see the woman who was in this room previously with you."

Why had I said that? In the few seconds she had bent over me, I already knew that she scared me. I didn't really want to see her.

"My apologies, madam. That is not possible."

Maybe that was a good thing.

"It is true that you are to see to my needs?" I continued.

"Yes, madam."

"And that Julius will have your head if you disobey me?"

He sighed and gave in. "Very well, madam."

The man bowed and left the room. Who were these people? They were clearly moneyed, old money from the looks of it, and I guessed had lived above the law long enough that they had lost all respect for anything. Was that it? Hadn't I read stories somewhere before about what the super rich did to stay interested in life? The weird games, the elaborate hoaxes? Maybe this Julius man was simply bored, and needed a new game. Had he been stalking me? Was he obsessed with me? Could it be as simple as sex?

I should never have gone to LonePine, never have involved Tucker in this mess. Maybe by some miracle he'd managed to escape, to get away from these monsters, but there was a foggy memory of a woman's voice asking if the cowboy had been eliminated. And the answer. Yes.

But Tucker wouldn't give up. He'd kick and fight until something gave way. A tiny sense of resolve woke up in me and my thoughts became more ordered. I had to get out of there. No matter what else happened, escape was the first order of business and the first step was to move the body, make sure everything still worked. I went through a quick inventory of major muscles and they all responded sluggishly. It was a start. Still lightheaded, I held the bedpost and stood, my blood tingling as it tried to circulate. At the window, I could see the welcome sight of towering skyscrapers. At least I had home court advantage.

I tried the door. It was locked from the outside. Damn. I assumed the old man would be back soon. I should have asked for something more complicated to eat, like lasagna with oven-roasted veal. How long could it take to boil potatoes? Not long enough.

I made a quick circuit of the room. No telephone, no jacks even. No electronic gadgets of any kind, no computer. Nothing that could serve as a weapon. The drawers were mostly empty, like a hotel room. And like a hotel room, there was a Bible in the top one. It looked impossibly old, and thinner than it should be. When I opened it, the layout was all wrong. If I remembered Sunday school at all, there was no Apostle Crinos.

There were two interior doors. The first opened into an enormous walk-in closet filled with designer clothes, lingerie, jeans, and sweaters. The clothes, shoes, even the underwear and bras were all, and only, my size. How the hell had they done that? These freaks had better taste in my clothing than I did. Lends credence to the stalking theory; it seemed they had been watching me for some time.

The other door opened to an elaborate bathroom with a claw-foot tub long enough to stretch out in. Shit, it was practically long enough to swim in. The sink was a marble pedestal and there was a bidet and toilet in a separate alcove. The floor was tiled and the pattern extended into an intricate mural on the wall. Piles of plush towels filled the shelves, along with scented oils, soaps, and creams. If I hadn't been in the middle of hell, I would have thought I'd died and gone to heaven.

Still, the hurried tour of my opulent prison provided no real clue as to what was going on or why they were keeping me. It was like I had fallen through the looking glass. If I could get out of the room long enough to do a quick reconnaissance, maybe I could figure out where and how to run. But how to get out? It wasn't like I could click my heels and go home. I was a prisoner. And they obviously had the means to keep me here as long as they wanted.

For now, it seemed like the best bet was to play along. Based on what had happened so far, they seemed to be required to do my bidding. Except for Julius. What was his game? His memory made me feel ill; how could I have ever let him close to me, tell him the details of my life. I could still feel his mesmerizing voice echoing in my ears. It sounded like . . .

There was a knock at the door.

"Who is it?" I asked, hoping I sounded stronger than I felt. I closed my eyes and told myself to remember the plan, to act regally and unafraid, to participate in their game as an equal, at least until I could escape.

"Your dinner is served, madam."

"Please enter." He set down a tray brimming with lavishly prepared dinner items. A voice in the back of my mind warned against drugs in the food, but I was starving. Besides, if they wanted to drug me, they could just hold me down and do it. He was so elegant in the way he made up the table, laid the silver, and poured the wine. And there was something almost gentle about him.

"What's your name?"

"Jenkins, madam." Even when he called me madam, it didn't sound funny. It sounded natural.

"Jenkins, why am I here?" I asked, sipping a glass of Pinot Noir.

In response, he simply smiled, bowed, and left the room.

The steak was cooked to perfection and I washed it down with the wine, which was fabulous. There was drawn butter for the crab legs, fresh sour cream for the potatoes. In a restaurant, this would've set me back two hundred bucks. After eating, I felt a bit better, and as I finished the last spoonful of chocolate mousse, there was another knock at the door.

Again, I reminded myself to act haughty, indifferent. "Now who is it?"

"Elita. You requested an audience."

Some plan. Now I would really have to wing it.

"Please enter."

I was stunned. This woman was gorgeous. Her dark, silky hair was pinned carelessly to her head, her ivory skin was smooth as satin and her green eyes glinted with suggestion. Her breasts spilled out of a white blouse and her short but perfectly tailored black skirt shadowed her hips, the exquisite ideal of a Madison Avenue model. She smiled at me. A flush spread from my throat, down my spine to my thighs, but I fought it under control.

She looked at me with a mixture of curiosity and boredom. "I'm impressed. The dose I just gave you would have made most Adamites cringe and beg and plead for me. Your kind can be most amusing."

In my mind, I told myself not to over-think this, to trust my instincts. This woman was powerful and, therefore, could be useful. Perhaps she was Julius' spurned mistress and sexual jealousy could be used to my advantage. "Obviously, you are not speaking to just any Adamite, as you so charmingly call us."

"Over the centuries there have been only a few who have not willingly given in to their passion for me. In fact, I could count them on one hand." She sounded almost rehearsed, speaking in a tedious monotone.

"I guess you'll have to move to the fingers on your other hand now. And just give it a rest, I'm not interested. The vampy trampy thing has been done. Frankly, uh, what was your name?"

"Elita."

"Frankly, Elita, after what I've experienced in the last few months, you could never measure up."

"Ah yes, with your little cowboy."

"Is he alive?"

"Why should I tell you?"

"Because I asked."

"As good a reason as any, I suppose. It would seem he is still alive." Relief welled up inside me. "Despite our best efforts, I might add. You must have made quite an impression on him. Or else he has a deeply entrenched survival instinct, like a cockroach. No wonder your culture has such a fascination with cowboys. But don't get your hopes up. He will be dead if he tries to find you."

My hopes were already up. Not in being rescued. Just knowing that he was alive gave me renewed energy to find a way out of this nightmare. What a story this would make for *Harrolds*. Definitely Pulitzer material.

"I have friends who will miss me."

"Like your photographer friend?" She smiled cruelly. "A shame he took your breakup so hard. Just couldn't seem to go on living without you." Her tone was even, but there was a perverse enjoyment hidden deep within.

"You killed him." It was not a question.

She smiled. "No. He committed suicide. I just helped."

I wanted to slap her face, tear at her hair for the ambivalence she was showing toward taking a life. But that was exactly what she wanted. She was trying to goad me and so I choked back the anger and sat quietly, composed on the outside, but my brain was reeling.

Her features darkened as she studied my calmness and so she pressed on. "Yes, it was a real shame about Ric. And you shan't have to worry about your dear cat. What was his name?"

"Felix," I whispered, my throat constricted.

"Your landlady was no longer able to watch over Felix, so I took it upon myself to offer a helping hand."

"And how is he?"

"Delicious. He was delicious."

"You ate my cat. I cannot believe you ate my cat. You are sick." Of course I knew that she didn't really eat my cat, but to even say such a thing! My rage was growing, which meant she was winning now and knew it. I was in a real mess here. I tried to change the subject and hoped my voice wasn't trembling like my heart. "I want a tour of this compound, or whatever it is."

"A tour? Forget it, Julius would not approve."

"Are you afraid of Julius?"

"Of course. Only an idiot wouldn't be. He has the power to turn."

"The power to turn?"

Elita smiled. "You'll find out soon enough." She moved close to me and whispered in my ear, letting the heat of her breath drip down my neck. "Are you sure you wouldn't like a little pleasure in these last hours of your mortality?"

"You are laughable. What I'd like, instead, little girl, is a tour."

"Yes, little girl," came a quiet voice from the door, "she'd like a tour. Give it to her." Elita pulled away, guilty at being caught. As I turned to face the voice, I felt inexplicably cold, a shiver wracking my frame. As I expected. Julius. He bowed.

"You owe me an explanation," I said.

"And you shall receive it. Soon," he responded, straightening. "Elita, take our future Queen for a stroll and then, Elizabeth, will you be so kind as to join me for drinks in the main parlor in, shall we say, an hour?"

"I'll bring her to you," said Elita.

"How kind. Plan on remaining a witness to our chat." Julius left the room almost as quickly as he had appeared.

"Don't get any ideas about escaping," Elita said tiredly, as we walked out into the hall. "It's impossible."

"I am the Queen. Don't tell me what to do."

"You're not the Queen until Julius turns you. Until then, little girl," she drew out the last phrase sarcastically, "you are merely a prisoner."

It was like no place I had ever seen. The splendor, the wealth. Impressive on a certain level, but it only left me cold. Cold and anxious to find a way out. I examined each door, wondering where it led: another hallway, another room? There had to be a way out. This was Manhattan, for God's sake. How could a woman of reasonable intelligence be kept prisoner among the teeming masses of New York? If these freaks really were Vampires, all I had to do was wait for the sun to rise, sneak out by day and bribe the guards. Bam, I'd be gone. What the hell was I thinking? They're not really Vampires. There's no such thing. I must be losing my mind.

"How did you get me here?" My voice was rising in spite of my best efforts.

"I'm right next to you, there's no need to yell. And frankly, I don't know why you think I should answer all your questions."

"Sorry. I'm a little off center. Kidnapping tends to do that to me."

She smiled in spite of herself.

"What does it matter, my questions? Like you said, I'm a prisoner."

"How we got you here is quite simple, and not very compelling. Barely worth the effort of retelling. In short, enough money in your pathetic, rational world will get you just about anything you want."

"Is that what this is all about? Boredom? Are you looking for some new kicks?"

"I wish it were that simple. If only you were just a new face for Julius' temporary amusement," she trailed off into silence.

"Why do you allow yourself to be held here by such a marginal looking man as Julius? You're a knockout, you could have anyone you want."

"I have spent centuries having anyone I want. After awhile, even newness becomes tedious."

"Why are you part of this, this game of Vampirism?"

"This is no game. No more questions. It really is quite boring."

As we walked down the hall, I noticed a heavy wooden door with metal bracing bars, bolted with an iron padlock.

"Where does that lead?" I asked my lovely, unwilling hostess.

Elita sighed, acquiescing to my curiosity. "To the ritual rooms below."

"May I see them?"

"No, they are sacred to our kind, not to be profaned by simple curiosity. Your turning will take place in them tomorrow night. Then you can see them firsthand."

"My turning?"

"Let Julius explain that. He's infinitely more articulate than I am."

"Julius, again Julius, I don't understand why you are so obedient to such a little pip-squeak."

Elita's face echoed the scorn in her voice. "Soon, my dear Queen-to-be, you will be completely in awe of Julius yourself." She paused and licked her lips. "I think I will greatly enjoy seeing your high and mighty attitude leveled. You have no idea what you're in for, do you?"

"No. But I hope it entails a Pulitzer."

Elita shook her head and opened the French doors off of the massive dining room. I followed her out onto the moonlit balcony. Delicately crafted wrought-iron furniture was placed carelessly about.

"All I know is that when the police find out, you and Julius and all your other freaks are in for some hard time."

Elita giggled. It was charming and unexpected from her exquisite face, but the girlish laugh and giggle somehow only made her even more seductive, lighting her face like a virgin.

"You are so naive," she stammered through another giggle, as I pushed past her and walked alone into the garden, "and for some unknown reason, that's rather endearing."

She stopped suddenly and with it, her humor faded. "I wonder if you are toying with me. Are you that smart?" she asked my retreating back.

I continued to walk into the wet grass; it was cold against my bare feet. At last, I turned to look back at the house. Elita cut an imposing silhouette in the moonlight, leaning over the balcony.

"How do you keep this place so peaceful?" I called to Elita. "What keeps out the masses?"

"There's a facade of rowhouses around the whole block. We own it all. We also employ a small army of guards who are paid handsomely for their services. They are full-time, so don't get any ideas about escaping by daylight. Some of them are part Vampire, simply biding their time until Julius chooses to turn them, others are descendants of families that have been under our protection and in our service for centuries. Very loyal. They live much better than any other Adamites and are promised safety on the day of reckoning."

"The day of reckoning?"

"It's closer than you think. And all because of you." There was a tone in her voice, almost mocking, but not quite.

How could I respond to such nonsense? If I wasn't a prisoner and they hadn't tried to destroy all that I loved, I would just laugh in their faces and cross to the other side of the street.

"Come back," Elita shouted, "we must go to Julius."

I was tempted to make a run for it, but Elita had let me get this far away and that probably meant we were being watched, or else she was really fast. Either way, my chances now were not good. Better to wait for something more promising, I thought. They may be crazy, but I didn't think they'd actually kill me. Why go to all this trouble just to kill the Queen?

"All right," I said instead, "let's go have a drink with your God, Julius."

He was waiting in the parlor, sitting in a leather armchair. Old-fashioned reading glasses were perched on his aquiline nose and he stared intently at a leather-bound book. He looked up and smiled as we entered, then serenely removed his glasses and placed the book on the oak table nearby.

"Time has dulled even my eyes a bit, but I can still see that before me are the two most exquisite creatures in the world," he said, standing.

He looked like a poor imitation of Mr. Rogers. "Could we just cut to the chase?" I said. "Why have you brought me here? You won't get away with it. The police are already looking for you, and by this time, for me too."

He gestured dismissively. "Lizzie, my dearest, to us these matters are no different than the buzzing of an annoying mosquito. Hasn't the demise of your photographer and the cowboy convinced you of this yet?"

My heart stopped. Literally. It was dead in my chest and the room swam. Then it skipped and stuttered, barely starting up again before I was able to mutter in response. "Tucker is dead?" I looked quickly at Elita, the bitch, why had she lied? Elita stared stonily ahead, avoiding my eyes.

Julius interrupted my hatred. "Please. This is not how I wanted our first conversation to begin. This is all in the past now. Your life is just beginning. May I offer you a drink?"

"No."

"Please. Sit." He motioned to the stool at the base of his chair. I sat, feeling tired and utterly defeated. Elita moved to the fireplace, warming her hands.

"There is much I need to tell you, my child, so much history, in order for you to understand who you are and why you will be our Queen, my Queen, and why together we will see the unseating of twenty centuries of Adamite rule."

I rolled my eyes, how could I do anything else? What an insipid old fool. Julius held up his hand, looked sternly at me. I couldn't help it, my gaze hit the floor, his look was just too intense, too difficult to master. But my anger was building, a rage that began to completely replace my fear of this situation. Soon, somehow, I would lay waste to his little kingdom and all that inhabited it. The fool spoke and his words wormed their way into my mind.

"Let me begin with your beginnings. Seventeen centuries ago, in a very different place, your ancestors were promised to me. For a variety of reasons, I have not yet chosen to claim what is rightfully mine. I intend to do so now."

EIGHT

I KNEW MY REQUEST was really putting Lenny under the gun, no pun intended, but I also knew that if anybody could help me in my quest to kill as many damn Vampires as it took to get Lizzie back, it was him.

"June," he said, "you'd better bring dinner to the shop. C'mon, Tucker."

The shop was where Lenny did his creating. In it, near as I could tell, there was a machine for everything except splitting atoms. 'Course, I wouldn't know what one of them looked like anyway. He opened up a fridge that had been a water heater in a previous life. It was icy on the inside and stocked with cans of beer, candy bars, and some vials of amber liquid I decided not to ask about. He popped two beers and handed me one. Between the horse medicine and the caffeine, my brain was in no condition for alcohol, but I started in on it anyway.

"The first thing we got to figure out is what killed that old boy. Fire or wood? Or was it the combination of the two?"

"Everybody knows wood kills them. You know, a stake through the heart," I said. "Least that's what Doc Near told me this morning."

"I wouldn't take nothing he says too seriously," Lenny said, taking a pull at his beer.

"Why not?" I asked.

He spread some recycled paper out across the table. "Because he's a government agent."

I pulled a stool up and dusted it off. "Doc Near is a government agent? I can't hardly believe that," I said.

"Believe it. It's too obvious. I don't know why you ain't already figured it out. Anyway, we got to get serious." He pulled out a worn-down nub of a grease pencil and sketched out a stick figure of a Vampire with oversized fangs, labeling it Dracula. Across the page he sketched out a rough image of a cowboy which, despite the lack of handsome distinguishing features, I assumed was me. "I figure it's a combination of both fire and wood. So, what we got to do is figure out how to get fire and wood from here," he underlined me, "to here," he underlined Dracula, "without you getting close enough for them to get their fangs into you." Just for emphasis, he circled the fangs a couple of times.

"Yep," I said, "that sounds like just exactly what we got to figure out."

His eyes started to glaze over and I grabbed my beer and wandered off. I could see that he was getting himself all worked up into one of those foamy creative states of mind.

The creative process has always been a mystery to me. Watching Lenny struggle with the technical muse was what it must have been like watching Michelangelo just before he painted the Sistine Chapel. I've painted my share of ceilings, but they was pretty small and generally of one color. Michelangelo painted a big old church with all kinds of little pictures and I reckon the difference between us, other than I can't paint little pictures whatsoever, is agony. Artists have to agonize. Creation springs from it. They have to torture themselves before they can work up enough interest and motivation to undertake such an endeavor. If they wasn't in agony, if they was just working at any old job and laughing and goofing around, they wouldn't be artists. I suppose that's what separates them from the rest of us folk. They don't mind subjecting themselves to the tortured state from which they can sit down and write *War and Peace* or paint the Sistine Chapel, whereas most of us would just as soon take a nap or else go have a beer.

Inconspicuous as possible, I watched Lenny. He drew stuff. He talked to himself. He flipped through books and laughed at jokes in his head.

He held his knees and rocked back and forth like a child. I just kept on drinking beer and stacking up the empties until his eyes sort of cleared and he said, "Come back later. I got some ideas."

By the time I got back to Dad's, it was getting on to dark. The sun was setting over the mountains and staining the clouds bunched up there, so I sat in the truck for a few minutes trying to memorize the beauty. Dad come out on the porch and waved me in. He set out a pot of beans he'd cooked up with a ham bone, along with some fried potatoes, store-bought tortillas, and fresh tomatoes cut up and a couple of deviled eggs from the Widow Johnson.

We didn't say much and I could tell he was troubled of mind. "I still think I should go with you, Tuck."

"Nope. I want you here. Lizzie may be trying to call or even come back. If she does, you got to take care of her until I can get back. I'll give you a call every couple of days to check in. Can I borrow the Casull?"

He looked at his prize pistol in its holster hanging from the bedpost. "What am I supposed to do if they come back for me?" he said.

"Give 'em some of these deviled eggs, I reckon."

He sighed, slumped down in his chair. "I hope Lizzie's okay," he said.

"Me too. Now let me help you with the dishes."

Afterward he turned on the TV so he could read a book and I gnawed off some more of that horse painkiller. Pretty soon it had me nodding and I curled up on the couch, letting my mind wander unchecked until it settled on Lizzie. It felt like I was somehow spanning the distance from LonePine to New York with just my thoughts. She was the focusing point, like my love was the sun shining through a giant magnifying glass and reflecting down into one tiny, burning, hopeful point. I tried to expand it, to make it real, but a terrible darkness stole over the sun like a wet blanket.

Something tugged hard at my heart and waves of sorrow and despair washed over me like a rock had been thrown into hell's pond and the ripples eventually come crashing up to pull me down. Underneath it all I could see the evil, smiling face of the Vampire I'd shot, with his arms reaching out for me. Behind him, growing faint, was Lizzie, looking beautiful and sorrowful and sinking away.

I awoke with a shout that startled Dad out of his chair. I checked the clock on the VCR and it was just after midnight. "Let's head back over to Lenny's, see what he's rustled up."

It was a quiet drive on a dark night. There ain't much traffic around LonePine at midnight, save the occasional folks returning from late-night social events hosted by women whose husbands work the graveyard shift. The lights were all off in Lenny's trailer so we idled on down to the shop.

He had fallen asleep over the workbench, but the sound of the door opening roused him. His hair was tangled over his face and littered with shreds of candy-bar wrappers and metal shavings; a pyramid of beer cans surrounded him. Dad nodded at him

"Lenny, how you doing?" I asked.

He stretched, rubbed his eyes and yawned. "Damn, Tucker, you owe me for this one." He pointed at a bundle on the table. "That's the best I could come up with on such short notice." He dumped out a bucket full of peculiar-looking shotgun shells and unwrapped a sawed-off double-barrel shotgun beside them. "I took apart these three-inch mag shells and replaced the buckshot with a seven-inch birch dowel. I sharpened it up and reinforced the tip with sterling silver so it won't splinter apart when it hits one of 'em. Silver is supposed to be disagreeable to all things supernatural. Of course, you can only use them in a breech loader like this here. Watch this."

He cracked it open and snuggled one of the shells into it, then put on some earplugs.

"Hold your ears."

We did and he shouldered it and took aim across the room at an easy chair against the wall. There was a roar and flash as bitter gunsmoke filled the air. The chair jerked backward as if kicked and the ragged end of a wooden dowel poked out of the fabric. "It ain't much good over about twenty yards, but up to that it'll shoot straight. 'Course the downside is, you can only shoot twice before you have to reload." He tossed the shells into a canvas bag.

"Now these," he unwrapped a box of more familiar-looking shells, "are from my own personal supply. They shoot a thermite load which, in case you ain't familiar, is magnesium-based and burns white hot at like a thousand degrees or something. I'd suggest one of each in the barrel. Stake them, then scorch 'em." He dropped them in the bag, too.

"Lastly, and this I'm particularly proud of, is some homemade thermite grenades." He laid a half dozen duct-taped balls on the table. "The engine case for a Volkswagen is pure magnesium. I ground one up and coated these here fragmentation grenades with the powder and then duct-taped it all into place. Once you pull the pin and give them a toss, you got about seven seconds to duck and run before the grenade blows, the magnesium ignites, and then rains down like lava. Expect about a twenty-foot kill zone and then add another forty to feel comfortable."

"Goddamn," I said, my mouth hanging open. "Where the hell did you get this stuff?"

"I have my sources."

"You scare me, Lenny."

"Ain't you I'm worried about." He headed for the door. "I think you're covered," he said.

"Any ideas on how to get 'em there?"

"You remember June's cousin Larry? He works for USExpress and he owes me for something big enough to get this all there overnight. I already called. You just need an address to ship it to. I penciled out some instructions on how to use this stuff. Let me know how it works. If it don't blow in your hands, we could start marketing it. I gotta go see if I'm still married, and if so, get some sleep."

I stuck the ammo and grenades in the duffel along with the shotgun, after wrapping it up in my denim jacket, then tossed the whole thing in the back of the truck. As we pulled out, Dad took a look at Lenny stumbling up to the trailer. "You sure have some strange friends."

NINE

"ALTHOUGH YOU MAY NOT believe me now, the information I am about to convey is critically important for you to understand. Please try to relax and listen. I shall start with some background to help you relate to us. You went to church as a child, did you not?"

Julius' voice was having the same effect on me as before, at that party. It was hypnotic. I left the question unanswered, although of course I had gone to church. My mother made me go every Sunday, no matter where we were. Did he know this already?

As if reading my thoughts, he smiled and I looked away.

"Before Adam or Eve, God created good and evil as a means of separating the souls of the world."

"What's the matter with you? Can't you tell I don't care?" My voice no longer sounded like my own; it was hysterical, in spite of my best efforts at outward control.

Julius continued, regardless. "The Bible called it separating day from night, a metaphor for separating humanity from Vampires. God needed a place in which good and evil could be manifest. This was the actual purpose behind what Adamites call the Creation. It was not simply the dispersion of the seeds of humanity, but rather a cosmic circumstance pitting good against evil."

"You're wasting your breath. Can't you see I don't give a shit about your little fantasy?"

"My dear," his shoulders slumped, "please refrain from commenting unless it is to ask genuine questions."

"I'll say whatever I choose," I snapped back, because I was truly afraid. "I think that is well within my Queenly rights," I continued. "I will not listen." I covered my ears with my hands.

Julius sighed again and made a slight motion in Elita's direction, a tiny nod of his head. I spun around to face her and she walked toward me, smiling.

"Someday," Julius intoned, "I will look back on this moment as Adamite parents look back on their child's toilet-training. As with those same parents, I look forward to the time when you are approaching my equal, Lizzie, and not merely a child."

Moving faster than I could resist, Elita sharply pulled my hands from my ears and handcuffed my arms behind my back. I sputtered and swore and she stuffed a gag in my mouth, a silk gag, but a gag nevertheless.

"Learn your place, little girl," she whispered in my ear, out of Julius' range of hearing, "and patience."

Bitch, bitch, bitch! I screamed inside. I kicked my feet, stood, struggled against the handcuffs, but to no avail. I was stuck, feeling more terrified by the minute. This was bad, really bad.

"Thank you, Elita. Now, I shall continue."

I sat back down but made a point of turning so that my back faced him. At least he couldn't see me cry. Tears chipped down my cheeks as I tried to find the switch in my mind that would shut them off. When I looked up, Elita was watching me, smiling like it was a big joke. Bitch.

"We shan't bind your ears, at any rate. Now, as I was saying, Vampires are a repository of evil. We are, in fact, a separate race of beings. A race to which cruelty, perversion, and exploitation of the weak are *noblesse*.

"This is not to say that humans do not possess evil. They do, as evidenced daily, and as shown rather elegantly by some quite remarkable men in your history. However, at heart, humans throughout history have always believed that good is the better of the two. At the bottom of all human evil there is always a nagging doubt, a recognition, an admission that what had transpired was wrong. Human evil is, thus, empty, wasteful and petty."

He paused. I could hear, although my back was still turned to him, Julius taking a sip of cognac. I watched Elita's eyes following his every movement with longing and expectation as he began to speak again. Her shoulders relaxed, almost imperceptibly. She was in love with him, or something resembling love, I thought.

"Vampires, on the other hand, have made a virtue of evil. It forms the basis of our moral code. To the undead, with our mirror-image morality, evil is our greatest aspiration. Anything good done within that framework is salted with the notion that at heart, it is still evil. Vampires are as convinced of their inherent evilness as humans are sure of their goodness."

Julius contemplated the weight of his own words. What a pompous pig. During the flow of his soliloquy, I had gradually turned so that I could now stare up at him, my mouth and hands still bound, but trying my best to burn my eyes into his soul. Wasn't there anything I could do to make him just a little bit uncomfortable? He smiled down at me like a paternalistic deity and continued.

"In the last several decades, with the destruction of your historic moral fiber and with no replacement waiting in the wings, a moral vacuum has been created. Inside of this vacuum, human civilization has spiraled downward. For the first time, Vampires are poised to replace humans as the ruling elite of this tired old globe and the morality of evil will finally replace the age-old morality of goodness."

He smiled, a huge toothy effort and to my surprise, leaned down and pulled the silk scarf from my mouth. His hand lingered on my cheek, traced the contours of my lips. Slightly parting my mouth, he inserted the tip of his finger inside. I fought the urge to vomit, to snap the end of his finger off between my teeth, but all the while he cautioned me with his eyes. One false move, one misplaced word, and I would be bound again. Again, an almost imperceptible nod to Elita and she moved behind me, pressing her body against mine so that I felt her breasts against my back. She unlocked the handcuffs and let them drop with a soft thud to the carpet.

"I'd like a glass of water," I said quietly, just after Julius removed his finger from my mouth. I wanted to wash out the stinking taste of him.

"Of course," he said, smiling at my acquiescence. "Elita, please take care of this request. And send for a snack, too. She should keep her strength up. There's so much to cover in such a short time. Your turning will be tomorrow night, no matter what." I felt Elita's nails through my blouse as she drew her hands up my back, lingering on my neck, beneath my hair. She left the room. Julius watched my eyes throughout.

"I have a question," I said, massaging my wrists. If I feigned interest, maybe he'd feel closer, personal, enough to let me go. Maybe I could convince him I could be his voice into the Adamite world, write a bunch of articles or something.

"Yes, my love?" he smiled, a parody of sweetness.

"What did you mean about the destruction of humanity's moral fiber?"

"Excellent question. Let me elaborate. Your world has been beset by sweeping social movements, wars, and devastating religious upheavals in the last several decades. While I certainly have my own personal hypothesis as to why, the only relevant point to this discussion is the consequence of these events. Unfortunately for humanity, your recent history has been your undoing. For many thousands of years, your intrinsic sense of good was steadily evolving, but it remained woefully incomplete. One need only turn to your history books and examine the difference between, say, Christianity now and during the Crusades, to see that humanity's sense of good has been evolving, slowly, toward a greater emphasis on love and tolerance. God gave you a code to live by and for centuries, under a wide variety of circumstances, it served you well in its many forms. Christianity, Judaism, Islam, and the many variants; underneath them all was one common element, namely, love both thy neighbor and thy God. Unhappily, your God-given code has all but crumbled here in the twenty-first century. In this country it has been amply demonstrated by the poverty of your inner cities, rampant crime, environmental destruction, drug dependence, the vanity of your politics, your flirtation with government-sponsored torture. It is by no means unique to this country, but the fact that this trend is now evident here—well, I rest my case. The once-proud society of the Adamites has become one of every man for himself."

It was hard not to hear inherent sense in what he said. Countless books and articles have chronicled this collapse of morality, the isolation of modern society, the loss of family, the hatred and rage. Wasn't that the reason everyone was in therapy, searching for meaning? But hearing it all from this man, this sick man, made

118

me want to vomit. How dare he pass judgment on anyone? His eyes burned into mine with condescension and he smiled. Had he again read my thoughts?

"Psychologically, humans are like children, controlled by peer pressure to be good. As with a child, this would have eventually matured into a framework, a moral code embraced by each individual, rather than enforced by religious coda. And then, quite frankly, Vampires might have disappeared. My personal belief is that this may have been what God had been hoping for, relegating Vampires to a role as the repository of true evil until, well, until Adamites matured into something more closely resembling God Himself. Then what need would there be for us?"

Despite myself, I was growing curious. Julius was a candidate for the funny farm, but he told a great story.

"Now, for the first time in history, Vampires have been given a chance to assume the mantle of power. Perhaps God is testing us both, for we, too, are His children. The balance in the Adamite world has tipped, very slightly and precariously, but it has indeed slipped toward the side of evil. What is it you Adamites are so fond of saying? He who hesitates is lost. Rest assured, I shall not hesitate."

"Why do you need me?" I asked, not sure I wanted to hear the answer.

"Lizzie, my dearest, your interest gives me great pleasure. Please understand that I am laying at your feet the most extraordinary adventure you could ever hope to realize in your simple human existence. You will be the envy of the entire world. You see, my sweet, you carry the blood of an ancient Vampiric family, royalty, and you are our rightful Queen. I am here to serve you, to guide you through the change. The world will be yours and you will belong to the world, a symbol of nobility."

He waited for my response. I tried to be as royal as possible by saying nothing. He smiled, again as if reading my mind.

"Yes, we still have a monarchy. What did you expect, yellow-dog democrats? Log cabin republicans perhaps? How quaint. But I get ahead of myself. First you should understand how it is you came to carry this royal Vampiric blood."

"Wait. One more question," I interjected. "What makes you so all-powerful?"

"Quite simple. I have the power to turn. I am the only one with this power. I choose who inhabits the elite world of the undead."

"The power to turn?" I pressed for more explanation.

Julius gently stroked my head, reminding me in a sick way of Mother and how she used to stroke my hair until I fell asleep. "Your questions will all be answered, but first, let us take a short detour through our history. Like you Adamites, we too have a bible. The recorded words of God that tell our creation story and establish certain mandates and universals, only from the perspective of our unique history and future."

Julius picked up the leather-bound book he had been reading earlier. "Let me read from the first few chapters of our Genesis. You may recognize some of the material." Julius cleared his throat, swirled a little more cognac back, and began to read.

In the beginning there was silence and God. God spoke and the silence was destroyed and from His words came the heavens and earth. God said let there be light and darkness and there was light and darkness where before had been only silence. And God saw that light was easy and bright and called it day. And God saw that darkness was challenging and hid-

den and called it night. Thus were night and day brought forth and it was one day.

He looked up long enough to ascertain he had my attention. He did, all of it. "I fear this shall become tedious, being somewhat familiar." His finger made a dry, whispery sound as he dragged it down the aged paper. "Let's move to the sixth day."

Then God said let the earth bring forth man according to his own kind who shall have dominion over the house of Day and all creatures who dwell within and so the earth brought forth a man and a woman and God saw that it was good and blessed them that they may be fruitful and multiply and fill the earth and subdue the Day and have dominion over all who move through it, all the birds and fishes and beasts and creeping things and plants that seek the sun. And it was so and it was the sixth day. Thus, on the seventh day God rested and beheld his work and saw that it was good and only good. Thus God spoke, and said let the earth bring forth Vampires each according to their hind who shall have dominion over the house of Night and all those who dwell within, and so the earth brought forth a man and a woman who were not like the first man and woman, but also not like the beasts of the earth. And God saw that they were not good and blessed them that they go forth and multiply and subdue the Night and have dominion over all that move through it. And so it was and it was the seventh day and God spoke and blessed the seventh day and hallowed it because on the seventh day, God gave flesh to evil that the earth be separate from the heavens.

I realized I was holding my breath. What sort of brilliant, twisted mind could create an entire world, including a creation story, for the sake of his Vampiric game? He put down the Bible.

"Let me summarize the next few centuries. From the dawn of creation, the two separate species have lived apart from one another. Vampires of course knew of and despised Adamites because our human brethren had the enviable quality of contentedness, due largely to the fact that time has a sense of meaning for Adamites. This is, of course, because they experience death. Time was measured by the extent of their lives.

"For the most part, Adamites have known nothing of the Vampiric world, except for those upon whom we preyed, mostly the weak and sick. We lived in darkness, shunning the light not because it would kill us—at that time we were not so sensitive—but rather because we were reptilian-like and it was more comfortable in the shadows. Our genetic material, lent from the cold-blooded serpent, predicated that we seek out dark and wet surroundings. We were like animals, reptiles, but with human attributes."

"From the serpent?" I asked incredulously.

"Yes. God experimented with our form in the early days. Whereas Adamites arose from the dust of the earth infused with God's breath, Vampires arose from the bodies of serpents bent by God's will into manlike form."

I couldn't help myself, I interrupted with a question. "Do you have an Original Sin also?"

"Please, Lizzie, think of what you ask. How could we have an Original Sin when sin has no meaning to us? We are sin. To a Vampire, the only sin is an act of genuine goodness. But there is a critical event that occurred for us and not for the Adamites. You see, we ate from the Tree of Life, which bore the fruit of eternity, not the Tree of Knowledge from which Eve tempted Adam.

"This was the cruelest joke God played, an irony that even now amuses me. With death, as reprehensible as it may seem to you, God gave Adamites the gift of context. And with the promise of an afterlife came meaning, a place to aspire to, a means of reinforcing your desire to do good. In contrast, we were granted eternal life. It should have been granted to those who ostensibly embody good, the Adamites. Rather, it was given to us, an entire race of men and women whose essence relies on spilling the blood of others. God intended it to be a balancing factor, but it backfired. We had no pride, no sense of ourselves as a cohesive people. Instead, we were little more than simple animals, living in the shadows of the Adamites. Scurrying about in the darkness and seeking blood where we could. A miserable eternal existence, don't you think?"

Julius motioned for Elita to bring the crystal decanter and he refilled his snifter. He smiled darkly before continuing. "Just over twenty centuries ago, this all changed with the coming of our Messiah. We call him Malthus. Our Messiah happened to exist about the same time as the Adamite Jesus. They knew each other. In keeping with the times, our Messiah also died on the cross, although not on the same day as Jesus, but shortly thereafter. He died not from simple blood loss or thirst, but rather because his body was raised upon the cross and as the sun rose, he burned to death. Thus came the greatest change in Vampiric history.

"There are many fables associated with his life, teachings and parables, but what is important to our story was his mission. He came to restore faith among the Vampires, faith in the morality of evil, faith that God had not forgotten us. He did this in two ways.

"First, he died on the cross to give us the gift of darkness. By embodying darkness, he gave power absolute to light. For the first time, those who accepted his teachings no longer found the sun merely uncomfortable. They found it terminal. In one stroke he managed to give form to the darkness of our heritage. By investing the sun with power to destroy us, he made us absolute rulers of the night. This may sound implausible, but no more so than the notion of one man dying for all humanity's sins.

"As Adamites ruled the day, the night now firmly belonged to us. For the first time, it seemed, we were on an equal footing. God had attempted this in the Beginning, but somehow we had strayed. Malthus showed us the value of one gift God had given us: Night. At the same time, he also gave us the gift of an afterlife."

"I don't understand," I said, "how could an afterlife have meaning for the undead? After what?"

"Our messiah died on the cross and was resurrected that night. Not three days later, as Jesus, never to be seen again. Each night we repeat and relive this miracle. Every day we are dead and every night we rise from that state to live again. He showed us that we could exist by being daily resurrected. For the first time, we had a spiritual life. Each dawn we die with the spiritual knowledge that we will be resurrected at twilight. It is a miracle. For the first time, our status as eternal beings had meaning; the now and the afterlife became one and the same thing."

"Does he still live?" I wished I could feign disinterest. I could not.

"As I already said, he died on the cross, by sunlight. His body turned to ash by the dawn. But his spirit was taken to heaven. He sits with God."

Julius was lost in the power of the tale he was spinning. His mesmerizing voice dropped to an even softer level. "Not only have his teachings survived, so have his progeny. You, my dear, as well as myself, are direct descendants of Malthus."

Elita offered a silver tray laden with cheeses, breads, mineral water, wine and chocolate truffles. I opened a mineral water and helped myself to a truffle, grateful for the diversion.

"Please, refresh yourself. Elita, join me outside for just a moment."

"My, my, I never knew you were such an actor."

"Really. You think it's going well?" Julius responded.

"It's hard to say. She is intelligent enough to not reveal what she's really thinking."

"Good point. But the truths of our bible and our ancestors are powerful. She can't help but believe. And the seeds of my deception are well hidden inside these truths."

Elita wrinkled her nose in distaste. "I don't see why you care. I say just turn her and be done with it. You don't need her cooperation."

"Ahh," Julius sighed, "but how much sweeter it will be to have it. Imagine Lazarus' face when he sees the new Queen at my side, a willing consort." Julius' face radiated with a childlike pride as he imagined such a victory.

"You want her to fall in love with you, don't you?" demanded Elita, trying hard to keep her jealousy covered.

"Call it what you will. Remember how much her mother cared for me? Such a silly, lonely woman. I'm surprised she was able to raise our daughter to turn out even marginally strong."

"Bad mothers often raise the most interesting daughters."

"Hmmm? What?" He had already skipped ahead by a memory. "Oh, yes, mothers and daughters. Well, now it's time for a really bad father to take over."

"Why not just tell her that she's your daughter? She'd be more willing to do your bidding."

"No, that won't do at all. Adamites are such prudes about sexual relations between family members."

"I guess I'm a little unclear on this part of your plan."

"Nothing short of total destruction of her innocence. She will give herself freely to me and when the truth arrives, it will be far too late. The rest of eternity at my side she will be as a mindless slave. A hollow shell of a woman. Nothing else can balance the scales with Lazarus for robbing me of my prize seven hundred years ago."

"Vengeance, while a laudable goal, should not be allowed to stand in the way of the greater evil to be attained in this circumstance," Elita added circumspectly.

Julius was lost in his own thoughts. "Imagine the sweetness of absorbing the power that she unknowingly carries in her blood. It will catapult me to the highest realm of power ever known in the history of Adamite or Vampire." He laughed. "And I get the pleasure of her body. I shall take her to heights she has never experienced; only then will I reveal the truth about her paternity. How devastating." Julius chuckled in anticipation.

"How utterly vicious and delicious," said Elita, grateful that Julius intended to destroy this woman. She would be nothing but a royal figurehead. There was no need for concern. Was there?

"Let's return to our protégé, shall we?" Julius said, offering his arm to Elita.

"With pleasure, master," she said.

TEN

By the time they returned, I was back on my stool as if I had never been eavesdropping. I had barely been able to make out sounds, and even fewer words, but I had detected a tone that put me even more on guard, a feeling that made me think this might be something far beyond a bunch of freaks needing new forms of entertainment.

"Please forgive our short absence. Shall I continue with my story?" he asked me.

I was not sure what to say or do. I felt more and more lost, struggling at the bottom of a dark hole with nothing to grab onto, no way to escape. And so I said nothing, swallowed my fear and feigned indifference.

"Silence certainly has its virtues," he said quietly "I trust you have eaten and drunk adequately?"

I nodded, not meaning to. It was involuntary.

"Good. Now, shall I continue the story of our Savior?" He didn't wait for my response, just sat in his chair while Elita resumed her position by the fire. "Malthus' secondary purpose was to provide us with new genetic material. His coming allowed us to finally separate ourselves from the bloodlines of the serpent, to rid our genetic constitution of the limits of this cold-blooded creature.

"While this purpose may appear purely biological at first blush, it was much more. In effect, he established a line of leadership in the Vampiric world to stretch into the unforeseeable future. There are only two family lines that have the blood of Malthus, all others remain tainted with the blood of the serpent. This, of course," Julius paused, and directed his eyes toward Elita, "makes them no less attractive."

Elita smiled, bowed her head to Julius, then quickly turned her back to us.

In one sentence, Julius had elevated me above Elita. She was no longer my superior, no longer even an equal. She was now my subject. I almost felt sorry for her. She must have sensed it, and turned her head around to glare at me, destroying any sympathy I might have maintained.

"Our messiah fathered many children..."

"But wait," I interrupted, "what woman existed who did not have reptilian blood?" If I could trip him up in his own story, maybe that would help to clear my mind, because I am beginning to believe some of the things he says. Must be the after-effects of the drugs they fed me or lack of nicotine. Julius smiled, pleased at my interest.

"Malthus was a powerful man. He made his mate."

"You just lost me," I said.

"Be attentive and all will become clear. He chose Mary Magdalene as a mate."

"What?" I said, heart pounding. "Come on now, Julius, this is getting a bit far-fetched. She was not a Vampire."

129

"No, of course not. Malthus had the power to turn full humans into Vampires. For all our history, he is the only one to have this power." He paused, before continuing, as if posing a question to himself. "Ponder for a moment, won't you, why the Christian church has so fearfully repressed its Savior's lover."

"This is nonsense."

"Verbal discussions of genealogy are always complex. You must listen carefully. Granted, the turning of Mary Magdalene was against her will, but Malthus then mated with her, and she bore twins, a boy and a girl. The boy was chosen by Malthus as our first King. However, there was an interesting twist. While the boy was fully Vampiric, the girl was part Adamite and part Vampire."

"I guess the Magdalene was more powerful than Malthus realized."

Julius smiled. "Perhaps. Malthus blessed this occurrence and gave the boy the power to turn the girl into a Vampire, should he choose, or to wait for any subsequent generation. His only directive was that subsequent Queens must stem from this original girl child of the twin birth, from this lineage. Our first King, my direct ancestor, chose to wait. He mated with this female several times and many children were born, all of whom had the genetic predisposition to be a Vampire but appeared human. There is an entire history in our Bible, much like Numbers in your Old Testament, in which the family tree stemming from our Messiah is clearly established."

"His sister," I gasped, "he mated with his sister?" Julius laughed. His laugh, as mesmerizing as his voice, made me feel foolish.

"My dear, such family ties have no meaning for us. Nor for your biblical Adamite ancestors. You need only take a closer look at your own Bible. I will admit, your naiveté is quite charming, so sweet." He smiled and cleared his throat. "Now, if I may continue. Our first King watched patiently as these children grew and finally selected a female to turn. There are stories of her extraordinary beauty, but other than that, no record of why he selected her. Thus, we have our first King and Queen and an explanation of our bloodlines. Mine, which is fully Vampiric and includes the gift of turning those with the predisposition for Vampirism received directly from the first-born male of Malthus. Yours, dear Lizzie, which represents the dormant Adamite line from which those of my lineage pick mates or companions to turn, originating from the first-born female child of Malthus. These two lines make up the Vampire elite, the ruling class. Then, of course, there is Elita's line, which predates the Royal lines and originates from the serpent in the fabled garden of Eden."

Elita stood abruptly and started toward the door.

"No, my dear," said Julius, "I am not done with you."

Bowing to him, she resumed her position at the fireplace.

He continued. "The bloodlines related to the Messiah are central to our destiny. They are bloodlines given the right to rule by God, the chosen ones. Their numbers, of course, are quite limited, certainly in comparison to the numerous reptilian Vampires, who are in essence, our masses, our rank and file, and who do not require turning. We have been rigorous in maintaining the purity of the Messianic lines. Interbreeding between the Messianic bloodline and the reptilian bloodline has never occurred. Nor will it. Reptilians only breed with their own. Although," with a nod at Elita, "that certainly does not prevent the sharing of sensual pleasures between Messianic Vampires and Reptilians, or even with Adamites. However, procreation between humans and Vampires is genetically impossible.

"Your world of cinema and fiction likes to pretend that we can create a Vampire simply by biting your fragile necks. If this were true, Adamites would have long ago come under the rule of the Vampire. I am the only remaining Vampire with the power to turn. All the others of my line are now gone." He smiled, like a child caught doing something bad. "The sun can be a mighty weapon when used correctly against your adversaries."

"There must be thousands, no, millions of possible Adamites that you could turn, that have this power to be your Queen. Your mate. Why pick me?"

"That is not important to you. Know only that you are critically important, to me personally as my chosen, and to the larger forces of our times. Many centuries ago, the Vampire world began to slowly disintegrate, infected, I fear, with the same apathy now plaguing humankind. While these various factions in no way rival the power I wield over my own group, they exist and are unhappy. You and I are a symbol of reconciliation, and our union will transform our world."

"Maybe you should tell her about Lazarus," Elita said defiantly from the fireplace.

Julius paused before responding, anger seething beneath his words. "All in good time, Elita my love, all in good time." He stood abruptly. "I grow weary of the sound of my voice."

Elita, her lips drawn tight, moved to leave with him. He held up his hand.

"No. I shall sleep alone this day. I wish to prepare for the turning."

He leaned down over me. Taking my hand in his own, he said quietly, his powerful mesmerizing voice now down to a sharp-edged whisper that was all the more hypnotic, "Tomorrow, we will be one, and the future will be eternally ours."

Julius left the room without another word or even a glance back. Elita moved stiffly toward the door.

"Hey," I said, "what am I supposed to do now, and who is Lazarus?"

"I will not help you in any manner," said Elita forcefully. "You are absolutely, utterly on your own. If Vampires prayed, I would pray that you were never turned." Her voice dropped to a level that only we could share. "I will see you vanquished."

I was left alone, bewildered, in the center of the room. My heart raced. Terror gnawed at the edge of resolve and the thin line between sanity and hysteria was bending dangerously close to irreversible damage. The absence of the suffocating sound of his voice was too much to bear, and alone with my thoughts, a scream was forming on the edge of my tongue.

"Are you ready for bed, madam? The sun will be up shortly." Frightened, I spun around and saw Jenkins standing in the open door behind me.

"I'm not a Vampire, I don't need to hide from the sun," I yelled.

"In that case, perhaps you would care for breakfast?"

ELEVEN

THE NEXT MORNING I woke up alone, the way I had woken up most of my life, only this morning it nearly broke my heart in two. Dad asked me how I was doing and I said not very damn good, so let's just get going. He drove us by the Sagebrush for breakfast. Hazel brought us my favorite, biscuits and gravy, scrambled eggs, and coffee. My body felt half starved from all the healing it was undergoing, and since this might be the last decent food I'd have for a while, I savored every grease-laden bite. After we finished, we strolled out into the parking lot and I give Rex the piece of toast I'd smuggled out in a napkin, after first balling it around a piece of pain pill.

The air was crisp, but the sunshine was warm enough to leave the windows down for the drive to Jackson. It was beautiful and it looked like winter was already making an early appearance. The trees were starting to turn golden and crimson. The uppermost peaks of the Tetons had a light dusting of snow and looked about as lonely as I felt. Wasn't a whole lot to say, so we just listened to the same sad old country songs on the radio. I knew Dad's pride was hurting because he couldn't come along to New York City, but he'd get over it. Life without Lizzie didn't seem too hopeful for me, but there wasn't no sense getting Dad hurt on account of my tragic love life.

At the airport, I coaxed Rex into one of them little dog carriers I bought. He didn't like it much, but the pain pill had made him limp and willing. He licked delicately at my hand through the wires and then curled up and went to sleep. His sides were moving slow with each breath and I watched him roll down the conveyor belt out of sight. Dad stood with me until I had to cross through security. The heaviness of both our thoughts kept us quiet until finally, he looked at me and sighed. "You find her, boy. Find her and bring her back."

"I aim to."

He reached into his jacket and pulled out an aged and weathered silver crucifix trimmed in brass. The middle of it was worn smooth by use, and seeing it brought a lump to my throat, for I recognized it well. "Thought maybe this'd help. It belonged to your mother. Her and God was real close."

I tucked it into my pocket and give him a hug.

"You connect with Lenny's friend?" I whispered in his ear.

"Yep, I did," he said as he hugged back tight and then slapped me on the shoulder, turning away without another word. I watched him walking down the terminal. His shoulders was slumped and his whole body looked as tired and sore as mine felt. I wondered what it would feel like losing a child, even one grown up and more or less able, like me. "I'll call when I get there," I hollered, and he raised his hand without looking back.

"Hey, Dad," I yelled, "one more thing. Could you see to Snort?"

"'Course," he yelled back. "Consider it done."

Seems like I'd barely been on that little plane long enough to finish my reinforced coffee and that little bag of honey-roasted nuts before it started its landing run in Salt Lake City. As it shimmied and shook, I thought about Lizzie and the Vampires I was going to have to go through to get her. Just to reassure myself, I took the crucifix out of my jacket, closed my eyes, and held it.

About that time the stewardess tapped me on the shoulder. "Are you feeling okay, sir?" she asked.

"Hell, no," I said, looking up in surprise. "Not since the Vampires come for her." Obviously that was too much information for her. I put the cross away and gnawed off a little more pain pill.

On the ground, I had a layover and stood in line for fifteen minutes to buy a ten-dollar hamburger, changed my mind and made my way to the bar where I paid five dollars for a beer that tasted suspiciously like what they serve at The Watering Hole for a dollar fifty. My head was so full of hurt and anger that I couldn't even finish it. I just sat and stared out the window at all the concrete and airplanes coming and going. Deeply involved in my reverie, I almost missed my boarding call, but heard the final one and made a dash for the gate. As I clattered down the hall, I hoped that Rex had made the connection.

For the life of me, I can't understand how airlines stay in business. What they call chairs I wouldn't even use as a footstool, and by the time they lowered that little matchbox-sized TV for a movie no one paid for the first time, my legs felt like they was broke in two. Between that and being sat in the crying baby section, I pretty soon had a tension headache along with dried-out sinuses. The voice come on to say buckle up, we'd started our descent into New York where the temperature was 59 degrees under a light drizzle. I raised up the little window slide and took a peek, curious and expecting to be inspired with an immediate sense of awe from my first glimpse of New York. But all I could see was a swirling mass of rain clouds, or maybe it was smog. I slid the window shut and prepared for landing by imagining giant fireballs of shattered metal pinwheeling down the runway, exercising my grip on the armrest until my knuckles turned white.

Once on the ground, it was so far to the baggage check that I wished I had Snort along for the ride and that made me sad and even more anxious to get at Rex. At the baggage claim, there was a little chute special for pets so I waited until a guy in coveralls come out and looked at me fiercely. "Your dog the one that threw up on everything?" he asked.

"More'n likely. Flying don't agree with him," I said.

Just about then, his little carrier came sliding down the ramp. The front of it, the wires and the door, was covered with has-been kibbles and Rex was sitting stiffly in the back, solemn and dignified, despite the wet evidence otherwise. He stood up when he seen me, give a little bark, and wagged his stump of a tail. I hoisted the carrier off and set it down, opening the door. He stepped forth gingerly, licked at my hand, and looked around the terminal at the new place we were in. What I meant to say was that I missed him, but instead I swatted him on the butt and said, "Look at this. I ain't cleaning it. It's ruined. You and your weak stomach." He jumped on me anyway, nuzzling his face under my coat until I had petted him enough and he could jump down and stretch. I just left the carrier behind.

Outside there was a line of taxi cabs clean out of sight around the corner and a line of people waiting even longer. A fellow in a uniform blew his whistle and motioned cabs up and people in, flirting with the women. He flagged us down a cab without flirting with me at all. The driver didn't speak much English, but didn't seem overly concerned about Rex, just grinned and motioned us in.

The first thing I learned about New York is that all cab drivers honk. It's the part of their job they seem to enjoy the most. He even honked at people that hadn't done nothing. Despite the ill effects it was having on my headache, it got us soon enough on a six-lane highway heading toward New York and, I hoped, Lizzie. The second thing I learned is that cabbies make significantly more than cowboys. That meter kept on ticking away dollars.

As much as it pained me to admit it, New York was a hell of a city. If a town was gonna be a city, then it ought to do it right and be a goddamn big city. New York sure seemed to have that part down. Skyscrapers tall as mountains and the whole skyline jagged with them and lit up. There was a certain sense of history in all that stone work that was hard to explain, but felt solid. And the air was heavy, too, with a strange smell of exhaust fumes, frustration, and garbage. Despite my preconceptions, I found it impossible not to be interested. I pressed my face against the window, trying to take it all in, and Rex did the same on the other side, somewhat relieved that in spite of all the people, there didn't seem to be any alpacas.

The cab rolled right on through Times Square, which looks a lot different by the light of day than it does on New Year's Eve on a black and white TV after several beers. The whole place was bustling with people and I got the sense that it was like that no matter the hour. Most of them were dressed like movie stars, which is to say the men were all in suits and the women were in as little as possible. Seeing that mass of people I realized how comfortable I'd gotten living in a town where I knew everyone by name. Here I was surrounded by something like twelve zillion people, people not really that different than me. All of us busy living and working and dreaming and struggling like everybody else in the whole world. And yet, here there was so many dreams it seemed easy to get lost in the mix of it. Out West, a man is judged by not being part of the crowd, which ain't too hard, given that the crowd is so damn small. That might explain, however, why so many people out East seemed to be trying so hard.

An hour and fifty-six dollars later, the cabby hit the brakes without warning and sat there smiling and pointing at the meter. I only hoped we were in the right place as I sadly peeled three twenties from my now seriously threatened cash reserve and slid them into the little drawer in the window. If there was any change left over, he wasn't talking about it, just roared off. I stood in the middle of the street and took a good look around. There was a fire station to one side and on the other was Lizzie's apartment building. Rex drifted over to the sidewalk and I hunched over in a doorway. After checking to make sure no one was looking, like anybody cared, I stood at the front door to the building, wondering what to do next. It was locked, and although there was a buzzer, there wasn't no one inside who would let me in. I put in a chew and hoped for a lucky break. The way my luck had been running, I reckoned I'd be here close to fifty years.

TWELVE

THE MANSION WAS STRANGELY quiet. Jenkins had told me earlier that only the humans were awake during the day. I responded with: didn't he mean the members of this group who were playing human? As if guessing my words were a means to disguise my plans, he reminded me that the building was completely fortified, no escape was possible, and that in fact, Julius had given orders that I was to be killed if I attempted to escape. Other than that, I was free to do as I wanted, within the confines of my room.

Lying on the four-poster bed, my breath came quickly and shallowly. I was tired, very tired. I hadn't slept since my forced arrival, but was afraid to shut my eyes even for a second. And now the whole day had passed, minute by torturous minute. From the window, I watched the setting sun, wondering many things. How did they get all these people to play along in this elaborate hoax? Who had scripted all that Bible genealogy? Who were these people? Last night's session with Julius had revealed precious little useful information, just a reinforcement of the depth of his insanity. But mostly, and sadly, I wondered what was to become of me.

The sorry fact was that it was unlikely anyone was looking for me. There was no one in my life at all who might miss me. Even the staff at *Harrolds'* thought I had taken a sudden vacation to Wyoming, and Tucker … my heart wrenched and I knew that I would have to put those thoughts aside for now. My survival depended on it. He'd understand, hell, he'd encourage it. I had to focus on how to escape.

Jenkins. How convincing he was as the attentive, yet serene butler. The right age, the right looks, the right manner; he could have been off a sitcom. Yet, despite his role in my captivity, I had the sense that on some level, I could trust Jenkins more than the others. He'd attended me all day as everyone else slept. Or hid. And although we'd talked only a little, a bond seemed to be developing.

Now, as night fell, he gave me his solemn promise that if I chose to take a bath, I would not, under any circumstances, be disturbed. Instinctively, I believed him and so I sat in the clawfoot tub, nearly overflowing, and the steam rich with the scent of lavender and rose essential oils. I placed candles around the edge of the porcelain, like votive candles in a church. As I lit each one, I said a silent prayer for Tucker. Lit by the sadness, nothing could penetrate the darkness inside me.

Steam collected on the glass surfaces around the room and yet, the water felt merely tepid. I scrubbed furiously at my skin, my hair, every inch of my body. I felt dirty, poisoned from the inside. I visualized it oozing silently and invisibly through my bloodstream, into my flesh, collecting in a thin veil that covered my skin. The image seemed to make me shudder as I stood. Why was I cold, so cold?

When I returned to the bedchamber, a thick towel wrapped around me, I spoke to Jenkins, who waited quietly to do my bidding.

"Jenkins, turn up the heat, or stoke the fire. Do whatever it is you do, but make it warm in here."

"Madam, I will of course do as you request, but it won't help. Your blood is already responding to the presence of Julius."

I ignored that idiotic and surely scripted line. "You're human, right?"

"Yes, madam."

"Why do you work for these people, I mean, Vampires?"

"My father, and his father before him, as well as his father, have served in this position. It has been a good life and not one that I have ever had any reason to question."

"You don't question the fact that I am being held here against my will? That they kill people? Ruin lives?"

His back stiffened. "There are certain aspects which I find distasteful."

"This is a pretty complex game you people play."

"It is no game, madam. No game at all."

I sat on the edge of the bed, crossed my legs. "You don't really believe that they are Vampires?"

"They are."

"They don't have fangs."

He turned to look at me. "Unlike the cinematic version of the undead, Vampires have no need for fangs. Their strength is such that natural teeth suffice. Or knives, if the circumstances call for such action."

He was good. Smooth. "Does a stake do them in?"

He built the fire up to a roaring pyre and I wondered how he could look so cool under those layers of stiff clothes. "Quite handily. As does sunshine. I'm sure you will learn about that soon enough."

"Don't count on it. What about garlic?"

"Miss Elita eats it raw. Claims it is good for her skin."

"Holy water? Crucifixes?"

"Regrettably, a decline in religious beliefs has led to their, how should I say, retirement."

Even though it was ridiculous, I was almost enjoying our conversation and stretched back onto the pillows. "I saw Julius sucking back booze like water, but what about regular food? Do they need anything besides blood?"

"May I sit?"

"Of course." I motioned at a chair and he pulled it around to face me.

"They do not require food, as Adamites do. But they enjoy it."

"I see. And sex? I mean, I don't want to make you uncomfortable, but the prospect of eternity without it seems a little dim."

He cleared his throat and arched an eyebrow. "Rest assured, the life of the undead revolves around two things, blood and sensual pleasure."

"Is it more pleasurable?"

"Really, madam, these are questions better suited for Miss Elita. I know nothing of their private lives."

"Okay, okay. Sorry."

He returned to the fireplace to stoke the logs, then moved silently around the room pretending to tidy, dust, and rearrange.

"They will come for you shortly," he said finally as he pulled a gown from the closet, motioning for me to dress. It was a light blue satin dress, long and sleeveless with a ribbed train of cloth from the waistline. At the sight of it, I was drawn to the painting above the fireplace, the one that looked like me. Jenkins watched the direction of my gaze and nodded. The dress was the same as the one in the painting. I stamped my foot and spun around silently, my back now to the painting. Remember, I told myself, all these people, Julius, Elita, all of them, are nuts. Just plain crazy. They are not Vampires. There is no such thing. There is no such thing. There is no such thing as Vampires.

Jenkins clearly had no interest in my nude body as he helped me dress. It was an odd feeling, but comfortable. After politely admiring the fit of the dress, he held out silver handcuffs with filigree around the edges. I faced him quietly, with the recognition that I had no power here. I would have to see this charade through to the end. There is no such thing. There is no such thing. There is no such thing as a Vampire, I chanted.

"Are you ready?"

I nodded. I didn't believe they would kill me. The worst, I imagined, was that I'd get cut a little, maybe raped, certainly terrified, but not murdered. At some point, Julius would have to get bored with me. I could only hope. And pray.

Jenkins gently pulled my arms behind me and cuffed my wrists together. He led me to the door.

"Elita will be along to take you to the ritual rooms."

"You're not joining in the fun, Jenkins?" I said with much more bravado than I actually felt. In fact, I was beginning to feel utterly and hopelessly defeated, ready to give in completely.

"No, madam. I have never entered the chambers and have no wish to do so now."

Quietly, I implored, "Why won't you help me? Please help me. Get a message to the police." I dropped to my knees. "You like me, I know, I can tell. I'm begging you, please, I'm scared. These people are crazy. Help me."

"For better or worse, we all must live out our destiny. Mine is to simply tend to the fire. Yours, however, is to burn. My sense is that you may do more good than you can possibly imagine. Soon, perhaps, you will have more power than Julius."

He held out his hands and helped me to a standing position. "What does that mean?"

"It's my way of helping you. Remember this conversation in your darkest moment, after you are turned."

"They must pay you a lot," I spat venomously.

There was a knock at the door. Elita poked her head inside the room. Her face radiated with life and health.

"Are we all ready, boys and girls? The fun is about to begin!"

I responded wearily. "How long will this little escapade last? And if I'm a good little victim, can I leave when it's over?"

Elita smiled. "Of course. Do as you wish. But I suspect that you will find it in your heart to remain with us. Your choices will be rather limited, you may find, at least for the first several decades."

"Turned, spurned, let's just get on with it so I can go home," I whispered.

As Elita led me down the stone stairs, the heavy door closed behind us and a metal bolt was dragged into place. It was difficult to make out anything besides a faint glow at the bottom of the stairs. Lifting one foot in front of the other, I walked mechanically, as if I were descending into hell, step by hideous step. Elita grabbed my arm roughly, pulling me faster.

Drawing back, I whispered at her, instinctively, "Don't touch me, don't ever touch me again. From this moment on, all who stand in my way are to be my enemy. As these events unfold, you had best be sure of your allegiances." Elita shrunk back, and I was filled with the joy of watching fear rise in her eyes. I felt the ferocity and power of my voice emanating from my eyes as I glared at her. But where had this power come from? Unquestionably, the words were from my mouth, but they came unbidden, as if I were listening to a stranger, an unfamiliar will inside my body and mind. *Don't worry,* I heard it whisper, *we are here for* you.

145

There was no time to listen. At the bottom of the stairs, Julius was waiting, enshrouded by shadows and barely illuminated by the dim light from thick, waxy candles placed around the cavernous room. It was difficult to make out much of the surroundings. There were no windows, only massive stone walls sweating beads of moisture, a cold floor, and two caskets against the wall.

Julius stepped forward and bowed low. Imperiously, I passed by him and circled the small room, arms still held behind me by the handcuffs. I could sense he was surprised at my sudden composure. This apparent confidence, despite the absurdity of my predicament, was equally surprising to me. I paused in my stroll at the second casket. Lined in lush purple velvet, constructed plainly but solidly of oak, stained a light brown, it was elegant, exactly the type of casket I would have picked out had I been in the position to shop for my own funeral.

"That was constructed with you in mind."

"It's attractive enough," I responded casually.

"It now belongs to you," said Julius quietly. He approached me like a cat, quietly but certainly. My body tensed as he came near. "It is time to begin."

"I'd like to cut to the chase here. Let's dispense with the ceremonies, the little arcane procedures and other notions you may have in mind for this evening. Just do what is absolutely essential."

He nodded. "As you wish. After tonight, after you have been turned, you will be mine, and you will do my bidding. For tonight, I will do yours."

"Whatever."

I turned to regard Elita. Making her uncomfortable had been one of the most satisfying things I had ever done, and now I wanted more of it. "Must she be present?" I said, my tone dripping with disdain.

"She is here to attend to you, to do your bidding as your lady-in-waiting."

"I want no one here but you," I replied.

Elita looked at Julius and something quiet passed between them. Elita nodded, bowed, and left the room, ascending the staircase. I listened carefully to Elita's footsteps, heard the creak of the heavy door, and waited for the next sound that I should have heard. I did not hear it. Elita had not bolted the door. My heart quickened at this unexpected turn of luck. Or was it luck?

Taking my arm, Julius led me silently to the center of the room to stand on a tiled circle inlaid in the stone floor. It was dark blue on the outside, with a red interior. At the very center was a single eye, green with a jet-black iris, fully open and staring up. Julius walked around me, circling several times, but said nothing, just growled deep in his throat.

Finally, he spoke, quietly, seductively. "I will remove your handcuffs." He did so and I remained motionless.

He purred and breathed and surrounded me with the sound of his voice. "Remove your clothing."

I obeyed, no longer thinking about what would happen or why. I was hypnotized by the timbre of his voice and was falling into his sound and melody, as before, only stronger.

My dress fell into a heap around my ankles. Underneath I wore nothing, Jenkins hadn't laid out anything else. An energy passed between us, palpable, and I heard his voice, unmistakably, inside my mind. "Be not afraid. What you will undergo has been passed down since the dawn of creation. Tonight, I will become your creator. I will be unto you as your mother, your father, your God, your husband, your child, your lover, your witness. I will be all to you for eternity. I will bring you into the darkness, will bring you into the world of the undead where you are to fully live and live fully, within your royal heritage and beside me forever."

He touched me gently on the small of my back, and turned me around three times in a counterclockwise direction. "Stretch your arms above your head as far as you are able."

Again, I obeyed without questioning, lifting my arms above my head. I felt blood rushing through my body, felt myself pulling involuntarily toward Julius, and felt the heat emanating from his body to mine as if our bodies spoke a wordless, sacred language unto themselves.

"Remain thus."

Julius removed a small knife from his vest pocket. It glinted in the candlelight. He looked intently in my eyes, holding them silently. There was a sudden ache deep in my womb—the pain so intense, I doubled over.

"No," said Julius hoarsely. "Keep your arms above your head or I will handcuff you again."

Above my head were iron hooks dangling from the ceiling, and I knew he would hook me, hang me from the wrists if I disobeyed. Despite the deep ache inside me, the searing pain shooting through my hips, I heeded his command, stretching my arms, my body, pretending that I was stronger than I knew myself to be.

Julius moved the knife close to me, looking still into my eyes. Damn you, I will not give you the satisfaction, I will not give in to the fear, I screamed inside my mind. His other hand touched my breast carefully, like a feather falling onto my skin. My breath quickened, I could breathe only shallowly, and I closed my eyes, knowing that I had to maintain my strength, my control, but a desire involuntarily swelled inside me, lying low beneath the pain in my belly, a desire so powerful I feared it would shatter me. Then, a quick cut and the skin and flesh parted. Blood welled and dripped from between my breasts. There was no pain, just a deepening of intense desire for him, for this man who was defiling me.

I dared not open my eyes. To look at him would mean the end of me. I prayed that he, too, would remain silent. I knew his voice would swallow me, would make me want him in a way beyond my control. One word and I would give in. No, no, I screamed silently, fight, resist.

"You cannot resist me. I will win you completely and you will be glad of it." His voice echoed inside my head.

Pain flared and crashed through me; I welcomed it as a weapon against my physical desire. I cracked open my eyes and saw Julius, head bowed before me. He placed his mouth over my wound, sucking the blood from me lovingly, longingly. The taste seemed to overwhelm him, the rich warmth of my blood flooded his hungry mouth. I heard him gasp and felt him shudder against me. He whispered, "How long I have waited for this moment." I weakened, felt his power moving inside me, much like the instant when a man first enters a woman, breath stolen by the wind. The flow of my blood draining from between my breasts mingled with the dull, insistent pain pulsating in my womb and the waves of desire for him that were swallowing me. I closed my eyes once again, allowed myself to be swept away, felt my blood thicken, knew that it was over. I was dying, yet in the midst of my death, I was lost inside the immensity of his power, of my response to him.

I heard a scream. From deep inside me. Tucker. It was Tucker. Screaming in agony, tortured, his pain at losing me ripped through my mind. In the span of a second, I was transformed. I looked down at Julius, still bent to my breast, and knew exactly what had to be done.

I arched my body as if locked in desire, mimicking the movements he wanted to see. Julius' mouth left my breasts and he placed his now trembling hands around my waist, pulling me to him. He pressed his mouth to mine. I tasted crimson and copper, felt my own blood being pushed back inside my mouth. "Swallow your own life," he said and I did, despite my revulsion. I felt a stab of pain in my womb and blood trickled down my thighs. Julius pulled back, his lips and cheeks red with my blood. He knelt before me, spreading my legs, greedily licking the blood from my thighs as it dripped from inside. I felt the roughness of his tongue, the glossy blood being twirled and teased in his mouth like wine.

He growled, making the noises that had mesmerized me earlier, but now sickened me. "Oh my love, my sweet, this is our union. Wider, spread them wider." He was completely lost in his desire for me. Again, I saw the glint of his knife. He cut himself, but I was not sure where. Cupping his own blood in his hands, he drank that blood, pooling it inside his mouth, and then pressed his lips between my legs, pushing his blood inside my womb, mixing it with my own. "My life is inside your life now. You are forever eternal. You are mine and I am yours."

Though I was repulsed, something involuntarily contracted inside me. My body shook, spasms ripped through my flesh and muscles, through every cell of my being.

Julius knelt before me, eyes glazed. "My love," he whispered, "my one true love. My Queen ... "

My body fell toward the floor. Jenkins' last words to me echoed in my head, and even farther away I heard Elita laughing.

I had no idea how much time had passed, but somehow I suspected it had been over an hour when I awoke. Power surged inside me, I felt very strong, a rush of adrenaline. The pain was gone. The wound on my chest had all but disappeared although blood was everywhere. Next to me, Julius lay in a crumpled heap, breathing deeply. What had happened while I was out? Never mind, I thought, don't think about it now, just get out.

Grabbing the discarded dress, I sprinted up the stairs, jerking the heavy door open. Jenkins was waiting. He peered past me and saw the crumpled form of Julius. Shit. Now what? I wondered if I could beat him, if my strength was greater than his. He placed his finger to his lips, motioning me to be quiet. He led me out of the house and into the darkened gardens. I struggled back into my clothes as I followed him. In the darkness of the garden, a shadow passed close by and the smell of cloves filled my senses. Elita. I paused, ready for a fight with the bitch, the adrenaline pumping through my body.

"Come quickly, my dear," urged Jenkins in response to my hesitation.

"Why are you helping me?"

"There are forces at work here that you do not yet understand, and I hope to be on the side of the winner."

"Me, a winner?" I asked incredulously.

"You will not be the loser."

"Explain yourself. Stop talking in riddles."

"Please, just follow me, we haven't much time. Listen carefully. There has been no time to instruct you properly. You will unfortunately have to learn the hard way, if you are to survive. You need food, blood. You must feed tonight. And remember, do not, under any circumstance, allow yourself to be found by the light of day. The sun will destroy you. You now embody the dark side, a side which cannot bear the light."

With these words, he opened the door onto the sidewalk and I found myself on the darkened streets of Manhattan.

Julius stood by the window, arms folded. "Tell me one more time how she escaped."

Elita sat, hands folded in her lap, near the fire. "It is unclear. She seems to…"

He cut her off with a wave. "I do not want supposition. I want to know where our security failed and whom I shall have to kill for this."

"Perhaps we…"

He continued. "Did I say kill? What I meant was torture. Who shall endure unspeakable agonies for this lapse in security?" He spun and faced her. "Well?"

"Julius, tell me what happened in the chamber."

"What happened down below is irrelevant."

"But…"

He cut her off with a savage wave. "Learn your place. Yours is not to question. Yours is to obey. She escaped from the chambers and that is enough. There is no excuse for her escaping the compound."

Elita bit back an angry retort and felt her body flush with anger. She nodded her head. "You are right, of course. Tell me what to do."

He sneered. "Do I have to spell it out? Find her. Kill who you must, but find her and bring her back. Now go."

Elita stood and crossed to the door and as she opened it Julius called out. "Wait." Her undead heart skipped a beat. "Where were you during the turning?"

She paused. "Are you accusing me?"

"I am simply not underestimating you. Where were you?"

"Feeding. Would you like to see the corpse?"

"Perhaps. Later."

She slammed the door and stood in the hall, fighting back the fear that was slowly infecting her mind. If Julius learned the truth, her life would be forfeited. She took a deep breath and lit a cigarette with trembling hands. He suspected. Of that she was sure, but it was far too late to stop it now. To have orchestrated Lizzie's escape so soon after her turning signed both of their death warrants. Alone and with no mentor to explain the change, Lizzie would perish. Of hunger or insanity, or from the sun. And if Julius found out the truth, she herself would be chained in the sun.

Elita was now committed to this risky course of action. There was no end to it until it ended itself. And hopefully, that end would be to her liking. Even if Lizzie miraculously survived and made it to Lazarus, she would still be far enough away from Julius to pose no threat to Elita. With Lizzie out of the picture, her place beside Julius would be secure for at least the next seven hundred years. Confidence returning, she stubbed out the cigarette and set about her task.

Back inside the study, Julius fumed. That Lizzie's escape occurred at all was his fault. This was undeniable. He had passed out. In the name of all things unholy, what was happening to him? His power had never taken an unexpected turn such as this. Like some feeble Adamite he had allowed his passions to claim him, had been

153

transported by the union he had forged between them. He had reached out for her soul with his own and felt them touch, briefly, and had succumbed to the explosion of unexpected power there. Unacceptable. He was the master, she a mere whisper of the potential that could develop in a dozen centuries under his tutelage.

And yet, when he woke, he had found himself alone and drained as if he were the acolyte and she the master. There was an emptiness in his soul, and he feared that perhaps she had seen something there and taken it from him. Something crucial and needed. The image of her swirled up from the depths of his memory, standing naked and proud before him, her breasts and thighs dripping blood, its taste hot in his mouth. An involuntary tremble racked him, nearly bringing him to his knees and he gasped unexpectedly at this convulsion.

He stood unsteadily and reached for the decanter of cognac. The liquid did little to quell the feelings unraveling in him. As ludicrous as it seemed, he felt like crying.

THIRTEEN

REX SAT QUIETLY BESIDE me for what felt like eternity, until an older gentleman with a cane came up the street. It had been my plan to wait for just such an opportunity and then grab the door after he went in. I was all kinds of inconspicuous, but he seen me anyway, pulled a can of mace out and held it ready as he keyed the door and pulled it shut with a click behind him. Clearly, my chivalrous manner of breaking and entering was not going to work in New York. I gave the door a solid kick with my boot heel and the lock gave with a satisfying pop.

Her name was stenciled above one of the mailboxes, 12b, and thank the lord or, rather, thank Lenny, there was my duffel addressed to Lizzie in the hall. I grabbed it, and backed into the shadows, then backed right into the elevator, one of those old-time metal cages with a sliding door. Even sitting still it was noisy, so I decided to take the stairs up to the third floor. The hallway was quiet and empty. Rex's nose was working furiously as we tip-toed our way down toward her door. It opened easy, since it wasn't locked. Inside, I was taken aback by the flood of recognition. There were pieces of her everywhere, and yet, she was nowhere.

The apartment was empty, like the cabin was when she first disappeared, only quieter and more still, like the bottom of a settled pond. I moved through it like a ghost myself, looking at what her life had been and trying to learn from the remainders. I was hoping to get some sense into where she might be now, but all I came up with was sadness.

The shelves were lined with little sculptures and photographs in silver frames, most of them of her and a woman I took to be her mother. Occasionally, there was a dog-eared book tucked here and there and I pulled one down to flip through. It was a thick old book by some Russian writer with a name I couldn't hope to pronounce. Reading at random, it seemed he hadn't led a particular happy life either, sorrow tinged his words like water damage to a carpet. I wondered if he had ever had the woman he loved taken from him by Vampires. If he did, I feared I too could end up a sad old Russian.

I went into the kitchen area, Rex trailing along. The sound of his claws on this strange linoleum, this strange kitchen, was somehow familiar and reassuring. Standing in the half-light of the opened fridge, I surveyed the contents and was dismayed to find it in a sadder state than any I'd ever seen. Nothing but a half-empty bottle of mineral water and some take-out Chinese food that might've been made in China itself and then walked over by an old monk. I rummaged around in the cupboards until I found a bottle of wine and a jar of old peanut butter that was almost edible. There was a corkscrew in with the silverware and I opened the wine, carrying it and the peanut butter into the bedroom. The bed was loosely made and I set down on the edge of it and drank straight from the bottle and scooped out peanut butter with a spoon.

Under the nightstand was a photo album, and I pulled it out and laid it open on the bed. There were more pictures of her mother, pictures of her as a kid looking far away like she was thinking something too secret to tell. There was other pictures too. Pictures of friends and boyfriends and scenery and toward the end there was even pictures of me, which brought a pain to my heart. I found myself praying that she was still alive somewhere and that I could find her and make everything okay.

Eventually, I couldn't look at her frozen memories anymore and dropped the album to the floor. Flipping through the closet, I found a sweater that looked familiar, one she must've once worn in LonePine, and I curled up with it on top of the bed, tucked the Casull under the pillow, and drew the covers over me.

They still bore faintly her scent so familiar to me. Rex was over-come by her smell too and wandered listlessly around until finally curling up at the foot of the bed. There we both dozed for upwards of an hour until I heard him sit up with a little growl, that same noise he started making back at the cabin. I grabbed the Casull from underneath my pillow. My body was stiff from the plane ride and sleeping bunched up, so I hobbled tenderfoot into the living room and could just make out two shadowy forms.

"Hold it right there," I said real quiet. I stepped in through the doorway, flicked on the light and raised the Casull up. Rex took up by my side, growling. They both turned and one of them smiled a toothy smile.

"You didn't die after all," he said, obviously recognizing me. I thought about the voices, the shapes around me when I was lay-ing for dead, and figured him for one of them. The thought of him taking Lizzie filled me with a terrible rage. There was a hesita-tion to him, like he wasn't sure exactly how this was going to work, me not being dead and all. I pointed the gun toward him, hoping maybe that would help make up his mind.

"This may not kill you," I said, "but it'll hurt like hell. That other old boy was squealing like a baby when Dad popped him."

"A lie. Your weapon is useless against us."

I pretended to think about it and nodded. "You're probably right." I dropped the hammer and holstered it.

They smiled and moved confidently toward me, taking it slow. I reached around the doorway and brought out the shotgun from behind, swinging it up to bear and thumbing back the hammers. They both winced simultaneously, dreading what they must've thought would be a painful inconvenience. I thought of Lizzie and the rest come easy. There was a hollow roar that near deafened me and the shotgun slammed back into my shoulder. The wooden missile reached out and tagged one of them just below the shirt pocket, damn near doubling him over backward as he clutched at the stub end of the shaft now protruding from his chest. I gave a silent thank you to Lenny for his wooden bullet design. That dark bastard dropped to his knees, black, foul blood trickling through his pale fingers, looking dumbly up at me.

"It's a … it's a …"

"It's a stake," I finished his sentence for him. "That was for Lizzie," I said, "and for Snort." I swung the barrel toward his companion. "You know I'll pull this trigger, don't you?" He looked at me, then down at his friend who was opening and closing his mouth like a fish on a line and slowly leaning back to die, spasms racking his body.

"I don't want to die," he said.

"You already are dead, ugly," I said and part of me wanted so bad to send him back to hell, to pull the trigger and engulf the room in blue flames. But that could wait. "Tell your boss that

158

Tucker is in town. Tell him I want Lizzie back. If I don't get her, I'll dedicate my life to hunting him down. Him and every other one of you blood-sucking freaks I can set my sights on."

His friend was turning to dust before our eyes. It was as if his body had not been made of flesh, even undead flesh, but rather had been made of dust and tumbleweeds now coming apart. I heard some sirens in the distance and someone yelling downstairs. Figured I better be making tracks. "I'll be waiting at the train station to see Julius."

"Which one?"

"There's more than one?" The undead one rolled his eyes at me and I felt like a country hick.

"Have a taxicab take you to the front of the Empire State Building and wait there," he said.

IN THE SIX CENTURIES she had known him, Julius rarely allowed his anger to show, yet now he sat rigidly at his desk, his face nearly transformed by rage. His gaze passed through Elita as if she wasn't there and when he spoke, it was to himself as much as her. "Things are becoming unnecessarily complicated." She simply nodded and he continued. "He lives."

"So it seems."

"And thus, we must fear the worst for Desard."

A sadness tugged at her heart as she nodded. "It would appear we have underestimated the cowboy."

"A mistake we shall not repeat. Take three to the rendezvous and deal with him, permanently."

Elita's eyes sparkled. "I have an idea."

"By all means," he snapped, his tone dripping with sarcasm, "share it. I am breathless with anticipation, as I am certain it entails sexual conquest and his inevitable, torturous death."

She smiled lazily in spite of the compliment. "Of course. But first, I propose we use him to," she sought for the proper word, "retrieve our errant Queen." Couldn't hurt to shake his suspicions and regain her position of favor, Elita thought to herself.

Julius regarded her for a moment, then nodded his head. "Continue."

"Apparently she loves him considerably. During her brief stay with us, she made that quite clear. If we can convince the cowboy that it is in her best interest for him to assist us, we can ..."

"Use him as the bait. Of course," Julius finished for her. "How deceitful. I truly admire the way your mind works."

"Oh, Julius. Flattery will get you everywhere."

"And though he appears to know our weaknesses, we know his."

"We do?" she asked.

"Of course. His weakness is love. How easy it will be to convince him that by joining us he will, in effect, be rescuing his dear recently departed."

"When he sees her, he'll be angry. He'll know we've lied."

"When we have her, he will no longer be of any use to us."

"Other than, perhaps, a continued point of leverage."

"I suppose we will burn that bridge, or not, when we arrive at it," he said.

They were silent for a moment. "Well then, send someone for him and make it clear he is to arrive safely."

"Certainly" She stood and stretched, arching her back.

Julius let his gaze linger upon the curves displayed there. "And Elita, one more thing." She swung her head around to catch his eyes. "In order for your plan to succeed, you must quell any notion of taking him. Do not let passion and hunger override our goals. Be a good girl."

"Only promise that he is mine once she is in our hands again."

He nodded.

FOURTEEN

I COULD LAND IN the middle of the Tetons with nothing but a book of matches and a pocketknife and be in Jackson for dinner time tomorrow, but for the life of me I had no idea where we were now. All I know was that we stopped in front of a row of brownstone apartments that didn't look much like a Count Dracula castle at all. It was really a little disappointing. One of the men got out of the limo that had picked me up and held the door open for me. "I must ask that you wear this blindfold," he said.

"I must decline," I answered thoughtfully.

"There is no other way for you to have an audience with Julius."

"All right but let's get a few things straight. You are going to walk in front of me with my shotgun pressed into your back. Anything strange, you die. Agreed?"

"Please try to refrain from pulling the trigger unprovoked."

They snuggled a silk scarf over my eyes and true to his word, he let me snuggle the barrel into his back and off we went. Judging by the feel of the ground and the sound of Rex's paws beside me, we walked up stone stairs and went into one of the houses, into what I figured, after hearing Rex's toenail click-clacking on the tiles, must be a lobby of sorts. We passed through another set of doors and I felt cool air on my face and, surprising, a sweet smell of grass and pine mixed up in the pungent odor of the city. We traveled down a sidewalk or a path, up a flight of low, deep stairs and back inside. The door closed behind me and I felt hands undoing the blindfold. We all breathed a sigh of relief as it became clear I wasn't going to accidentally blow a hole in nobody and, at least for now, my blood was safe.

"Julius is waiting," he said. "You may leave your bag here. Your gun as well, if you feel safe enough."

I laughed and kept walking, gun and bag in tow. He caught up to me and led me up a spiral staircase carpeted in what seemed like a foot of red velvet. Rex padded along beside me with a strange look to his eyes caused, no doubt, by being so deep in the heart of the wild kingdom. We walked up three flights and the whole way I couldn't help but think someone was watching because the hair on the back of my neck was standing up and waving at the hair on my shoulders.

He pointed to a massive door at the end of the hall and scurried off. I strolled on down to the door, took a deep breath, grabbed the brass handles and yanked. The doors swung open to reveal a man sitting behind a mahogany desk, a man who seemed pretty much used to getting things his way. There was a quill pen and old-time brass inkwell sitting on the desk next to a sheaf of heavy paper.

He stood. "You must be Tucker," he said, tugging a crease straight in his pants. He came out from behind the desk and crossed the room slow and controlled, like a big cat after a little bird. He offered his hand.

"Yeah, that's right," I said, taking it. It was cold like marble and the strength of his grip was barely contained. He could've squeezed my hand to jelly if he'd wanted.

"I'm Julius," he said. "I'm … a friend of Elizabeth's."

"Where I come from, friends don't do what you done."

He smiled, but there wasn't much to it. "I'm afraid there has been a bit of a misunderstanding."

"Naw, I don't think so. In fact, I think I understand pretty well. You're a murdering Vampire that took my woman and I aim to get her back."

"I see you're a man not afraid to speak your mind. All a matter of upbringing, I suppose." He gestured at the bar behind him, set into a mirrored alcove and glittering with row after row of bottles and crystal tumblers. "Care for a drink?"

"Look, I ain't here to dance around with you. I come for Lizzie. That is," I said, hating to look a gift horse in the mouth, "unless you got some whiskey in there somewhere." What the hell, no sense hurting his feelings before I killed him.

"Maker's Mark all right?"

I nodded and watched as he poured a triple shot. He handed it to me and drifted over behind the desk again.

"Damn, that's good," I said, taking a sip. "Thank you much. Now whyn't you save us both a load of trouble and tell me where Lizzie is?"

He gazed absently out the window behind his desk. At last he said, "We no longer have her."

I set my glass down, empty. "What the hell you mean you don't have her? You took her."

"We did take her. She got away."

164

"You're lying," I said. "Don't pull that shit on me, Dracula. You're gonna get her for me, now. And you better pray to whatever God you call your own that she's all right."

A storm cloud come across his face and I could tell he was fighting to choke back rising anger. I half expected him to come for me and half hoped he would. I was ready.

"Tucker," he said slowly, "you cannot frighten me. I have been a part of this world for nearly eighteen hundred years. I have seen many powerful men." He looked at me with a barely contained sneer. "I assure you, none of them did me any harm whatsoever. Your wrath is—please don't take this the wrong way—laughable."

The whole time he was talking I was reaching nonchalant for the crucifix tucked into my waistband and I drew it out with a flourish and shoved into his face. "That's right," I said. "Not so high and mighty now are you. How's that feel?"

"Painfully embarrassing, actually," he said, plucking it out of my hand. "For you."

Not exactly the reaction I had been hoping for. I had kind of planned on standing over him as he writhed in agony, getting the information I needed, then standing on his neck while I drove a stake right through his evil heart.

"What the hell? I thought crosses made you burst into flames or something."

"More whiskey?"

I slumped back onto the couch, dejected. "Yeah, I reckon."

He dropped the crucifix into a brass trash can and then refilled my glass.

"Hey, wait a minute, fetch that out, it was Mom's."

"Think about it, Tucker," he said, casually retrieving the crucifix and then sitting down opposite me. "You're a man of the world, a horseback philosopher so to speak. Why would a crucifix, in this day and age, cause me even the slightest pang?"

I felt kind of like a kid in school when the teacher is asking a question and I didn't know the answer 'cause I hadn't done the homework, since I'd been out hunting rabbits. I crossed my legs and looked hard at my boots, the duct tape unraveling there. "I always figured it was because God didn't like y'all much."

Julius dismissed my notion with a wave. "God created Vampires."

"Not the devil?"

"Have you ever read the Bible? I have some particularly rare copies. Perhaps I could lend you one. Satan was not a creator. He was just, how should I say, misunderstood. He was an angel, in fact."

I was feeling a little stupid now, and getting loose from the whiskey. "How come them Hollywood types make it look like crucifixes work?"

"A long, long time ago they did. In the dark ages, man believed fervently in God. He had faith in a higher power of good. The crucifix was a dramatic symbol of this belief. The cross, symbol of your good God, was believed power enough to ward us off. To our everlasting shame, we believed man was right only because Vampires are as prone to erroneous beliefs as humans. Now, however, humankind has as much faith in God as they have in their legal system. It's a dim, barely conceivable notion that once made sense. The crucifix no longer holds the power of faith for you, so why should it have any power over us? It has to work both ways. Do you understand?"

I nodded, shifted uncomfortably in my seat. Deep inside the front pocket of my jacket was one of them duct-taped grenades and I looped my forefinger around the pin. I felt the bulk of the explosive and it was only slightly reassuring. If I popped it in this room, we would both be gone. It was obviously going to be a damn site more effective than a crucifix. Just to keep the conversation going I said, "What about wood? How come that works?"

His voice took on a hollow echo as I reckoned he was thinking about them two boys of his now gone to ash. "Unfortunately, we do not understand its mechanism ourselves."

"What about sunlight?"

"Sunlight is the bane of our existence. Its rays are as a poison unto us. This is the price we pay for immortality. When I was a young Vampire, a hundred years old, I tested the sun. I fought the urge to blackness, fought death. At dawn, as the sun crept over the horizon, I held my hand past the windowsill." I could see the memory slipping into his eyes and I knew it to be real. "The pain was remarkable. I'll never forget it. It was like holding onto damnation. I fled to my coffin and have never been as close to the sun again." He ruminated a moment. "Enough questions."

I nodded. "You're right. Let's get down to brass tacks." I pulled the grenade out of my pocket and yanked out the pin, tossing it on the desktop. "So quiet you could've heard a pin drop," I said.

All trace of civility disappeared. There was open scorn in his eyes. "And what is that?"

"This is a thermite grenade. You up on current military technology?" He waved the question away as if absurd. "It's liquid fire. Enough to turn this office into Mt. St. Helens."

"You'd be destroyed as well," he blustered and believe me, it was a sight I enjoyed. Probably been a couple hundred years since anyone ruffled that smooth exterior. Never underestimate a cowboy.

"I'd rather die than live without Lizzie. You make the choice."

His eyes took on a look like when you drop a rock onto real thick ice and the fractures drive down and out. "Put the pin back. No need to do something we both will regret. I am sorry about this," he chose his words careful, "misunderstanding, but know that we allowed you to live. It's an act of good faith."

I didn't make a move for the pin, just let him watch my fist and how close it was to our deaths. "Misunderstanding or not, y'all took Lizzie and you killed my horse. I want her back. And there has got to be a reckoning for my horse."

"As I said, we do not have Lizzie. Again, I apologize for my associates. They were a little, shall we say, enthusiastic."

"They damn near enthused my head right off my shoulders."

He cut me off with a chop of his hand. "No one was supposed to get hurt. Their instructions were simply to bring Lizzie to me."

"What do you want with her?"

"Quite simple, really," He looked at me levelly. "She is our Queen."

That shut me up. I really didn't know what to say, so I just put the pin back in and stuck the grenade back in my pocket, but I kept my hand around it.

He continued. "She didn't know. She has lived her life until this point unaware. It was our intention to, ah, remind her. Wake it up in her. Unfortunately, we were unprepared for her response."

"What exactly was her response?"

He sighed. "She chose to part ways with us."

"That's one thing she's done right so far."

"I guess that depends on your perspective."

"Let me tell you something about my perspective. I'm pissed. I'm a long way from where I belong, looking for someone that would still be right beside me if y'all hadn't waltzed in and screwed up everything. So I guess my perspective is you better come up with a pretty good reason why I shouldn't burn this goddamn place down around you and shoot everything that tries to run out the doors." Man, saying that felt good.

He just sat stock still and tried to keep from jumping over the table at me. "While we may have been a bit overeager, the fact is, she is crucial to my people."

"Keep going."

He pressed his fingertips together, as if meditating. "Lizzie represents a union between two of the most venerable bloodlines of Vampire genealogy. When this is made known to the Vampiric world, she will be able to assume the royal mantle waiting for her and put an end to the entropy that has gripped our world."

"Just out of curiosity, does she have a say in any of this?"

"She is a figurehead, an instrument of history. She has no choice but to honor the legacy she represents."

I still didn't believe him. There had to be more to it than needing Lizzie for a Vampire princess. I kinda shook my head real hard, rattled around the rocks inside. Lizzie was not a Vampire. "Just for the sake of conversation, let me tell you how things are gonna work out. She don't want to be your Queen. Hell, she don't even want to see you ever again. When I find her, I aim on taking her back to Wyoming. And if I ever see any of y'all sneaking around her, you're dead. And I mean dead like forever, not just during the daytime. Are we clear?"

I suppose he wasn't used to being talked to like that, but seemed to take it well. He nodded. "I think that would be for the best. However, I feel a certain sense of obligation in finding her. After this revelation, she must certainly be feeling confused, lost. I am scared for her, as I know you must be. Perhaps," he tilted his head inquisitively my way, "we could be of mutual assistance to one another. There's no reason we couldn't work together. At least until we find out for certain what she wants."

"Reckon I'll have to think about that."

"Please do so. You are welcome to stay here. You must be exhausted after your trip."

"Yeah, but I'd feel better out looking for her."

"New York is a big city. My people are looking at her familiar places. If they find her, she will be brought here and you will be notified immediately."

"I don't know…" The thought of a few hours of shuteye was sounding pretty good.

"You will be quite safe here, both you and your dog. You have my word."

I hoisted the shotgun up in one hand. "I know I'll be safe."

He smiled thinly. "There are others here, mortals. They will see to your needs during the day. Tomorrow night, we shall talk again."

FIFTEEN

A COLD CHILL RACED through me, like someone had just stepped on my grave, as I followed the old man up the stairs. "You know," I said to his crooked back, "you're working for a bunch of monsters."

"I suppose that is a matter of perspective, sir," he said. He opened a door into a room like out of one of those bed and breakfasts I could never afford to stay in. "This shall be your room. I trust it will be to your liking as there is an extensive liquor cabinet. Fresh towels are in the closet. Is there anything else I could provide for you before I leave?"

"What's the chances of you rustling something up to eat? Maybe a couple of sandwiches. One for each of us." Rex perked up at that bit of news. Being right in the middle of castle hell was making him a little forlorn.

"Sandwiches? You wouldn't care for some pasta perhaps, or a Caesar salad?"

"Naw. Just some sandwiches. Roast beef if you got it."

"Very good, sir. Two sandwiches." He backed out of the room, closing the door behind him.

"Make that three," I hollered as I examined the room. The bed was an antique four poster with crisp linens and ruffles in descending layers. Rex jumped right up on it and sat on a lacy pillow like it was meant just for dogs. "Should've got a hotel," I said to him as I stretched out. "At least there'd be a TV."

Knowing Lizzie was still alive made me feel a little better, but not much. Directly there came a knock at the door and after I managed to shut Rex up from barking, I opened it to a young lady with a tray full of sandwiches, some potato chips in a silver bowl, and a pitcher of ice water with matching glasses.

"Thank you," I said, taking it from her. She smiled and curtsied and I wondered if she was alive as I watched her slip away. I set one sandwich onto the carpet and pointed Rex down to it. He looked at it, then back to me like I was fooling, but I nodded and he dove into it straight away. In two bites and a swallow, he was done and looking up at me with mustard on his chops. Patience won out and I got tired of him staring so I gave him the rest of mine and stretched out on the bed. I started nodding off, but not before first double-checking my shotgun and laying it out beside me. Rex hopped up on the other side and sprawled out after first licking my face to make sure I was okay. What I meant to say was I was a little scared too, but what come out instead was a bunch of grumbles and threats to kick him off if he didn't get still.

A dream came quick and it was of Lizzie. There was a blue and terrible sadness coloring the edges of my mind's picture of her as she floated just out of reach, inside some quiet, stone place. An earthquake came and the walls shook with a rumbling sound that slowly turned into Rex's growling. He was standing over me and snarling way down low in his throat and I snapped full awake, fumbling for the shotgun. It was no longer beside me.

"No need for violence," a woman's voice whispered and Rex exploded forward, barking furiously.

"Lizzie, is that you?" I called out, knowing in my heart it wasn't but desperate to believe. I sat up, confused and drenched in sweat, trying to reach my arms around Rex and calm him down. It was so dark I could barely make out a form across the room.

"Better than Lizzie," she said. I could see the cold shine of my gun cradled in her arms, then her leaning it softly against the wall. There was a whisper, a scratch, and a match flared to life, illuminating a vision of dark beauty.

It was a Vampire woman, pale and cold, barely dressed in some sort of emerald green lingerie that sparkled in the dim light of the match. The skin not covered, which was most of it, was pale as pearls and I could see the dark outline of her nipples brushing against the flimsy fabric. As the match burned down to her fingertip, she touched it to a candle in her other hand. The flame caught and she dropped the match, taking a step forward.

Rex was lost in a rage that silenced him, hackles raised and trembling with a desire for her soft throat. "What a cute puppy," she said. "Is he housetrained?" I nodded dumbly, lost in her eyes and the mesmerizing sound of her voice. "Why don't we let him out to play?"

"Lady," I said, "I don't know what your aim is, but I got me a grenade here that would turn us both to french fries if you take another step."

She threw her head back and laughed, her black hair swirled like smoke. It was a throaty and melodious laugh that clouded my brain. "Talk about a lady killer," she said. She seemed to float forward on strings. "I am Elita. I mean no harm. I only want to talk about," her voice clicked coldly, "Lizzie."

Seemed reasonable to me. Midnight, a half-dressed Vampire vixen in my bedroom and wanting to talk about my true love. This ain't smart, but there was no harm in talking, after all. "All right, but keep your distance. What do you know?"

"Everything," she said. "May I sit down?"

Her mocking eyes never left mine and leaning over from the waist to place the candle on the dresser between us, her gown gapped forward, not so inadvertently showing the pale upper curve of her breasts. My blood quickened of its own accord and a sleepy sort of giving up was stealing through me. I pushed a disbelieving Rex away.

Close as she was, an arm's length, I could feel something hot and dark coursing from her. It was like standing in the middle of a grass fire, feeling the deadly heat and extent of it raging about me. She was pure power, ruinous. Her scent was narcotic and as I dragged my eyes away from the shadows between her breasts, her eyes were fixed on mine.

"Yeah, help yourself," I said weakly, then pointed. "The chair."

She sat down and leaned forward, resting her elbows on her knees and her chin in her hand. Her hair hung down to frame her face and dancing eyes.

"So you're the mighty Tucker."

"Mighty pissed off," I said, "and looking for answers."

"What do you want to know?" She leaned back into the chair, legs apart and hands resting on the leather arms.

I knew my mouth must be hanging open at the sight of her. I jerked the bedspread off and threw it her way. "Would you cover yourself up?"

She laughed again and wrapped it around her shoulders, somehow managing to make even a damn blanket look sexy. "Is that it?"

"No. I want to know where Lizzie is, and if she's okay."

She sighed. "Your devotion is so touching." I couldn't tell if she was still mocking me or just downright mean. She sighed. "She's fine, I guess. Though speaking as a witness, the change is," she flicked the tip of her tongue around the edge of her lips, "most unpleasant. In fact, I imagine wherever she is right now, she is terrified, suicidal, and very, very hungry. So in answer to your question, no, I guess she's not okay."

I sat up in bed. "What the hell are you talking about?"

"You are boring me, Tucker. And boring is so very disappointing. She's a Vampire now. She's dead. She's gone from you. You cannot get her back. She is no longer of your world."

Despair and rage swept through me and tears came. Rex barked and I swung around like I aimed to cuff him. He looked up at me hurt, and hunkered down out of sight. I leaped up and in a bound was standing over the woman. I took her by the shoulders and lifted her up from the chair. The blanket fell back and the strap of her negligee slipped down from her pale shoulder revealing more than the round tops of her breasts. Her body was flushed and scorched my fingers. Smoldered with a life I feared had recently belonged to someone else. "That's a lie. That's a goddamn lie," I shouted into her face.

She laughed and I hated her for it. "It's true. Elizabeth Vaughan is no more, Tucker. Look into my eyes." I made the mistake of doing just that and my breath came short and shallow. The rage was burning in me, threatening to burst out, and I knew that was exactly what she wanted. "You know I speak the truth."

I dropped her and she made no move to cover herself or sit up, just watched me. My mind was reeling like I was about to black out and I steadied myself against the wall, held my hand to my head and cried, the tears falling into the shadow. I begged God that this whore was lying. That Lizzie was all right, and that she was human still. Nothing made sense, and I mourned for the death of sense and of love. Then a hand slipped around my waist.

It was Elita, standing now. Rex ran around us barking and tangling me underfoot so that I staggered into her, but she supported my weight easily. She guided me to the bed. Her hand was small and even through the thickness of my clothes I could feel the heat of it against the small of my back.

"Poor Tucker," she said. "So sad." She laid me out and crawled on top of me. "I can help you. Lizzie is lost to you. At least until she learns the power of her condition. It takes years. A century. You'll be gone and forgotten. She will be forever."

Her words snaked deep into my thoughts and I pictured me old and alone and Lizzie as beautiful as last week up in the mountains with the sunlight in her hair, and then Elita was tugging at my shirt and it was gone and her body was pressed to mine so that I could feel the contours, the heat. Her hands slid across my chest, nails raked into my back and her mouth glided along my abdomen. She bit at me, teased my nipples with her tongue and I knew this was terribly bad, but my limbs were frozen with a dreadful paralysis like I wanted to die then, and by her pale hands. The realization that Lizzie was lost from me forever unhinged something in my heart and it howled like a wolf and tore at the soft underbelly of my mind.

She was tugging at my belt and her hands, on fire with pleasure, caused an unearthly desire to swell in me. She was wild. Her mouth was all over me and then, finally she pressed it to my mouth and it burned like fire on my lips. I could taste the sweet, bloody taste of death on her and something in my soul recoiled.

Rex saved my life, once again. About the time I had all but given up, he come flying over the bed like a canine missile and slammed into her side. It jolted her good and she tore her hands off me and swiveled her head around, a savagery painted there. Rex darted out of reach and she regained her composure, turning her attention back to me.

She redoubled her efforts, but my mind was clearing now, slow, like muddy water. I let my body be borne backward by her momentum, carrying us across the bed and close enough to reach the Casull out from under the pillow. She was tugging on the waistband of my jeans as I thumbed the hammer back and pressed the muzzle to her temple.

"A dozen of you ain't worth one of Lizzie," I said. A terrible, hoarse shriek ripped out of her throat and her whole body trembled with rage like an animal. She would have gladly ripped my heart out and made me watch while she ate it, but I kept the pistol up against her tight. "Now get off me. I love her. And I aim to get her back. Your behavior only tells me I ain't too late."

I was surprised at how quick she regained herself. Like when a cat falls and pretends it was what she'd meant all along. She stood, her hair in wild disarray and lingerie falling off at the shoulders.

"You have no idea what you're missing. The pleasures I would have shown you."

"I have a pretty good idea," I said, keeping the pistol leveled right at her black heart. "Whyn't you just save us both some trouble and tell me where I can find Lizzie."

"If I knew where she was, do you think I would have come to you?"

"I'll find her. If I have to take this whole goddamn city apart, I'll find her."

She leaned close to me, unwavering. "You may not like what you find."

177

"You're right. I'll love what I find. All them years you been around, guess you still don't know what that means." She spun with a wordless curse and was gone.

Rex jumped up beside me, wagging his little stump and trembling. What I meant to say was thanks for distracting her, but instead I said, "What? I didn't do nothing." He curled up into a ball and kept one eye disdainfully upon me. "You're the one who let her sneak up on us." I eased the hammer back down and stuck the pistol back under my pillow "I didn't do nothing," I said again as I closed the door and retrieved the shotgun, double-checking that it was still loaded. "Don't be like this."

No answer.

"Fine," I said, pulling over the blanket still smelling of her, "but if any more of 'em get past you tonight, I'm gonna get me a cat."

SIXTEEN

"I DON'T HAVE ANY money." The cabbie was looking at me with open hostility. He started to shout.

"You crazy bitch, then what the hell did you get in my cab for? I'm gonna run you straight to the police station is what I'm going to do, you rotten rich bitch. That designer dress probably cost two grand and you tell me you can't pay for a lousy cab ride? Crack is an expensive hobby, you bitch."

My eyes burned into him and the heat scorched us both. He froze, mouth open. "I don't have any money. They took it. They took everything," I said quietly.

"Go on," he stammered, "get out, get out of my cab, what are you, some kind of witch or something? You got the evil eye. Get out, get out," he yelled, slamming the cab in gear and screeching away from the curb even before I could shut the door.

The church loomed over me, imposing in the dark, and my body trembled. Sanctuary was within, a place where I could think, hide. Can't go home, can't go anywhere I've been, I thought. They would find me. I had to collect my thoughts, figure out what to do. Call the police or somebody, anybody, to help me.

It was locked. Shit! Of course, why wouldn't it be? This was Manhattan, even God locked his doors. Oh God, why won't you let me in, I silently implored. What was I supposed to do now? I felt so faint, so scared, I knew I wouldn't be able to go on much longer. I had just escaped from the craziest people in the world, I had survived, I was alive, but now was to be undone by a locked door.

No, a voice screamed inside me, the same voice that had reverberated during the turning. *Your will is your power.* Tentatively, my hand reached out to the heavy door, grabbing the handle. Inside my mind, I visualized the lock buried within, watched it turning, resisting as I pushed it with my thoughts, squeezing a slow, steady pressure on the oiled but reluctant parts. It clicked and I pulled the door open and entered the church. My church.

The silence of the empty church felt quieter than what I imagined it would be like inside a coffin. Yet, it felt comfortable. I hadn't been here for years, but it was something familiar. If only I was still that little girl coming here with Mother.

Halfway down the darkened aisle, I lay in between two pews. No one could see me there, and I thought it might help to be still for a minute or two, long enough to figure out what to do next.

The marble floor was cold against my cheek. I was so cold in this dress. My mind slipped back to the cabin where Tucker and I had last made love, and the passion we had shared. Tucker—where was he? I could only hope he was still alive. Queen of the Vampires, it was absurd. Tomorrow, I would stand fully in the sun, proving Julius to be a foolish old man.

I knew that to even see tomorrow, I first had to move, to get rid of this coldness, this stiffness in my limbs. I stood, stretching my arms toward the moon visible through the skylights. Beneath the

chill, my body felt foreign, like the movements belonged to someone else. Elita. The movements were like hers, sensuous and without thought. I stretched even higher, hoping to somehow feel like
myself, but a new sensation broke free. I could feel liquid power
surging from my fingertips, crackling and twisting. Before I could
even comprehend it, the sensation began to change. Suddenly, I
could see it, and pure light began to stream from inside me. Over-
whelmed, I fought against it, but in that instant I could see inside
myself from the light, just as I had seen the mechanism of the lock.
Nothing was hidden, no aspect of my life was locked away, all was
open. Everything I had been, everything I had ever wanted to be,
everything I would never be was all displayed, illuminated by the
light. I was there in the church, but not there at all. I was inside the
light and outside, connected to the air, the granite walls, the clouds
and on into the blackness of space.

The glaring noise of the light gave way to the rhythmic rise and
fall of voices, the words echoing inside my dizzied mind. I could
hear them, as if they were part of me, stretching from the past,
and beyond into the future. *We are glad,* they said. *We come to
you through the light. Nothing is outside of you. The light is you. We
mean no harm, we will protect you. Leave your body here, enter our
world by the light of your fingers. Come with us now. Fly, fly through
the stars, through the ether of human souls, taste their pains, their
lusts, their sicknesses, insanities, and love. Feel the futility of human
life, understand its power, the power of God. See dead souls struggling to leave the underworld, touch the fire of a new soul burning
itself into the flesh of an infant. Understand all of humanity inside
your flesh, not with your mind or heart.*

As suddenly as it began, it was over. With a lurch, I was sucked
back inside my body with a violence and pain that were almost
unbearable. I fell back to the floor, unsure how much time had

passed. Minutes, hours? A fire burned inside my veins, raging and trapped by the constraints of my body, at that instant little more than an aching prison of flesh. Too much knowledge, too much pain. I was certain I was dying, and nothing, no one, could help. Please go away, I begged the voices, make it stop. Mother, Tucker, God, make the pain go away. And the cold. I was shivering, my body felt as if it had no bones, the floor was so cold.

Blood. The taste of blood will warm you.

"No," I screamed at the voices. This is not real, a hallucination, I don't want blood. It must be a hallucination, I wouldn't let my mind do this. I told myself I wasn't, but I must be crazy.

Eat, or you will die.

"Go away," I screamed at myself, at the voices, "leave me in peace."

Eat or you will die. You must birth yourself.

"The pain will kill me," I shouted, pounding my head, "let me die here. Please, God, let me die here in the arms of sanctity."

From the corner of my eye I saw movement. It was a rat, scurrying through the shadows. My hands lifted of their own will, pulsing with the light. The veins on the back of my hands had begun to recede into the flesh like parched streambeds and the skin was sallow, yellow, illuminated by the red and green kaleidoscope of moonlight streaming through the stained glass windows. Soft light mixed with the harsh primary colors of the Crucifixion of Christ, Mother Mary and the Magdalene cowering at the base of the wooden Cross.

The tiny heartbeat of the animal filled my thoughts, I could feel it move. The will to survive eclipsed rational thought. In a flash, my now foreign hands darted forward and seized the rat. Brutishly, I brought it to my mouth, unbelieving as it squirmed in panic inside my mouth. My teeth broke through the skin, crumbled the bone and I devoured it, tearing off its fur and sucking every last drop of blood from it.

Good, the voices sang in harmony, *you eat, and watch. Be inside the light, until you can bear the change.*

Again, I was pulled outside myself, witness to my own madness.

The warm taste of copper flooded past my teeth, coating my mouth as I flicked my tongue across my fingers, licking up every drop. The blood melted into my flesh and my senses heightened to an unbearable pitch. Each drop slid down my throat, dripped into my belly and womb, coursing and mixing with my own blood. Such an insignificant little vessel of flesh and blood, and yet such profound events. What had I done? The voices shouted in my head with joy and wild abandon.

The pain was gone. The light was gone. My body was quiet. I felt warm for the first time since escaping. My mind was once again my own. "Oh, Lord, my God, help me," I yelled out loud, falling prostrate on the marble, but there was nothing I could do except choke back a cry for Tucker.

Again, the voices entered my mind. *Beneath the church. Hide. Sleep. Be cautious and learn quickly. We will only be with you a short time.*

Like a zombie, I moved stiff-legged toward the door into the catacombs. As I descended the worn steps, though, a fury began to consume me, fueled by the blood, anger at the God that Julius had described. Could that God be the same as mine, the same whose house I was in? How could I have been so blind? How could I have trusted, believed in a God who would so casually create a world pitting good against evil for His amusement? What other reason could there be? And so much heartache due to it. This was too much for me. I never considered myself smart, or religious, just a woman trying her best to keep cat food on the table and dress well. "I am not special," I screamed aloud inside my mind.

"Mother, Mother," I cried, "you must have known. Why didn't you tell me?" If everything Julius had said was true, Mother must have known everything. Then I remembered and my shoulders sagged. She had told me. Just not all of it. The safe deposit box. The letters. She had made me promise not to read them until night became day. If I had only known, if I had only understood those words, I would have broken that promise in an instant. At the time, I thought she was going senile, but she must have known that if this day arrived, I would figure it out.

That thought filled me with despair. Was her whole life then a lie? Had she made a deal with the devil, with Julius, to save herself by sacrificing me? Surely not. There had to be more to it, things I didn't yet understand. That thought was strangely calming, ludicrous as it sounded. Something unknown that I could believe in, have faith in, unlike the God I now despised.

No, none of this was real. I decided to rest there a moment or two. The sun did not frighten me. I would rest a few minutes, before the dawn. I was not afraid. I could walk into the light and it would mean nothing to me. I had been brainwashed or drugged. Vampires were not real. The rat was madness. Madness was better than believing. Tomorrow, by the light of day, I would get the answers. Tomorrow I would get the safe deposit box.

But even as this confidence grew, a darkness was gathering in the coils of my mind—a darkness that deepened and embraced all but a pinpoint of light. In this light was the thought of Tucker. It was a pure thought of love and empathy. I felt a dread and horror as to what kind of death he might have experienced. "Please, make him be alive, make him come back to me. I need him," I prayed to a God I could no longer trust as I crawled into an ancient corner. God responded with a holy darkness and all was lost as death overtook me.

SEVENTEEN

Funny how by daylight the madness of night seems so far away. I woke up after noon, well rested, and then tumbled Rex off the bed and stood up, stretching and groaning. The pain in my ribs wasn't so bad anymore so I left the horse pills in my bag. Gradually, I was growing accustomed to the weight of the pistol under my arm and studied it under my jacket to see if it was noticeable. It wasn't.

I moseyed on down the stairs, pausing along the way to admire the various swords, guns, and vases encased behind glass along the way. Last night, it had been so dark when I was brought here, but by the light of day it was really something. The walls were covered with paintings, and not those velvet kind, either. I stopped at the window at the end of the hall. The whole thing was set in a few acres of good grass with some tall, old trees drooping around and I couldn't quite figure out how I got there since the last thing I seen was a bunch of tiny little apartments. There was a stone wall circling the grounds and beyond it, reassuring in an odd way, skyscrapers poking up like jagged teeth.

I happened upon the old man from the night before and he smiled painfully at the sight of Rex trailing beside me. "We was wondering if there was any breakfast to be had around here?"

"Of course, right this way, sir." He limped down the hall and I followed along. "I trust you slept well?"

"Yeah, except for the rodents."

"Rodents, sir?"

"Place is crawling with rats."

There was a table set next to the kitchen and a little placemat for Rex on the floor with a handsome silver bowl full of some sort of dog food. We both put away some grub, including a couple of croissants I slipped down to him, and then I figured it was time to take a look-see around town. The old man, whose name I found out to be Jenkins, led me through the front door and down a winding pathway to the stone wall.

"Unlike your bosses," I said as we got close to the imposing face of it, "I can't fly. So I wonder if you could let me know what you're planning on doing. Putting me up against the wall and shooting me?"

"Nothing quite that drastic, sir. Simply turning you loose into the city, may God help you both." He reached toward an otherwise blank section of the weathered marble and with a press, a door swung open. "This way."

Rex and me followed along with him after pausing long enough to remind each other that Vampires sleep by day and also checking the fit of the Casull under my jacket.

The passageway was narrow and damp, but short-lived. Another door stood at the end of fifteen uneasy paces and as Jenkins held it open, I walked into a surprisingly modern little apartment which was exactly what I wasn't expecting. There was a large man watching us silently from behind a row of video monitors, a particularly nasty-looking assault rifle in his lap. Jenkins acknowledged him with a nod.

"This is Mr. Tucker," he said, not offering an introduction. "He has immunity. Allow him egress at his word." The man nodded and returned to his monitors.

"And my dog as well," I added.

Jenkins pointed at the front door. "On the other side of this door is Bay Street. 126 East 2nd Ave. The apartment you need to enter is 4E. Will you be back for the evening meal?"

"Couldn't say right off. But I will be back by sundown, count on that." We stepped out into the gloom and noise and stink of a New York day.

"Sir, I am to remind you of your obligation to bring Miss Vaughan back to us. Julius believes she requires our assistance."

"Will I be followed?" I asked as I walked down the stairs.

"I imagine so. One more thing, sir," Jenkins called, "there is a leash law." He pulled a leash and matching collar out of his pocket.

"Thanks, Jenkins. I appreciate that, I really do." Outside we sat down on the front step and I snuggled the collar around Rex who looked at me like I was committing a cardinal sin. Club Vampire was completely gone. Down the block both ways was nothing but apartments and the mansion was now completely hidden from sight. Neat trick. How many years, I wondered, had this compound existed? Probably since New York was just a little pissant town wishing it was London.

Despite many mutterings to the contrary, I don't have nothing personal against big cities. 'Course, I don't have much use for them either. In my limited experience, and that based on Louis L'Amour novels, news reports about violent crime, and big city tourists turning Jackson into one big art gallery, New York City is about as big as a city can get before it turns into its own country. Sometimes as a form of amusement on winter nights, I try to think about what all those people living cheek to cheek think about, what their lives are like. I've yet to come up with a clear picture in my head.

Near as I can figure, it all boils down to lack of space. America became the greatest country in the world by being so damn open. All our ancestors come sailing over from England, which must've seemed pretty full at the time. They landed out east and stepped off the boat and said I'll be damned, look at how many folks ain't here. Things progressed and cities grew up and some folks decided to keep on moving on account of looking for open space. The Indians, in the worst case of there goes the neighborhood, ended up on little graveyard-sized pieces of land, while the settlers eventually run out of room at the West Coast. To make a long story less interesting, my kinfolks decided to stay out in Wyoming where brutal winters and intolerable summers kept out most civilized folks. Having lots of space was never a problem.

That's why it never made sense to me how people live all cramped up in tiny little apartments looking out at more tiny apartments and breathing in smog while they hurry up and get in a traffic jam on their way to a job they don't like anyway. Give me sagebrush and clear skies any day of the week. 'Course, if everybody thought that-a-way, they'd all move to LonePine and things would be no better off.

First order of business was getting a cup of coffee and losing the skinny fellow in the cheap suit that Julius had stuck on to me. I'd watched him trying hard not to look at me and hoped losing him wouldn't be too much trouble. I detoured into a little shop with a neon sign out front flickering *coffee, coffee*—then left out the back door, circled around front, and went back in the front door.

That seemed to do the trick. I watched him running down the back alley looking this way and that. Just like in the movies. Now, time for a cup of coffee.

There was a big old chalkboard behind the counter with all these strange names I couldn't hardly pronounce and prices ranging from too expensive to intolerable. The girl at the cash register had a shaved head and a ring in her nose like the kind we use on bulls we can't control. She smiled and asked what I'd like.

I said a cup of coffee, black, which seemed pretty straightforward and she give me about sixteen different choices, all of which sounded nothing at all like what I normally buy at the supermarket.

"Just coffee," I said again, "and whatever kind tastes like it's been sitting around the longest."

She poured me up a cupful and I reluctantly give her the two dollars she asked for, and I'll be damned if that coffee didn't taste exactly like Hazel's. And they had to fly theirs all the way from Ethiopia.

Coffee in hand, I walked out onto the sidewalk and was immediately swept up by a crowd of people all mumbling and shoving and walking with their heads down. I just stood in the middle of this human river and wondered how in the hell I was going to find Lizzie.

Across the way, bells chimed on the hour. Church bells ringin' out deep and clear above the crowd, the traffic, the cursing and struggling. I looked up and seen a flock of pigeons on wing as if borne up by the message of the bells and the commotion around me dissolved away. It seemed as if a shaft of sunlight touched those birds, lighting up the soft grays and whites, and time stopped for a heartbeat. Church bells. The church. Where her father's funeral was held. Her sanctuary. Now what the hell was the name of that church she told me about? It was a long shot, but what else did I have to go on?

There was a phone booth nearby and Rex and me fought our way over to it, but there was no phone book. Nor at the next one nor the next after that. Finally I went back into the coffee shop and asked the girl with no hair if she had a phone book. She pulled out this monstrous old thing the size of a small car. I sat down at the window, Rex under the chair, wondering whether maybe alpacas wasn't so bad compared to Vampires and New York City. I found churches in the back and there must've been ten thousand of them so I got a refill and something called a biscotti, which I think is Italian for really hard, old bread with chocolate on it.

Down the list I drug my finger, hoping to find something familiar. Synagogues, Zen Buddhists, Catholics, Jehovah's and other churches I had never heard of such as Dr. Dingle's Church of the Blue Light and the Church of Elvis. All righty. Down toward the bottom of the first page, my finger stopped and my heart skipped a beat. The Church of the Holy Trinity.

I run back up to the counter and egghead must have thought I was some kind of crazy man. "How do you get to this here church?" I asked, pointing.

"The cross street up the block is 13th so you got to go up to it and take a left and it's over from there."

"Thank you very much," I said. "By the way, I like that earring in your nose," I said.

"Thanks. My girlfriend likes the one in my nipple." She smiled sweetly and I reckoned I must have blushed. "Are you a real cowboy?"

"Naw," I said, backing out with Rex. "I play one on TV."

It was a walk but I figured we could use the exercise, so we took off. It took awhile and Lord Almighty, the characters I seen. There was ratty old women pushing shopping carts full of useless junk, talking to themselves, and old men sucking bottles of wine in the alleys. Nervous-looking young toughs in leather and chains and all kinds of fat, pale men in suits, carrying briefcases. Finally, there it was, the Church of the Holy Trinity. It was tall and gray, with a dozen spires all pointed and tipped with crosses. Arching windows looked down onto the street and there was a considerable amount of greenery around it.

Rex and me scouted around the bottom of it and found a back way in. The inside was quiet and mostly empty and we took a seat in the back pew. Sun was streaming in through the stained glass and in each corner was a bunch of candles. Directly I got up, bidding Rex to stay, and lit me one of them candles and said a few words in my head directed at God concerning Lizzie's state of health. Every little bit helps. When I come back, Rex had found a tattered old piece of something to chew on which turned out to be the remains of a rat. I give Rex a disappointed look and kicked it under the pew in front of us.

I sat down and watched people come and go, hoping one of them might be Lizzie, but they wasn't. Like when I was a kid, eventually my ass got tired of sitting on them hard old pews and Rex got kind of fidgety and had to go pee, so we went outside, and while he was looking for the perfect bush to pee on, I stewed in my own disappointment. As he was sniffing around, his butt started twitching like it wished there was a tail to wag and he come dashing over to me, then back to the bush and back to me. He had her scent, I was sure of it.

There was a sign that said "Catacombs," with an arrow pointing down. The door was old and rusty, braced over with iron ribs and padlocked. I looked to make sure I was alone, then hammered it open with a rock. The door gave a groan as I pushed it open and musty air rushed out and mixed in with it was a familiar scent, all but lost in the mildew. Almost without thought, the Casull was in my hand and cocked. Steeling myself for the worst, I called Rex close and started down the slick stone steps leading away into the darkness below.

I'm not sure what a catacomb is exactly. Near as I could tell it means a really narrow, dark place that smells funny, probably from people sneaking in to have sex and drink cheap wine. Rex was sniffling out loud, his uncanny senses working overtime, and I let him race on ahead and tried to keep up. We got deeper and deeper, and the city scent was replaced by a musty smell of old clothes or something. Whoever built these tunnels must not have believed in electricity because try as I might I couldn't find a light, so we just groped and stumbled and cursed our way deeper into the bowels of the church. There was a book of matches in my jacket, probably left over from having Lizzie out, and it filled me with sadness to pull one out and light it up.

It filled me with even more sadness that my match failed to light up much of anything at all. We stood there, me looking at the feeble circle of light and Rex looking at me. I sighed and petted him. "Think she's here, boy?" I asked. He sat down and sniffed the air with gentle motions of indecision. The match burned out.

Seemed like the tunnel went on forever. Now and again I'd stop to light a match but it only revealed more of the same old stone, so mostly I just stumbled along in the dark with one hand against the cold surface, slowly making my way deeper through the twists and turns of the catacomb. Along the way was all these little nooks and crannies that I eventually realized must've been for burying folks in. I lit another of my dwindling supply of matches and held it up to reveal a crumbling archway with a little brass plaque badly tarnished by age that must've bore names of the dead. There was bigger rooms too, like them little houses from graveyards with bench-like shelves around the walls where I reckoned coffins was supposed to sit and occasionally saw some stone ones with lids sealed tight.

Before long, my matches was down to one and so we continued in the dark, hoping we were making progress and not just walking around in dark circles. The only thing I was counting on was Rex's nose which I could hear working and also the click of his claws on the stone surface. It was like sleepwalking in a way and soon there was nothing more than the rise and fall of footsteps, the certainty of motion and the gritty feel of progress as the wall slipped away under my palms.

Lulled by the sameness, when my hand slipped off into empty space I almost fell over. Rex gave a bark of sorts as I stumbled in and dropped down to my knee. I crawled forward until I felt a door of sorts. There was a padlock on it too, but Rex kept sniffling and barking, so I jammed my knife in it and pried it open as well. There was an even smaller room, one I had to hunch over to get into. I got to feeling around it, and there was a little ledge of crumbling wood running the length of the wall. I felt my way around the room until I was at the back wall, patting along like I was making biscuits and hoping not to find some rotten old coffin. All of a sudden, my searching fingers come upon hair. It curled around my finger like wire and twined up to my wrist. "Goddamn," I hollered, dropping the gun altogether and, scooting backward on my ass, hit the wall with my back and dust and decay dumped down my collar.

There ain't much I'm scared of. After facing down Vampires, not much can hold a candle. But I've always had a thing about bodies. It ain't logical. Dead is dead, at least that's what I used to think, but damn, they give me the creeps anyway. They say the hair keeps growing after death and I feared I'd just put my hand into a big pile of it. I imagined some old damn monk covered in hair with dead fingernails a foot long rotting inside and out into nothing but teeth and dust.

In spite of myself, I had to know. I flicked that last match to life, preparing for the worst. It was more worse than anything I could have prepared for. It was Lizzie that was dead, not some old priest. Dead and cold, and curled up on the ledge like a baby.

A scream ripped loose from me involuntarily, a scream heavy with pent-up hopes now dashed to bits and all the hope I'd been holding back and holding on to all these last days and all my life. It was a scream both loud and long, and the catacombs took it and echoed it and that old church shook and rattled all the way up to heaven itself. It was a scream that served notice to God Himself that I was through with Him. That I could never forgive Him for the sight of Lizzie lying before me in the dim light of my last match.

I had enough sense to cast about for something flammable so as not to be lost altogether in the darkness. There was a long piece of splintery wood on the casket behind and I ripped it loose and set the tip ablaze. By the light of that bit of wood, I could see a flaky old candle set into an iron cup just outside the door and I lit it up and placed it by her beautiful head, kneeling down to cradle her in my arms. Rex was beside himself with grief, whining as I took her cold and stiff in my arms. I swore and gritted my teeth because this ain't the way it's supposed to end. The cowboy always saves the girl before the credits roll. The cowboy always wins, even if only to ride off alone into the sunset. But that's by choice and here I was sitting in the middle of the last sunset with a whole movie full of mistakes playing in my head. The cowboy is supposed to win and I had just lost everything.

Hard to say how much time I spent down on my knees that way. Could've been hours or seconds or days. A whole lifetime of hurt give way and I knew my life was over, just like hers. She looked so peaceful, so calm and sure and it was mighty tempting to join her there. I let go of her just long enough to find the pistol discarded behind me, and place the barrel up against my temple. I cocked the hammer back and all I lacked was an eighth of an inch of resolve, but it was close. Mighty close.

Something stayed my hand, and that something was vengeance. A terrible and fierce vengeance swept through me like a thunderstorm of fire and rage, gradually eclipsing the hurt until nothing seemed more important than balancing the scales, in laying waste to the whole rat's nest of Vampires. Blotting them from the face of the earth and making one tiny detour into right from this freeway of wrong. Nothing else seemed to matter, not even my sorrow or the salvation that me joining her offered. I would set things right. Then I would join her.

But that was spare comfort now. I gathered her close to my heart and buried my face into the cold, sweet stretch of her throat. Rex kept edging up to sniff and lick at us as if the effects of his tongue might change the course of nature, then, failing each time, would retreat into the shadows with a whimper. At last I stretched out beside her and imagined us back up at Widow Woman Creek that last night with the sun setting and her in the firelight, so alive and lovely. Now, in my arms she felt so cold and forgotten. I reckon I must've cried myself to sleep in childlike fashion.

When I woke, for the barest of instants my mind convinced me it had all been but a terrible and long dream and that Lizzie was sleeping in my arms. But as I brushed the hair back from her face and pressed my lips to hers, they were cold and that terrible numbness came running back to me. She was dead as my heart.

Out of the depths of this tragedy, the oddest thing happened. My hand was splayed out over her chest and I felt a tiny stutter, faint as distant thunder. A bare and halting echo of a rhythm that struggled and lapsed and fell back on itself, only to start over. I drew back in absolute alarm and fear as her eyes fluttered open. There was life in there, an empty kind of life that was unsure of itself. Hungry life, but life just the same.

Her lips parted and she struggled to form words. "I knew you'd come," she whispered. "I knew it."

PART TWO:
RESURRECTION

He stood at the window, resting his hands on the cool adobe, the sweet smell of sagebrush and night washing over his face. A shooting star fell, blazing fiercely, then disappearing. The silver glow of the moon lit up the hills and twisted juniper silhouetted there. It brought a smile to his weathered face.

There was movement behind him. He turned too late to see who it was, but on the table was a tray with a steaming mug of coffee.

"Thank you," he called into the air and pulled up a chair. He took a sip and continued to look out the window. A coyote howled.

There was a knock at the door and a tall, youthful man with wise eyes and pale skin stood in the shadows under the arch. He was dressed simply in blue jeans and a plain cotton shirt.

"Carlos. Come in."

Carlos bowed respectfully and pulled up another chair. "It's a beautiful night." The older man nodded. Carlos continued. "Any news?"

"According to Jenkins, the turning has taken place. Shortly thereafter, she escaped. Elita believes it was by her doing."

"We should be there," Carlos said.

"We must not allow impulse to rule. Every action taken now will have serious implications."

"He will try to get her back," Carlos said.

"Of course."

"What if he is successful?"

"It is a distinct possibility. New York is his element. The more important question, however, is can he convince her to follow him?"

"Julius can be quite persuasive. Naturally, she will be confused at this early stage."

The older man sighed. "If she believes him, chooses to follow him, then she will have chosen her destiny, as well as that of billions of Adamites. But the choice must be hers and we will wait." Smiling benevolently at his young friend, he added, "After all, what meaning has time to us?"

Carlos rested his elbows on the table and cradled his head in his hands. "I can't help but fear for her," he said sorrowfully. "I remember my own turning well. If you had left me to my own devices, I would have lost my mind."

The old man contemplated his cup, harkening back to his past. "There are worse things than the turning." His eyes clouded darkly like the shadowy cave that still, after so long, made up the bulk of his memories. He pushed his chair back and stood, returning to the windowsill, leaning against it.

"Her lover is alive and seeking her in New York. He is aware, to a limited degree, of what he is up against and yet has gone anyway."

"He is either very brave or very stupid."

The old man shook his head. "He is in love, that is all."

"What will that mean to us?" Carlos asked.

"He loves her, and she him. That is all I know. Who can predict the effects of love, even with the unique historical perspective that you and I enjoy?"

Both men were silent for a time, the softness of their words barely missed by the wind outside. At last the old man turned from the window. "We have seen much together, yet I believe our proudest moments still lie ahead."

Carlos stood and made for the door, pausing long enough to say, "I hope so, Lazarus. I truly hope so."

EIGHTEEN

"WHAT HAVE THEY DONE to you?" Tucker whispered as he stroked her hair.

She struggled to find words. "You must get me something to eat. You must hunt for me, I can't do it."

"Hunt? What do you mean?"

"I must have blood," Lizzie said. The hunger in her body and soul was almost crippling.

Tucker stared, unable to comprehend the truth of the matter. He wrapped his arm around her. "Honey, you didn't have no pulse. And now you want blood. What have they done to you?" he repeated, his eyes wide and heart heavy.

Her hands trembled and her voice grew shaky "I didn't believe. Last night, I thought it was all a game, but the light came out of me, and the voices. Then I ate a rat. I needed the blood. And I died. I died, Tucker. I was dead until just now." She looked into his eyes, terrified. "Tucker, what are we going to do?"

"I have no idea, sweetheart," he replied, his mind struggling to keep up with a heart that at the sight of her breathing had immediately and without question resigned itself to her changed cir-cumstances. She was living, in a way. He could talk to her, touch her, kiss her, and for this he was grateful, but she was something grotesque too, something he would never have believed if he had not lived through the past few days. "I guess we'd better get you fed," he whispered.

"I can't kill anyone, I can't do it."

He swallowed hard. "We'll do it together. I'll help," he said, "and then we'll kill them all, every last one of them blood-sucking bas-tards."

Out on the streets of Manhattan, they strolled silently, hand in hand, safe in the seclusion that only a huge city can offer, hiding their emotions awkwardly behind the immediacy of her needs.

"We have to break into a blood bank somehow," said Lizzie, more to break the silence than anything else.

"Blood bank?"

"Yeah, one of those Red Cross deals."

"Red Cross?"

"Tucker, this is a shock to both of us, but do you think you could get more than two words out at a time?"

"More than two words?"

"That's a start. That was four words." She smiled at him.

"You better not get me started. I could go on and on." His lips were tight. "This'd be a hell of a topic for one of them daytime talk shows. You see, Oprah, I'm involved with this real nice gal, kind of the girl-next-door type. The problem is, every time the sun comes up, she dies. Now, I don't mean she stays in bed all day, I mean she's dead. No pulse, no blood pressure. Blue lips. Dead. Now if that don't beat all, when she does finally come back to life, the first thing she's thinking about is finding someone to suck the life out of . . . "

"Okay, okay, I get the picture." She cut him off. "We can talk about that later. Let's go to one of those places that stays open all night to buy blood from the winos and junkies when they need a few bucks." Lizzie hailed a cab. She pulled open the door fiercely and the hinges groaned.

"Hey, lady, what are you, a body-builder? Careful with my cab," said the driver. Lizzie was startled, surprised at her own strength. She jumped inside the taxi.

Tucker stood on the street corner. Lizzie looked at him from inside the cab. Now was the time to leave, and they both knew it: get himself out of this mess. Lizzie looked away, into the traffic on the street, resigning herself to the idea that maybe he should go. She could go it alone, if she had to. And it would certainly be better for him. Turning back, she saw that he was watching her intently, as if memorizing her features for some distant, future time when he would have to struggle to recall her face from a long-ago dream. Rex jumped into the cab next to Lizzie. He barked. She smiled weakly and stroked his head.

Tucker shook his head and climbed in the cab. He scooted over close and planted a kiss on her lips, then glared at Rex. "Like you're so goddamn smart. Stupid mutt."

The tired volunteers moved with graceless efficiency through the spent bodies of the blood donors, all willing to give up a pint of their life for a few dollars. It was a square room, sterile, with a stained gray carpet and once white walls turned sickly yellow with time and inattention. There were a few worn-out, upholstered chairs, intravenous devices for blood-letting, and several stacks of coolers where the yawning nurses placed the pouches of blood. It wasn't very busy, only two people giving blood, with a receptionist and a nurse overseeing the process.

"I wonder if I could give my own blood and then drink that?" asked Lizzie.

"Naw, that'd be like some kind of Vampire eating disorder. And besides, what'd happen if your blood is green or something even more disgusting? It would be a dead giveaway."

She slid her hand inside his coat pocket in a familiar fashion, felt the cold edge of metal, the gun she had yet to see.

He took a hard look at the blood bank. "Well, it sure ain't the Betty Ford clinic. Goddamn, this is depressing. And I thought LonePine was a sad little town."

Unexpectedly, Lizzie's knees buckled and she sagged toward the sidewalk. Tucker caught her and held her up.

"What's the matter?" he asked.

"I don't know, I'm dizzy. My head feels like it's filled with light." But it was light and voice combined, the now-familiar cacophony of female voices urging her to feed, to take a victim, Tucker if she must, but to survive at all costs.

"Leave me," she whispered, "I don't want to do anything bad."

"Hold on. Just a little longer."

"I'll try."

He pulled away and walked toward the entrance of the blood bank, his boot heels striking hard on the pavement. "Be right back."

"What are you going to do?" she asked.

"I could use a little extra cash. That should at least give you a snack to tide you over."

"I can't drink your blood."

"Why not? I'd just as soon you drink mine as some other cowboy's."

She smiled faintly and watched him walk inside. Kneeling on the sidewalk, she put her face close to the store-front window.

Her breath formed a veil on the glass, a mist through which she watched his every move.

Inside, Tucker smiled brightly at the receptionist who noticeably cheered when she saw a cowboy had just walked in. Lizzie scowled. The receptionist handed him a clipboard with a paper and pen and pointed to a chair against the wall on the other side of the room, smiling radiantly at him all the time. He smiled too, from ear to ear, shuffled his feet a little and, as he passed through the center of the small, understaffed room, paused. Planting his feet, he pulled out the shiniest, biggest pistol that Lizzie had ever seen. It was long and sinister and glinted in the harsh light and she wondered how he had managed to conceal it, her finger remembering the edge of metal in his pocket, what must have simply been the tip of the iceberg.

"Nobody move, this is a hold-up."

As it turned out, nobody moved because nobody believed him. "Come on," he yelled louder, "get against the wall."

A bedraggled street man looked up from his seat, needle in his arm slowly dripping blood into a bulging pouch. "What gives, Tex? Are you nuts? It's a blood bank, not a money bank. Who the hell steals from a blood bank?"

"I do." Tucker backed toward the stack of coolers. Pointing the gun at the nurse, he yelled, "C'mon, c'mon. I'm on a schedule here. Open one of them up."

The nurse began to cry. "Oh, damn, I'm sorry ma'am," he said, feeling guilty. He rummaged through his pocket for a tattered old handkerchief and moved close to comfort her, but then Lizzie tapped her nails against the glass and he caught himself. "Look, this is hard on me too. Just move it. Open that cooler." Inside were at least thirty pouches of blood in an orderly stack, jewels as far as he was concerned. "All right, everyone, stay where you are, I'm taking this cooler and getting out of here." Again no one moved, largely because they were still astonished that they were being robbed. Tucker struggled to hoist the cooler onto his shoulder with one arm while still managing to wave the gun around in a mostly comical fashion. Lizzie turned, hailed a cab and waited for Tucker to emerge from his robbery

"The things a man will do for love," he said as he got into the waiting taxi.

Lizzie reached into the cooler and tore open a bag. She gulped down the blood, so greedily that it dribbled out her mouth, down her chin, on to her now-ruined blue dress. That first one gone, she looked up at Tucker, half embarrassed, half relieved. She grabbed another and drained it, too. Her weak frame and ashen face, that only moments ago had convinced Tucker that she could die at any moment, were quickly transformed as the fresh blood flushed her skin and her eyes began to glimmer. Her lips turned deep crimson before his eyes. In a matter of seconds, she was radiant. Tucker was transfixed by her beauty, and simultaneously repulsed.

"Hey, you plan on telling me where you're going?" asked the driver.

Startled, Tucker responded, "Just drive for a while. And it's tomato juice, really." The cab driver only shrugged his shoulders and pulled out into traffic.

"Ah," she said, wiping the crimson juice from her lips with his shirt sleeve.

"Feel better?" he asked, looking at the stain on his shirt with an arched eyebrow.

"Much. Thanks, Tucker."

"How long will this last you?"

"I have no idea. Guess we'll learn the ways of a Vampire together." She paused. "And I have a feeling there are many things to learn. I don't know if I can eat regular food. And will I still have my period? Will wine still make me tipsy? Just how strong am I?" She stopped talking, asking more questions inside her mind and emanating a blood-satisfied vitality and exuberance. Tucker was quiet. All he cared about was what it all meant for them and just how long it would take Julius to catch up.

"I have to tell you about the safe-deposit box," Lizzie said, assuming a business-like tone of voice. "You'll need to get into it tomorrow during the day sometime, while I'm sleeping."

"Sleeping? Honey, it ain't sleeping. Let's call a cow a cow. You'll be dead. And while you're dead, you want me to rob a bank. Isn't a blood bank enough? You want me to break into a real bank during the light of day?"

"No, honey. I have a key. And I'll need some clothes too."

"But we can't go back. They gotta be watching your apartment."

"I'll call the landlady. She can do it for us and just meet you somewhere."

Her landlady was not particularly happy to be disturbed in the middle of the night, but after the initial surprise and the promise of fifty dollars, she agreed to meet Tucker the following morning with a suitcase full of clothes and the desired key.

The next day while she slept, he took the key to Lizzie's bank and opened the safe-deposit box. There were two letters, yellowed by age, both with Lizzie's name neatly inked on the outside. Tucker shoved them into his pocket and beat a quick retreat from the bank. Hungry as hell, he grabbed six hot dogs from a corner vendor for the cab ride back to the church. There wasn't any need to rush as she'd still be in her dead sleep, but watching over her would give him more comfort than wandering aimlessly among the streets of Manhattan with six hot dogs. Plus, he wanted to make sure she fed right off the bat.

That thought brought up a problem. Their stolen blood booty was rapidly dwindling and he knew that they would have to do something soon to get more. More precisely, he would have to do something to get her more. The concept of blood had little impact on him, he had long ago butchered too many cows and skinned too many deer for the gore to bother him, but supplying her was another matter. Would he be able to do what, ultimately, he guessed he would someday have to do? Could he kill an innocent person for Lizzie?

She was like a child now. She didn't know anything about this new life, this new death. In order to survive, she would have to learn and she would definitely need some help—help, he feared, she would seek in him. How in the world did he get himself into these situations? Nursemaid to a baby Vampire?

He sat on a park bench to eat and watched the pigeons. Maybe it would be best to contact Julius after all, pondered Tucker. Maybe he could cut a deal, get Julius to teach him what to do, and he, in turn, could teach Lizzie. Then, after she was stronger, and knew which end was up, maybe she would choose to join Julius. Or maybe not. He guessed that Julius would agree to just about anything to get his little Queen back, or at least, the hope of getting her back. Yeah, he thought, what could be the harm? I hold all the cards on this one, and Julius ain't got horse shit.

It was getting on toward late afternoon by the time Tucker made it back to the Vampire compound, thankful that they would be safely in their coffins. He rang the doorbell to apartment 4E. To Tucker's surprise, Jenkins himself answered.

"Hey, Jenk. What'cha doing getting the door yourself? Where are all your underlings?"

"I have been instructed to wait for you."

"I got a message for your boss. I want…"

Jenkins interrupted. "Where is your dog, Mr. Tucker?"

"My dog? Rex is with Lizzie."

Jenkins was deadly silent. Tucker felt suddenly uncomfortable, uneasy. What was going on?

"Your message?" inquired Jenkins.

"Well, maybe I should write it down. It's kinda important."

"There is no need. Every word we say is being videotaped."

Tucker regained his composure, smiled for the invisible camera. Jenkins looked mildly embarrassed for him.

"Tell your pale-faced master that I'll maybe put in a good word for him with Lizzie, under one condition."

"Yes?"

"He's got to teach me the ways of a Vampire."

"And you, I presume, would provide lessons for Ms. Vaughan?"

"Pretty bright, Jenkins."

"At least one of us is," muttered Jenkins in response.

"What was that?"

"I shall relay the message. And how will Master Julius contact you?"

"I'll come back here tomorrow, same time, same place."

"Very well, sir."

Tucker left the compound. Pretty damn smart of me if I do say so myself, he was thinking. Better get back quick, he thought. He hailed a cab. He was surprised at how quickly a yellow-top made it to the corner. Jenkins, of course, was not at all surprised, as it had been dispatched from the garage beneath the compound.

It was getting dark quickly now, and Tucker wanted to get back to the church straight away, but he was figuring he might have been followed.

"Hey," he said to the cab driver, "I'll give you an extra fifty bucks to drive like such a lunatic that no one could possibly be following us."

"It will be my pleasure, sir," answered the cabbie, smiling. "It's quite infrequent that I'm able to amuse myself in this line of work."

"Finally, a cab driver who speaks English," sighed Tucker, too unfamiliar with the urban immigrant jungle to know that a cab-driver speaking Oxford English definitely was out of the ordinary. He gloated as the cab sped off, anticipating the surprise he would give Lizzie when he told her he had figured out a way to be her tutor in the ancient art of Vampiring.

He settled back into the seat, feeling like he was starting to get the situation under control. Now, all he wanted to do was get back before she woke up. That part of her sure hadn't changed, he thought—not based on what had happened the night before. Before, it was coffee and cigarettes she had craved. Now, it was blood. At least, she seemed to have quit smoking, although he wondered if it mattered. Could cigarettes shorten the undead life of an eternal Vampire? Somehow he doubted it. Ah, the irony of love, he thought, always something to worry about. He wondered if he should tell Lizzie about his visit to the compound and his message for Julius. Nah, he thought, he'd wait and surprise her when he gave her a first lesson in Vampiring.

Back in the catacombs, he waited, looking at the letters. Sealed in linen envelopes, one was clearly marked with what he guessed was her mother's handwriting and said "open first." He rattled the envelopes around. There was something in both of them. He was aching to rip the letters open, to find out everything before she woke up and use the information to somehow make it all better. Instead, he decided to wait until she regained life, until she drank her fill of stolen blood. And then wait, he hoped, until after they'd made love.

He wondered if the future held any hope for that physical side of their love and whether Vampires even wanted to roll around in the hay. Then he remembered Elita and his question was answered. Rex crawled up, snuggling against his neck. He shoved the letters into his jacket pocket, took Lizzie's cold, distant hand, and nodded off.

Within the hour, she moved. She awoke with the same feeling from the night before and wondered if it would always be the same. First, the darkness touched something in her soul, then tickled behind her eyes until they opened. Seconds later, there was an ecstatic feeling, a sense of completion, and the power and mystery of the universe seemed to fill her. But this glorious sensation lasted only a minute or two, replaced, overcome, by the need for blood. This time, she was ready. This time, she had it under control, or at least close. It was like Christmas as a little girl, lying in bed and knowing that Santa Claus had filled her stocking with presents. Desperate to dash into the parlor, anticipating the happiness of a new doll or violin in her hands. Back then, she had fought to control her impulse to get up before the sun. She felt the same now, only it was her desire for blood that she was struggling to control, and the battle was in a scary and grown-up world with consequences more dire than a gentle scolding from her mother.

As the shadows coalesced into forms and the night became visible, she looked over at Tucker. He was holding her hand and sleeping, quietly and without moving. He looked dead himself. Rex's eyes followed hers and his stump of a tail banged softly against the floor. She smiled in spite of her hunger, happy that she could keep her blood-lust from destroying her two heroes.

She saw the bag of blood in Tucker's other hand. Sweet Tucker, he had remembered to keep the blood well within reach. Her mind and spirit soared in ecstatic anticipation. Quietly, she took the bag from his hand and ripped a hole in the tough plastic, sucking the contents down. She hoped he wouldn't wake up, suspecting he would not find this exactly a glorious moment. Watching her lust be so easily satisfied with the crimson heat might make him jealous. Or her ashamed.

"I have the letters from your mother," he said quietly.

She sat bolt upright. He had been awake after all, but for how long, she wondered. She wiped the blood from her mouth like a child wiping away a milk mustache. "Give them to me. Please." She was embarrassed to the point of anger, snatching them from his hand.

She tore open the first letter. Inside was a black and white photograph. She turned it over, reading the words written faintly on the rear. It was a picture of her mother and father, an unfamiliar one that must have been taken many years ago. Odd. Her mother had always told her there were no other photos of her father. But now with a start, she realized who it was. Her face turned pale. She handed the photo to Tucker.

"Who is it?" he asked, yet to look.

"My mother and father, my real father, before I was born."

He looked at the image and swallowed audibly. "Lizzie, that man, it's Julius."

"Yes, it certainly is, isn't it?" Lizzie pulled a note, hastily written, from the envelope, then paused. "Wait a minute. How do you know what Julius looks like?"

"It's a long story."

"I have time." She looked at him expectantly. "All eternity, in fact."

"Read your letters first." Tucker felt a vague discomfort about his visit to Julius this afternoon. Maybe total separation would have been better. Never mind, he thought, I can just not go back.

Lizzie read:

Dearest Elizabeth,

You once swore to me that you would not come to this box unless day had turned to night. If you still do not know what that means, if you have not been contacted by Julius, Elita, or Lazarus, I beg you not to open the next letter. Burn it immediately. I know, dear daughter, that your natural curiosity will be overwhelming, but you must trust me. Your life would be better served to live without this knowledge, and I will rest more comfortably knowing that my past actions continue to protect you. I am with you always.

Your loving Mother

Lizzie ripped open the next letter. A simple, well-worn pendant on a gold chain fell out. Her hands were shaking, but she felt a resolute calm, the calm that comes before the storm, the calm of impending knowledge. The pendant was a crucifix with a thorny rose wound around it, the full, heavy bloom hanging just in the center, and a crescent moon perched on the top, through which the chain passed.

My darling Elizabeth,

I am so sorry. Since you are reading this letter, you are surely tormented by the newly found knowledge of your heritage. My heart is breaking for you. I tried hard to protect you from the past, but it seems I have failed. All I can do for you now is to tell you everything, absolutely everything, so you will have the power of knowledge to face what lies before you. And what lies before you is grave indeed. I wish I could be with you, and hold you as if you were a child. But you are no longer a child and it would certainly offer you little protection but right now, comfort may be more important than protection. I dearly hope that there is someone in your life that you can trust, someone who will look after you, but I guess that is too much to hope for.

Please wear this locket, and know that I am always close to your heart. It was given to me by my mother and to her by her mother, your ancestors. I only wish I could have told you about them, about the power and magic that was their lives. The moon will be your sun for the rest of your days. Always let the power of the cross guide your actions, and pray that something beautiful blooms in your heart.

Lizzie paused from her reading and looked up at Tucker. He was staring closely at the photo, looking a little ruffled.

"Tucker, did you eat today?"

"Don't worry about me. I'm fine. I had some hot dogs." He scowled. "Besides, I could always try some of this." He held up a bag of blood.

"Don't be disgusting."

"Probably better for me than what was in them hot dogs."

Lizzie shook her head, laughing. The sound was foreign in the void of sadness around them. "I love you, Tucker. Just Tucker."

"Read your letter, sweetheart."

She turned back to her mother's words. The recognition of her handwriting evoked a longing, a tenderness.

Do you remember when you were a little girl and hurt yourself? You used to be so fascinated by your own blood. It nearly made me faint to see you suck at your cut finger, knowing what I know. Many years have passed and you are all grown up. I cannot tell you what course of action to take now, but I believe in you. Believe you can, must, make the right decisions and handle what has happened in your life. Trust in yourself.

The Book of Revelations in the Vampiric Bible prophesies a new Savior, one who will carry on the legacy of Malthus. The wording is vague, typical of the mysteries of the Bible, but it is believed that the power which will create the Savior will stem from a descendant of the first Queen. Revelations predicts that the Savior will be created from the powers given to a girl-child born of that noble line every seven hundred years. The world will know of her coming because she will be the only girl-child born in that generation. Further, the father of the girl-child must be descended from Malthus' first-born male. The girl-child must be turned at age thirty by one who is capable of becoming the Savior, that is, someone who has the power to turn. But the Savior does not come into his powers, does not become the reincarnation of Malthus until one more critical event occurs. This event is related to part of Malthus' legacy, bringing new blood into the Vampiric lineage.

Exactly twenty-one days from the girl-child's turning, she will have her first menses as a Vampire. The blood that leaves her body that first night is where the power of the future Savior lies. If he who turns her also drinks that blood, then it is prophesied that he will have the power to turn a full-blooded Adamite into a Vampire. If no one drinks this blood, the power will pass back into the Cosmos. Revelations also says that the Savior may in fact be the girl-child who carries the blood, if she chooses to drink it herself.

The girl-child prophesied by Revelations is you, my love.

Julius has always believed strongly in the literal truth of the Vampiric Bible. I am not sure if these prophecies are true or not. It doesn't matter. All that matters is that Julius believes in them and has spent the last thousand years manipulating lives so that he would be the only one capable of becoming the Savior. He will stop at nothing to have you under his control during your menses. He believes that he is Malthus reincarnated, and it is his fate to assume the powers soon to be manifested in you.

As you know by now, turning can only occur for those who carry the Vampiric bloodline. If full Adamites can be turned, the consequences for the world will be devastating. If an individual has the power to turn both Vampires and Adamites, they ultimately have the power to rule the world. And it's not just humans who would suffer. Not all Vampires are like Julius and his people. The world needs Vampires.

As I already said, I cannot know precisely what Julius' plans are. I do know, however, that he will unquestionably seek to drink your menses in order to have the dual power. He has been waiting a long time for this moment.

Lizzie handed the first few pages to Tucker. "You'd better read this too," she whispered.

Julius is your real father. I mated with him because this was the only way he would agree to allow me to live my life as an Adamite, which I wanted desperately to do. I had no idea what he really intended. While not all those with Vampiric blood are selected to live this destiny, once Julius decides, there is no more choice in the matter. My ancestors, our ancestors, had lived both as Vampires and Adamites. I believed the Adamite life preferable. He duped me into thinking that he gave me this choice because he loved me. At the time, I thought I loved him and very naively, I did not understand the significance of what I was doing. Julius had been systematically mating with all possible candidates who could carry the second girl-child, given that the seven-hundred-year interval was then fast approaching. Shortly after you were conceived, I was visited by a Vampire named Lazarus, who explained Julius' scheme. I did not believe him at first, did not want to believe him, but in time I learned the truth. I left with him and lived under his protection until you were born. I had expected you to be a boy, as were all of the children born to Julius' hundreds of consorts.

If it is even real, I believe that the power of dual turning is very dangerous; and should be allowed to simply pass away into nothing. You, of course, must come to your own decision.

Lazarus and I agreed that, ideally, you would simply be able to live your life as an Adamite, never having to face these awesome decisions. We also realized that if there was any hope of you living an Adamite life, you could not be raised in the Vampire world. You and I left Lazarus when you turned three and lived quietly, supported by him, protected by him, hidden by him. The separation was very difficult for me, for I had grown to love him very deeply. It was of him that I spoke when I talked of your father when you were a child, for he is the father of your heart. I never saw him after we left.

Lazarus is powerful, with an entire army and billions of dollars. While Vampires may seem monstrous in the context of the human world, some manifest their vow to embody evil in a manner very different than Julius and his factions. You will come to understand this when you meet Lazarus. Like Julius, he too has the power to turn. You must seek him out now in order to protect yourself. He has sworn to see you through this if you have the will to stand up to Julius, to not give in.

I wish there was some way I could have saved you from this. I tried. But now it is up to you. Good luck. I love you.

Tears were streaming down Lizzie's face, dripping onto the white paper, smearing the ink. She cried quietly as Tucker finished reading the last pages. He leaned over and brought her hand to his lips, kissing it softly.

"I don't understand. How could she have kept so much from me?"

"Doesn't seem like she had much choice."

"Why keep me in the dark? She should have prepared me."

"She prepared you pretty damn well. You're smart and tough as nails, and that's more'n most can say. And after one day of being a Vampire you already got a cowboy robbing the Red Cross for you."

A hint of a smile escaped from Lizzie's tortured face.

"She loved you, honey. She was your mother and although I ain't a parent, my guess is she wanted to protect you as best she could. She thought giving you a chance, however slim, that you might be able just to live a normal human life was the best way."

Lizzie did not respond, and her sad silence screamed through the catacombs and through Tucker's heart. Tucker just let it be, figuring that sooner or later she would break it herself. LonePine behavioral psychological training in action, yet again. Plus, although he himself was still reeling from everything that had happened in the last few weeks, he had to admit that at least he did not crave blood nor disdain the sun. She was the Vampire, not him, and she had more things to get used to than he ever would. Give it time, he thought, give it time, sweetheart. You got a lot of that now, might as well put it to use.

Finally, Lizzie handed the locket to Tucker and lifted up her hair for him to clasp it around her neck.

"It's strange being back here, in the church I mean," she said, "odd that all this should occur here in the church catacombs. She always told me that this church was where my father's funeral had been. But obviously he didn't die. He was already dead." The emptiness of this statement rang in her heart. "We used to come here every Sunday whenever we were in New York and sit in the back of the church. She never sang, or went up to pray. Just sat in the same pew and listened. No one knew her, not really. Not even Mr. Sully, and he was always sitting next to us every time we came here, without fail."

She looked around them. "It was my mother who showed me these catacombs, told me that they were secret, that I should remember them. When I was little she used to tell me that this would be a great place for hide and seek. When I got older, we still came down here from time to time, just to visit. She had an arrangement with the parish priest. I think she even contributed money to the church so that they would never be sealed off. But I finally stopped coming altogether when I started college, although Mother attended this church until she died."

Tucker stretched his legs out in front of him. "Who was this Sully guy?"

"I don't know. Some strange old man that was always at the service."

"What do you mean, strange?"

"He never said a word to us though we sat next to him on and off for years. And," her voice trailed off, "we only came to the evening masses, well after dark." Her eyes widened as a new-found realization began to sink in. "And Mr. Sully never got older. Even after I'd gone away to college, so that made it about twenty years we had been coming here on and off, he looked exactly the same." Lizzie paused, tempered excitement in her voice. "Tucker, I think that Mr. Sully was a Vampire. He must have been. He must have been connected to Lazarus."

"You don't think he's still coming, after all these years?" asked Tucker, incredulously.

"I don't see why not."

Tucker's shoulders slumped. "God, my mother would have loved you."

"What?" she asked, confused. "Why?"

"She always said I needed a woman who'd make me go to church."

LAZARUS LOWERED HIMSELF INTO the small pool of still water. Several hundred years ago when he moved to this part of the world with the Spanish, he designed and built this pool specifically for his body size, and other more subtle concerns. It was constructed of local materials, nothing more than a deep hole reinforced by strategically placed red sandstone from the desert, and located just outside his private quarters in his carefully maintained interior gardens. Far from elaborate, a circle only four feet across and exactly five feet, eleven inches in depth, it was perfectly tailored so that when he soaked he could stand upright, feet resting on the soft sand at the base, with the water just up to his neck. These days, however, his ever-expanding belly threatened to overflow the edges of the pool. Each time he soaked, he was unpleasantly reminded of just how desperately jolly looking he had become. He shook his head and ripples spread out around him.

His one luxury for his modest pool was, after the technology had developed several decades ago, refrigerated coils wrapped around it beneath the surface. This kept the water just above freezing. Vampires, as a rule, despise the cold. Through the years, however, Lazarus had discovered that the cold was a tremendous aid to controlling his appetites. It had become his nightly ritual. Each evening as the sun set and he was resurrected, he came first to his dipping pool to cool his body and his hunger. He was then able to think clearly about the coming night.

Tonight, like all other nights, as he soaked, the frigidity of the water took his breath away for an instant. He felt his heart skip a beat, but continued resolutely to immerse his body into the water. Moonlight streamed in through skylights carved out of the solid stone above, and Lazarus looked up into the blackness of the night sky, the millions of stars blazing there. The desert sounds passed through his entire being, the quiet certainty of the life moving there, the insect hum, the warmth of the wind, the slow but certain shifting of the sands.

At last he let out a deep breath. His mind was cleared of the cobwebs collected during the long, empty day before. Yes, he thought, the die has indeed been cast. Last night, he had completed the process of putting his contingent of supporters throughout the world on full alert. He honestly did not know what to expect from Julius and his New York world of darkness, but expected it would be drastic. The real wild card was that he had no idea how much Lizzie knew, if anything. Whatever she knew, the power was building in her body, power that would issue forth in twenty-one days—no, it was more like eighteen days now. Oh, women and their periods and their other mysterious processes. If the Adamite women only knew about the power of Vampire menses. What a magnificent article he could write for their tabloids, thought Lazarus.

One of his greatest pleasures in life was reading the tabloids. Daily, his minions made the trip to a convenience store outside Santa Fe for the sole purpose of purchasing the latest issues, as well as chocolate milk and HoHos. In the glossy, shocking pages were luridly captured the real interests of the Adamites, the subtleties of thought, their childlike worries, their strange attachments. Unlike the mindless and polished void of respected media, the tabloids were a direct link to their psyches. Often, he ghost-wrote articles, telling the truth about Vampires, ancient biblical prophecies, and the like. Imagine if he told them about the pain of existence for Vampiric women, the pain that kept them so slim and firm. And forever young. "Stars Flock to Try Fantastic Vampire Blood Diet!" What a headline. He smiled even wider and in doing so, began to laugh. Lazarus liked to laugh, even if it was at himself.

"Sir, would you care for your tea now?" Carlos asked.

Lazarus lazily opened his eyes. "No. Bring me some whiskey instead. I suspect I may have to learn to enjoy it, based on what I know about cowboys."

"Do you think they'll be here soon?" he asked hopefully.

"I reckon I don't know."

"Sir?"

"Never mind. I'm just practicing. I would like to be able to relate to my girl's main squeeze."

Carlos laughed. "Your ability to pick up the nuances of languages never ceases to amaze me."

"If only they had accepted my offer to translate the parts of the Dead Sea Scrolls in Aramaic. I could have turned the academic world upside down with an accurate translation. Instead they have that poppycock version full of educated guesses. It's my mother tongue, for God's sake. Oh well. I guess my enthusiasm does rather intimidate the Adamites."

"Sir, with all due respect, they thought you were a fanatic. When you started speaking Aramaic—words that, in this day and age, have been experienced only as an ancient and dead language—they thought you were crazy. An academic groupie, if memory serves, is what the professor called you."

Lazarus waved his hand, dismissing the memory, although his eyes took on a gleeful sheen, and his mouth turned up in a familiar smile. "Fetch me that whiskey, pardner." He ducked his head under water and held his breath as long as he could. When he emerged, a bottle and glass on a floating tray were pushed toward him. Lazarus poured two fingers and took a long sip. "I have to admit, I'm awfully excited to see her, to actually be able to talk to her. It's been so long."

"I wish it could be under different circumstances."

"It surely is a double-edged sword. Nevertheless, I remain optimistic. We can protect her. But she must seek the sanctuary here by choice. I will not force it on her. I owe her mother that."

"I understand. But no one has been able to find her since she left Julius."

Lazarus let out a belly laugh. The water around his naked body shook, sending waves out from him, circles of water undulating from the force of his laughter, ripples cresting over the edge of his dipping pool, spilling carelessly and pointlessly onto the hot desert sand.

"That's my girl."

"By the way, he telephoned. Several hours ago."

"Oh, he did? What did the old fart have to say?"

"He was very polite. Asked if we had seen his protégé."

The waves of undulating laughter again engulfed Lazarus' pool. "Fortunately, you were not put in a position of needing to tell a falsehood."

"Julius was not at all pleased."

Lazarus sighed. "No, I imagine not."

"Now what?"

"We must be certain that every opportunity is available for her to contact us. It must be simple, once she makes the connection, once she understands what is happening."

"We have Vampires out all over the world."

"Is Sully still in New York?"

"Sir, Sully has been in New York, attending the same church on the same night every week for the last twenty-seven years. I hardly think he would stop now."

"Yes, excellent. Remind me to send Sully a reward for his hardship posting. I suppose his assignment has been rather tedious this last decade, after she stopped going to the church altogether. I'm guessing it's about to get considerably more exciting."

The sounds of the desert deepened in Lazarus' ears, mixed with the warmth of the whiskey in his mouth.

"Bring the Book of Revelations into the library. I'd like to read it again."

"I reckon I can do that, pardner. Pardner-Sir."

Lazarus let out another laugh that shook the stars.

NINETEEN

Lizzie pushed the letters to the side and slumped back against the wall. She looked down at the tattered and soiled shift she had been wearing since her death and subsequent escape. "Look at me, I'm a mess."

Tucker looked up from petting Rex and studied her closely: the way a particular strand of hair hung over her sparkling eyes, the way her pale hands folded together like she was praying unconsciously, the way the material seemed to pick which curve to cling to and which to reveal. An interesting idea formed of its own will on a level beyond comprehension. "You look fine to me. Better than fine. But I did bring you some clothes from your apartment."

She brushed the hair back from her face so that now it was exquisitely framed. He stood up and moved over to sit beside her.

"What?" she asked. Tucker said nothing still, so she asked again.

He sat down and stretched his feet out in front of him, crossing his boots at the ankle. "I been thinking."

"Oh, you have, have you? About what?" Her voice had taken on the ghost of a smile, a coy sort of happiness that he had feared had been erased.

"Well, I've only really ever kissed you when you was dead. Now that you're alive—well, more or less," he winked, "and there ain't no one chasing us or trying to kill us, I think I might like to see what it would feel like to kiss you for real."

She laughed, a real laugh. "Dear *Penthouse*, I never thought this would happen to me, but there was this dead girl . . ." she let her voice trail off and scooted into his arms.

"That ain't funny." He craned his head around to press his lips to hers and they were surprisingly warm and pliant, unlike before. His rational mind wrestled a brief instant with the thought of someone else's blood coursing through her, but before it could take hold, she pushed him roughly back to the wall and leaned her body into him. With one hand in his hair, she pulled his head back, exposing his throat.

Nipping at it playfully, letting the tips of her teeth and tongue tease the skin, she paused long enough to look laughing into his eyes. "Are you scared?"

"A little."

"Why?" She nipped at his cheek and ear. "Afraid I'll hurt you?"

"It ain't that. It's been a long time," he whispered hoarsely. "I'm afraid I might be a little quick on the trigger, if you know what I mean."

She ripped his shirt open, ran her burning hands across his chest. His back arched involuntarily. "Don't worry, I'll be gentle. The first time." She raked her nails down the tender skin of his chest, raising welts. He gasped in surprise. She kissed the marks quickly and took his head in both hands to rain kisses on him, kisses that took away his breath and made his heart hammer in his chest.

228

Raising herself enough to untangle the shift bunched between her legs, she fumbled at his belt buckle. He slumped almost helplessly as her hands encircled his desire. With her guidance, he entered her and they remained locked there, her atop him, rocking gently.

All his pent-up anxiety and frustration of the last week disappeared in a swirl of pleasure and a physical reaffirming of all the love he held for her. He closed his hands around her waist, the skin as soft as her hot breath in his ear, as he pulled her close again and again. Lizzie trembled in his grasp, twisting and moaning as memories of mortality mixed with heightened responses heretofore unimaginable. A whirlwind of ecstasy ribboned inside her, lifting her to dizzying heights that stretched every sense into a taut, quivering wire of rainbow extremes. The myriad colors stretched tighter and tighter until they snaked around Tucker as well, his wrists, ankles, arms, and eyes. They rewove themselves into a solid arc of joy that bent from one heart to the other and back again.

Time retreated, ashamed at becoming a simple bystander, as they were pulled higher and farther away from all constraints of the physical. The church held them loosely in the arms of sanctity and in that holy silence of bodies joined, love laid its claim on the future. A wave of pleasure crashed over them, so intense it burned like fire, and Tucker melted into her with a groan and she blazed around him, trembling as her body took him deep within. And then it was done. Time rushed heedless into the void that had been created. She fell onto him, and he held her tightly in silence.

At last his back started hurting from the position and he pushed her gently to the side. "Good Lord." He thought about it a minute. "Think it's sacrilegious to, you know, do it in a church?"

She shook her head. "I don't think He would mind very much." Tucker's eyes started sliding closed, but he fought against it.

She traced the tips of her fingers against the stubble of his cheek.

"Tucker?"

She arched her eyebrow. "I think I might go grab a bite to eat."

He sat bolt upright. "A human?"

"No," she responded, "but maybe I could do an animal of some kind, one that would die soon anyway..." her voice trailed off.

"Can't you just have a cigarette or something?"

"I thought you were trying to help me quit."

"Yeah, well that was before."

"It's just that I feel so alive right now."

"Well you ain't," he grumbled matter-of-factly, rolled over onto his shoulder and pulled his jacket over him. Rex, who had watched their writhing with typical disdain, curled up against him. "You're dead," Tucker said.

TWENTY

"Darling, you look fantastic."

"Are you sure? I don't need just a little more eye shadow? I'm never sure if I have too much or too little. You'd think all my time on stage would have given me more skill with makeup, but I guess I'll have lots of time to practice now, you know, with it being eternity and ..." Mathilda babbled.

"That purple shade is just stunning on you," interrupted Sully as he leaned down to kiss her lightly on the cheek.

"You're sweet."

"I'm so excited about tonight. I have the most delicious target."

"Who, Sully? Tell me."

"First, let's move to the balcony. It's a perfectly lovely night and I have a bottle of champagne waiting."

"Champagne?"

"Yes, precious, we're celebrating tonight, are we not? It's your first full year under my tutelage. Sadly, you'll be moving on shortly. Has Lazarus told you where your next assignment is?"

Mathilda gasped in response, so unexpected was this news. He gave her no time to respond, however, ushering her through the apartment toward the balcony as he continued. "No, no, not another word. Wait for the champagne and then I can tell you absolutely everything."

The elegant uptown apartment belonged to Sully. Unlike many Vampires in Lazarus' tribe, Sully enjoyed standing out in manner and dress. He was small, tiny really, with a shock of thick, wavy blond hair, but no facial hair. Rather, he was childlike in appearance, almost angelic looking, pale skin with tender features. Unfortunately, his sweet blue eyes were covered by thick, horn-rimmed glasses. He was, in fact, nearly blind, but managed, nevertheless, to move through the world more confidently than most.

The balcony, like the rest of the apartment, was immaculately cared for, an extension of the grandeur of the adjacent dining room. Sully had spent the last thirty years lovingly nurturing this garden, largely to pass time during this Manhattan posting. He had artfully arranged various plants to create a cloistered feeling so that the city down below was nearly nonexistent while the sky above was wonderfully overwhelming. Many of the plants were exotic and some even deadly. There were countless varieties of blooming potted orchids that Sully replaced weekly with fresh blooms from a greenhouse devoted just to his pleasure. On the balcony he had also planted hemlock, belladonna, Venus fly traps, bittersweet nightshade, baneberry, death camas, foxglove, sumac, lupine, and many other deadly varieties. The plants had been carefully chosen to reflect the trivial nonsense that Adamites believed about Vampires. Sully loved to watch the mortals he lured here react to his plants. It was such a delicious way to lay the foundations of suspicion, which later would blossom into terror. Of course, by that time, it would hardly matter anymore. Lazarus knew of his gardening interest and periodically had Vampires from around the world send Sully magnificent seeds from the gardens of Europe and elsewhere that Sully meticulously cared for. This time of year it was a bit cool to use the garden, but tonight was unseasonably warm and Sully thought it might be the last chance for a while.

As Sully uncorked the Dom Perignon, he thought about how to break the news to Mathilda that she would be moving on to her next Master. Lazarus had contacted him last evening to say that events were transpiring quickly and there was no room in the scenario for the naiveté of a recently turned Vampire. He wished there were time for a few more lessons in the sophisticated hunt—it was so crucial to a balanced lifestyle. Sometimes he pitied new turns like Mathilda, still at the very earliest stages of understanding their craft. They were forced to rely solely on their still crude and evolving instincts to ferret out the Adamites who possessed that particular brand of evil that emitted a scent so familiar to the undead. Their absence, these mortals, benefited the world and helped maintain the intricate balance between good and evil.

"Drink, my dear, to your very successful first year," Sully toasted her.

Mathilda was going through the very extensive training required by Lazarus. The first year was often difficult—the reason Lazarus matched young Vampires with Elders, rather like an apprentice to a master or a savior to a disciple. Absolute obedience and submission were required and every need of the young recruit was seen to, from how to hunt to drying tears when an Adamite family member was missed, to correcting their occasional over-zealousness. Once the initial adjustment was made, the real purpose of the training was to teach a young Vampire their role in the world and to pass on the moral codes from the Bible, balancing impulse with purpose. Lazarus and his adherents believed strongly in the Original Purpose of Vampires, the purpose laid down in the Garden of Eden.

Silly Adamites, thought Sully, why live by the notion of an Original Sin when an Original Purpose is so much more compelling. Their purpose was to embody evil, literally, by devouring its flesh, sucking its life-blood, watching it writhe in agony, containing it. It was a noble pursuit, protecting the Adamites from themselves.

"I've been tracking my latest victim for nearly four weeks. Another Wall Street banker, but really he's just a tawdry con-artist. Yesterday, he convinced a sweet old woman to invest $60,000 toward an ostensible real estate venture in Phoenix. What a fraud. After the check cleared, he immediately wired it to a personal account in Weehawken. He's been pulling the same scam for years now and has bilked countless seniors out of their hard-saved money. He has over $3,000,000 in that account alone."

"How did you find all this out?"

"I broke his security clearance on his online banking system and put a bug in his phone."

"But how did you spot him at first?"

"The same way you young-uns spot the petty criminals, liars, potential rapists."

"Young-uns?" Mathilda interrupted.

"Forgive my colloquialisms. I'm practicing a new dialect at Lazarus' instruction. What was I saying? Oh, yes. I spot the evil by its smell, just like you. But with more years of training, your sense of smell matures. With this refinement, you will be able to sense a less gruesome, but perhaps more deadly, type of evil in your Adamite prey."

"Like last week. You took that man who was poised to rape his teenage daughter."

"Exactly. He was quite simple, really. I first scented his evil during a stroll along Madison Avenue where he was shopping with his daughter. I followed him for only two hours, observing his interactions with her. Even a well-adjusted Adamite probably could have predicted that one."

"His daughter will now live a better life. All because of you, Sully." Sully hardly heard her, momentarily lost inside his fantasies about his later rendezvous with the banker. He smiled gleefully, like a little boy, and clapped his hands together in anticipation. "Now, my dear, enough about me, did you take your snack earlier? You know you are not strong enough yet to control your urges. You must drink the packaged blood at least four times a night."

"Yes, Sully."

"And this evening?"

"I'm going to the nightclub again. I enjoyed that immensely."

"Good choice." Sully refilled her fluted crystal glass. "You will enjoy your new Master, or rather Mistress. She has led an extraordinary life. Make sure she tells you her stories from the Sun King's reign at Versailles. What a deliciously evil time."

Mathilda stuck out her lower lip.

"You will be leaving for Paris tomorrow, my dear," Sully went on.

"I was supposed to be with you for ten years. Are you displeased with me? Why can't I stay with you here? I love you, Sully. No one has ever been kinder to me."

"Don't sulk, sweetheart. If you promise to smile, I'll tell you a secret."

"Oh, Sully," she exclaimed, "I love secrets. And you know I can keep a secret well."

Yes, I know, thought Sully, that's one of the reasons Lazarus chose to turn you. That and to contribute to his pet theater project in London's east side. She was indeed a fine actress. Sully uncer-emoniously downed his champagne and threw his glass onto the floor, startling Mathilda with the shattering glass.

"I just love to do that," he said, giggling. "Oh, the time. I must be off. I have to attend my church service before I meet my banker."

"Sully, you promised me a secret," pouted Mathilda, the sound of her high heels striking the pavement lost in the slam of the door as it shut behind him.

TWENTY-ONE

Soon, she would have to go, but not just yet. She wanted a little more time to look at Tucker. He was sleeping quietly—sleep, she suspected, that he desperately needed. He looked so peaceful, his face years younger, free of the recent lines of worry that she had caused. She loved him more than she thought possible and now wanted to remember every pore, every line, every mark on his face. She did not touch him for fear of waking him, fear of what he might say; but her hand moved just above his body, mimicking his shape, the hard edges, as if she were stroking him.

She knew he would never leave her. If the thought had even entered his mind, it was now gone, replaced by a certainty that would keep him beside her. Perhaps it was his sense of honor, something deeply bred in his bones, having to do with cowboy codes and happy endings, that prevented him from getting himself out of this mess. There would be no happy ending here, the letters had proven that. At worst, she would live for all eternity like an animal. At best, after contacting Lazarus, she would let the sun have its way with her and be done with it. No matter what, Tucker deserved better and she was going to see that he had it.

It was as simple as leaving him now, finding Sully and Lazarus, and then, well, whatever. Tucker could go back to LonePine, find a good woman, have a baby or two, and chase off his alpacas. That was the life he was meant to live.

Should she write a note? Yes. Otherwise he might wait here for days, or worse, put himself in danger looking for her. She took the photo of her mother and Julius, scribbled on the back of it: *Tucker, I love you. Please go back to LonePine. Don't forget me but don't wait for me. Thank you from the bottom of my heart for everything.*

As she moved closer to him to put the photo on his chest, she realized that he was awake, following her every move with his eyes.

"You running out on me?" he asked quietly.

"I, well, what I, I …" she trailed off in confusion.

"Answer the question."

"Yes."

"Well, that ain't an option."

"Ain't isn't a word," she sniffed. "And this ain't a cowboy movie. You should go home, live a real life."

"Find some new girl, you mean?"

"Yes. Someone who doesn't drink blood."

"Look, let's be clear here. I ain't going anywhere. End of story."

"What if I want you to?"

"Do you? Really?"

"Yes." Lizzie was resolute. She stood. "I'm going to church now."

"Got your Sunday best on, I see." She looked down at her tattered clothing.

"It can't be helped. I have to meet Sully. I don't want to see you again, Tucker. Ever."

"What about Rex?" Rex wagged his stumpy tail hopefully.

"I'm serious. Go home." She spun around and stomped out the door, heart heavy that she was leaving Tucker behind. He smiled and shook his head, muttering.

Outside the door, Lizzie walked up the stairs out of the catacombs, into the church nave. There was no sound of Tucker behind her. Good, she thought, at least he listened. Damn him for listening.

She made her way through the sparse crowd, back to the pew where she had sat with her mother, so long ago. Or was it the one behind? She could not quite remember. A few churchgoers eyed her suspiciously as she sat down, torn clothes, bare feet, and exhausted eyes, but she ignored them and bowed her head.

"My, my, my. You look like you've been through the wringer," came a familiar woman's voice. "And I had so hoped we would never meet again."

Lizzie turned to look over her shoulder and Elita smiled coquettishly at her from the aisle. Before Lizzie had a chance to respond, Elita spoke with great ferocity in her voice, but without losing the smile. "This entire church is surrounded. You cannot possibly escape. Just come quietly. Please."

Lizzie stood up in frustrated obedience. She noticed Mr. Sully sitting demurely two pews behind. Her eyes met his, and he nodded almost imperceptibly. Lizzie looked quickly away, her face resigned as Elita led her out of the church.

Just then, Tucker slipped in one pew behind Sully, his massive pistol leveled at the base of the diminutive Vampire's neck. "You Sully?"

"Yep, pardner. Reckon I am." Tucker was startled for an instant, then shook his head and lowered the gun out of sight. "Any ideas?"

"Oh, yes," said Sully, lapsing back into his normal speech pattern, "but I think she'll need some inside help."

"You saying I should go with her?"

"It would be most convenient if you allowed yourself to be captured now."

Tucker paused thoughtfully before responding. "See you in a little while then?" Tucker asked hopefully.

"Oh, most definitely," responded Sully "We will be there at," he checked his watch, "nine-thirty tomorrow night. It would be most helpful if you could create a small diversion of some sort."

"I'll see what I can do." Tucker stood and squared his shoulders as he walked toward the door. Once outside, he shouted, "You'll never take her alive," and rushed headfirst at the mob of Vampires hustling Lizzie into the waiting limo. Rex ran behind, barking furiously.

Inside, Sully laughed heartily. He, too, would be quite an addition to Lazarus' theater project, and so handsome. If only Lazarus could turn the cowboy.

By the time the confusion ended, Tucker and Lizzie sat facing each other in the back of the limo. Tucker's guns, he noted with dismay, were on the front seat, which was separated from them by a thick layer of plexiglass. Their hands were manacled behind their backs and Rex was tied to the door handle with a length of rope. He looked forlornly at Tucker, then back at Lizzie. On either side of them was a silent Vampire. Elita sat in the jumpseat, directly behind the driver, idly flipping through the latest issue of *Cosmopolitan*.

Lizzie glared at Tucker. "I told you I never wanted to see you again. What the hell were you thinking? You just don't know when to give up, do you?"

Tucker shrugged his shoulders. "I didn't believe you."

"Well, do you believe me now?"

"Naw…"

"You are so pigheaded and ridiculously stubborn."

He leaned toward her. "Ain't that kind of the pot calling the kettle black, darlin'?"

"If my hands were free, I swear I'd choke the life right out of you. Don't you see, whatever happens to me will be bearable as long as I know you are all right?" She leaned closer too, their faces inches apart now "But no, you had to waltz in and ruin everything."

"That's some gratitude for a guy risking his ass to save yours," he yelled back.

"Who asked you to?" she screamed.

"Enough," Elita yelled. She threw the magazine and it bounced off Tucker's head, falling onto Rex, then she pushed them back into their seats. "You two are driving me out of my mind. You sound like an old married couple." She looked into Lizzie's eyes. "Like he could just turn his back on you. He loves you. And you," she turned to Tucker, "don't you see she was trying to protect you?" Her shoulders slumped. "Oh, God, this is so nauseating." She retrieved her magazine and slumped back into the seat.

Several minutes passed. Tucker glared at Lizzie, who glared back at him. Finally she said, "You'll never take her alive. What the hell does that even mean?"

"It's all I could come up with, all right?"

Elita shook her head behind the magazine and scowled.

"Why didn't you just stay at the church?" Lizzie asked tiredly.

He arched his eyebrow. "'Cause I didn't want to *sully* our relationship."

"Our relationship would be a lot better off if one of us hadn't been captured by these goons."

Tucker rolled his eyes. "No, our chance of escape would have been *sullied* if I'd stayed behind."

"Oh," she said at last, understanding. "I get it." She nodded.

Elita looked up curiously and started to say something, but the limo came to a stop outside the facade of rowhouses. Shrugging, she opened the door, ushering the captives outside. Elita took the rope restraining Rex and dragged him along. They were led through the darkened gardens, pushed roughly by their captors. Tucker balked, and the Vampire behind him punched him in the kidneys. The force of the blow dropped him to his knees.

He struggled back up and glared at the sinister face. "If my hands were free," he grumbled, "I'd whip your ass."

The Vampire grinned. "I would be delighted to accommodate you," he said, driving his fist into Tucker's gut. All the air rushed out of him and he doubled over. "Some other time, perhaps."

"You piece of shit," Tucker mumbled through gritted teeth. He spit and straightened up. "What's your name?" he asked, as he turned toward the mansion.

"I am called Revor. Why does this concern you?"

"I like to know who it is I'm going to kill." Revor jerked his arms savagely and laughed.

Julius was waiting in the lobby and smiled victoriously as the party entered. "Elizabeth, so good to see you again. And Tucker, loyal Tucker. My heartfelt thanks at leading us straight to our Queen."

Tucker glowered at him. Lizzie quickly surveyed the room and Julius' face, quietly assessing what the situation was and how to best play the few cards they had.

"I don't think this is a suitable way to treat the Queen of the Vampires," she said.

Julius chuckled. "Don't get carried away, my dear. You proved your allegiances when you chose to flee. Come, bring them." He gestured expansively up the staircase. "We have prepared a special room."

"Thanks, but I was getting used to the church," Tucker said and Revor pushed him forward.

"I will admit, you have a certain charm," Julius said. His face quickly darkened as he took the first step and turned to regard them. "Let me tell you the way things are to be now. You are my prisoner," he said, pointing at Lizzie. "You will be held here until I have what I want from you. Depending on your level of cooperation, I may let you live after that. You," he pointed at Tucker, "are my hostage. If Elizabeth disobeys my wishes, you will be killed in an extremely painful way." He smiled at Revor who stood close behind. "Of course, Elizabeth, you will be obligated to watch his demise." He paused, lost in the force of his own words. "The dog dies now. A reminder of the seriousness of my concerns. Elita, he is yours." She scooped Rex off the floor and held him tight in her arms, beaming at Tucker.

"You bitch," Tucker roared. "Let him be." He lunged at her but Revor lashed out with his fist, connecting with Tucker's temple. He collapsed to the floor with a groan. Lizzie took an involuntary step forward, but Julius seized her by the shoulders.

"If you cooperate, he lives. For now."

She stared hard into his face then shook herself free. "Whatever you say, Father."

Julius paled even closer to white and took a hesitant step back. "Who told you that?" he stammered. Then his eyes fell on the pendant glittering on her throat. He snatched it away, regarded it briefly, then smiled and placed it in his vest pocket. "It would seem I underestimated your mother. I'll keep this for now."

"Take me to my room," she replied, moving past him, trying to keep him off balance as long as possible. Revor hoisted Tucker over his shoulder and carried him to the top of the stairs. A door stood open and he dumped Tucker unceremoniously inside. Lizzie stepped in as well and Revor undid first her manacles, and then those of Tucker. Julius stood in the doorway, his face tight.

"Do not try to escape. It is impossible."

"Don't kill the dog," she said, "it will be your undoing."

"A dog? Don't make me laugh." He stepped out of the room, pulling the door closed behind him. He opened it again briefly. "You do not deserve the privilege of a coffin. Lie so that you will avoid the sunlight, as our wild ancestors once did, hidden in the shadows." He pulled it shut and she heard the lock click into place.

OUTSIDE, JULIUS SPUN AROUND to regard Elita triumphantly. "That certainly went well."

She allowed herself a tight smile and readjusted her grip on the collar of the dog under her arm. Rex lolled his head passively, his wide eyes on the room where Tucker lay, now sealed tight.

"I must give you the credit for this, my dear. Your plan worked splendidly," Julius said.

"I am so happy for you," she said. "Your little princess has returned. It will be interesting to see if you let her escape again."

His hand closed involuntarily around the doorknob and brass squeaked and groaned under the pressure. "Mind your tongue, Elita." He took a threatening step forward and she shrank from him. Given the blood to spare, she would have flushed. Even Rex, almost catatonic from fear in her arms, bared his teeth in alarm at Julius. "I will not tolerate your ridiculous jealousy and petty sarcasms. If you find this situation no longer to your liking, feel free to leave."

"Maybe I will," she said shakily, her chin raised in defiance.

"Don't let me stop you." He brushed past her down the hall and called over his shoulder. "Enjoy the dog. Consider it my parting gift."

Elita stood frozen in the corridor, her face transformed by shock and despair. As the grief played itself out, she stared down at Rex and snarled at him through her sobs, "I almost hate to take this out on you. But not quite."

She carried him through the mansion and down the spiral stairs into the heart of the underground complex, passing scores of other Vampires who smiled enviously at the burden in her arms. She said nothing, walking straight to the elegant door of her room. Keeping one hand on the collar, she laid him down and reached up to open the handle. Rex lay completely motionless as the door swung open. She tugged him forward by the collar. "This is going to be too easy," she said, bending low to envelop him.

With a snarl and alarming speed, Rex came to life.

Where a second before, he had been lying still, feigning resignation, now he was extended in a jump that allowed him to clamp his own fangs into the soft flesh of her breasts. It surprised her more than hurt, but she fell backward and swatted at him as he disengaged and bolted for the door, scooting around the corner just before it swung closed.

She howled in rage and looked down at her torn blouse. Liquid seeped from the teeth marks on her half-exposed breast, staining the torn fabric. She pulled the pieces back into place and, fumbling at the door latch, opened it in time to see Rex disappearing down the hall. A dozen bewildered Vampires turned to see who had made so much noise as Rex negotiated through them at breakneck speed.

"Get that damn dog," she screamed, startling them all into motion, but it was far too late as Rex was already bounding up the stairs. She charged after him, shouldering through the confused Vampires. "Idiots," she snarled. When she cleared the landing, he was nowhere in sight so she paused, listening deeply. The faint click of claws across linoleum reached her ears. The kitchen.

She sprinted down the hall and smashed through the swinging doors in time to see him darting across the dining room. A string of curses formed in her mouth but were cut off as the doors swung back and sent her tumbling. She sat on the linoleum and raged. "I despise dogs," she screamed at the empty kitchen. She let her senses flood out of her, seeking a cowering, flea-bitten, canine form, but finding nothing.

One of the Vampires entered the kitchen. "Miss Elita, can I be of assistance?"

"Of course you can be of assistance. Find that goddamn dog."

"Perhaps he went outside."

"Well, go outside and look for him."

The Vampire hurried to the garden's main door and held it open, surveying the darkened grounds outside. A furry flash streaked past him with a yelp and the Vampire uttered an exclamation. "He's out here now, Miss Elita," he yelled, sprinting after him.

Elita raced out into the night and felt a strange thrill coursing through her veins despite the ridiculous nature of this game. There was a time, back in her wild, untamed youth, when the hunt was the joy of her life. Not simply prowling the streets for some young, sexually desperate man to take home, but running the woods and taking her prey with tooth and claw. A worn-out cowboy's worn-out dog was a far cry from the knights and highwaymen of the Dark Ages, but it was still invigorating. So be it, the hunt was on. With a laugh, she threw herself into the darkness, felt the cool air against her face and the wet grass beneath her feet. Reaching out, she found the scent of fear, and finding it, increased her speed until it was almost like flying.

TWENTY-TWO

TUCKER OPENED HIS EYES into a memory. When he was a child, he'd slept under apple trees in an orchard on the ranch, planted back in the days when the stagecoach used to come through. Lying in a thick bunch of grass, he would stare up through the fruit-heavy branches at the sky and clouds, standing every so often to pick an apple, eating it slowly and savoring the fresh, tart surprise of it.

Waking now in the darkness and holding Lizzie close, he felt the same warmth and peace as in the orchard. There was even a faint trace of apple, of sunshine trapped in her hair, and he buried his face in the nape of her neck, which was cold as spring water.

After a moment, he disentangled himself from her stiff and un-yielding limbs, grimly marveling at the wonder of it all. He peered through the heavy drapes to fix the position of the sun, well estab-lished in the smog of the Manhattan sky. He moved slowly, careful not to let any of the sunshine touch her sleeping form. Settling back onto the bed, he pursed his lips to give Rex a wake-up whistle and then realized with a numb sort of horror that Rex had been taken last night. The last thing he remembered was Elita yanking him away by the collar and a fist that came out of nowhere. The rest was all blackness.

He massaged the lump on his skull as this most recent disaster sank in. What the hell else could go wrong, he wondered. If past experience with Elita had taught him anything, Rex was gone, empty as last night's beer can. With a hoarse cry, Tucker attacked the door, swearing and kicking and raging until his voice was ragged, threatening all who lived or unlived in that accursed mansion if anything happened to his dog. If anyone heard, no one responded, although shadows moved underneath the door. His energy at last gave out, leaving him slumped against the door, disheartened and with a lump in his throat.

Knowing the Vampires were dead and tucked away rankled Tucker the most. Now, by the light of day, they were utterly defenseless, except for the well-armed servants and guards. If he could escape, he could spend all day exacting revenge, do it right; but the door held tight. He kicked it again out of force of habit and sat down on the edge of the bed. Lizzie sure wasn't going to be any help, being so dead. He ran his fingers through her hair and wished she was alive enough to at least smile the way she used to when he kissed her in her sleep.

Slumped over her, he almost missed the inquisitive scratch at the door. It was a familiar sound, one that made him instinctively stand to let Rex out. Halfway to the door, he realized that Rex wasn't in the room. In fact, he was supposed to be dead. But squatting down, he could see furry paws under the crack of the door. What he meant to say was "Goddamn I'm glad you're alive," but what came out was "What the hell took you so long?"

Not that Rex's arrival could necessarily change things. There was still a locked door between them and figuring a way out. Tucker lay down with his cheek to the floor and watched Rex's haunches backed up and sitting there, measuring the situation. He thought about all the times Rex had sat and looked forlornly at the trailer door until, aggravated, Tucker would open it so that Rex could go out and stare at it from the other side.

"Try the handle," he whispered.

Rex didn't move.

"Try the handle, Rex," he whispered, a little more loudly. He raised up and looked through the keyhole. Rex was looking at the door like it was about to do a magic trick.

He jiggled the knob. "Try the goddamn handle," he whispered so loudly that Rex shrank back, momentarily, then jumped up and caught the handle in his mouth. Their eyes met through the keyhole, and there was a mighty pool of determination reflected there. Rex hung from the handle, jerking and twisting his whole body in the air for extra leverage. The lock mechanism creaked and clicked under his weight and Tucker stepped back and gave a mighty kick. It swung open and Rex, still hanging on by his teeth, crashed into the wall with a muffled thud.

"Sorry about that," Tucker said as Rex limped out from behind the door. He was muddy and bedraggled, but didn't appear much worse for wear. Tucker gave him a pat on the head, nonchalant, as if he hadn't been heartbroken moments before. Rex sat down to lick himself.

There was no one visible up or down the hall, despite the noise of the door. He held his breath and waited for the sound of running steps which would signal the arrival of the guards, and with them, their guns. All was silent. They tiptoed out, with one look back at Lizzie lying safely dead in the shadows. Tucker examined the doorknob, the metal twisted out of shape. He whistled under his breath. "Them's some powerful jaws you got there, boy."

Rex wagged the stump of his tail.

Unlike the room, the hall was bright with sunlight. They crept cautiously to the stairs, and up toward the study. Tucker was anxious to find his guns and hoped Julius had left them in the drawing room where he had been set up that first night. What an idiot I was, he thought as they reached the upper landing and, the doors unlocked, entered the study. The blinds were wide open and the whole room seemed almost cheerful, although underscored by the faint stench of death. A quick look around did not reveal the guns. He sat down in the swivel chair and propped his feet on the desk to plan his next course of action. There was a box of cigars in the top drawer and he pulled one out and lit it up. Rex hopped up on the desk and sat facing him like they were having a conference.

The door suddenly opened and Tucker tensed. It was Jenkins. Tucker glared over the point of his boots and blew a stream of smoke at him, waiting for a cry of alarm to be sounded.

Instead, Jenkins stepped in and closed the door, looking disdainfully at the placement of Tucker's feet.

"Morning, Jenkins," he said, without stirring.

"Good morning to you, sir," he answered. "I see you have escaped."

"I have indeed. You got a problem with that?"

"Quite the contrary; I am delighted." His face took on an odd expression. "Though I won't go so far as to say I shall miss your company."

"I smell a rat, Jenkins," Tucker said and swung his feet down. "How come you ain't called for the guards?"

He took a step forward. "Quite simple. I do not wish you to be discovered."

"Whose side are you on?"

"Not yours," he answered.

"Not Julius' either."

"No. I serve another master. One you have yet to meet, although I suppose you will soon enough. I only hope this matter is resolved in such a way as to preclude the opportunity of you and me remaining in close contact."

Tucker smiled at this. "Any idea where my guns are?"

"In the cabinet behind the desk."

"It's locked."

"I have the key." Jenkins bent and unlocked the antique cabinet and swung the doors open. Inside, the guns gleamed in the sunshine.

"Damn, did you clean these?" Tucker asked, pulling them out and giving them a cursory examination.

"Yes. I took the liberty of having them cleaned and oiled."

"Thanks, I appreciate it. You know, you're all right."

"You have no idea what that means to me. If I may be so bold as to make a suggestion, you should wait until nightfall to attempt an escape. During the day perimeter security is extremely tight, but after the masters of the house arise, this security is relaxed somewhat. If there is any hope of successfully escaping, it would be early in the night."

"Around 9:30?"

"Precisely."

"Interesting coincidence. You gonna help?"

"I already have. Anything else I might do would be foolish and ineffectual. I am an old man, after all."

"I guess you're right. But do you think there's a chance we could get something to eat?"

"I believe you are familiar with the layout of the kitchen. If you wish to risk discovery for the sake of a meal, it is your choice. Now I must go." He checked the hall and then turned. "In truth, I hope we shall meet again. If we do, the plan will have succeeded." He bowed short and pulled the door shut.

Tucker sat and pondered Jenkins' curious words, eventually rising to check the hallway. Satisfied it was not some kind of trap, he called to Rex. "Guess I wasn't as hungry as I thought. C'mon, let's go check on Lizzie," he whispered, guns in hand.

There wasn't much to check on. She was still dead. Back inside, he pulled the door shut, locking it as Rex watched in disbelief. He pulled a chair around facing the door and sat down to wait for sundown, the shotgun in his lap. It was a long wait, with many hours to kill before Sully and his boys showed up. He made a mental note to buy a watch. Without one, he hoped he would be ready when the action started. He passed the time imagining what a normal life with Lizzie might have been like. By the time sundown rolled around, there was a powerful pain and anger in his heart.

Later, he heard voices down the hall and he tensed. When a hand grasped the knob he smiled grimly, hoping Lizzie would wake soon, thinking that he should probably remember in the future not to make plans that depended on her waking up on cue at sunset from her daily death. Sooner or later, her internal body clock would probably get it right, but that could be awhile off.

The door swung open to reveal a tall Vampire standing there smiling as he contemplated the evening's festivities.

"Pardon me," Tucker said levelly, "do you have the time?"

He looked oddly at Tucker and checked his watch. "9:24."

"Thanks," he said, swinging the shotgun up to bear on the Vampire.

"Lord Julius, the cowboy…" was all the man had time to get out before Tucker squeezed the trigger. The wooden stake blasted out and caught him low and hard, the force lifting him up on tiptoes and slamming him out the door. Behind Tucker, Lizzie stirred.

"Sorry about the noise," he said, reloading. "Did I wake you?"

"Tucker," she asked nervously, "is that you? What's going on?"

"We're getting out of here, that's what."

She sat up, the blankets drawn around her, still dazed from the newness of the resurrection. He pulled the pin from a thermite grenade and lobbed it through the door. "Cover your eyes," he called and squatted down to hold his hands over Rex's eyes. Rex, surprised at the attention, rolled over on his back and wagged his stub.

"Why?" Lizzie asked.

"Just do it," he yelled. There were some mumblings and general sounds of confusion outside and then came a blinding flash of light, like a thousand suns. A wave of noise and white fire swept down the hall, momentarily covering the shrieks of the dying and muffled shouts from farther away.

Tucker grabbed Lizzie's hand and pulled her into the smoking ruin of the hall. Everything that wasn't burnt up was still on fire; the drapes and carpet, bookshelves, and chairs, even the paintings were flaming and dripping trails of flaming oil. In and among the ashes were scattered pieces of bodies, a smoking hand or a smoldering foot. The acrid smoke stung their eyes and lungs. Rex picked his way carefully through the embers. Though Lizzie was barefoot, she didn't seem to feel any pain, only a dazed sense of wonder at the carnage.

In the midst of their retreat, the door at the far end of the hall flew open and scores of Vampires spilled out into the smoky ruins, eyes glittering like knives. He dropped to his knee and fired as fast as he could, the steady beat of the shots only interrupted by the act of reloading. Some were pierced by stakes, others scorched by the thermite, the blue fire balls belching down the hall like giant, deadly Roman candles.

Lizzie paused, looking back over her shoulder at the destruction, as Vampires blazed and fell like moths too close to the flame. Some ran screaming and leaped through windows, falling away into the night in a rain of broken glass. It was a grim and terrible sight, and she pressed her hand over her mouth to keep from retching. Tucker, still kneeling behind her, was mechanically feeding shells into the shotgun with trembling fingers.

The way behind them was clear and she shook him by the shoulder and pointed. Together they fled down the stairs, Rex close behind. It was like a long and terrible dream, the screams and the smoke, the crackling of flames and the sounds of pursuit. Wide-eyed, Jenkins bustled past with a fire extinguisher, ignoring them as he hurried toward the worst of the inferno. At the bottom landing there was only the large foyer to cross; through the smoke, it looked deserted. As they crossed that short space, a rough hand clamped onto Tucker's shoulder and spun him into the wall. Lizzie's hand slipped away and Rex lunged frantically at Julius, standing defiantly in front of him.

Revor was beside him too, burly and menacing. Tucker swallowed hard and swung the shotgun up. He had Julius dead to rights and one squeeze of the trigger would have ended it forever. Funny, he thought, how you can make the wrong decisions so damn easily. And knowing he was doing it again, he made the wrong choice. He shot Revor.

It wasn't common sense that pulled the trigger—it was the promise he had made to kill Revor that pulled the trigger. Wounded pride pulled the trigger. A long history of mistakes in his life pulled the trigger. And this was one more to add to the list.

"Guess what, asshole? My hands aren't tied anymore," he yelled.

The shotgun bucked in his hands and Revor folded over like a house of cards in a hurricane, his face twisted in pain and disbelief. Julius stared in open-mouthed rage at his companion and then looked back as Tucker smiled grimly and swung the barrel around to cover him. Without a moment's hesitation, he pulled the trigger. The hammer fell forward with a dry click that echoed in the chaos of the room.

Misfire!

In the time it took for both men to realize the implications of fate, Tucker began fishing in his pocket for another shell and Julius threw himself forward with a roar, faster than the speed of darkness. Tucker's fingers wrapped around a shell and fumbled it into the breech, snapping it shut and pushing up and out so that the barrel came to rest against the Vampire's chest even as Julius closed his hands around the cowboy's throat. They froze, half a breath from the end. The room was silent save for the crackle of the fire and their slow, hoarse breathing.

"I always wanted to be one of those movie heroes that has some smart ass thing to say," Tucker whispered, "but the only thing I can think of is goddamn you to hell."

His finger tightened on the trigger and Julius snarled, eyes glittering. Time stopped, and they stood like statues in that rich, burning room. Eternity passed as his finger made that short arc. The trigger released the hammer and even as it swung forward toward the firing pin, Lizzie screamed as a shadow slammed into Tucker, a shadow of muscle and hatred.

"Tucker," Lizzie cried desperately, as Elita crashed into him.

The gun discharged over and above Julius, who scuttled sideways. The wooden missile roared out and splintered against the ceiling, dislodging the chandelier that fell with a crash and spray of glass shards. Elita bore Tucker over backward onto the stairs. He came up fast, swinging the empty gun at her head. She ducked and brushed it aside easily, laughing as it flew out of his hands. Lizzie lunged toward her, but Julius intercepted her and with a snarl, she scratched at his face and neck. He staggered under her attack, but kept her arms pinioned against her sides.

Elita smiled down at Tucker, her intentions clear in her burning eyes. "You're the meanest bitch I have ever met in my life," he said, drawing for the Casull.

"And you are about to become my favorite kill," she laughed chillingly. "I should have taken you that night in bed," she shrieked, lunging.

His hand fisted around the cold butt of his pistol but already she had closed the distance, driving her hands straight toward his heart. Some deep instinct for survival made him twist at the last second so that her hands raked across his forearm and punched deep into his side. He felt a wet rip and pain flared throughout his frame. He staggered away from her, leaning against the wall, and she stood over him, hands dripping blood, mouth bared to finish him. His right arm hung limply at his side and he reached clumsily with his left, still trying desperately for the gun. Elita laughed and bent low over him, and he braced for the worst.

Her hungry smile was replaced by a look of astonishment as she was suddenly lifted up. Lizzie, having managed to free herself from a distracted Julius, held Elita firmly by the neck and ankle and tossed her sprawling body through the wall. With an undignified shriek, Elita disappeared in a cloud of plaster and paneling. Julius looked steadily at the doors, listening intently to the noises that were fast approaching.

Tucker staggered toward Lizzie, unable to stand steady. Blood was soaking into his jeans and pooling in his boots. The strangest things enter the minds of the dying. Even as his vision began to fade, Tucker was ashamed that his boots were in such bad shape and his blood would spill from them like a sieve. Strong arms slipped around his waist. It was Lizzie. She held him close and whispered that it was going to be okay, that she would take care of him.

He struggled to frame words, wanted to tell her how beautiful she looked and how much he loved her, and that he was sorry it had to end like this. What came out was "I don't need no woman nursemaiding me." And then in a spray of blood, he collapsed.

The heavy door to the outside crashed open and the sound of combat filtered in. A worried Sully stood at the head of a group of Vampires armed with crossbows. Sully himself wielded a rough-hewn oak stake and advanced on Julius who, face twisted with fear and eyes wild, fled up the burning stairs.

TWENTY-THREE

"GO QUICKLY, QUICKLY," SULLY hissed in alarm. "There are far too many of them for us to fight here." Lizzie hurried through the garden, carrying Tucker, while Sully and his contingent kept their enemies at bay. Nothing could keep her from getting Tucker to safety. Adrenaline rushed through her body, she was fearless, and her eyes dared anyone to stand in her way. Underneath the thought of Tucker's safety was a burning desire for revenge. She'd be back, back for Julius, if anything happened to Tucker.

Once outside, Lizzie saw the waiting van with an agitated Vampire standing beside the open door. Sully's troops scattered quickly into the darkened streets of Manhattan as Sully himself turned to help Lizzie lay Tucker into the van. They stretched him out on the floor and Rex jumped in, whining and licking anxiously at his pale face.

"We have to get him to a doctor," Lizzie said, holding her hands over the wound to staunch the blood. It pooled over her hands and the warmth of it felt oddly comforting, though her concern for him far overrode even the hunger.

"And we will," Sully said breathlessly. "Go, go," he shrilled to the driver who ground the ignition to life and roared down the street. Behind them, a crowd of Vampires spilled out into the street, some carrying automatic weapons that twinkled in the distance. The rear window shattered, the sound of breaking glass mixed with the screaming sirens of police responding to the battle. Lizzie involuntarily covered her ears, then laid herself over Tucker and shielded Rex, but no more bullets reached the van as they screeched around the corner, out of sight.

"Well, well, well, that was surely exciting," Sully said, breathing heavily. He turned and beamed at Lizzie. "Lizzie, so good to see you again. You look absolutely stunning."

Lizzie looked down at herself, the tatters of her dress, soil smudged deeply into her skin. "Mr. Sully, I believe we owe you our freedom, if not our lives."

"Never mind that, it's just so nice to see you. You have grown so enchanting. The turning has done you wonders."

"Please don't take this the wrong way, but could you please get us to a doctor. We will have time to catch up on our lives, or deaths," she corrected herself, "after Tucker is seen to. And if I'm not mistaken, we don't have much time until the sunrise."

"Right you are. So practical. Dakalus," he called to the driver, "to Dr. Vesu's."

Dr. Vesu, as Sully explained on the way, was a doctor of most impressive credentials. He was a Vampire of immense learning, having studied with Hippocrates himself. Though of course his leanings were, understandably, directed toward the Vampire physiology, Sully was convinced he knew more of Adamites than all their textbooks and practitioners combined. His penthouse overlooked the Hudson as it emptied into the bay. As Dakalus and his

260

crew spread out in the shadows to post guard, Sully buzzed the intercom by the door.

"Yes?" a rich, baritone voice inquired.

"Vesu, it's Sully. I need your help. It's an emergency."

"Of course, of course, let me open the door." The lock clicked and Sully led Lizzie, carrying Tucker in her arms, and Rex into the lobby. They took the elevator to the top, Sully's nonstop conversation blending subtly with the drip of blood from Tucker's still form.

The elevator opened into the foyer of the penthouse, onto Dr. Vesu's worried countenance. He was tall and thin, his features pinched as if the immense knowledge in his mind drew heavily from the flesh. His hair was gray at the temples and he wore a severely cut frock coat that sparkled with hidden highlights. His eyes flared at the sight of Lizzie and the limp body in her arms.

"Heavens," he exclaimed, striding quickly to relieve her of the weight. "This way, quickly." He looked back over his shoulder to catch Sully's eyes and his look mirrored surprise. "This is an Adamite."

"I know," Sully said. "A very important one."

"Can you help him?" Lizzie asked. "He's hurt very badly."

"Indeed, indeed," Dr. Vesu said absently, laying him on a leather-covered couch. He pulled the shirt away gently and fresh blood welled up. "Oh, my."

"What? Is it bad?"

The doctor stripped his coat off, rolling up the sleeves of his starched white shirt. "It appears to be superficial, extensive, but superficial. It has been so very long," he said, shaking his head.

"So long? What has been so long? You mean since he was hurt?"

"I mean since I have worked on an Adamite. Fascinating." He looked up at Lizzie. "For the last several centuries, I have confined my practice to certain maladies that affect the Vampire mind and extensive research into, well, the effects of sunlight and sharp wooden implements."

"I do so hope you are making progress in those areas," Sully said.

Dr. Vesu shook his head. "Not as much as I might hope." He hurried off, returning with an old-fashioned black bag which, when opened, revealed shining rows of surgical instruments. After a thorough examination and a litany of mumbles and exclamations, he began to clean the wound with alcohol and old-fashioned gauze swabs. Tucker groaned from the depths of his unconsciousness and Rex barked fiercely at the doctor. Lizzie held him to her with one hand, reassuring him. He sat down to regard the doctor with open hostility, but deferred to Lizzie.

Dr. Vesu held a compress to Tucker's wound while probing underneath in the ripped flesh. "What did this?"

"Elita," Sully said with a conspiratorial nod of his head.

"Ah, so this must be the infamous cowboy, making you," he nodded at Lizzie, "our very special concern, whom Lazarus has gone to great pains to locate. I see he has found you."

"He hasn't found anybody until Tucker is okay. He is going to be okay, isn't he?"

"It appears she missed vital organs, though I can't quite remember exactly which are vital and which are not." He withdrew a thin silver needle from the bag and pulled a piece of surgical thread through the eye. Setting the compress aside, he began sewing meticulously and silently. Once completed, he turned his attention to the gash on Tucker's arm, already crusted shut. "Luckily he sleeps the sleep of the dead," he said, now stitching down the gash.

"Which, if I am not mistaken, we also will be doing before long." He glanced at the window and the hint of dawn evident there.

Lizzie could feel the pull of death already in her mind and body "But I can't leave him alone."

"I assure you," Dr. Vesu said as he examined the contents of a dark cupboard and finally selected a smoky colored bottle, "he will be quite all right by midday. I had the good fortune to spend several centuries under the tutelage of a renowned Taoist healer who came remarkably close to distilling immortality." He held the bottle up and swirled the liquid contents. "The tonic properties of this elixir are astounding. Though your paramour will undoubtedly be in a considerable amount of pain, his vitality will be quite high." He opened it and it seemed to Lizzie a vapor of emerald smoke escaped as the doctor tipped the bottle into Tucker's mouth. Tucker's body twitched and Dr. Vesu covered him gently with a starched sheet.

"I have to leave him a note," Lizzie exclaimed.

"Too late for that," Sully said, taking her by the arm and pointing at the window. The sun peeked over the edge of the horizon and a terrible raging pain filled the room.

"He'll wake up alone," she said, reaching toward him, but already shafts of first light lanced through the window and gnawed at the blackness settling into her mind.

Sully and Dr. Vesu pulled her into the inner chamber and the comforting darkness there. "Quickly, into the casket," Sully said, helping her in. "He will be there when you arise."

TWENTY-FOUR

ALONE AND IN AN unfamiliar room, Tucker cracked open his eyes. His memory of last night was nothing more than a blur. He stared at the strange ceiling and tried to piece it back together. Judging from the way he hurt all over, whatever had happened, he must have lost. As his scattered senses began organizing themselves, he took stock of his surroundings. He was lying on a strange leather couch with a stiff sheet over him. Swinging his feet over the edge, he nearly stepped on Rex who was sprawled beside a pile of bloody cloth which he vaguely recognized as his shirt. Beside them were his boots, also bloody.

"Wonder if all that blood was mine," he mused, trying to stand. A wave of weakness forced him to hold the edge of the couch. "Guess so."

Limping over to the window with Rex close at his heels, he saw an expanse of dirty water and boats. He pushed the sliding doors aside and stood on the balcony. The air was cool as he leaned on the railing and looked down. They were on the top floor of what appeared to be a very exclusive stack of apartments. "Where the hell are we this time, Rex? And where's Lizzie?" Rex didn't answer, so he limped back in to look around.

"First things first, let's see what there is to eat." The fridge was barely stocked with mineral water and little else. Rex looked up at Tucker inquisitively, but Tucker just shook his head. In the cabinets were bottles of wine with vintages ranging from old to extremely old, but no food. Definitely a Vampire, he thought and that thought, foreign at first, jolted his memory of the night before. A twinge of pain radiated from his ribs and he cursed Elita under his breath.

Off the main room, he noticed a heavily lacquered door and pushed it open. Inside the windowless room was a row of coffins, all handsomely built and all occupied. Lizzie was lying dead in the center, one hand reaching toward the door. On one side lay Sully and on the other, a man Tucker had never seen before. A handsome man with gray at the temples, wearing a blood-spattered white shirt.

"Must be my blood," Tucker whispered to Rex. "Guess he's a doctor."

A wave of jealousy welled up in him at the sight of her with her own kind and him on the outside. He took a breath and held it, trying to straighten out the twist in his thinking. Sully had saved both of them from Julius, and the tall one had probably just saved his life after Elita's attack. Still, the separateness clouded his mind.

Rex sat by his foot and Tucker slid down the wall to sit beside him. He peeked under the bandages at the wounds, surprised to see there wasn't much healing left to be done. Good Lord, he thought, I hope they haven't turned me into a Vampire, too. Just to be sure, he looked directly at the sun and it didn't have an impact, except that it brought tears to his eyes.

He kept petting Rex and questions and images flooded his thoughts, images of Lizzie and happiness and darkness stealing across the face of the moon.

Maybe Lizzie was right, he thought. Maybe he should just walk away right now. Rex nuzzled his hand as if reading Tucker's thoughts. "Well, why not?" he asked Rex. "When she woke up, she'd understand. Sure, she'd miss me at first, but what the hell, she'd have the rest of eternity to deal with it. It ain't like I have that much to offer anyway, not compared to these guys. No power. No air of mystery. No desire to suck the life out of innocent folks. All she could really look forward to with me was a whole lot of nothing but cold winters and hot summers in a Godforsaken little town in Wyoming. Not much thrill there."

Rex lay down at Tucker's feet, staring up, a look of genuine pity in his brown dog eyes.

"Don't look at me like that. You expect me to be happy about watching her stay young and beautiful while I get more and more ruggedly handsome with the years? Having to keep her stashed by day and never being able to have the boys over for a beer at night for fear she would eat them?"

Tucker shook his head, his words now continuing as thoughts. She was right. He had seen her through the worst. There was no shame in that. Besides, she had left him at the church. It was her idea. Their lives were no longer compatible and the smart thing to do would be to just walk out. To just find a clean shirt and walk right out. Put his hat back on and gather Rex up and just walk on out. That would be the smart thing to do. To just walk out that door and leave her there with her new buddies. Just walk on out, that's the thing to do.

Instead, he called Dad.

"Hello."

"Dad, it's me."

"Tucker, where the hell you been? I thought you was dead," he said.

"Well, I ain't, but it sure does feel like it."

"Ribs still hurting you?"

"Naw, they're fine, but this little Vampire bitch stuck her hands damn near through me."

"Did you find Lizzie?"

"Ain't you worried about me?"

"You're talking on the phone, ain't you?"

"Yeah."

"So how's Lizzie?"

"Well shit, Dad, she's dead."

"What?"

"Yeah. I was too late."

"You telling the truth?"

"I swear. She's dead as a doorknob and laying right in the other room."

"Well, you don't sound too perturbed."

"I am. Mostly 'cause she won't stay dead."

There was a moment of silence. "What the hell are you talking about boy? All the smog out there caused your brain to vapor lock?"

"Naw, Dad, she's a Vampire now."

"Like that boy we shot in my kitchen?"

"Yeah. Only she's the Queen of the Vampires or some such thing."

"She always did seem a little high strung. But I would've never figured her for a Vampire, much less a Queen."

"You hadn't even seen a Vampire till you shot that one. Besides, she wasn't a Vampire when you seen her. Not for real, anyway."

"What the hell happened?"

"I don't know exactly. All I know is when I got out here, there was Vampires all over the damn place, all looking for her. I found her first but it was too late, and then on account of my natural willingness to see the good in people, I kind of got us caught, and then I had to shoot a whole mess of them to get us out, but in the process one of them got a little friendly with my internal organs."

"Where are you now?"

"Damned if I know. Some fancy penthouse."

"How's Rex?"

Tucker reached down to pet him. "Fine. Antsy to get back, I reckon."

"So, you heading this way?"

"I don't rightly know. I guess after she wakes up tonight we'll figure it out."

"I wouldn't mind seeing you soon. There's a big stretch of fence down and winter is coming and all."

"Yeah, I know. You miss me."

"Hell, I don't miss you. Especially since you ain't got no place to live now. I just got more work than one old man can do."

"They're all talking about some other old boy, a Vampire, lives out in New Mexico."

"Always wanted to see that part of the country."

"I'd just as soon stay in LonePine. If she's got a better idea, I'll call and tell you. Otherwise, I imagine we'll be out that way soon enough."

"I'll put a pot of beans on. I suppose I can't put no onions in it."

"Why?"

"On account of Lizzie being a Vampire now."

"It ain't onions, Dad, it's garlic. And besides, none of that stuff is true anyhow."

"I didn't know."

"I gotta go."

"All right. Talk to you later then. Give my best to Lizzie."

Tucker hung up and pulled a mineral water out of the fridge. It would be a while before she woke up, so he turned on the TV and flopped down in a leather easy chair. He flipped through the channels until he found a horror movie. A Vampire was chasing some girl through a cemetery. There was organ music playing in the background and the Vampire's fangs gleamed in the moonlight. Tucker started to laugh. It made him feel a little better, although the wound opened up and blood began seeping under the bandages.

CARLOS FLEW FROM THE parlor into the living room. "She's been found, oh Master, she's been found!" he stammered. Lazarus was dozing, his spectacles slipping down his nose and a *National Enquirer* strewn across his lap.

"What?" he gasped, as he struggled to wake. "Where? Who has seen her? Dammit, Carlos, tell me everything, word for word." He was completely awake now, commanding in his massive, physical presence as he stood to his full height. Carlos shrank back instinctively, like a man confronted by a grizzly bear. Intellect and memory quickly overcame instinct and Carlos continued, cautious but confident of his master's benevolence.

"Doctor Vesu. He just called. The cowboy was seriously injured and there has been a narrow escape, but they shall be leaving soon."

"On their way here?"

"He thinks so, although it is ambiguous. He is providing them with transportation and supplies. Where else would they go?" His enthusiasm carried him away again. "There is still so much to get ready. I'll have to make a special casket for her. I wonder if her favorite color is still purple. I still have the stuffed bear, the pink one, that she used to sleep with here. Yesterday—it seems like just yesterday, but it was nearly thirty years ago. Oh, Master, I am overcome."

"Calm yourself, Carlos. Sit. How are they getting here?"

"By car."

"Good. That is by far the safest way. Who is with them?"

"Sully."

"Even better. He will know the safe-houses along the way." Lazarus smiled, reminded of years ago when he had inadvertently become involved in the Underground Railroad, funneling escaped slaves to the North. His legions had quietly helped destroy certain narrow-minded whites hampering the process. It had been a small aid, but one he liked to think had helped bring about the defeat of the South, as some of its most prominent advocates slowly lost their minds and their life's blood. He had discovered, over his many years, that it was sometimes better for humanity to have its most evil men destroyed slowly, rather than killing them outright. Immediate death often left martyrs, thereby allowing certain evils to gain even greater momentum. During his help with the Underground Railroad, he had admired the established network of safe houses, all within a minimum distance from each other, so that the escaped slave could avoid exhaustion and minimize the probability of capture. It was a battle strategy he had since implemented in his skirmish with Julius. Many were the fledgling Vampires he had enticed away from Julius and smuggled to various sympathetic locations throughout the world. He hoped that this system of safe-houses would prove valuable to Lizzie and Tucker on their way west.

"Yes, Carlos, we must prepare. You see to the requirements of their lodgings. I will see to the protection of her power. Have the jet prepared."

"You are leaving? Now, at such a time?"

Lazarus continued, patiently, but with a slight annoyance at being questioned by Carlos. "It will take them at least two more days to arrive here, probably longer. I intend to pay a personal visit to Julius before their arrival."

Carlos was stunned into silence.

"What are you waiting for?"

Haltingly, Carlos spoke, "Master, it has been so long."

Lazarus was quiet, a memory moving painfully through his soul. When he spoke, it was gravely, but to himself, as if no one was in the room. "Even the passage of these seven hundred years has not changed my feelings about those events."

Carlos was quiet, afraid to say anything in the face of such sorrow.

Lazarus waved his hand futilely, whispering, "I cannot change the past, but I can change the future." He knelt down, overcome, and touched his forehead to the ground. Eventually he spoke to an invisible presence, one forever close to his side. "I promise you, I will do now what I should have done then. Forgive me. You were not evil."

Carlos stood completely still and breathed quietly. "I am deeply sorry for bringing this up now I know you still mourn for the loss of MaryAnne. I apologize."

"MaryAnne," Lazarus consented. A moment passed, all was quiet. Abruptly, he rose. "Enough." Though his voice was strong, his eyes were weak. "Julius lost his power base by his own sordid, greedy hand. He has been trying to make up for it for centuries, laying the foundation for the event that will occur in—" Lazarus moved to his desk and paged through the calendar, silently counting the days, "by my reckoning, her first menses will be due in just about sixteen days."

"What shall you do, Master?"

"Do? What anyone would do in such a case."

"What do you mean, what kind of case is this?"

"Indeed, Carlos, have you not figured it out? This, my faithful servant, is war. Between myself and Julius. Only one of us can survive."

TWENTY-FIVE

Lizzie rejoined life with an anxious curse, springing from the coffin and rushing into the front room where Tucker was dozing on the couch. He awoke to her smothering him with kisses and brushed futilely at her, laughing.

"I was so worried," she said breathlessly. "The sun was coming up and we had to leave. Dr. Vesu swore you would be all right."

"I am, I am," Tucker grumbled, embarrassed at the affection with the two Vampire men so close. "C'mon, let's get this show on the road. I reckon we should be on our way to New Mexico."

"I'll call ahead to Madame B. We can stay there tomorrow."

"Naw," Tucker responded. "We ain't stopping. It'll be harder to find us if we're always moving."

Dr. Vesu kindly offered his Land Rover to the expedition. They were loading what little supplies Dr. Vesu could provide, aseptic cartons of blood and clean clothes, into the car.

"Oh, Lizzie, it will be wonderful to spend such uninterrupted time with you," Sully was rambling. "I just know I'll lose you altogether once we get to New Mexico. There will be a line to see you and I'll never get more than five minutes of your time," Sully said, holding her arm. Tucker glared at his back and Lizzie, laughing, looked back to catch his anger. She was briefly puzzled, then realization dawned and she sighed and shook her head.

"Sully, it's nice to see you too, but don't think you get to monopolize me on our little trip. I want to spend as much time with Tucker as possible."

Sully looked mystified and hurt until Lizzie tilted her head toward Tucker, who was mad enough not to notice. Sully nodded and smiled, then waited for Tucker and caught his arm. Tucker looked at him like he was a walking disease.

"Now, my sweet cowboy, don't get your bandana all knotted up. If anyone should be jealous, it should be our Queen." Lizzie giggled.

To emphasize his statement, Sully winked and squeezed Tucker's arm.

Tucker pushed him away, and might have lashed out, but Sully, with his supernatural agility, was already ten feet away. He blew Tucker a kiss. Lizzie came to stand next to Tucker. She wagged her finger at Sully in mock seriousness.

"He's sold goods, Sully."

Tucker nodded his head furiously, grabbed her hand and slapped it on his ass, where Sully's had just been. "I surely am sold goods," he said.

"He's just having fun with you, Tucker," Lizzie said.

"That ain't funny," he said, but realized how misplaced his jealousy had been.

In the time it took for Tucker to get a chew in and Lizzie to find a cup of coffee, a group of eager young Vampires pulled a small trailer into the parking garage. They hitched it to the Land Rover and loaded into it a pair of coffins.

"Would you like one?" Dr. Vesu asked.

"Uh, no. I think I'll pass," Tucker answered.

"They really are restful."

"No, thanks, but answer me a question. Why do you use them anyways? Seems like just being in a dark room is good enough protection."

"It is, but the coffins are an extremely convenient way to allow our humans to move us during the day, if necessary. Unfortunately, carrying what seems to be a dead man in a bag or a cardboard box is usually reason enough to be stopped by the authorities," Dr. Vesu replied.

Tucker spit onto the pavement, yawned, and opened the back door. "I think I'll do like my Adamite ancestors have done for the last hundred years—sleep in the back seat." Rex hopped in ahead of him.

"I guess I'll take the wheel for now," Sully said. He opened the door for Lizzie, then walked around and slid behind the wheel. "Although, I much prefer coaches to cars."

"Versailles was a different world," Dr. Vesu said as he waved and walked into the shadows.

Within minutes, they had bid their farewells and left the skyline of Manhattan behind. Tucker sat in the back seat with his shotgun across his lap. They all breathed a sigh of relief when the Land Rover passed through the Holland Tunnel and made its way firmly into the particular loneliness of the interstate highway system. Only then did Tucker relax and stretch out. Under their agreement, Lizzie and Sully could "sleep" by day, while Tucker drove. At nightfall, Tucker could sleep in the back seat while they drove. This first night, Lizzie quickly traded places with Rex and lay beside Tucker. Rex sat in the passenger seat with the window open, comparing wordlessly with Sully the strange and wondrous scents of the night.

They didn't feed in front of Tucker. Lizzie could tell by the look on his face that it still didn't sit well with him. Not that she was feeding on humans yet. She couldn't bring herself to take that step, much to Sully's consternation. Dr. Vesu had provided plenty of blood, jokingly taking credit for the ancient practice of bloodletting, but watching her feed on the little pouches still left Tucker pale and rattled. As for larger animals, the savagery of the act upset him, but not as much as Sully's little outings into the night. His forays were definitely not after animals, given that most of them occurred in metropolitan areas.

When they stopped at a rest area, Sully took Tucker aside. "Tucker, I know you love her, which is why we have to talk. She has to feed soon, on a human. Her soul depends on it."

Tucker leaned on the car hood and spit, silently gathering his thoughts. At last he spoke. "If you think I'm going to encourage her to kill someone, you got a long spell to wait."

"She has to in order to survive."

"Now listen here. Against my better interests, I'm starting to like you. But don't tell me what she needs to survive. She was doing just fine before you and your kind mucked everything up."

Sully sighed, a heaviness filled his limbs. "My kind had nothing to do with it. We tried our best to let her live a normal life. We tried, we really did."

"That may be true, but you failed. Things are bad now, but I cannot, with a clear conscience, turn her into a murderer."

"What are you guys talking about?" Lizzie asked, materializing from the shadows of the restroom. She was dabbing crimson from the corner of her mouth.

"Nothing, darling."

"Why don't I believe you?"

"C'mon, let's get rolling."

Miles fell behind them in this fashion, and time. Soon enough, the motion of travel became the standard. Such was the case when Tucker awoke in the back seat, surprised by the stillness, the lack of motion and the quietness of being parked by the side of the road. He stretched and stepped out into the cool morning, the sun barely up and, as yet, ineffective. Rex jumped out and pissed on the tire, yawned, and stretched lazily. Tucker sighed heavily and thought about breakfast.

After checking on Sully and Lizzie in the trailer, he took over the daytime driving shift. Pushing the car another fifty miles along, he found a little town with an equally little restaurant, and went in for a cup of coffee and a plate of biscuits and gravy. Not bad, he thought, must be getting farther West. He pulled the map out and spread it on the table, tracing with his finger their route thus far. They were making good time and so far, no sign of trouble. He looked longingly at the state of Wyoming. He made a decision, probably not his best, and after paying the bill, crawled back behind the wheel. Rex sat in the front seat and Tucker used the button to lower the power window on the passenger side. "Smell that, boy? I think it's time for a little detour."

By the end of that day, the car and its load were no longer on a direct route to New Mexico. Later, when the sun set, and Tucker heard Sully and Lizzie rattling around in the trailer, he pulled over.

Sully crawled into the front seat and looked at the odometer. "My, you've been busy."

Tucker nodded. "Yep."

Sully opened the map and clicked on the cargo light. "Where are we now?"

Tucker sucked in his breath and stabbed his finger down. "I'd say right around here."

"But, but, that's … we're going the wrong way. We're going north."

"Yep. Thought maybe we should swing through LonePine. Just for a day or two. See Dad."

"But they'll look for us there. They'll be waiting."

"Like they won't be waiting in New Mexico. Figured this might throw them off a little. Besides, I can't leave Dad up there alone."

"That's just unacceptable. Too risky. Tell him, Lizzie. We can't take chances like this. Tell him."

Lizzie, still outside the car, looked at Tucker with shining eyes. "I'd love to see LonePine again."

Sully snorted in disbelief. "But darling, it's just not safe. Am I the only one with any sense left?"

"Sully, it's important to Tucker, and he's important to me. I'm going with him. You don't have to come along."

"Not come along? My Lord, my God, Lazarus would have my head. I have not been going to that ridiculous little church for nearly three decades now to miss out on the best part of this assignment," he said indignantly, then continued in a soothing voice, "Lizzie, dearest, you must think beyond yourself now. You have tremendous power and Lazarus is very anxious to see you. I hardly think that a detour to that ramshackle little ghost town," he winced and looked at Tucker, "quaint as it might be, is critically important at this time."

Lizzie's eyes seemed to suddenly catch the moonlight, as they flashed defiantly at Sully. "Let's get something straight. Nothing, I mean nothing, will come between Tucker and me. Got that?" Sully nodded, taken aback by the vehemence of her words, and by the fact that the door handle was crushed flat in her grip.

Tucker stared in open-mouthed awe, then grinned from ear to ear. "Reckon we're heading to LonePine."

Sully swallowed audibly, then hurriedly studied the map. "This looks like the quickest route," he whispered.

Tucker smiled. "Don't you just love a road trip? Always unpredictable." He got in the back seat and Lizzie crawled in on top of him.

Sully looked at Rex and rolled his eyes.

By midafternoon the next day, Tucker pulled across the Wyoming border and gave a little whoop of joy as he did. A passing truck driver blew his airhorn and waved, and Tucker breathed deep, happy to be back in a place where people were naturally friendly and there was room for deep breaths. There weren't many miles to go now. Tucker figured he could get Lizzie and Sully to LonePine before they awoke. He pulled on his denim jacket so he could leave the window down and enjoy the mountain air, cooling quickly as the afternoon stretched toward evening.

His pleasant reveries were interrupted by the harsh sound of a siren: A quick check of the rear-view mirror revealed a police car, lights blazing. The driver, Tucker realized, looked just like Melissa Braver's little brother Bart. He was just a kid when Tucker had spent time over at the Braver's. Used to ride to the Dairy Queen for ice cream, most of which Bart had managed to drip on the seat of Tucker's truck. Smiling at the memories, Tucker pulled the car and trailer over to the side of the road, but the tenor of their reunion was quickly defined as different than Tucker had expected.

"Tucker," he called out in a business-like voice, "keep your hands up where I can see them and remain in the truck."

Bart pulled his standard-issue police automatic out of the holster and pointed it toward the driver's side window.

Tucker opened the door and started to climb out. "Bart, what the hell do you think you're doing? It's me."

In response, Bart cocked the hammer in a traditional Western greeting and things became substantially more tense. "If you take another step I swear to God I'll put a bullet in your knee."

Tucker raised his hands, eyes wide. "Bart, have you lost your mind?"

"No, but it seems you have. Now turn around and put your hands on the hood."

He did. Rex was sitting on the front seat, watching curiously through the open door. "Hey Rex," Bart said, "how you doing, boy?" Rex thumped his stumpy tail. Bart kicked Tucker's feet farther apart, keeping the muzzle of his automatic leveled at belt-buckle height. He ran his free hand up Tucker's legs, around his waist, and under his arms until it bumped into the Casull. Bart's whole body tensed and he gingerly pulled it free and dropped it, giving it a kick with his boot.

"Jesus Christ, Bart, take it easy. That's Dad's gun."

Bart poked his pistol into his ear. "Take it easy? I ain't screwing around here, Tucker. I don't want to have to shoot you."

"I don't want that either, Bart. Just tell me what the hell this is about."

"Keep your hands behind your back." He slapped the cuffs on. "What's going on is you're wanted for questioning."

"Questioning, for what? What the hell's going on? Can I turn around now?"

"Yeah." Bart holstered the piece and stepped back to regard Tucker. "Murder. Seems you got into a little bit of trouble out in New York."

"I sure did. But I didn't kill nobody. Not people, anyway."

"According to our bulletins, you're wanted for questioning in the disappearance of one Elizabeth Vaughan. She's plumb vanished and folks at her work are getting a mite concerned."

"Oh shit. Of course she disappeared, but she ain't dead. Well, she is dead, technically. But I didn't kill her. Julius did. Even though she ain't dead. This ain't coming out right."

He nodded. "Maybe you should wait for a lawyer. For the time being, let's just say you're under arrest. And anything you say…"

"…can be used against me. I know, I know, I watch TV. But she ain't really dead."

"Tucker, you can't be kind of dead," Bart said. Then he leaned against the truck and put a chew in and started petting Rex.

"That's what I used to think, Bart. But things ain't so clear anymore."

"Well," he said slowly as he spit, "they're pretty clear in the eyes of the law."

"Aww, Bart. How long I known you?"

"Ever since you started squirreling around with my sister."

"Bart, listen to me. You know I ain't a murderer. I didn't kill my girlfriend. I didn't kill anyone. Anyone that wasn't already dead."

He looked at Tucker for a while. "I think maybe I'll take a look at your load."

The thought of an impartial observer with a badge and a gun finding two corpses made Tucker wince. "I don't think that's a good idea, Bart. And don't you need a search warrant or something?"

"I just arrested you, Tucker. You ain't got no rights." Rex came out good naturedly and followed Bart to the back of the trailer.

The sun was still perched dangerously far from the rim of the mountains, and Tucker hung his head and prayed for the earth to turn a little faster. Just my luck, he thought. By the time Lizzie and

Sully arose, he'd be in lockup, Julius would send his legions, and his little trip home would be the end of them all. He hunkered down by the tire, the cuffs pulling against his wrists.

Bart unlatched the back door and it swung open. He sucked in a breath and whistled it out. Sometimes the sight of a coffin will do that.

"Tucker, you better start talking." There wasn't anything to say, so he just listened to the thud of boot heels climbing in, felt the truck shift under the weight and heard the scrape of one of the coffins being opened. "C'mon back here, Tucker."

"I'm mighty comfortable here."

"I insist."

He struggled up and walked around the corner. "Do me a favor, Bart. Just keep it out of the sun."

"There ain't no sun, it's done set," said Bart, and Tucker realized, gratefully, that he was right. He prayed that Lizzie wasn't going to sleep in tonight. He and Rex watched as Bart opened the coffin wider. "Jesus Christ," he exclaimed. "This must be your girl-friend. She's real pretty, Tucker." He held his fingers to her neck to search for a pulse. "And real dead."

Rex jumped up on his hind legs and licked her face.

"I can explain this."

"Let's do it down at the station."

Tucker looked forlornly at the night sky "I'd rather do it right here." Bart shrugged and pointed at the squad car.

In the car, Bart listened politely and attentively to everything Tucker had to say. When he got to the part about Vampires, Bart smiled and nodded and even acted interested. Tucker stretched the story out as long as he could, even going back a couple of places to emphasize certain things about Vampires, all the while waiting for Lizzie to make an appearance.

At last, he ran out of words. Bart smiled patiently and started the engine. "Bart, what're you doing?"

"Taking you to jail." He pulled the radio loose and held it up to his mouth. "Dispatch, this is 112."

"Go ahead, Bart," the radio crackled.

"I just picked up …" There was a tapping on the window, like a raven gently rapping. Bart looked up into the beautiful face of Lizzie, smiling down into the squad car.

"If you two are almost done, we really should get going," she said.

"Jesus H. Christ," Bart shrieked and the radio slipped from his hand.

"She's dead. She's dead," he stammered. "There wasn't no pulse …"

"Bart, you broke up, Bart," dispatch crackled. "Please repeat."

Tucker slumped forward in the seat and sighed with relief. "I told you, Bart. I told you she was dead."

"If she's so dead, how come she's standing right there?" he stammered. Lizzie smiled and waved, shielding her eyes from the headlights. Bart paled considerably and Tucker raised his wrists up, nodding toward the handcuffs.

"Can I go now?"

"How the hell am I supposed to write this up?"

Bart and Tucker huddled together in the cab of his squad car, trying to come up with a plan. Lizzie leaned regally but impatiently against the Land Rover. At last Bart drove off, leaving Tucker standing beside the road.

"About time. You want me to drive?" she asked.

Tucker rubbed his wrists and looked cross. "Took your own sweet time getting out of bed. I could've been hauled off to jail by now."

"It's not a bed, honey, it's a coffin. Besides, I figured he was a friend of yours."

"Hell, sweetheart, everyone around here is a friend of mine."

"What did he say?"

"He said he was going to pretend none of this had ever happened. He said he was going back to the station and break that rule about cops drinking on duty. He said we had three weeks before he called the FBI. And he also said you was real pretty."

"Really? That's sweet. I'm just glad Sully didn't come out. I can only imagine what he would have thought then." Hearing his name, Sully slammed the trailer shut and wandered over to the front door.

"Good evening, Tucker, how was your day? You must be exhausted, all that driving." He took a deep breath. "Smell that air. It's so invigorating, so wonderfully pine-scented. Where are we?"

Tucker crawled back behind the wheel, muttering. "We're outside of LonePine. God's country. And I call it God's country because until only recently, there wasn't no Vampires here."

"Tucker." Lizzie gave him a nudge in the ribs. If Sully heard, he chose to ignore it.

After New York, LonePine looked small and lonesome in comparison. The lights of the main street, those that were still on as they pulled into town at nearly 10:30, were few and far between. There was no traffic, other than between the town's two bars. Tucker's eyes glazed over and Lizzie took his hand and gave it a squeeze. "Ain't it beautiful?" he said.

"It's something, all right," Lizzie said. "Looks just the same as the first time I saw it."

"Something to be said for things staying the same."

She swiveled to face him, the conversation taking a turn for the worse. "Change is good," she said, cutting him a hard look.

"Whoever said that probably had it pretty bad to begin with," Tucker suggested, still unaware of the underlying discussion they were having.

"Or maybe they just didn't realize things could get better." She let go of his hand as he reached for the gear stick to slow down for the turn onto Dad's road.

"Maybe that only applies to people who are bored," Sully chimed in. "You know, if you're bored, any kind of change seems exciting and new. For example, I have been alive for what, twelve hundred years, and I am constantly amazed that I have yet to grow bored. Of course, I am always trying to find new things to keep my interests up…"

His conversation with himself lasted so long, Tucker began to wonder if Vampires needed oxygen. Lizzie stared icily ahead as they pulled up in front of Dad's. Tucker felt a vague sense of making a mistake, that he needed to say something to reassure her, but decided that, as close as they were, she should be able to tell that he was sorry and hadn't meant anything and was just tired from driving all day.

The door to Dad's house cracked open and the barrel of his old ten-gauge goose gun poked out. "Tucker, that you?"

"Yeah."

"You ain't a Vampire now, are you?"

"Naw."

"If you are, I'm gonna shoot you right now. I didn't raise my kid to be no Vampire."

"And what exactly is wrong with being a Vampire?" Lizzie asked as she appeared beside him.

"Aw, Lizzie," he said, the gun barrel dipping. "I didn't mean nothing by that."

"I should hope not," Sully added as he crawled out of the truck. "We're not all like those awful Vampires you met before. Some of us are quite civilized and rather enjoyable to be around. And I must say, I love your cabin. It's so charming. It reminds me of this little hunting chalet I used to stay at in Austria whenever the Viscount and I went after stag or fox. It was remarkably warm and on those lovely Austrian nights..."

"Tucker," Dad said, "who's that?"

"That's Mr. Sully. A friend of Lizzie's."

"Does he ever shut up?"

"Only in the daytime."

He nodded and opened the door, motioning them in. "Well, come on in. Coffee's on."

"Reckon it's been on for a week now. I almost hate to ask, but do you have any of them beans you promised?"

AT THIS STAGE IN his life, Lazarus did not particularly enjoy the sophisticated veneer of city life. While he had rarely visited this Manhattan compound in the past, he had on occasion been pulled to New York by its easy hunting. Thus, he had the comfort of coming to a place he at least understood well. He wished his task here was one of a reunion of old friends, rather than of confrontation. Had things gone differently seven hundred years ago, that might be the reality. Lazarus rang the bell. The door creaked open warily. A man that Lazarus did not recognize, but clearly a Vampire, poked his head through the narrow slit between door and frame.

"What do you want?" the young Vampire asked menacingly. He was rough-looking, unshaven, with greasy black hair. Downright ugly, thought Lazarus, as he considered Julius' low standards.

"I wish to see Julius."

"Go to hell," the greasy Vampire responded and started to shut the door. In less than an instant, Lazarus pulled it off the hinges. The young Vampire stood motionless, suddenly afraid. "You are one of us," he whispered, "I thought you were Adamite."

"Your master's training has always been woefully inadequate. Why were you unable to sense me?" Julius' underling did not respond. "Never mind, it's none of my concern," said Lazarus. "Run along and fetch Jenkins for me."

"Jenkins no longer has any responsibility in this household."

Lazarus felt his cold blood chill further. Jenkins no longer in a position of power? Something was seriously amiss. His patience exhausted, he pushed the young upstart aside and walked into the compound. The Vampire had enough sense to push the alarm buttons so that as Lazarus entered the gardens, he was immediately surrounded by a dozen Vampires, accompanied by several brutish Adamites, all heavily armed.

Lazarus was merely annoyed. It had been too long since his last visit and obviously these minions had not been told that there was another Vampire as powerful and strong as Julius. From their perspective, he imagined, he was simply a fat old man breaking into the fortress, someone they thought they could have a bit of blood-sport with. He sighed deeply. The events of the last few days had tired him, the plane ride had been particularly bumpy, and he was not in the mood for a full-scale fight. Oh well, he thought, best to get it over quickly. How lovely the poppies are, he thought, and how unusual to be blooming at this time of year. But the flower beds were in dire need of weeding, the beautiful pale-orange treasures were nearly choked to death. He bent to touch their delicate petals, deeply disappointed that this once extraordinary garden was in such a state of disrepair. As he drank in the odor, his senses blossomed, fully heightened and aware of the group of mercenaries moving steadily toward him, jeering and threatening.

Unexpectedly, but very welcome to Lazarus, the leader of the posse group suddenly fell on his knees and touched his forehead to the ground. The rest of the guards looked on in amazement, then quizzically followed suit as their leader screamed at them in terror to kneel or be certain of never being resurrected again. Thank goodness, thought Lazarus, immensely relieved. He would be able to avoid at least one fight.

Jenkins emerged from the house. He was very drawn, his skin hanging loosely over his face, his once-sparkling eyes now weary and blank. Upon seeing Lazarus, he was momentarily reinvigorated, but it lasted only an instant before the weight of his own flesh seemed to press him down closer toward the earth, his back bowed in submission to his body's demands.

Lazarus moved quickly to his side, recognizing the signs. "Jenkins. Why is he doing this?"

"I imagine it's because I am becoming too old and no longer am of much use to the family. I expect that this is in fact what happened to my father as well."

"But Julius always kills."

"Yes, that's generally been true, but he is instead choosing to feed on me only once a day, very briefly, and never enough to kill me. Not yet, at least. He has relieved me of all other duties. He claims he has no time for the hunt and wishes to be certain of the quality of blood he is consuming. During his feeding ecstasy, he mumbles about preparing his flesh for new power." Jenkins labored to finish his last words, breathless with fatigue.

"Has he said anything else?"

"Strange words that I cannot understand. Mostly about Miss Vaughan and her blood, a new world order. I wish I was able to tell you more but it is very difficult for me to maintain consciousness during the feeding. He does occasionally mention Elita, cursing that she is of the serpent line."

"Jenkins, please forgive me. I never thought that Julius would stoop to using those in our service and under our protection for such a purpose. I would not have posted you here had I thought it would come to this."

"I served you well, did I not? I helped her escape."

"You have done more than I ever expected. We are all in your debt. And now I wish to repay you. Leave now, and I will ensure that you have safe passage to the door. One of my men will take you to Dr. Vesu, who will bring you back to health, to Adamite health. Then you shall have anything you desire."

"I have no wish or need other than to serve. It is my fate, my choice."

"I would be honored to have you in my personal service in New Mexico." For an instant, it looked as if Jenkins would cry, then he collected himself and started to move toward the compound's exit. "One more thing, Master Lazarus. Julius fainted during the turning of Miss Vaughan." Quietly, he turned and walked away. Lazarus watched until he was outside the compound.

"I would have given him to you. You needn't have stolen him," said a voice quietly from behind. Lazarus turned to find Julius smiling at him. "I've known for some time that he remained loyal to you. It was a personal game, seeing if I could sway him."

He stepped closer and motioned for the prostrate Vampires to rise and disperse. "All this power sometimes makes existence a bit tedious and we, you and I that is, must invent games to entertain ourselves." Julius smiled demurely. "Alas, I realized I was not to win this one. Adamites can be so stubborn. So I changed the rules, changed the entire nature of the game. He has served me well these last few weeks. So few Adamites today lead such healthy lives. His blood is of a rare quality." Julius was glowing, his lips full and red, his skin radiantly pale, his hair dark and silky, his body trim and fit. Lazarus felt a pang of jealousy. How did the Vampire stay so damned thin? As if reading his mind, Julius said, "And you, you've gotten fat. How amusing."

Lazarus rolled his eyes in response and then said, "Let's go inside, Julius. We have much to talk about."

"Actually, Lazarus, I can sum it up in just a few words, and I'd prefer to do just that, to minimize the time I must spend in your presence. Correct me if I'm wrong. Our Queen has managed to make contact with you and is on her way to your compound. You, in your quaint, chivalrous manner have decided to protect her. And you are here to threaten me in hopes of avoiding a show-down. Am I right so far?"

Lazarus didn't answer. He suspected it might be better to find out how much Julius knew before responding. History had taught him that Julius had always been a bit of a show-off. It had gotten him into trouble in the past and, perhaps, would do so now.

"I shall take your silence for assent, dear chap. But you shall fail." At this, Julius' tone turned acidic and his eyes burned with rage. "You beat me once before. I did not anticipate your displeasure with my plans. I won't make that mistake again. You have hidden her from me these last three decades out of spite, pure spite. Nevertheless, despite the intentions of you and her insipid mother, I have in fact succeeded in turning her. Thus, my pathetic, fat Vampire friend, you failed in the most critical part of her protection. All that is left is drinking her menses and she becomes totally irrelevant. You can have her when this is done. Do with her as you wish, make her your consort, eliminate her, I don't care. But be forewarned, nothing will stop me in my quest for her blood. It has been ordained. I am fulfilling the prophecy of Revelations."

"I will kill you first."

"Don't be ridiculous! You have been unsuccessful for centuries."

"You misunderstand. I have never tried to kill you. Until now, you have posed no real threat. You have been nothing more than a game for me, too. A means to combat eternal boredom. You have served a useful entertainment purpose. Now, however, I, too, am changing the rules. The stakes are too high. The accumulation of your atrocities merits your destruction. You have surrounded yourself with the very evil we are ordained to absorb, cultivated it. You have sickened the word of Malthus," Lazarus said quietly, but with depth of conviction.

"No," screamed Julius, enraged. "I have upheld his word while you have weakened it, infected it with the foolishness of the Adamites. We are not meant to balance good and evil for the sake of the Adamite world, the Adamites exist for our desires. Good is weak. Evil is strong. In the final battle, we will, we must vanquish them. With the Queen's blood, I shall have the power to do just that."

Lazarus shook his head. "My Father's house is a great house, as noble and as powerful as yours."

"You shall not stop me in this. You may have once, when I was young and foolish. But I have learned my lesson. This I have planned for the past seven hundred years while you, you slept in ignorance. Your Western solitude has softened you, left you weak." He pointed at Lazarus' prominent belly. "Proof that my plan is already implemented."

"I will hide her from you until the menses pass."

"You cannot hide her from me. I can smell her."

"A lie. Vampires can only smell Adamite evil, or its absence in Vampires."

"It was a power that came during the turning. At first, it was weak, and it did not help me in locating her when she escaped previously. But in the last few days it has become very strong. I expect that it will continue to do so, and that by the time of her menses, I'll be able to find her anywhere in the world. While I certainly have no need of proving this fact to you, I shall do so simply for my own amusement."

"How?"

"I know where they are this exact moment: Sully will not make it to New Mexico. At least, not if he remains by her side."

Lazarus felt a pang of worry for Sully, but kept it to himself. Slow thoughts crept into his mind. Had he let sentiment get the better of him? He had loved Constance, and by extension Lizzie. He had optimistically, and now he feared, naively, thought Lizzie could live without detection. He realized now that he may have made a fatal mistake in not turning her himself. He had allowed Julius to gain powers that he did not have. He said none of this, of course. He did have Lizzie physically and of her own volition, or at least he would very soon. That would count for something. And Julius had fainted during the turning. Was there a chink in his powerful armor that would allow Lazarus to dispense with him without harming anyone else in the process?

"She will be under my protection and will not under any circumstances be released to you," Lazarus said.

"I will allow her to stay with you until two days before her blood starts. Then I shall come for her. With my army."

"You will not succeed. If I must, I will kill her myself."

Julius scoffed. "Come now, we both know you won't do that."

"Have you forgotten the past so easily?"

Julius laughed coldly. "No, no, you need not remind me. Those events are forever etched in my mind. But you know as well as I that you have regretted that action ever since. You may have killed the only other woman to have this power in the last seven hundred years, but how it has haunted you. Elizabeth is different. She represents a chance for you to redeem yourself. You love her. You didn't even know the other one, despite the fact that she was your own daughter." Julius paused to gauge Lazarus' response to this painful memory, taking great pleasure in the emotional distress.

He continued in his reminiscences. "MaryAnne was such a sweet child, such a surprise that you birthed the power, you and your little messiah. She was so young, such gloriously golden eyes. I could have easily molded her to my will. She would have been an excellent figurehead. Her blood would have given me the world. I remember that night vividly. You were still powerful, not yet flabby. The locals fled in terror as you and your men descended on the caves. I was caught unaware. When you sucked her dry of her blood just hours before it had the power, how she cried out to you, begging you to spare her. I even told you who the mother was and still you drained her. She didn't even know why. She had no idea that she had the power of uncreation in her blood; but then, neither did you. MaryAnne. You do remember?"

"Your assumption that I have any interest in reliving the past is grossly unfounded."

Julius laughed again and began to mimic the voice of the girl long ago killed. In a soft whisper he brought the memory vividly to life in Lazarus' mind. "Please, don't kill me. What have I done wrong? I want to serve you. I will love you if you'll let me."

Lazarus glared at Julius. Both knew that the murder of Mary-Anne had been the greatest crisis in Lazarus' life. In those days, Lazarus had lived differently, with greater decadence. He had kept a harem, small but adequate, and while he was very kind to the women and their offspring if they had any, he felt no bond. Julius had, unknown to Lazarus, taken a girl child from one of the women, the only girl child born of that line at the seven-hundred-year mark, raised her, and then turned her at age thirty. Lazarus had not even known such a child had been born in his dominion.

Now, in a way, he had as much at stake as Julius. Julius wanted Lizzie's blood in order to create an empire. Lazarus wanted Lizzie's blood to prove that he had not killed his daughter in vain, that he had not spent the last few centuries watching a crazy Vampire who threatened the world only in his imagination. He wanted Julius to be something worthy of opposition, worthy of the amount of energy their conflict had demanded.

"In an odd way, I should thank you for murdering that innocent nymph," continued Julius finally. "Back then, the world was still naive. I would have gotten very little support when I took control. Now, with the shift in morality away from religion and family, I will have no problem attracting Adamites into my service." Julius laughed. "Just think of it. The silly young things will be clamoring to have me turn them into Vampires. It will be far more—what's the word—cool, than a nose ring. The Adamitic world is so imbued with apathy. Anything to excite their pathetic lives. As I told your dear Elizabeth, the time is right, and I shall seize it. It is so much easier to have willing victims, don't you think, Lazarus?"

Already, Lazarus was tiring of this game. He had changed in response to those events seven hundred years ago, had considered many things, had brought together strands of experience earned through many centuries into a wisdom, an understanding of the world and the morality necessary for its survival. Waiting Julius out had always been difficult to do; now it was even harder to listen to his infantile posturing, but he guessed that soon Julius would tip his hand.

"By the way, you couldn't kill Elizabeth Vaughan, even if you wanted to. Her power could be greater than either of us. She just doesn't know it."

"Impossible."

"The ancient voices speak through her. I heard them at the turning. Ask her."

Lazarus did not respond, but his mind was reeling.

"My moment has come, Lazarus. Nothing will stop me. I will come for her, this I swear, and I will take her and I will destroy anything that stands in my way."

"You will never get inside my fortress. I have an army at the ready."

"Please, don't insult the very notion of army. My war machine is built of former Adamites who were by nature bloodthirsty and ruthless, and those of the Serpent tribe. Yours is a gathering of poets and judges. Who do you think will win?" Julius laughed. Then, he turned and walked inside the house, saying over his shoulder as he walked, "And really, Lazarus, lose the weight. You look ridiculous."

Lazarus turned and walked slowly toward the outer wall. The trip had been worth it. As expected, Julius' ego had caused him to reveal his entire strategy, a tendency he had repeated through the ages. The ancient voices? They had not spoken through him since the time of his resurrection more than two thousand years ago. As far as he knew, Julius had never heard them and could not understand their purpose or power. That is why he had fainted, Lazarus was sure of it. Only Malthus, himself, and now Lizzie, had heard them. The voices would know what to do, they would be able to guide Lizzie. The voices to the past, he hoped, would be considerably stronger than his army of poets.

TWENTY-SIX

When the Wyoming sun rose, the shades to the spare room were drawn tight and Tucker had stapled a blanket over the whole window. He crawled out of the bed, stiff from the driving. Pulling on his hat and boots, he wandered out into the kitchen, still in his underwear. Dad had one hand wrapped firm around a cup of coffee and was using the other to guide powdered sugar-covered donuts toward his mouth.

"Can I join you?" asked Tucker.

"There ain't a whole lot left."

"I can see that." Tucker poured a cup of coffee and pulled up a chair. He grabbed a donut from the box on the yellow linoleum-covered table, trailing a line of white powder behind. Absently, he wiped it up with his finger and became lost inside the reflective plastic patterns, memories of what seemed like millions of childhood meals trickling into his mind.

"Dad?" said Tucker.

"There ain't no more donuts."

"I know. What do you think about all this? Sometimes, I can't hardly make sense of it."

"Ain't it the truth. The Gas 'N' Get don't stock nearly enough of them donuts."

"That ain't what I was talking about."

Dad thought for a minute. "There ain't much I know for sure. But I do know that life is precious, a gift from the creator that we can't ever truly understand. You just got to do the best you can, no matter what comes along."

"Even if it's Vampires?"

"Remember that two-headed calf was born a few years back?"

"You mean when I was twelve?"

"Yeah. I would've never believed in something like that until I saw it with my own eyes. But I did. I suspect this ain't much different."

Tucker thought about that for a while, then said, "That don't make no sense."

"Dammit, Tucker, I'm no good with this sort of stuff, telling stories with a moral. We both seen them. They took your girl. Nothing else matters."

"Now that I understand." He grew quiet again. "Do you think Mom would have liked Lizzie?"

Dad didn't say anything, just leaned back and studied his coffee cup. "I reckon," he said at last.

Tucker wanted to ask more, to say something else about his mother, to talk about the biscuits and gravy she used to make in this kitchen, about how she'd be mortified to see her boys eating store-bought powdered sugar donuts on her linoleum table. But he said nothing. Something had changed in Tucker in the last few weeks, something quiet but big. He knew now what love was, but also that a deep and final sadness came with it, and that sometimes you had to be quiet to keep it from turning to that dark side.

"How about we go do some shooting while our guests are sleeping?" asked Tucker. Dad smiled and nodded.

They drove up to the gun range and shot up so much ammo at beer bottles that they had to drive back to town to buy more so as not to be unarmed by night. After lunch at the Sagebrush, they drove back home and then cleaned all the guns they had used earlier, one of Dad's favorite pastimes.

They were sitting cross-legged on the floor with guns taken apart and scattered across the living room among the beer bottles and burger wrappers when Lizzie came in, paler than ever, irritated, and sort of dazed. She looked at the mess. "I have to feed," she said.

"Good morning to you, too, sunshine."

She tried her best to smile. "Hi. Sorry. I'm starving."

"Want some beans?"

"Maybe later. I have something else in mind."

"Please don't kill anybody," Tucker begged. "These are a nice bunch of folks around here." He paused. "Well, except for my neighbor."

"Oh, Tucker," she beamed, "you just gave me the best idea. Sully, are you coming?"

Sully sat down on the couch. "No, my dear, I think I'll stay here with the boys. You run on ahead." Dad stood up and arched his back, the joints creaking in rebellion. He took a seat by Sully.

Lizzie planted a cold kiss on Tucker's cheek and disappeared into the darkness. In the wake of her leaving there was a brief moment of uncomfortable silence that Dad and Tucker hoped would stretch into several minutes, but Sully would have none of it.

"I've never met an honest to goodness cowboy," he said.

"Can't say as I ever expected to meet an honest to goodness Vampire either," Dad grumbled, stretching out across the couch.

"You have such a life out here on the frontier. I still remember those heady days when it seemed everybody and their uncle were loading all their supplies into wagons and heading West. The excitement was absolutely dizzying. Of course, I only read about it in the penny-dreadfuls. I could never have left the East Coast. My attachment was not due to birth as I was actually born in Germany. The real Germany, the one before the Reformation. But I have always been drawn to America and your rugged idealism. I have such a soft spot for you cowboys. I used to imagine myself out on the range with you. Unrolling our bedrolls under a sky full of stars. The coyotes calling and an old owl sitting in the oak tree ..."

"The West wasn't like that," Dad said.

"It wasn't?"

"Not the West I know," he said. "Never was, never will be."

"But what about John Wayne and the Marlboro man? The Last Cowboy, my God, what a brilliant piece that was, and you looked so handsome in those pictures," he said to Tucker.

"Mind if I grab a beer?" Tucker asked.

"Help yourself," Dad grumbled. "It ain't like I bought them for myself." He was getting cranky since it was past his bedtime.

"You see, Mr. Sully," Tucker said, popping the top of the can, "cowboys ain't no different than any other man. We work hard and never make much money. We fall in love and make other mistakes. It's the same way for people all around the world. Cowboys ain't special, we just do what needs done. Only difference is the setting."

"And the hat."

"That too."

"How, then, do you explain the romance of the West? Everybody loves cowboys," Sully said.

"Speaking as a real live cowboy, I ain't got the foggiest," Tucker said. "Guess it has something to do with the wide-open country and an honest sort of labor that beats sitting inside all day."

"But what about the Code of the West? The unspoken law of the land? Virtue and all that?"

"I suspect that there are certain things that all men should do, want to do, in the name of what is right. And since they can't, they think there ought to be one kind of man or another that just naturally does right."

"And that would be my cowboys?"

Tucker nodded.

"There must be more to it than that," Sully said. "I have the advantage of a certain historical perspective, which you lack. And what I have found is that at the heart of all myths lies a single, often-overlooked truth."

"Maybe you're right," Tucker said. "Maybe at the heart of the cowboy myth is…"

"Heart," Sully interrupted. "At the heart of the cowboy myth is just that, heart."

"Y'all are making my head hurt," Dad said. "And where's that woman of yours? How long does it take to kill someone and drain their blood?" He looked at Sully for an answer.

"Not that long, really. But understand, we only feed on bad Adamites. That is what I am supposed to be teaching her. That's why I've asked your help."

"You only feed on bad guys?" Tucker asked.

"And bad girls."

"There ain't no bad people around here."

"Oh, you'd be surprised. I sensed several as we came through town."

"Really?"

"Oh, yes. Several 'shocking' incidents will be avoided because of my stay here, and the good citizens of LonePine will have no clue."

"I can tell you one person that's gonna turn real bad if he doesn't get some sleep," Dad said. "It's all well and good for you youngsters staying up half the night."

"Youngsters," Tucker squawked. He pointed at Sully "He's a thousand years old."

Dad stood up and grumbled his way toward the back bedroom. By the time he had reached the end of the hallway, the front door flew open to reveal Lizzie; her hair was disheveled and clothes askew. She was flushed, eyes burning bright, and there were traces of blood still about her mouth.

Dad paused, his hand resting on the knob. "I bet they'll have something to talk about at the Sagebrush Cafe tomorrow," he said quietly.

"Aww, honey," Tucker moaned. "Who was it? Was it Mr. Harlan? Even he didn't deserve to die like that. I ain't sure I even want to think about your mouth sucking on him. I mean what if I was sucking on some old gal?"

"Tucker, relax. I didn't kill anybody." She dabbed at the corners of her mouth but then abruptly stopped and ran for the bathroom, her hand cupped over her mouth. The sounds of her throwing up filtered into the living room to the three men standing there. When she walked back in, she was pale and looked weak.

"I guess alpacas don't agree with me," she whispered. Tucker's eyes flared open and he smiled, then the smile turned into laughter.

"You got one helluva woman there, boy," Dad managed to stutter out in between guffaws.

Tucker laughed even harder, knowing it to be true.

ELITA ENTERED THE PARLOR. She said nothing, sitting down quietly next to Julius on the red leather settee in front of the fireplace. It was a cool evening, the leaves were beginning to transform themselves from the greenery of summer into the vibrant colors of autumn.

"I am in a famously good mood, darling Elita," said Julius. At the sound of the word darling, Elita was overjoyed. She waited, moving closer to Julius as he toyed with her hair, twining it this way and that.

"You know how important you are to me, how much I need you. It was not by accident that through the centuries I have killed every female of Malthus' line so that you could reign supreme, beside me. Once I have the power that my darling daughter possesses, I will destroy her as well. But now, I must ask you to do something for me." He paused, adding drama to his words, kissing her lightly on the forehead. "You must exterminate Sully."

Elita gasped. Julius held his frozen smile. Destroy one of Lazarus' key men? That would mean an end to the antagonistic peace, the uncertain but at least respected truce, that had existed between him and Julius for the last seven centuries. It could plunge the Vampiric world back to a place more hideous than before Malthus, a time she remembered well. Vampire against Vampire. And

Lazarus would see to it that she would pay for this trespass, pay dearly with her own existence. He was no fool. Despite his softening in the last few centuries, Lazarus was still capable of evil on a grand scale. Everyone in the Vampiric world knew of the legends that surrounded him, including his turning, and his resurrection by the hand of Jesus.

Elita looked carefully into Julius' eyes. Nor was Julius a fool. He was sending her to her doom, knowingly. Had he guessed her involvement or was he simply tired of her? Julius smiled sweetly, his motivations hidden. For the last several hundred years, Elita's only happiness lay in the knowledge that she had power over Julius, the power of his love for her. She would risk anything for him, had risked everything to be with him. Nothing brought her any pleasure outside of his tortured devotion and his constant need to test her loyalty.

"You will leave tonight to assure that you join their little party prior to their arrival in New Mexico. My senses tell me they have returned to that little town in Wyoming."

"It pains me to be away from you."

Julius arched his eyebrows.

"Remove my shoes, dear Elita."

Elita knelt to do as she was bid. She remembered the first time he had asked her to do this. She had been exhilarated by his desire for her, his willingness to let her touch his body so intimately. Now she was unsure. His pale toes wiggled out of his nylon socks like jaundiced infants, seeking the sunlight.

Her mind flashed on the comic dog chase from just a few nights ago. She had indeed felt a moment of exhilaration chasing that insipid dog, however brief—the first time in centuries she had felt anything at all outside of Julius' presence. Perhaps she could feel that again. Perhaps it was time to reconsider her allegiances, time to reconsider her life.

"Yes, Master," she said, as she bent down to take his toes in her mouth, "I will go to LonePine."

TWENTY-SEVEN

LIZZIE AND TUCKER SPENT the next five days pretending to have a normal relationship. They held hands and took walks by moonlight, went out to eat in the finest restaurant LonePine had to offer, rented movies. Tucker changed his schedule around, started sleeping in way past sunrise and staying up way past sundown. For the briefest time, it was an oasis in the desert of calamity after calamity that was befalling them. In that quiet corner of the country, they grew closer than ever.

Sully and Dad gave them plenty of space and, in the process, came to be friends. As it turned out, Sully was a fine shot and there wasn't much Dad respected more in a man. Dad even started taking naps during the day so that at night they could set up cans on the fence post down in the gully behind the house. There, by the headlights of Dad's truck, they initiated a contest of moonlight trick shooting. They got pretty elaborate. Dad took to shooting between his legs and Sully, showing off his Vampiric abilities, was once able to strike a match at twenty yards.

All the shooting eventually attracted Lenny, who has a sense for all things gun-related. He drove up in his old truck with a case full of automatic weapons, infrared spotting glasses, and a laser scope.

They were having the time of their life and the hillside trembled under the onslaught. "So, you say you're a Vampire," Lenny said, the laser scope on his .45 winking crimson in the half light.

"Yes."

"I have a hard time believing that." He popped off a long string of shots that rattled the log they had propped up.

"It's true," Dad said, holding his ears.

"Maybe you're just allergic to the sun."

"Oh, no, I am undead. You can shoot me, if you like. With one of the little guns. And not in the face."

Lenny pulled off his hearing protectors. "No. I couldn't do nothing like that."

"I could," Dad said. He raised up the little .22 pistol his own father had given him and pointed it at Sully's chest. "Can I?"

Sully nodded and looked to the side. Crack-crack-crack. Three times the little pistol discharged point blank. Lenny's mouth hung open and he struggled to find words.

Sully winced and slapped at his chest dramatically, then tittered. "Oh, my, that smarts." He pulled his shirt aside and Lenny bent forward to examine the wounds. They were already healing closed and as they watched, the misshapen bullets popped out and into Sully's open palm. "Now do you believe?"

"Definitely. I would say I definitely believe. I would also say I am definitely going home now. Very pleasant meeting you."

"Are you sure you have to run off so soon?" Sully asked, slipping the lead projectiles in his pocket. Dad was laughing so hard that he had to hold his sides.

"Afraid so," Lenny said, as he climbed in to his truck.

"Look at him go," Dad snorted. "Like he seen a ghost."

"That was kind of cruel," Sully said. They both popped open a beer and walked back toward the house, unaware that they were being watched from the deeper shadows.

Meanwhile, Lizzie and Tucker had driven down to his place for old times' sake. They were walking through the thick grass and past the burnt-up remains of his trailer. Most of it had been hauled away while they were in New York, and all that was left standing was the barn and the water tank, and most of the fence. Mysteriously, the alpacas were shying away from the downed wires.

Rex rolled in the familiar grass, covering himself with the smell of home, dusting his coat with memories. Tucker's eyes took on an eerie shine as the power of his land transferred through the soles of his boots into his soul. Lizzie slipped her arm around his waist and led him toward the barn.

"Naw," he said, dragging his feet, "I'd just as soon avoid it for now."

She looked at him quizzically, then just shrugged her shoulders and they kept walking for a while without saying anything, both knowing there was too much to say.

"Is it because of Snort?"

"I guess so."

She sighed deeply. "I'm afraid if I start crying, I might not stop."

"Well then, you better not start."

"I don't want anyone, anything, else to die."

"I suspect that a whole lot more people are going to, sweetie. But not you. You won't die. You're eternal."

Lizzie made a funny scoffing noise, something between a laugh and a sob. She moved close to Tucker and kissed his neck softly.

"Lizzie, you got to make up your mind." Sully's words echoed in his thoughts. "You got to live in your world now."

"I've come to one decision already," she whispered as her hands moved down to his belt and even lower. Tucker's breath came shorter, but he pushed her back gently.

"What are you going to do about your period?"

"I'm not sure yet. I'm not sure I even believe it."

"Julius does. And that's all that really matters."

"I'm surprised he hasn't shown up here yet."

"He will. Or New Mexico. We have to figure out what we're doing."

"The only thing I want to do is live here with you."

"That's a start. Let's work backward from that. How do you want to do that? As a bored housewife Vampire, feeding on an occasional alpaca and waiting around to nurse me through Alzheimer's? Or as a Vampire Queen ruling the earth, being true to the higher purpose inside you? If what they're saying is right, you can do a great deal more good making sure all that power don't get in the wrong hands."

"Why should I worry about the whole world?"

"Cause we owe the world a favor."

"For what?" she asked bitterly. "Look what it's done to me."

"For bringing us together. And there is one advantage in you drinking your own blood," he said quietly.

"What's that?"

"You could turn me into a Vampire."

"I would give anything to be able to spend eternity with you, Tucker. But I don't believe that you would much like the things you have to do."

He sighed. "You're probably right."

"How about this? We go to New Mexico. Take Lazarus up on his offer to protect me until my period comes. If there really is a power, we let it go back to the cosmos. Then no one has it. After that, we can come back here and live out your life together. After that, I suppose I'm on my own."

"Seems a little simple. Julius and his army won't let it end that easy. There's bound to be a scrap of some sort."

"We'll deal with that. The important part is my knowing we'll be together. That's all that matters to me. Besides, I thought you liked it simple."

"It does have a certain beauty to it. I'm guessing Lazarus could help us figure out how to do it all."

Lizzie smiled. "At least, we have some goals to work toward now."

"We'll make staying alive number one. No, we'll make staying in love number one. How's that sound?"

"Good, really good. But let's move making love to number one. Just for now?" She nuzzled her face into his neck and Tucker kissed her. Breathless, he unbuttoned her shirt, letting the moonlight shine on her pale skin, her breasts sparkling like magic. Taking his hands, she led him back down the hill and toward the barn, never once taking her eyes from his.

Inside, they made love in the loft, clothes spread out on the hay and smelling the sweet smell of summer. Afterward, he heard her sigh, and then, much to his drained surprise, he heard something else. Another voice, other voices. Distant and mumbled.

He will not be easily vanquished. Protect yourself. Go to your childhood. The dark woman will aid you.

Tucker bolted upright. "What? What did you say?"

"Nothing, I said nothing, it was the voices again, I swear."

"What did they say?"

Lizzie pulled her clothes on roughly and fast. "We've got to find Sully and go. I need to get to Lazarus." They drove quickly back to Dad's place, the truck rattling in the deep ruts.

"Dad, Sully," Tucker yelled as they entered his house, "time to get moving. You finished horsing around with your target..." His words died in his throat.

Dad and Sully were both bound to chairs, both pale, and both marked with blood-tinted wounds on their throats. Sully was still as a statue, eyes closed and breathing shallowly. Dad was conscious, eyes burning but drained.

Elita lay back in the recliner with the television remote and a beer, Dad's gray Stetson perched on her head. She was wearing a skimpy black satin cocktail dress and red cowboy boots, her feet propped on the table. She laughed her throaty laugh when she saw their surprised faces. Tucker muttered an oath and reached for his gun, but Lizzie stayed his hand. Her back was rigid and fury blazed in her eyes.

Elita showed no sign of concern, just kept flipping through the television stations and sipping her beer. "The reception out here is awful," she said.

Lizzie walked to the center of the room where Dad was, leaned down and untied him. He stood up, his old body tense and ready to lunge, but Lizzie stopped him too.

"Stand by Tucker." She said it quietly, but with a dark strength that left no room for argument. Lizzie moved to Sully. She knelt down beside him and whispered in his ear as she untied his hands. His eyes fluttered open, and he mustered a tiny smile.

"What happened, Sully?" she asked tenderly.

He coughed weakly and could hardly get the words out, but finally managed to whisper a response, all the while looking at Elita, his eyes burning with a mixture of rage and terror. "She fed on me."

Those words appeared to be Elita's cue. She jumped up from the recliner, flipped the hat far back on her head, and stood, hips pushed forward. "Lizzie dearest, I suppose you don't yet know how to kill a Vampire. While it's rather challenging for Adamites," she explained, grinning maliciously at Tucker, "it's quite elementary for a Vampire. Simply take their blood. All of it. Generously, I have refrained from killing Sully. I stopped in time. He's only stunned. He'll be back to himself by tomorrow night. That is," she purred, "if I choose not to feed again before he has regained his strength." She smiled demurely, looking at her nails.

Lizzie stood. Her power was awesome, light seemed to flow from her. Surprisingly and oddly, she was calm. No rage, no angry words. It was as if she had the power of time and gravity wrapped around her little finger.

She turned. "Tucker, please help Sully to his coffin. He needs to rest." He hesitated, unsure if he should leave her alone, but then decided he should at least take the opportunity to get the others to safety.

Between Dad and Tucker, they managed to support Sully and carried him toward the basement door and the coffin waiting below. "It's gonna be the catfight of the century." he said, looking over his shoulder one more time as they negotiated through the doorway.

TWENTY-EIGHT

It was clear to Lizzie that Elita could have killed Tucker's father and Sully. The fact that she had not meant that the true purpose of her visit to LonePine had yet to be revealed. As if reading her thoughts, Elita spoke.

"I could have killed them both."

Lizzie simply nodded. Elita began pacing the floor, slowly, seductively, the black satin of her tiny dress clinging softly to her swaying hips. Neither spoke. Finally, Lizzie broke the silence.

"Don't drag this out. Tell me why you are here."

"Julius sent me. To kill Sully."

"Julius sent you to kill, yet you have not done that. Though a killing may yet take place tonight."

Elita turned abruptly to face Lizzie, the taunts and teasing half-formed on the tip of her tongue quickly dying. There was a deep calm on Lizzie's face and Elita felt a sudden, profound fear.

"I miscalculated in telling you how to kill a Vampire."

"I'm beginning to understand a lot of things, to even accept certain aspects of this role that has been thrust upon me. But understand this, Tucker is sacred, as is anything dear to him. It would seem I have no choice but to enter this little fantasy world, but Tucker will not become a victim, no matter who I have to destroy."

She stood very close to Elita, whose startled eyes betrayed her outward composure. Elita sensed the power in her, the same power that had flashed to the surface the night of the turning, and she knew that any advantage she might have ever had was rapidly disintegrating.

"Do you understand why all this has happened?" Elita asked Lizzie.

"I understand enough and the remainder I choose to have explained to me by Lazarus, not you."

"There are some things that Lazarus cannot tell you, some things that only I know, as Julius' long-time companion."

"Lover?"

"Yes."

"Are you in love with him?"

"In the way that you are in love with that cowboy?"

Lizzie nodded in response.

"I am a Vampire. Love is more complex for us."

"Love is always simple. I assume ours is different only by duration."

"I thought I had found the ideal man."

"And now your ideals are changing?"

"Maybe."

"He may have only been ideal in the sense that he knew how to keep you attached to him, unlike the hundreds…"

"More like thousands," interrupted Elita.

"All right, thousands of saps who have passed through your clutches. Enough of this prattle. What good is killing Sully?"

"Julius sent me to kill Sully, as a demonstration to Lazarus that he, in fact, can sense you, and thus you cannot escape him. He knows where you are all the time."

Lizzie's heart stopped at this news. The voices had been right. She must get to Lazarus quickly. She needed protection, powerful protection. "Why have you disobeyed Julius?"

She shrugged and tossed the cowboy hat onto the table. Lizzie took it and carefully turned it crown down, a movement she had seen Tucker repeat a thousand times. "I no longer am convinced Julius will emerge victorious in this war."

"War?" asked Lizzie.

"Oh, my little Queen, you know not what events you have set into motion."

Tucker walked back in. He was surprised to see them calmly talking. "Honey, everything okay?"

Lizzie nodded. "Let's get started for New Mexico right away. And Tucker, I think your dad should come with us. He's not safe here anymore."

"I could be of service to you," said Elita. She paused and then added, "You are, after all, my Queen, and I am quite intimate with the ways of your King."

"Elita will be joining us but," she added, turning to face Elita, "if any harm comes to anyone by your doing, I will personally destroy you."

"I understand."

"Um, Lizzie. Could I see you outside for a minute?" On the porch, Tucker stared at Lizzie dumbfounded. "What are you thinking, asking that witch to come with us?"

"She has a tremendous amount of knowledge about Julius and his operations. The voices said to trust the dark woman. Who else could that be? And despite it all, I'm starting to like her."

"Maybe you should pick someone a little less dangerous to have as your girlfriend. Like Medusa. What about Sully? He'd make a great girlfriend. Or I could introduce you to a whole handful of cowgirls right here in LonePine."

"I bet you could. But somehow, I'm guessing they would not be quite the type of friend I'd like. Anyway, she was only a threat as long as she was attached to Julius. She's disobeyed Julius and therefore cannot return to him. She has no place to go. Her only hope is to be accepted by Lazarus and myself."

"Honey, she tried to kill Dad and Sully."

"If Elita had wanted to kill either one of them, they would be dead. That was just to prove a point to me."

"And that point would be?"

"That she could control her desire to kill, that she could go against Julius' wishes."

"But how do you know it ain't all a setup? Maybe Julius is just planting her inside so that she can spy on us?"

"I suppose that's possible."

"It's an awful big risk. She's dangerous."

"Tucker, is there anything you need to tell me about you and Elita?" Tucker stammered for an answer. Just then, Elita joined them on the porch.

"I tried to seduce him once. But he remained true to you. He's the only Adamite male that has ever refused me."

"Really?" asked Tucker, chest swelling with pride. "The only one?"

Lizzie shook her head and rolled her eyes. He looked like a rooster.

"Thank you, Lizzie," said Elita quietly.

"For what?"

"I really wasn't sure how this evening was going to turn out."

"Could have been a lot worse."

"More than you know," Elita said. "Even if I had vanquished you, I would have been forced to destroy myself. Killing Elizabeth Vaughan before the onset of her first menses would have made me a pariah in our world, accepted by none. I want to help you now. You must believe me." Her last words were directed at Tucker, who just rolled his eyes in disbelief.

"Let's get moving. I'd like to be in New Mexico as soon as possible," said Lizzie.

"C'mon, Rex, load on up," yelled Tucker as he walked toward the Land Rover. "Hey Dad, remember that vacation I always promised? Hope you got lots of ammo."

PART THREE: REDEMPTION

TWENTY-NINE

"Man, Lenny would love to see this place," Tucker drawled. The Vampire at the gate motioned them inside while speaking into a wireless transmitter jutting off his ear. Lizzie and Tucker watched with open-mouthed awe as laser-guided machine guns swiveled noiselessly to track their car. As soon as it had passed inside, a series of tire-shredding vehicle barriers popped up from the pavement behind them. There were other men just outside the walls, laboring with shovels to plant mechanical devices in the sand. Tucker figured correctly that they were laying a mine field. Periodically, immense arc lights would swing around, brighter than day in the middle of the night.

Lizzie took Tucker's hand and held on tight as they were led inside Lazarus' compound. Elita, Sully, and Dad followed close behind. Rex slunk in last, what was left of his tail between his legs. Another dog barked from somewhere nearby.

Inside the main house, the architecture and interior design reflected the austere tradition of the Southwest, with local clays and wood used for both substance and decoration. Underneath this facade was every imaginable necessity and more than a few luxuries. Lizzie paused, held tighter to Tucker's arm, and marveled at how the furnishings, plants, fireplaces, and bookshelves combined to form a perfect whole. There was even a computer monitor built directly into the adobe in the main room, an input jack for the keyboard barely noticeable below it. There were no wires visible, no phone cords, no extraneous items. An absolute marvel of interior design, and, she realized slowly, rich with half-forgotten memories.

Carlos, entering from the hallway, sensed the revelation within her and smiled. She remembered him. "How long has it been, Carlos?"

He sighed happily, and took her in his arms for a hug. "Too long, my little angel. Too long." He held her back to study her. "You are so beautiful now, so grown up. I remember when you were but three, and ..." His voice trailed off and he took Tucker's hand. "You must be Tucker. It's an honor to meet you. We owe you a great deal for saving Lizzie's life. A great deal."

"Shoot," Tucker said. "Weren't nothing." Lizzie smiled tenderly at his hidden pride.

"It was to us," Carlos continued, "and we will be forever in your debt, no matter how this turns out."

"Is it that bad?" Lizzie asked.

"It's very bad. But let's not talk of that now. Come see your room." Before leaving, he turned to the others in their group. "Please wait here for just a moment. Someone will see to your needs very shortly." Lizzie smiled comfortingly at everyone, putting humans and Vampires at ease.

Carlos escorted Tucker and Lizzie to a room at the end of the hallway. It was decorated with pink curtains, ruffles, and stuffed animals, more a nursery than a room. It hadn't changed in twenty-seven years. Under her pillow were strings of red and black licorice, her favorite candy. There was a framed photograph of her when she was two, with her mother and a man she presumed to be Lazarus.

"Well now, weren't you the cute little bloodsucker," said Tucker.

"I realize that you are no longer a child," Carlos explained, "but being your nanny all those years ago, I couldn't part with the memories. I hoped that having them around would make you feel at home."

"Thank you," Lizzie said. "I do feel at home." Tucker sat on the bed, exhausted from the drive, and Rex hopped up beside him to chew on a licorice whip. Lizzie wandered through the room, touching pieces of her childhood, remembering her mother.

"Your father and Mr. Sully will room together in another wing of the house. Elita will sleep down below, so that we may more easily gauge her allegiance. If you need anything, there is an intercom on the wall here." He pointed at a slightly raised pattern in the tile work trim. "There will be someone here instantly. Now, I must take my leave. There is still much to attend to." He paused at the door and nodded first at Tucker and then addressed Lizzie directly. "Welcome home."

And oddly, she did feel at home here, in a way that she had never before experienced. There was a dimly remembered connection to the house, to the land, to the crisp air of the Southwestern landscape, to the dry feeling hanging from the juniper branches, to the light that dripped from the stars. The sensation of belonging was increasing with each passing moment. She wanted to revel in it, to relax, and languish inside the protective fortress, inside the love she felt for Tucker, inside the walls of protection from Julius that Lazarus provided.

Time passed quickly there, but in three days and as many nights, Lazarus still had not sent for her. He saw to their every comfort, made sure that they wanted for nothing, but he himself had yet to appear. Tucker, in his usual fashion, wanted to go and find him. Knock on a few doors, step on some toes; but Lizzie felt there was a certain protocol that should be followed, one she understood on a deep, instinctive level. He must come to her, not because she was Queen, but because he was Master. She had no right to seek him if he chose not to be found.

The only good thing to come out of all this, so far as Tucker could see, was that Rex had found a girlfriend, a Russian wolfhound, a Borzoi, whose name was Alexandra. According to Carlos, she was Lazarus' dog and she was a beautiful combination of style and grace. She seemed a little out of place in this wasteland of rock and cactus, but was possessed of a sweet temper and kind disposition. What she saw in a no-good old cow dog like Rex escaped Tucker entirely, but Lizzie told him that she understood completely.

In hope of gaining some small advantage before push came to shove, as it was bound to very soon, Tucker tried his best to get to know the terrain. In a matter of days, he had familiarized himself with every crag, column, twisted scrub pine and cactus within a ten-mile radius. The most noticeable natural feature was a steep canyon with sheer walls, not far from the compound. Near the top end, where it joined the bald mountains, there were Indian ruins of a sort unfamiliar to him. Below the ruins, and running the length of the canyon, was a little spring that made a brief appearance before the desert heat forced it back underground near the mouth of the canyon.

It was there that they ended up, Tucker and the dogs. While the dogs panted and splashed in the water, he explored the ruins. There was an eerie silence surrounding them, but it suited him somehow. After climbing a broken, weathered ladder, he sat among the shadows looking at the shards of pottery mixed in with the dust and gravel. Studying the lines etched into the clay, he found them curious and unlike others he had seen, less symmetrical, the pattern quietly unnerving. The walls were smooth and cool, and the curious pattern was repeated more intricately there.

The dust was thick over the walls and with his hand he swept it off, revealing a series of figures painted there. These, too, were unlike other Indian paintings he had seen. What differed most was their faces. The artists had taken great pains to illustrate a sense of motion and expression. The motion was mostly that of running, seeming to be retreating; and the expressions on most of the figures were that of horror. There were exceptions. A small cluster of figures were leaning over a prone woman, and they appeared to be eating her.

Tucker leaned back on his heels and thought hard about the significance of this discovery. The Vampires were here before the Indians had left. One of them might well be Lazarus. Seeing this record in stone drove the point home to Tucker that all the recent past events were more than just talk. Here it was, old as the hills— older, even, than the discovery of the New World.

A cold shiver trembled through him. He stood up and regarded the sun, dipping close to the purple-tinged mountains across the way. Sundown, now, was when his life really began. He clambered down to the dogs. Halfway down the canyon, Rex spooked a gangly jackrabbit, all ears and back legs. It bolted down the streambed, Rex hot on its tail, but losing fast. Alexandra took the opportunity to show her new boyfriend what sets wolfhounds apart from other breeds. She sat for a moment like she was bored, giving the rabbit and Rex a sporting chance. When they were almost out of sight, she stood and licked delicately at her forefoot, then disappeared like Superman after Lois Lane.

As Tucker watched in amazement, she passed Rex in a blur of gray. Surprised, Rex lost control, veered to the side and tumbled into a cactus. Even though his nose was full of stickers; he stood up to watch as Alexandra passed the rabbit too. Once well in the lead, she stopped to let it catch up, only to pass it again. On and on they ran like that until the poor rabbit gave up and plopped down, its ribs heaving from the strain. She sniffed at it and ran a few teasing steps to see if it would start again, but it refused, so she trotted back to see about Rex. She didn't even look winded, unlike Rex, who looked like an out-of-shape pincushion.

"Damn, that girl can run," Tucker said to Rex, who was looking at him over a row of stickers in his nose, eyes welling tears. "C'mon, we got to get you back to the house and pick those sons of bitches out."

"I STILL DON'T BELIEVE you."

Lazarus was immersed in his pool, his body cool and relaxed. Elita stretched out beside him. She rested lightly but certainly on the sand, her back arched and head thrown back to drink in the moonlight, her breasts uncovered and sprinkled by the light of millions of stars sparkling in the darkness. A thick beach towel was bunched below her waist. She rolled over onto an elbow and regarded Lazarus coolly.

"But Lizzie does."

"She is not yet able to make those sorts of judgments."

"She believes that she is."

Lazarus harumphed and motioned for her to join him. She arched her eyebrows and then shrugged delicately, the towel falling from around her, and she slid into the pool.

"Oooh, it's cold." She shivered and then relaxed.

"I must tell you, Elita, it is not often I have the pleasure of such a beautiful bathing companion."

She smiled. "It's not often I have the honor of relaxing with the self-proclaimed champion of free Vampires." Lazarus had been with so many beautiful women through his eternity, no aspect of feminine beauty remained a mystery to him. Elita was able to fully relax with him, knowing her charms meant little.

"We have lost touch, you and I, over the years."

She nodded, her face shining from the invigorating coolness of the water. "I suppose many Adamites felt the same way during the great schism of the church. Two popes and all that. One in New York, the other … where are we exactly?"

"New Mexico, my dear."

"Oh, yes." She dipped her head under the water and then re-emerged, running her hand through her hair. She smiled, revealing her perfect teeth. "So what must I do to gain your trust?"

"You can't. Only historical perspective will allow that luxury. Come, I have something to show you." He hoisted himself from the pool and Elita studied the ample folds of his body as he pulled on a thick robe. She smiled, but wasn't for a moment fooled. There was more power concealed in that body than most Vampires could dream of. More, she sensed, than even Julius. She pulled herself out to follow, padding barefoot down the hall, still naked and as comfortable with it as a child.

They wound their way deeper into the recesses of the sandstone underground. At an unassuming metal door, he pressed a section of the wall and the door slid open to reveal a bare room lined with video equipment. There was a folding table in the middle and he gestured at one of the chairs. "Please sit."

She did while forming a question. "Tell me. Why have you not seen Lizzie yet? You should be as anxious as Julius to see her, and yet, here it is, what, three nights gone by and you still refuse. Why? And do you have any cigarettes?"

"No. I'll send for some, if you like."

She nodded. "If you don't mind."

He pressed a switch on the wall. "Cigarettes," he said simply. "In the meantime, have some HoHos." He pulled a bag out and slid it across the table. "It's not that easy, seeing her, I mean. She's so young. She has no idea."

"Of what?"

"How important she is."

Elita rolled her eyes. "You sound just like Julius. Anything to keep our Queen happy."

He shook his head sadly. "As intelligent as you are, Elita, and you haven't figured it out. Haven't the centuries taught you anything? My God, woman, you have lived a dozen lives as blindly and stupidly as the most ignorant of Adamites."

She blanched. "I do not need a lecture, Lazarus."

He nodded, a peculiar look of scorn and remorse on his face. "Indeed. What you need is a heart. Look inside yourself. Hasn't a real thought entered that pretty head of yours in the last thousand years? Haven't you just once tried to figure it out, the purpose? This is not some silly accident we live in. It's life. Eternal life." He pushed the HoHos aside and leaned close. "There is a reason for this, for the evil, the violence. It is no game of chance that we were born Vampires. We are needed, we are necessary."

A knock at the door interrupted him and Carlos entered. Glaring at Elita with undisguised hatred, he dropped a pack of clove cigarettes on the table as well as a book of matches.

"I hope these are to your liking." As if an afterthought, he also dropped a silk robe onto her lap.

Elita slipped it on, knowing that she was perceived as disrespectful, appearing before Lazarus without clothes. Despite his hatred, Carlos clearly was not as disinterested in her body as Lazarus. She smiled at Carlos and pulled the robe tight, accentuating the curve of her breasts and the silhouette of her nipples. She used one lacquered nail to split the package, slowly extracting a cigarette, lighting it and blowing a stream of clove-scented smoke at him.

"Carlos, you remembered." Her taunt lacked conviction, however, and he smiled tightly and left without a word.

"You still enjoy silly games, don't you, Elita? I'm surprised you have yet to realize that your power extends far beyond your sexuality." Lazarus sighed, and leaned back in his chair, took a bite of cupcake and contemplated the moist crumbs and cream filling.

"Tell me something. Did Julius explain the rationale behind his desire for Lizzie?" asked Lazarus.

"At first I thought it was simply to have a Queen by his side, but now I realize it was something much more practical. World dominion."

Lazarus laughed. "Exactly. Exactly. A new dawn for our kind. No longer confined to the shadows. An earth of Vampires, that sort of thing."

"There is a certain beauty to it," Elita replied casually.

"But that is where you are wrong. There would be no beauty. There would be nothing but evil, awful, terrible torment. We have a role, you and me, and those like us. We are to consume evil. It is our legacy. Those that live forever must necessarily be evil. There is no other choice. We have a taste of the infinite and it is blood, and there is no need to seek higher ground. We have no time limit. We live forever, and in doing so, are answerable to no one. Do what thou wilt shall be the whole of the law."

"Aleister Crowley," Elita said, recognizing the words.

"Yes. A human who wished he was a Vampire, that human moral concerns need not apply to him, just as they do not apply to us."

"And what is the problem?" she asked.

"The problem is that we do have a purpose, and Julius has strayed far from that place. Malthus came to us with a message of hate, just as Jesus and other Adamite prophets came with a message of love. We must hate so that love can exist. We must be evil so that good may exist. Ours is to contain the darkness that others may contain the light. Without the light, though we cannot see it, this world is not worth living in. Without friendship and love and laughter and joy, how could we go on in our lives of death and decay?"

"These are all just words, Lazarus, words like those of Julius. Words do not matter in the end. Words don't keep your mouth full of blood, your gut full of blood. I know my purpose when I see the fear in their eyes, taste it in their agony. That is my purpose."

"Then you are worse than an animal."

She laughed, a throaty laugh that ricocheted through the room. "More words. What good do they do me?"

"Not words, Elita, faith. I can't convince you with my words, but I can with my faith. I have faith that we are not animals with minds. I have faith that we do serve a purpose, that we are not mindless killing machines driven on by urges we cannot control. I have faith that these urges, this immortality, this power, is not ours by accident. We have a reason, Elita. It may be unclear, but we have a reason."

He leaned back and laced his fingers together behind his head, staring at the ceiling. "You remain in this world, you are here with me now, because I have faith in you. Don't look so surprised. I need you."

"Me. What could you possibly need from me?"

"Look around you. This is my war room. My sanctum sanctorum. It is from here that the battle against Julius, when it comes, will be waged. But at another level; it will be fought from here." He thumped his fist on his chest and the undead heart beating below. "My heart against Julius' mind, his ego. His thoughts against my faith. When the heart and the mind are at war, there can be no winner. I imagine neither of us will survive. But you will. You always survive. And if you survive, the faith will survive with you."

"Don't be ridiculous, I have no faith," she snapped.

"But you have the capacity," Lazarus said gently, "for I know that you love him. What else could it be? Why would you have stayed with him all these years? Why would you have tipped me off seven hundred years ago with MaryAnne if not from a hidden desire to protect the world. All these years you have loved him and that would be impossible without heart."

Her chin trembled slightly and tears fought their way to the corners of her eyes, but she swiped them away viciously. "You are out of your mind. A dreamer. A hopeless romantic. I tipped you off because I was jealous, as petty as that may sound. When Julius denied me the chance to share in the girl's blood, when it became clear that he and I would no longer be equals, I decided the girl had to be done away with. So, you are wrong. It was jealousy, pure and simple," she said. "You are so wrong." She ran out, slamming the door behind her.

He could hear her retreat as it grew distant. "For your sake, I almost wish I was," he said softly, reaching for another HoHo. He touched the button in the wall. "Carlos, it is time."

THIRTY

"I MUST APOLOGIZE FOR making myself so scarce," Lazarus said as he entered the room. "Matters concerning your safety, and all of ours, demanded my attention." It was the start of a new night and Lazarus was speaking to Lizzie and Tucker, who were sitting before an open fire. Rex and Alexandra were curled together at their feet. Elita was sitting across the room, glaring at Lazarus as he spoke. Dad and Sully were playing checkers across the room, but stopped when Lazarus came in.

Lazarus walked briskly to Tucker and offered his hand. "You must be Tucker." His grip was firm and cool.

"Yep. And you must be Lazarus. The real Lazarus? I mean, the one from the Bible?"

"The same." Tucker whistled under his breath and Lazarus moved to Lizzie, who stood. "Elizabeth, what can I say? I have waited a long time."

Lizzie said nothing. She was too nervous to speak. It threatened to be an awkward moment until Lazarus broke the tension by enveloping her in his massive arms.

"I've missed you, child. Not a day passed that I did not think of you."

"Then why didn't you come get me sooner?"

He nodded gravely. "I was tempted. Sorely tempted. But Constance … your mother thought it best to keep you far from the world of the undead for as long as possible."

"Great plan," Tucker mumbled.

"Ah, my cynical friend." He turned to face Tucker, a wry smile on his face. "How unfortunate for you to become enmeshed in our world, especially poised at the brink of such change. But how lucky you are to receive the love of Lizzie. You must agree, she is an exceptional woman."

"Yeah, I guess."

He bent over to pet Rex. "What a charming animal, already becoming close with my favorite hound."

"Careful," Tucker called, "he don't cotton much to Vampires. He might …" Rex rolled over and let Lazarus scratch his tummy. Tucker sighed. "He might slobber all over your hand."

"I wish that this was a social visit. We could talk about old times and drink too much, stay up until dawn. But unfortunately, it is under much more regrettable circumstances."

"Regrettable?" Tucker blurted out. "We got most of the Vampires in the world chasing us. A month ago I thought all I was gonna have to worry about was someone using my toothbrush and drinking my beer, and now I don't even know if I'm going to live until tomorrow, and you say it's regrettable. And I thought I was good with understatement." Lizzie elbowed him in the ribs. "What? What?"

"Mr. Tucker is right," Lazarus continued. "By my reckoning, your period will start in about two days, maybe three."

"Sometimes it's late," Lizzie said. "I mean, it's not like clock-work. I even skipped one once, and I thought I was pregnant, but I wasn't."

"Who'd you think the father was?" Tucker asked. "I mean, was this before me? Way before me?"

"Tucker, stop it. It was nobody. Well, it was somebody, but compared to you, it was nobody."

"Whether it is late or not," Lazarus interrupted, "Julius can't afford to miss it. He must have you under his control before it starts. He will be here by tomorrow night. He may already be close. At any rate…"

"Why don't we just ask her?" Tucker said, glaring at Elita. "I'm sure she knows his plans."

She smiled lazily, infuriatingly, at Tucker.

"Elita has switched allegiances."

"Never switch horses in midstream, that's what my dad always told me."

"He also told you that approaching headlights on a dark road were giant man-eating insects called hootenhoppers," Lizzie said.

"You told her about that?" Tucker asked Dad, who nodded sheepishly in response. "Well, I never believed it. Not for long, any-ways," retorted Tucker.

"From what Sully told me, Elita could have killed him and your father both," Lazarus added.

"Stop talking about me like I'm not here," Elita said. "You'll hurt my feelings."

"As far as I'm concerned, you ain't here."

"Tucker, stop it. She's one of us now. Trust me."

"It ain't you I don't trust," he said. "You didn't try to poke a hole through me." Elita eyed her fingernails circumspectly and beamed over at him. "There ain't no way I can trust her. You can't teach an old dog new tricks."

As if to emphasize his point, Rex sat up and scratched, then plopped back down beside Alexandra.

Lizzie took him by the arm. "The voices told me to trust her. So I will. End of story."

He sat down, his shoulders slumped.

Lazarus pulled up a rocking chair fashioned from twisted, unfinished pine. "The voices, you say? They told you of Elita? Then I was right. I was right." He clapped his hands together in glee, looking at a confused Elita. "You see, my dear, I am right."

Elita lit a fresh smoke and now tried her best to pretend she was alone in the room.

"I don't hear no voices other than the ones that tell me I'm loco for sitting here waiting for Julius to come traipsing in and rip us all into shredded wheat. For Chrissakes, this place looks like something out of *Better Homes and Gardens*. I mean, sure, a big fence and some high-dollar machine guns on the wall, but goddamn it, in case you forgot, we're talking about Vampires here. What the hell are we doing sitting on our thumbs and waiting?"

Lazarus grimaced, as if the seriousness of the subject pained him. "There is no safer place in the world, my friend. Don't let appearances fool you. This entire compound is built with one thing in mind, defense against the Vampire. As you already know, the entire structure is surrounded by a minefield. I understand you are familiar with the workings of thermite. The mines are thermite, with delayed delivery systems that trigger at waist height. Quite nasty. The machine guns you noticed on the turrets are laser-targeted 40-mm miniguns, firing at a rate of close to 1,000 rounds a minute. Not to be grisly, but they are capable of inflicting such damage as to be almost lethal to a Vampire. The entire perimeter area is monitored by a variant of global positioning grid technology. If a leaf falls, my men know it. Speaking of men, I have quite a contingent here. Four hundred strong, well trained, and equipped with some of the finest military hardware money can buy. Incendiary, projectile-edged weapons. You name it, we have it. Does that make you feel any better?"

"Maybe. But I don't understand why we're just laying low. Don't that make us kinda like sitting ducks? Sounds like you got quite a fortress all right, maybe better than anything in the world, but it strikes me to be a mite simpler just staying ahead of Julius until her period is over. Why not put us on a plane to Tahiti or Katmandu?"

Lazarus began to respond, but Lizzie interrupted him. "Julius knows where I am all the time. He can sense me. There is nowhere to hide."

"I was not aware you knew this," Lazarus said quietly.

"I have been experiencing some profound shifts in my sensory perceptions. I can sense him as well."

"Is he close?" Tucker asked. "Can you sense him right now? Is he outside listening?"

She shook her head. "Unfortunately, it is not very accurate yet. Only occasional whiffs, so to speak."

"Can you sense anything else? Anyone else?" Tucker asked.

"Only you."

There was a heavy silence in the room. Lazarus broke it. "It appears Tucker has imprinted on you."

"Well," said Dad from across the room, "looks like you're going to have to toe the line, boy."

There was nervous laughter, but underneath it was a mixture of fear and resignation emanating from all those present. The knowledge that Julius was aware of her exact location at all times was difficult to comprehend at this late date.

"I think I'd feel better if I could call in a friend of mine. A specialist," said Tucker.

"An Adamite?" asked Lazarus.

"Of course an Adamite. I don't have any Vampire friends." He looked at Sully. "No offense. He's a genius when it comes to weapons. Couldn't hurt to have him on our side for this."

"That's right," added Dad. "Maybe he can bring down some of the local militia. Them guys are fearless."

Lazarus shrugged. "Make the call. I can send a plane. He'll be here by morning."

"I'd appreciate that. And a cup of coffee."

"Me too," Dad chimed in, "and could you put a dollop of Jack Daniels in there?"

Lazarus nodded and spoke softly into the wall speaker. In moments, Carlos carried in a tray with drinks. He handed the coffees to the Adamites, a hot chocolate with peppermint schnapps to Lazarus, a carafe of blood to Elita, and a porcelain teapot with a matching cup to Lizzie. "It's ginger tea. I overheard you complaining about a touch of indigestion."

"Carlos, that's so sweet. Thank you." She took a sip. "Do you really think he'll come?"

"Oh, he'll come," Lazarus said, wiping a bit of whipped cream from his lip. "There are a few things from the past that I should tell you about. Provide a bit of perspective, context. This is not an entirely new scenario between Julius and myself. Many years ago, a situation very nearly identical to this developed. A young woman believed to have the power was turned by Julius. Julius wanted her power then as badly as he wants yours now. I was unaware until the last minute of his plans. Had I not received word from an inside source," he shot a look at Elita that only Tucker caught, "things would be very different today."

"Who was the girl?" asked Tucker.

Lazarus sighed before responding as Elita laughed, quietly and cruelly. "She was my daughter." He cleared his throat and tried to gather his emotions. "Although, I did not know this until just before she was destroyed."

"Would it have made any difference in your actions?" asked Lizzie.

He weighed his answer carefully. "I have asked myself that question again and again. I do not believe it would have made a difference, at least, not back then. I was willing to do anything to stop him. I was impulsive because my knowledge of his plans came so late. I had little time to consider the implications of my actions. In my unfortunate zeal, I decided my only option was to sacrifice her. It is a mistake I have lived with for a long time. Now I have a chance to rectify that. With you. It is very important that I make this work for you."

"Not to be critical, but how could you have killed your own kin?" asked Dad.

"Historically, we Vampires do not recognize the bonds of family as you do. Our primary relationship is with the one who turned us. No, my mistake in killing MaryAnne was that it ultimately meant that I succumbed to Julius' view of the Vampiric world. My beliefs and those of my followers allow us only to consume Adamitic or, as necessary, Vampiric evil that threatens mortal goodness. In destroying MaryAnne, I went against my own moral precepts, and thus, Julius won. He will not win this time."

Dad said, "Seems a mite complex. I'm guessing Julius didn't exactly feel much like a winner."

"Definitely not," responded Lazarus.

They were all silent for a minute. Tucker stood up and looked at Lazarus. "I can sort of see your point of view, and I appreciate all you're doing for us, but don't ever come between me and Lizzie. This whole world ain't worth nothing to me, next to her. There won't be any sacrifices. Not this time. Understood?"

Lazarus put down his hot chocolate and wiped the whipped-cream mustache from his lip. "Perhaps it is time to be more direct. Lizzie, what is your decision about the power you possess?"

Without hesitating, she said, "I choose to let it pass back into the Cosmos. Unused."

"You have the strength necessary to let it pass from you? The internal strength?"

"Yes."

Lazarus continued. "I have said before that I am not wholly convinced of the literal truth of Revelations. We may in fact be dealing with a fantasy richly embroidered by Julius' mind."

"Seems too big a risk to take," said Dad.

"Spoken with the true sense of a man of the land," responded Lazarus. "Assuming the words of Revelations to be true and that this power does move in your veins, you must remember we know nothing of what is about to occur. It is new in our history. The manifestation of this power in your blood may be very painful to you. Especially unconsumed." Lizzie nodded wordlessly. "Very well. This makes our plan somewhat simpler. Now, we must only prevent Julius from having access to you for the duration of your menses."

"I'd suggest we err on the side of caution and prevent any Vampire from having access to Lizzie during that time," Tucker drawled.

"The only ones that could use this power are Elizabeth and those Vampires who have the power to turn," responded Lazarus.

"I understand that," said Tucker, staring evenly at Lazarus.

"Tucker," snapped Lizzie, "what are you saying?"

Lazarus waved his arm, a dismissive motion. "I rather like the fact that someone is thinking completely about your safety. While there is no reason for you not to trust me, I understand that the cowboy code you live by requires that such trust be earned. I respect that. Since there will be little time to earn this trust, however, we will establish a way that Lizzie can remain isolated from anyone except those of your selection during her menses. In the meanwhile, my contingent will keep Julius at bay. Frankly, I expect there to be many losses and for the battle itself to be quite brutal." He sighed. "I believe we can hold them off. If not, we will abandon the fort and escape through the tunnel system that leads to the Indian ruins in the hills. From there, we will continue on foot to rendezvous with reinforcements who will see that we all are able to escape to a place of our choosing."

"Why will we have to run once my period is over?" asked Lizzie.

"Julius is not a gracious loser," interjected Elita before Lazarus could respond. "His power to sense Lizzie may be gone once the menses pass, but his failure will enrage him and he will unquestionably continue until he has utterly destroyed this compound and wreaked revenge upon each of us now in this room."

"And you especially," said Lazarus, looking at her. "Particularly if it occurs to him that you are the reason for his previous failure."

All eyes turned to Elita. Elita glared at Lazarus. "That was supposed to remain our secret," she hissed.

"There is no leisure left now for secrets, my dear. All cards must be on the table." He turned to face Lizzie. "Elita was the one to inform me of Julius' plans last time. She does have a heart, although she seeks to hide it. Once this is over, you will need training in order to exist in this world. I ask that you rely on Elita to help you understand your role."

"My role?"

"While you will not have the power to turn full-blooded Adamites, you will still have the power to turn, as do Julius and myself. Thus, for better or worse, my dear, you will be assuming an important role in the world of Vampires."

"Why don't we just take it one step at a time?" suggested Lizzie. "Let's get through this battle and then we'll see who I turn to for guidance. My inclination, Lazarus, is that I would prefer to be under your tutelage." Lazarus smiled while Lizzie struggled to find the words to continue speaking. Quietly, she said, "I will need some help. I have still not had my first kill." She felt embarrassed, admitting this to Lazarus and Elita. Surprisingly, Elita was the one to respond.

"You need not worry about that. It will happen of its own accord. Much like losing your virginity as an Adamite."

"Spoken like a true elder," said Lazarus, smiling. "Now, shall we move into the dining room for a meal?"

"Yes, please," said Sully, finally breaking his silence. "All this talk has left me starving."

Dad smiled at Sully and slapped him on the back. "Great idea," he said.

Sully choked, fell slightly forward and then made a comical attempt at slapping Dad in return. For a moment, all eyes were on this camaraderie.

Dad looked a bit embarrassed. He shrugged. "War makes strange bedfellows. But before we run off feeding Sully, I got one more question," said Dad. "How is it you can so easily send these Vampires of yours off to meet their Maker?"

Lazarus sighed. "This has been very hard. I have been honest with them all, and they know that the possibility of their demise is very high. However, my army is made up entirely of volunteers."

"Volunteers?" asked Tucker incredulously. "You sure you don't mean mercenaries?"

"No. Julius' army is made up of mercenaries and those who fight for the spoils of war. Most of them have certainly not been told they are fighting against brother Vampires. My soldiers are fully informed of all facets of this situation as well as the strength of the enemy. The truth, my friends, is that the Vampires in my army are fighting for what they believe in, as well as for the chance to feel mortality, something you Adamites take for granted. Eternity can prove to be a very lonely existence. The specter of death, as you call it, holds little fear for my men. In fact, for many of them, I suspect they view it as a long-sought-after companion."

There was a heavy silence in the room. There was little else to say and they moved toward the dining room—all except Lizzie. She took Lazarus by the arm, holding him back. "I'd like to know why you are doing this for me."

"I truly believe that Vampires must maintain their role as the vessels of evil. Containers. Those that consume evil in order to lessen its presence in the world. That was our original purpose as handed down in Genesis."

"You could find some other way. Continue your existence as that repository, fulfilling your philosophies in different ways, ways that would not put yourself and your followers in such danger," Lizzie charged. Lazarus did not respond. "Answer my question, Lazarus," she demanded quietly.

"I have lived an eternity, Elizabeth. And frankly, every century I exist, I become more and more puzzled by the nature of good and evil in this world. Naively, I once thought that, sooner or later, I would have all the answers, all the wisdom of God at my disposal, if only I lived long enough. Much time has passed and the only thing I know for certain is how little I know. But I do know that

I loved your mother, and by extension, I love you. These feelings are the only ones that I have experienced that I know to be wholly real, to exist outside of any philosophical speculation. They are not good, they are not evil, they are the simple essence of my soul. I will do anything in the service of that love."

The room was quiet. Tears streamed down Lizzie's cheeks "Thank you," she whispered, "I am grateful."

"Come," he said, wiping the tears away with his massive hand. "Let's join the others."

LOST IN A PRIVATE world of fury and dream, Julius gazed out the window, watching the lights of the Midwest give way beneath the airplane. That he missed Elita bothered him, but only mildly. What he missed most, he suspected, was merely a sounding board: a visual diversion, a habit much like the whim for a fine cigar or cigarette. He was certainly not experiencing desire for her. Desire was something only felt as part of a quest for power, not as foolish Adamites experience it, through passion and love. Even the word "love" felt strange and distasteful in his thoughts. He took comfort in his knowledge that Adamites are fundamentally impaired in terms of intelligence. They were like children. His dominion over them would certainly relieve them of the pain of their pathetic lives. The thought of this power caused tremors in his body and he experienced something close to ecstasy as he lapsed into the thought, the fantasy, of the force that would course through his veins when he took Elizabeth's blood. Suddenly, he felt faint, his breath came quickly and, with a start, he was reminded again of the instant he had blacked out during Elizabeth's turning.

Julius shook his head fiercely, forcing away the images of her during the turning, replacing them with images of her as she would be soon, legs spread wide, spilling her blood into his waiting mouth. He fiercely pinched the inside of his wrist, squeezing the fragile skin together until it tore. That brought him back quickly enough. He snapped his fingers for the steward.

"A cognac."

"Would you like it warm?"

"Yes," answered Julius, "allow it to flame, but only for an instant."

"Right away, sir," responded the young steward, "anything else?"

"As soon as I have finished the cognac, bring the girl from the back. I shall have her now. And I desire a bit of a struggle, so do not drug her or bind her in any way. Just let her wander the plane for a while. I shall entice her to me."

"Yes, sir, as you wish."

Like a spider, I shall bring the sweet thing into my web, he thought, although he realized the challenge was mostly a facade, given that she was a prostitute and would be expecting some type of aberrant behavior from him. Certainly, even her jaded nature would eventually be surprised when, in the moment of her sexual ecstasy, he drained her blood.

The idea of this pleasure gave him only temporary respite, a conscious diversion, from the darker thoughts plaguing his mind. The inexplicable blackout at the turning and now this faintness distressed him greatly. Thus far, he had thought little of it and, even now, he knew that he could not allow it to interfere with his plans. He smiled at the fact that fat Lazarus would never in a thousand years guess that the first wave of his attack was already assembled and would come during the day, when the sun was at its height. An army of dull-witted but well-armed Adamite mercenaries had been remarkably easy to assemble. With a wave of gold and cash, members from terrorist groups from around the world had willingly signed up. By noon tomorrow, they would surround the desert fortress. By nightfall, he would walk over the bodies of his enemies to reclaim Elizabeth.

The sweetness of victory, however, would be slightly lessened by what he had last seen in Lazarus' eyes. Julius sighed deeply, feeling a tinge of sadness, if it could be called that. That moment of sadness passed quickly, however, as he realized that with nothing to lose, Lazarus would be twice as dangerous.

He had seen that look on others, the look of weariness from living a life of such enormous proportions. When time has no meaning, meaning itself is slowly eroded from life. Those were the ones who walked, finally, into the sun, turning themselves to dust, leaving eternity behind for endless darkness. It was never a problem for those newly turned, but slowly, the Vampires of old, the ones who had attained a high degree of instinctive power, were simply annihilating themselves. It had to be stopped. Where once Julius himself had ruthlessly exterminated some of those older Vampires, those who could have possibly challenged him, now, he saw that wisdom was a desired commodity.

In the end, it was this weariness that Julius was seeking to fight. He wanted to create a purpose, a reason not to desire the sun. He had felt twinges of it himself, but more importantly, he believed it was his duty as sovereign and descendant of Malthus to reenergize the world of Vampires. With the power to turn Adamites, a new chapter in the history of the world and the Vampires would be possible. A new energy to do evil would emerge.

He idly twirled the pendant between his thumb and forefinger, the pendant he had so recently taken from Elizabeth's neck. He held it up to the light to better study it. The metal felt heavier than it should, and hot, as if imbued with some hidden life. There was motion behind him, and he let the pendant fall back into his shirt, coming to rest at the end of the chain like a just-extinguished ember.

The young woman walked down the aisle, curious, in awe of the wealth of her latest trick. She was robust, with tan thighs and an ample bosom. Yes, she would do nicely for the evening, thought Julius. If Elita were here, they could enjoy this kill together as they had so many in the past. Was she dead now? Ah, well, no matter. He smiled serenely at the girl. He was drawn into the rhythm of her breathing flesh, felt the beat of her heart. His mouth began to water.

THIRTY-ONE

LIZZIE AND TUCKER LAY tightly wound in each other's arms. They had pushed the two single beds together to give them more space, but still only used part of one.

"Honey," whispered Tucker, "we need our own plan."

"What do you mean?"

"A fallback. I got a bad feeling about all this. We may end up needing to rely just on ourselves. And Dad. And Lenny when he gets here."

"What do you suggest?"

"The only thing that is keeping us here is the fact that Julius can sense you. There has got to be some way to create a decoy so he thinks you're still here while we sneak out the back door."

"While that may be ideal, I don't think it's possible. Vampiric sensations are quite strong, I'm coming to realize."

"There's got to be something we can do. I'll bet Lenny can come up with..." Lizzie put her hand to Tucker's lips.

"I think we should trust Lazarus' plan. Tucker, we have more important things to talk about."

"Like what? What could be more important than …"

"I think maybe you should leave." Tucker started to speak in protest, but Lizzie held her hand over his mouth. "I mean it this time. It's possible that I'll survive this ordeal, since only a limited number of things can kill me and Julius wants me alive. Neither of those is true for you."

"I ain't leaving you. End of discussion."

She sighed and squeezed his hand. "I didn't really expect anything else. But what about your dad? Is this really the way that you want him to die?"

"No, but I'm guessing I couldn't talk him into leaving either. He's pretty fond of you."

"All right, a compromise. You, your Dad, and Lenny stay with me under whatever arrangements Lazarus makes. I can offer a certain amount of protection, since Julius can't afford to destroy me outright. And you can protect me from attack, should the pain of the process overwhelm me. But promise me, Tucker, no heroics. I want you alive."

Tucker kissed her. "Okay, no heroics. Truth is, I want to stay alive too. I'd like to spend a few decades with you under more normal conditions. I mean, normal as life can be with a Vampire."

Lizzie sat up. The outline of her nude body was silhouetted against the backlight of the moon shining through the curtains. Tucker leaned up and kissed the cleft of her breasts as she stroked the top of his head. "Make love to me, Tucker. I want to feel you inside me before the sun rises. I want your body to be my last sensation before I die."

Tucker pulled her down close to him and their bodies melted into one another.

When Tucker awoke, the new day was well hidden. The special glass in the windows sealed the rays of the sun out tightly, as

349

dark as the inside of a coffin, he guessed. He reached for the lamp by the bed and, under its light, studied Lizzie's pale form with a smile that was half sadness. Rex and Alexandra watched him as he dressed, then padded quietly down to the kitchen with him, where Dad was already sitting with a cup of coffee and an irritable scowl.

"Shit, boy, thought you was aiming on wasting the whole day."

"I was. Wish I'd never woke up."

A matronly cook set a plate of eggs, beans, and corn tortillas in front of him, smiling briefly as he nodded in appreciation. "Thanks, ma'am."

She disappeared as silently as she had come.

"Probably tonight, you know," he said to his father.

Dad nodded and hoisted a black case onto the table. "Ran down to Hoback Junction while you was in New York City." He flipped the case open. A new Casull with an eight-inch barrel lay nestled in protective foam. There were two cases of ammo beside it. "Thought this might come in handy. Didn't have time to give it to you before."

Tucker whistled and pulled the pistol out to admire it. "Damn. It's beautiful."

"Should be. Cost more'n you'll make all year. There's a holster too. That, I made." He pulled it out, a beautifully tooled leather affair with flowers cut into it. "I was kind of bored while you were gone."

Tucker's eyes shone. "I don't know what to say."

"How about thanks?"

"Thanks. Now you eat while I load it up." He filled the chamber and then shoved cartridges into the loops around the waist. Afterward, Tucker stood up and cinched it around his lean waist. It was a perfect fit, hanging low on his hip. He pulled it free with a couple of quick draws and then snugged it home inside the holster.

"Hope I don't have to use it."

"You will."

"Listen, Dad, things are about to get rough. Ain't no way Julius and his gang are gonna rest until they get what they want, or else we put 'em down."

"Tell me something I don't already know."

"I don't want nothing to happen to you."

"I don't want nothing to happen to you, either."

"Shut up and listen. You are too old for this kind of shit." They glared at each other a long minute. "All right, here's the thing. I got you into this mess, and I don't want nothing bad to happen."

"It's my choice."

Tucker nodded. "I know. But I want you to promise me something. I want you to stay with Lizzie, no matter what. If I can't know that she's okay, I can't do nothing. You're the only person I can trust. She's worth everything to me and I want you to guard over her like my life depends on it. 'Cause it does."

"Fair enough. But I don't want you…"

They were interrupted by a commotion outside, and a young, tanned guard burst in. "Your friend is here, Mr. Tucker."

"All right! Reinforcements. Let's go say 'hey' to the boys."

As it turned out, the boys consisted only of Lenny, who was already inside the gate, a pair of massive duffel bags in the dust by his feet. He was eyeing the perimeter defense with unabashed awe.

"Lenny," Tucker called as they ambled out onto the porch, "over here. Glad you could make it."

"Where the hell is the rest of the LonePine militia?" Dad yelled.

"I'm it," he said sheepishly. "You know how militias go. Bob was off to see his kids. Red had too much work to be done, and Frank, well, Frank just wasn't too keen on fighting Vampires."

351

"That's okay. We'll be fine. At least you made it. I'm surprised June let you come."

"She didn't, uh, she said it'd be fine."

"Goddamn it, Lenny, you didn't tell her, did you?"

He nodded absently. "More or less. Are those miniguns? I've never seen these new ones. Can I take a closer look?"

Tucker shook his head and put in a chew. "Whyn't you have one of the boys show you around and then let's talk. We're expecting company tonight."

"I brought some party favors," he said, grinning and nudging one of the duffles with the toe of his military-surplus combat boot.

After his tour, they all sat on the veranda sipping beers with the dogs curled up in the shade. Lenny spread his arsenal out on the planking. "That's a .300 WinMag. Bull barrel, two-ounce set trigger and an 18 x 200-power floating scope. You can damn near read a license plate at over a mile."

"Sounds handy," Dad said. "If I wanted to read license plates."

"It also shoots a 300-grain bullet at close to thirty-five hundred feet per second. I've used it in thousand-yard target shoots and shot three bullets so close together, you could cover the holes with a silver dollar." They whistled appreciatively "Of course, I brought several shotguns modified to shoot wooden ammo, including this little number." He pulled a nasty-looking gun from a shoulder holster. It was a sawed-off double barrel, the stock cut away and wrapped in duct tape to look more like a cheap version of a dueling pistol. The points of the wooden bullets were visible in the shadowy holes. "Plus, I built something special." He pointed at an immense, vaguely gunlike object.

"Looks like a spaceman gun. One of them lasers," Dad said.

"This here is a precision stake shooter. Very accurate. It's an A-10 that I salvaged off a Warthog from Desert Storm. Normally shoots 30-millimeter projectiles really fast at enemy tanks. I convinced it to shoot stakes, 30-millimeter stakes. Accurate to three hundred yards."

"How do you keep 'em from turning into toothpicks?" Dad asked.

"Well that's the beauty of it. I encased the wood with machine-tooled metal jackets so thin and light that they shred away on impact. They're snugged down into the original brass, reloaded with a lighter load. It's beautiful. Just beautiful."

"Lenny," Tucker said, "you are a genius. You been busy since I left."

He nodded. "Figured you'd be needing some help soon."

The noontime heat took its toll as the day dragged on. The three men sat in the shade and contemplated how many beers would be okay without impairing their abilities, come the evening. The Adamite security force sweated silently, patroling the walls and peering out into the shimmering waste. Down below, in the comfort of air conditioning but with nerves frazzled by tension, more humans scanned monitors or else sat rigidly, listening through electronic ears.

Despite the wall of electronic defense, Rex sensed them first. He sat up to sniff at the air, a puzzled look on his face. Alexandra opened an eye to watch him.

"What's wrong with your dog?" Dad asked. "He's acting funny."

"He always acts funny," Tucker replied and pushed at Rex with his boot heel. Instead of lying back down, he whined and looked anxiously toward the gate. Alexandra sprang up, looking back and forth between the shimmering sky and Rex.

"Rex, what the hell's the matter with you?" Dad said.

"Aww, shit," Tucker swore. "They're here."

"They can't be. It's the middle of the day."

"I'm telling you, Rex ain't never wrong. Take cover." He grabbed hold of the dogs and pulled them close as Dad and Lenny looked around bewildered. "Get down, I mean it."

As if in confirmation, the first rocket fell. It looked like nothing more than an errant firework, some lost remnant of the fourth of July drifting lazily over the adobe walls.

"What the ..." Dad started to say but Lenny leaned across the table and took him by the arm, dragging him under.

"Incoming!" he yelled.

The explosion ripped through the courtyard, sending shards of sandstone through the air like a swarm of angry bees. Smoke swirled thick and there were cries of alarm as armed soldiers moved toward the walls. The mounted guns swiveled in unison and began to chatter with an endless roar that rained burning brass in glittering arcs.

"Jesus Christ," Tucker shouted as the hiss of another rocket filled the air.

Lenny scooped up the massive sniper rifle and clambered up the wall, bolting a live round in and scanning the desert. Across the vast expanse, he sighted in on a dusty cloud of rocket vapor and a group of grim-faced men in desert camos. One was already staggering back under the impact of launch. The miniguns locked on to the descending missile and a hail of bullets intercepted it, detonating it harmlessly in front of the walls. Lenny sighted, gently stroked the trigger, and with an echoing blast, sent a bullet racing across the desert. It caught the soldier just above the belt and drove him stumbling backward, the launcher falling to his side. The rest of the group scattered, their faces mirroring disbelief. He racked another round in and drove a shot into the launcher, smiling with tight satisfaction when it jumped sideways from the impact.

Dad crawled up beside him on the wall, lugging the modified stake gun. "Shoot them bastards with this, shoot them with this. They won't stay dead."

"These ain't Vampires. They're human." As if on cue, a contingent of camouflaged men rose up out of the dust and scrub of the desert, their heads swathed in mesh and leaves. They leveled automatic rifles toward the compound and round after round crashed into the walls and skipped off the stones. Two men fell away, mortally wounded. A third cried out and spun away from the wall, clutching his shoulder.

"Shit," Tucker said, joining them, "I don't think Lazarus figured on this."

"When you say Lazarus," Lenny said, calmly, feeding another shell in, "you don't mean the real Lazarus, do you?" He squeezed off another round and another man fell.

"I sure do," Tucker responded, shouldering a Steyr bullpup offered by a frightened young man ducking out of view below them.

"So this guy actually knew Jesus?"

Tucker rattled off a long burst and grimaced at the responding shriek of agony. "Knew him, hell, Jesus raised him from the dead. Made him a Vampire."

"This sure does change things." He pointed at a box of ammo at the table below and Dad handed it up to him.

"You mean the battle plan?"

"Naw. We're fine, long as they don't have any choppers or many more of them missiles. I'm talking about Jesus." A bullet slapped into the edge and he winced, the slivers of stone cutting into his cheek. "The whole thing has always seemed so mysterious, but this guy knew the real thing. No mystery. No faith. Historical fact. Damn, Tucker, the implications are astounding."

Tucker slapped a new clip in and peeked over the wall. "The only implications that astound me are how it's gonna feel to be dead." The mercenaries outside fell back to the cover of some monolithic sandstone columns, just out of range of the miniguns but still well within the range of Lenny, who was casually drilling holes through whoever was stupid enough to reveal themselves. The sun bore down and the minutes dragged by. Tucker slipped away long enough to lead Dad and the dogs to Lizzie's room. Though reluctant to miss out on the action, Dad pulled up a chair, rested a thermite-loaded shotgun across his lap, and held the Casull in one hand. Rex and Alexandra cowered under the bed.

Back on the wall, Lenny was watching the activity through the lens of his scope. "Uh-oh," he murmured.

"What? What?" Tucker demanded anxiously.

"Nothing, just get your head down."

Tucker ducked, but not before seeing the mercenaries spring into view, a pair of them holding rocket launchers. The rest concentrated heavy fire along the wall, pinning the defenders down. "If they launch another in here, we're toast," Tucker said and already the whoosh of a missile cut through the small arms fire. Then another.

But instead of falling into the compound, they exploded forty yards in front of the main gate. Simultaneously, a new sound could be heard. A popping sound. And then electric flashes of intense light. "Jesus Christ," Lenny mumbled. "They've ignited the bouncing betties."

They both peeked over to see that indeed, the explosion had triggered the sensitive mines. Hard rubber balls the size of plums were springing up from the sand and exploding with a sizzle, splashing thermite that with its intense heat fused the sand to glass.

"Crap. They ain't here to kill us. They're just softening us up for tonight."

Tucker nodded grimly. "It's gonna be a long night."

"It won't be long if there ain't no mines left. The Vampires'll be able to walk right up and ring the doorbell like trick-or-treaters."

"I got an idea. There's a tunnel runs from here to some ruins over in those distant hills behind the bad guys. If we can find it, you could take that long rifle and hunker down in the rocks. I bet you could flush 'em out in short order."

"Sounds like a real plan," Lenny said. "Where should we start looking?"

Tucker peeked out across the landscape and tried to imagine the tunnel lying cold and empty below the rocks and cactus. He jumped down and entered the house, Lenny close on his heels, stuffing ammo into the oversized pockets of his cargo pants. They wound their way down into the cool caverns beneath the house and ran from door to door, opening them into various rooms. Some were lined with books, others with pale-faced men watching video screens or else working at keyboards, manipulating the guidance systems of the guns. Other rooms were empty save for the bodies of Vampires, peacefully dead to the onslaught above.

After fifteen minutes of searching, they had yet to find any sort of access. Tucker squatted down to think next to the dark pool of water where Lazarus so recently had soaked.

"Jesus, where the hell could it be?" He scuffed a pebble loose and dropped it in the water, staring at the rings it made.

Lenny was leaning on his gun. "We're running out of time, Tucker."

"I know. I know." He threw another stone savagely into the still water. "Has to be somewhere that's easy to get to, but well hidden. He wouldn't trust Lizzie's only line of escape to something obvious." The empty chamber echoed his frustration as he swore under his breath. "Where the hell would I hide a tunnel?"

Lenny scratched his ear. "Someplace obvious. Someplace you could look right at and still not know." He looked up and Tucker was staring at him.

"Christ, Lenny." He jumped into the water, his boot heels sinking into the sandy bottom. He ducked his head under and felt around the smooth walls. Near the bottom was a hole not two feet across. He came up for a breath and then dove under. It was a tight fit into a narrow tube that horseshoed into a similar pool, this one rough and unfinished. Beyond the edges, lit by a smoky torch, cavern walls reflected slightly in the gleam. Walls, and a blackness. The mouth of a tunnel.

He returned to the other side and when he broke the surface, Lenny was already wrapping the gun in a plastic bag, the contents, Tucker assumed, of one of the many pockets of his combat vest. He clipped a flashlight to his waist and without a word jumped in. He clapped Tucker on the back and disappeared with a splash.

Tucker raced back upstairs, commandeering all the able bodies he could muster. Armed and ready, they squatted out of the line of fire and waited. He imagined Lenny making his way through the tunnel, prayed he was in shape enough to make it fast. Fast indeed. Twenty-one minutes after parting ways, the first shot rang out.

From that distance, the report took several seconds to carry across. He saw a flash of smoke from the distant rocks. Then a man screamed and tumbled prostrate into the open. Only then did the low rumble of the shot reach his ears. From there on, the fighting took a turn for the grim. Trapped between an unseen sniper and a well-armed contingent, Julius' mercenaries struggled to hold their own, and lost. Those who made a break for it were cut down by the men on the walls, and those who sat and prayed were only waiting in line for the next shot. Faced with no choice, they chose the obvious. They surrendered.

Tucker watched through field glasses as one of them waved a white flag. Some thirty of the mercenaries, barely half of those that initiated the assault, slowly walked toward the compound, weapons left behind. Once in range, the laser-guided mounts swiveled noiselessly to cover them, and Tucker stood on top of the wall and shouted.

"Howdy, boys, glad you could make it. Now I want all of you to strip down to your skivvies and then keep your hands up high. You got to know that you're beat. Don't make us slaughter you." The mercenaries obliged, swearing up a storm, and Lazarus' men moved out to usher them inside. Half naked and wholly demoralized, they were herded into a storage facility and locked up tight.

Lenny came up from the basement, dripping wet, cradling the rifle. His eyes were glazed. "This is some nasty business, Tucker. Nasty business."

"I reckon it'll get worse." Tucker eyed the horizon and the sun hanging poised there. "I reckon it'll get a lot worse."

When Lizzie awoke, Tucker was holding her hand and already speaking, but the words were soft and incomplete, barely penetrating the fog of death slowly clearing in her head.

"... baby ... got to wake up ... baby ... wake up ... it's me ..."

"Tucker," she said sleepily. She squeezed his hand, careful not to crush the bones. "I missed you."

"I missed you too, now get up. They already attacked and we are in a bad way."

This time, the words were instantly understood and she sat bolt upright. "Oh my God. He's here?"

"No, worse. He sent some Adamites ahead to—shit, I can't believe I just said that."

"What?"

"Adamites. I said Adamites. They wasn't Adamites. I'm not an Adamite. They were humans. They were not Vampires." He shook his head. "Anyway, we had a pretty rough go of it for a while. Didn't lose many men, but we lost damn near all of our defenses. When Julius shows, the only thing between us and him is the wall."

She was silent, then quickly stood to dress. "That won't be enough. He's close. Confident. We have to run. We can stay far enough ahead until the time has passed." She tugged his aim. "C'mon." He didn't budge. "Tucker, let's go. Get Dad and Lenny. And Elita. Let's go."

Tucker shook his head, his features drawn thin by lack of sleep and accentuated by the shadows. "It's too late for that, Lizzie. If we leave here now, we're goners. Ain't none of us would make it through this except you and then only 'til he was done with you. We're stuck here for the time being."

A moment of panic coursed through her face like a flush but she swallowed deeply and regained herself. "Has Lazarus been told?"

"Dad went to find Sully and him both."

As if on cue, the sounds of frantic activity from below swelled into a commotion as the Vampires burst into their version of life. They could both hear Lazarus, his voice booming over the confusion as he organized the chaos into a last-ditch defense.

Thundering footsteps stopped outside the door. It was Sully and Lazarus, Dad following, winded, behind. Farther still was Elita, her normally calm face showing faint traces of fear as she looked over her shoulder. If this defense failed, she would perish. Julius would never suffer her to live. Old habits die hard and the will to live, taken for granted for close to three thousand years, was deeply entrenched and not something she was in a hurry to break.

Lazarus drew to a stop, his features pinched. "We have little time." He took Tucker's arm briefly. "Again, we owe you a great debt. Without you and your friend, all might have been lost."

Tucker shrugged. "Pretty much everything was lost anyway."

"True, the perimeter defense suffered much. But lives were saved."

"Guess it's better than waking up dead."

"Lazarus," Lizzie said, brushing past Tucker, "we have to leave. I can't put the rest of you at risk."

"Out of the question. We have made our choice. No one is here against their will. We can defeat Julius. You will be safe here. Now you must excuse me." He turned and raced down the hall, followed by a group of Vampires with determined faces.

The ragtag group stood outside and inside Lizzie's room, unsure of what to do next, but sure that doing nothing wouldn't help. Lizzie looked down the hall at Lenny lugging weapons toward them. He offered one to Elita, who curled her lip in scorn, then examined her fingernails as if offering confirmation of her weapon of choice.

Sully was not so proud, taking a shotgun and shoulder bag of ammunition, and slinging it over his shoulder.

Lenny passed the same equipment to Dad, who took it and leaned with his back against the wall just outside the door, making it clear he was on duty again.

The Adamite assault had perilously weakened the defenses and Lazarus now attempted his best to repair them before the final assault. All hands were enlisted to replace and repair the damage until they reached a point where little else could be done except wait. And wait they did. Every pair of eyes cast nervously about. Every pair of ears strained against the silence. Every nerve was drawn taut, but nothing stirred in the desert. No motion. No sound, not even the call of coyotes or nightbirds. Even the wind seemed dead, or at least undead. Hidden away.

Those who had more to lose than just their lives, more to lose than immortality, gathered together in the drawing room to say nothing.

"You okay, darling?" Tucker asked Lizzie.

"No, not so great."

"It is probably the power inside you," Lazarus said.

"It's probably those goddamn cigarettes," Tucker said, nodding his head toward Elita who leaned on the window sill, smoking her exotic cigarettes and staring nervously into the night. She was dressed for war, a leather miniskirt paired with a sleeveless denim blouse and men's combat boots shined to a mirror-like state.

She looked beautiful, which irritated Tucker to no end as he watched Lenny watch her as surreptitiously as possible. He glared over at her. "I don't suppose you'd go outside to smoke those?"

She smiled coolly "I'd love to, but I might just run off. I'm not trustworthy, you know."

"I'm well aware of that."

"Let her be," Lizzie said. "We're all nervous."

"Only thing I'm nervous about is dying from secondhand smoke before the Vampires kill me," Tucker grumbled.

"They aren't going to kill you," Lazarus said. "We are ready for them." His voice lacked conviction, however, and his face showed the strain of two thousand years of living.

"Speaking of that," Lenny said. "Reckon I'll go make another circle." He hefted the odd gun over his shoulder and headed for the door.

"Mind if I tag along?" Dad asked.

Elita took his vacated seat beside Sully, who instinctively shrank away from her. She stubbed out her cigarette and laughed, a sound at once welcome yet strangely out of place in the solemn room. "I can't believe it comes down to this."

"You don't have to be here," Lizzie said quietly.

Elita allowed herself a quick, wry smile. "This is not about you any longer. It's about me. About choices. About mistaken assumptions I've carried around for a thousand years."

"About love?"

A tiny glimmer of a tear appeared at the corner of her eye, surprising them both. "Yes, about love." She looked at Tucker until he was uncomfortable and had to look down, then her eyes turned to Lizzie. "Sometimes you have to live with the truth for a long time before you can accept it. I thought love was a game. Now I see that it isn't."

Lenny climbed up the adobe wall and, resting on his elbows, scanned the desert with infrared goggles. The view blacked out and he ripped them away from his face to see a Vampire, one of Lazarus' men, standing in front of him. "They don't work on us," he said simply. "Unless we have recently fed and then they only reveal faint traces. Try these." He offered an elaborate set of binoculars to Lenny. "These are motion sensitive and amplify ambient light. Much more effective."

The landscape they illuminated was silver and surreal. He panned them slowly across the sand and rock until a tiny comet ripped across the viewfinder, trailed by a streak of blue. He sucked his breath in sharply and tensed, but as the comet slowed, it was only a rabbit. Lenny smiled and slithered back down to the ground inside the wall.

Had he continued to watch, he would have seen the rabbit crouch in sudden fear as a pale hand darted out to snatch it back into deeper shadows.

"Nothing moving," he said to Dad. "Maybe they ain't coming after all," he started to say, but then froze in midsentence. "Shit, I hear something." From inside the house, muffled barks echoed confirmation and already a distinct thrumming filled the air.

"Choppers," Lenny whispered, then shouted a warning. "Choppers. Choppers."

The war machines flew in fast from behind the mountains, running without lights and blacker even than the night so that the blades were barely discernible, their presence made real only by displacement of the stars. "Hit the lights," Lenny shouted and a dome of light burned away the darkness. The air pulsed with the mechanical throbbing and fifty feet overhead, the sinister bellies of the airships gleamed like giant dragonflies. And then, impossibly, it began to rain Vampires.

They threw themselves from the open cargo doors, howling like lunatics. No ropes or parachutes, just freefalling the distance, laughing all the way. They crashed into the sand with an impact that would have finished a mortal, only to pick themselves up and charge headfirst into the stunned defenders.

"Holy shit," Dad whispered to Lenny "If that don't beat all." "Get to Lizzie and Tucker," Lenny said. "I'll cover you."

Already, Lazarus' men had recovered somewhat and the sound of the battle filled the air. Lenny raised up and blasted a wall of stakes in front of Dad who was hightailing it through the courtyard. The high velocity stakes cleared a pathway for him, but more and more Vampires crashed around him. One fell from the sky and landed in his path, instinctively grabbing his ankle. Dad tucked the end of his pistol barrel under the Vampire's chin and blew most of its face away. The creature clutched the ragged remains and moaned, leaving Dad free to sprint for safety, as fast as a seventy-year-old man can sprint.

He joined Tucker, who was on the porch and had a shotgun in each hand, dispatching the invaders as quickly as he could reload. Dad leaned on the railing, winded. "Some vacation this has turned out to be," he wheezed.

"You okay?" Tucker asked.

"Hell no, I ain't okay. It's raining bloodthirsty Vampires and you want to know if I'm okay? Watch out on your left. My only boy is dating the Queen of the undead and you want to know if I'm okay? There's another'n . . ."

"I'd hate for you to get this far only to die from a heart attack."

"Get the hell out of my way, boy. I can still teach you a thing or two." He stomped inside. The dogs made a show of hackles and growls as he entered, but then came with tails drooping to his side, scared and confused. Elita glared savagely at him as he approached Lizzie, who sat pale and quiet on the bed, a stake in her hands.

"Help her," Elita said simply.

"You okay?" Dad asked.

She shook her head slowly. "I don't think I will ever be okay again." She looked at the stake. "I could end this all right now. If I was dead, dead for real, all this would stop."

Dad took the stake from her. "You do that, you'd be dooming a lotta folks to a worse fate. Ol' Julius wouldn't give up. He'd just figure out new ways to do bad things. And do you know what'd happen to my boy if you did that? You'd be killing him too. You'd be killing hope and that's the one thing everybody needs." He looked at Elita. "And I do mean everybody."

Lizzie shook her head, her long hair swaying. "I should be out there."

Elita intervened. "You should be where your chances of survival are greatest. Not only to thwart Julius. There is a nation of my people who have lived for centuries in the shadows. If they ever are to see a new world, it will be up to you." She paused and then added with quiet respect, "Against all odds, you have survived what should have destroyed you."

In the moment of silence that followed, the sounds of battle raged outside. Lizzie peered out the window. "I hope Lazarus knows what he is doing." She looked back at Elita. "It seems I have much to do in the coming eternity, but," she added, "I will need your help."

Elita smiled faintly.

More and more Vampires fell into the battle, despite the almost constant roar of the miniguns and flash of the defenders' rifles. From his place on the wall, Lenny could see some of the invaders break away from the engagement to claw their way into the bunkers and the security devices below. "This ain't going our way," he murmured, laying aside the Warthog and unshouldering an M-203. Sighting in on the closest airship, he sent a 40-mm high explosive round streaking into the underside. The explosion shook the compound. Shards of metal rained down and the other choppers, rattled by the shockwave, wobbled off to set down in the desert outside the circle of lights. Lenny, catching Tucker's eyes across the way, gave him a thumbs up. Tucker returned it jubilantly, but his smile turned to horror as a shadowy figure loomed up over the adobe and pulled Lenny out of sight into the darkness beyond.

"Lenny," he screamed, wading oblivious through the death around him. He reached the wall unharmed and vaulted up onto it, but there was no sign of Lenny, and he screamed in frustration, sweeping up the gun and spinning to shoot stake after stake into the melee below. Abruptly, all the electronic security devices stopped. The miniguns died. The massive lights went out. The heavy gates swung open. The night was lost.

THIRTY-TWO

LENNY NEVER SAW HIS assailant. His eyes had been on Tucker and half blinded from the explosion. Judging from the strength of the arms now clamped around him, it had to be a Vampire that was dragging him over backward.

They landed with a bone-jarring thud and he planted his feet and drove his head up and back, feeling the Vampire's nose give way with a crunch. He was dropped involuntarily, but as he spun around with the rifle in hand, the undead combatant was smiling through this minor pain. He thrust a massive hand out and crushed the barrel as easily as clay, turning it up and away from his chest.

Lenny let it go and darted out toward the temporary safety of the rocks and cactus, praying that no mines were still active. He heard a laugh and then heavy footfalls behind him, closing fast. He fished a Browning Hi-Power out of his gear vest and emptied it behind him without turning to gauge the effects, knowing already the nine-millimeter ammo would be practically useless.

Just for fun, he threw the empty pistol behind him and almost laughed when he heard it strike something solid and elicit a groan of pain. The footsteps drew even closer and, though he was running his fastest, he knew the Vampire was toying with him. At the last second, he dropped into a ball and felt the shins of his pursuer collide with his sides, tripping the Vampire and sending him flailing and stumbling face-first into a large saguaro cactus. There was a howl of pain as the needles sank into undead flesh, but Lenny didn't linger to gloat, he was already loping farther into the rocks and shadows.

In the deep pockets of his combat vest there was a lone thermite grenade. Against a highly mobile target, it was practically useless. There was no way to keep it close to the target without toasting himself. Then his fingers closed around a roll of duct tape and an idea came to him. He unclipped the Vietnam-style tomahawk from his belt and leaped over a rock.

The Vampire was still silent, though enraged. His nose was broken and would take all night to heal. The cactus needles stung like hell. And he was hungry. He was looking forward to feeding on this little man and scented the night wind. The Adamite was close. He leaped over a wind-smoothed boulder, landing softly. His hand streaked out to Lenny's shoulder and he spun him around.

Lenny turned with the impetus, raised the brutally shaped hatchet overhead, and drove the diamond-pointed edge between the Vampire's eyes. The Vampire dropped to his knees, stunned. His glazed eyes refocused in time to watch Lenny pull the pin from the grenade taped firmly to the handle of the hatchet.

"Oh, shit," the Vampire said, clawing at the deadly bundle.

"Yep," Lenny said, diving away and covering his eyes. There was a whoosh of ignition and he turned to see half a body, from the waist down, slowly topple over through a bank of chemical smoke.

Alone and weaponless, save for a knife, he eyed the now-distant compound and the eerie flicker of gun light dying out within. Parallel to him and a little over a mile away, the black helicopters were disgorging a swarm of Vampires that ran screaming toward the now-open gates of the compound.

"Christ," he muttered, "looks like Lawrence of Arabia." He broke into a trot toward the idled choppers.

Amidst the din of the battle, the brief flare out in the darkness was lost to Tucker, who was feeling the first real loss of the combat. A numbness filled him as he imagined living to tell June that it was his fault Lenny was gone. He crouched down in the shadows, the rage now vanished and nothing coming to take its place. He watched the enemy pour through the gate like water from a cup, watched Lazarus, his massive frame clearly visible through the sea of bodies, throw himself into the breach.

In the midst of this undead engine of siege came Julius, the battle reducing him to little more than an animal himself. A violent, powerful animal with a cunning mind, but an animal nevertheless. His hands flashed through flesh and bone, tearing and snapping, and all who crossed him died or else shrank back. All except Lazarus.

Separated by the sea of bodies locked in immortal combat around them, their eyes met. Lazarus, standing like a mountain of retribution in the swirling chaos, saw his most ancient of enemies and began a laborious approach. His eyes burned brightly as he made his way forward, bodies of attackers tossed carelessly away like firewood. Julius snarled and rolled his eyes, redirecting his whirlwind of destruction in a straight line toward Lazarus. Vampires fell under his onslaught like wheat before a scythe, until the two stood face to face, only a dozen yards of casualty-strewn sand separating them.

Lazarus threw himself like a battering ram into his lifelong enemy, his very frame transformed into a weapon. Julius staggered back with a snarl and a look of stunned surprise. Lazarus reared over him and dropped again, like a giant eagle. Again and again the ancient foes struck, clothes shredding and flesh tearing away to reveal bone and muscle. Any mortal would have died a dozen times, but the two kings continued on.

The other fighting died down as all eyes turned to the chaos before them. Elita stood on the porch, her hands bloody from stacking up the dead before her. The savagery painted on her face began to dissolve into awe as she watched Lazarus and Julius. Lizzie walked slowly out to lean on her, her body bowed and a look of exhaustion on her face. Drawn to the sight of her, Tucker raced past the soldiers stilled by the spectacle and regained her side. He took her hand.

"How you doing?"

"Weak."

"If Lazarus takes him, I think it'll be over. Without Julius, the others will leave."

She squeezed his hand.

Lazarus had the upper hand. His weight was wearing on the much smaller Julius, who was on one knee and bracing for the next charge.

"At last," Lazarus bellowed. "After all these centuries, it comes down to this. A simple contest of strength." He drew back and, then threw himself forward, hands outstretched.

"Nothing is ever that simple," Julius hissed, pulling a golden crucifix from inside his tattered clothes. One end had been hammered to a dull point and as Lazarus descended, Julius thrust it up and into his heart.

"No," Lizzie screamed from the porch.

Lazarus staggered back, staring at the holy icon with a morbid curiosity. The night was completely silent as he looked over to the porch. "Ahh, I'm sorry," he whispered to Lizzie. "I failed you. I never thought…"

He pitched face down into the sand, his own weight driving the instrument of death farther in, until it protruded from his back, glistening in the half light.

"How quaint," Julius said as he stood, unconsciously rearranging the shambles of his clothes. "He still believes."

In the silence that followed, Alexandra howled pitifully and threw herself toward her fallen master, but Rex blocked her way and Tucker reached down to grab her collar. A roar broke out from Julius' men, who set upon their foes with redoubled vigor. Julius strolled casually toward the house, his damaged flesh already slowly regenerating.

"Well, wasn't that entertaining? Elita, I trust you are well?"

"Never better," she replied.

"You know, there is something that has been bothering me," he continued. "Maybe you could set me straight. Just whose side are you on? I sent you out to kill Sully and yet I see him cowering in the shadows there. I can't imagine him getting the better of you. So, tell me, whose side are you on?"

"Yours, of course."

He nodded. "Just getting close to the prey, I suppose?"

"Exactly."

"And all this?" He gestured at the bodies around them. "For the sake of show, I suppose?"

"I wasn't sure you could beat him."

"And if I didn't, I guess I can't blame you for wanting the power yourself. How else would you move up the social ladder? Poor little girl, always from the wrong side of the tracks." He smiled at Tucker and Lizzie. "At any rate, I know you well enough to know you are on my side now, since I have won." He motioned and she smiled and moved into his arms. "I did miss your company. You can be so amusing."

"You traitorous little bitch," Tucker hissed, swinging a shotgun up.

"Tucker, no," Lizzie said, stopping the arc with the palm of her hand.

"Yes, wait," Julius agreed. "Perhaps you could kill both of us, but I rather doubt it. The potential of the uncreation is racing through my blood. But even if you did, my men have strict orders." He pointed at the multitude of faces gathered beyond the house. "If I die, so will you, your father, Sully, the dog..." he paused when he noticed Alexandra, "dogs, I should say. And," he added dramatically, "Elizabeth, who as an immortal, can endure the rigors of rape and torture for a very, very long time." He smiled magnanimously. "I have given you a great deal of time to play out your little games and now they have come to an end. I have won. The power will be mine and your lives are forfeit. All that remains are the details of your dying."

He kissed Elita lightly on the cheek. "I rather fancy the feel of world dominion."

His gloating was interrupted as the first of a chain of explosions rocked the distant choppers, each one igniting the one next to it. The firestorm lit up their faces and dazzled their eyes, and as Julius turned his head in annoyance, Elita twined her fingers through his hair and jerked his head back savagely. "Run," she screamed, and then plunged her nails deep into his exposed throat. Julius pitched backward with a shout, dragging them both into the crowd of surprised Vampires that closed around them like a curtain.

Tucker seized Lizzie by the arm and dragged her inside, with Dad and Sully close behind and bolted the iron door in place.

"We have to help her," Lizzie cried, pulling her arm free.

"Too late," Sully said, grabbing her by the waist and scooting her forward. "If we linger, her heroism is in vain."

Already the door was echoing the sounds of forced entry and a clamor of voices could be heard outside.

Through the house they fled, down the stairs and into the chambers below. Past the bodies of the dead and dying, past the occasional live representative of the undead still lingering in the shadows.

Tucker steered them through the maze of corridors and burst breathless into the darkened garden where the pool shimmered faintly. "Through here."

"Through where?" Lizzie asked.

"The water. It leads to the tunnel." He helped her jump in and then handed a reluctant Alexandra to her. They disappeared and Sully climbed in next. Rex watched the whole thing with bewilderment and balked when Tucker reached for him. "You have to go, you idiot dog. Want I should leave you here with the Vampires?"

Rex didn't answer or move, so Tucker motioned Sully through. "You're next, old man."

"This is a good set of clothes, Tucker."

"Get in." He pushed Dad, who fell sputtering into the pool. "Take Rex."

"Come on, you dumb mutt," Dad called, but Rex backed away and eyed them like they were crazy.

"He never did much like water. Go on, I'll drag him through."

Dad disappeared and Tucker grabbed Rex by the collar and dragged him to the edge of the pool. He climbed in and his grip loosened. Rex darted out of reach and sat down, trembling. Tucker stood chest-deep in the water and shook his head. "What the hell are you doing?" He pulled a pair of grenades out of his pocket and laid them on the edge. "See these. I'm gonna pull the pins and take off and so help me God, if you're still sitting there, you're gonna get blowed up." He waited, but Rex sat motionless. "I don't need this. There's plenty of other shit going on, and I shouldn't have to be talking to you like a little kid. Now come on." Rex didn't budge. "I ain't joking. Once I pull these pins you got ten seconds to make up your mind."

Rex lay down and put his head on his paws.

"Aww, for Chrissakes, Rex," Tucker said as he crawled out, dripping water. There was a roar outside, and the thunder of footsteps.

With a yelp, Rex shot past Tucker and made a mighty leap into the water, disappearing. Tucker pulled the pins from the grenades, tossed them toward the entrance, and dove into the churning water.

SANTA FE, NEW MEXICO

OCTOBER 30, 11:22 P.M.

JULIUS STOOD IN THE rubble of the hallway, scattered fires burning around him. He massaged the side of his neck, which was savaged and raw.

Elita's attack had left him drained to the point that he could not, as yet, sense Elizabeth's whereabouts. He knew they had retreated deep into the caverns and had destroyed the entrance to this particular cave. Were they waiting breathlessly on the other side, he wondered, or was there another means of escape?

He reached out with his mind, felt nothing of Elizabeth. Instead, he felt a weakness, and crouched down disoriented. There was something else. Voices.

He heard the voices for the first time. Faint, but there nonetheless. They were laughing. Mocking him.

He pressed a knuckle to his temple and fought against the ache blossoming there. The ache and the voices.

And the whisper of insanity.

He must find her. He would find her.

THIRTY-THREE

THE FLIGHT DOWN THE tunnel was harrowing and dark. Dad, claiming his heart was failing, brought up the rear just in case the explosion had failed to plug the hole. Tucker argued but was overruled, and he, Lizzie, and Sully followed the dogs through the darkness.

"Like being in the catacombs again," Tucker grumbled, straining to make his way as they ran. Alexandra had obviously made the trip a number of times and loped ahead, only to turn back to encourage them on, circling through the survivors in search of her master, then running forward again.

Tucker caught up to Lizzie and pulled her to a stop. "Listen," he panted, "don't you need a rest?"

She shook her head, watching nervously behind. "No, I'm fine."

"Are you sure?"

"Positive. I was exhausted earlier, a little sick, but I'm fine now."

"Really?"

"Really. C'mon, I think I see the end."

He bent over and sucked air deep into his lungs, pushing Rex out of his face. "Maybe you just don't feel tired, even though inside you are and need a little rest."

"Okay, fine," she said, understanding at last. "We'll rest."

"If you really need to. But just for a minute," he wheezed.

"Somebody's coming," Sully snarled. The conflict had peeled back the effeminate mannerisms he had crafted over the last several hundred years so that all that remained was the essence of a survivor.

They swiveled their heads in unison to see a dark, misshapen figure carrying a sputtering torch making its way toward them. The tattered shadow was moaning and cursing and Tucker whistled a sigh of relief. "Just Dad. What the hell are you carrying on about?"

"My damn underwear's wet and I got sand in it."

"No sign of anyone?"

"Not yet."

"Good, 'cause we're almost out of here. Smell that?"

A cool breeze was drifting among them, rich with the smell of juniper and pine. In a matter of minutes, they came to the end, a rough-hewn square cut into the sandstone above and a splintered ladder leading to it. Tucker crawled up first, hand over hand, into the night air to see that it was safe. He found himself in the ruins of an ancient pueblo high up in the canyon, the one he had explored just a few days earlier. From this ledge, he could see the trees and hear the faint muddle of the spring down below.

"All clear," he whispered. "Come on up."

Lizzie was halfway there already and stretched her hand through. Her strength was ebbing quickly, due, she feared, to a lack of blood. Tucker helped her through and let her lean on him as he sat her down against the wall. Dad struggled up next and then Sully leaped up in a bound.

"I gotta get the dogs. Be right back." Tucker disappeared momentarily then struggled up with Alexandra. Sully lifted her from his arms and waited as he returned for Rex. Rex fought off his attempted assistance so that Tucker had to crawl up with the greatest of difficulty to deposit his dog unceremoniously on the hard floor.

Standing at the window Tucker could see over the edge of the canyon and all the way to the compound and beyond. In between, the wreckage of the helicopters still guttered and smoked. He kicked at the spent cartridges littering the floor and smiled. "These were Lenny's," he said to no one in particular.

"Hope he's all right," Dad said.

"He's the one who set those whirly-birds alight. He must be okay."

Lizzie regarded the ruined compound, the activity still visible there. "So many lives lost, all for me."

"The alternative ain't so great. And I don't mean just for me. I mean for the whole world," said Tucker.

"He's right, honey," Sully said as he came to take her hand. "It has to end here. If Julius becomes keeper of the uncreation, I shudder to think what will happen next."

"Lazarus certainly believed so," Lizzie said.

"If memory serves, Lazarus wasn't all too keen on getting resurrected. Maybe this turned out to be sort of a blessing."

"It's nice to think something good came from his death."

"Now you have to take his place," Sully said.

Lizzie was incredulous. "Don't be ridiculous."

"Yes," Julius said, stepping from the shadows of a ruined anteroom. "Don't be ridiculous, Sully," he said, his spirits high. "No one could ever replace me."

Sully responded first, his near-animal-like reflexes driving him into a defensive crouch and then hurling himself at Julius faster than the human eye could follow. Even faster, Julius caught him with his fists in midair and threw him, like Satan from heaven, out the window and into the open space of the canyon. Sully disappeared with a scream, a rattle of stones, and a distant thud.

"Son of a bitch," Dad grimaced, drawing his pistol. Julius swatted it away with a casual gesture that broke the bones of his gun hand like Styrofoam. Dad howled in pain and Julius drove a stiffened finger through the flesh of his chest, the force of it driving Dad back into the wall where he slid down with a groan.

"Dad, goddammit," Tucker screamed. He fired the shotgun from his hip, both barrels discharging simultaneously with a deafening roar. The wooden stakes streaked out, but Julius stepped to the side like a ghost, snatching one from the air. He twirled it around his fingertips with a flourish, then balanced it in his palm.

"Goodness," he said to Lizzie, "simply being near you makes me feel a thousand years younger."

He hurled the wooden missile and it plunged deep into Tucker's shoulder. His mouth dropped open as the shock grabbed him, collapsing beside Dad, who drew him close and pressed his good hand over the wound, the butt end of the stake poking out from between his bloody fingers.

"Tell you what," Julius said, seizing Lizzie around the waist, "let's leave the boys alone for a while. We've got some catching up to do… daughter." He leaped out the window, holding her tight, and sprang out of sight, dropping into the ruins below.

In the quiet left in their absence, Dad pulled Tucker closer to his shoulder. "This is bad, isn't it?" he said, his face pale from the pain. "Real bad."

"At least he hasn't killed us."

379

"Yet."

He pulled Tucker's hand aside to examine the wound. "Hurt?"

"Yep," he grimaced.

"Reckon you'll pass out?"

"If I do, how'm I gonna save Lizzie?"

"I don't know. Got any ideas?"

"Naw. How 'bout you?"

"Yeah. I should've stayed home," he said, cradling his broken wrist.

Tucker straightened his legs. His voice was strained. "Too late for that."

Dad nodded. "S'pose Sully's dead?"

"No more'n usual."

He regarded the stake for a moment. "Think we should pull that out?"

"I'd probably bleed to death."

"We gotta do something 'sides just sit here."

"Even healthy, the two of us, we ain't much of a match for super-Vamp."

Rex crawled up to lick cautiously at Tucker's bloody hand. Tucker pushed him away absently. "And you sure weren't much help, you idiot dog. I shoulda got a cat."

Dad petted Rex on the head. "Wasn't nothing he could do."

"He could've bit him."

"Hell, we couldn't even shoot him."

"Whose side you on?"

"Lizzie's."

At that, Tucker sighed. "I best get down there." He stood unsteadily and Dad pulled himself up alongside. Leaning together, they made for the front ladder.

"You hear something?"

"Just the wind."

"I must be losing my mind," Tucker said. "I could have swore I heard voices."

———

Lizzie leaned on her hands and knees, her hair hanging down almost to the floor of the moon-drenched pueblo several levels below where the battle had taken place. The roof was long ago claimed by the wind and weather, and the night sky served as a backdrop for Julius, who paced around her in a frenetic circle.

"So, tonight it ends. And here, of all places. Most amusing." He stopped in midstride to gaze blankly at the walls. "If all these centuries have taught me anything it's that fate does indeed control our lives, more so than most can imagine."

His pacing continued. "Many, many years ago, I had a young lady, also of the blood, and through her I had hoped to gain the power of the uncreation. I might have if Lazarus had not interfered. To make a long story short, he killed his own daughter." His face was manic and twisted. "The guilt destroyed him. He has grieved ever since. Came to this desolate place and never left."

He gestured at the pictographs. "His arrival so terrified the natives, they left their homes and farms by the thousands. One of the 'mysteries' that has bothered your historians ever since. And now we are at the crossroads again, and this time, in his backyard. Pity you're not his real daughter."

"He was a good Vampire," she said, brushing her hair back and rocking back onto her heels, "a good man."

"He was weak. Pathetic. He should have long ago killed you, when you were just a baby."

She shook her head, jaw set in grim determination. "He did what he had to do."

"As did I. Including the rape of your silly little mother. If it had not been for Lazarus' continual interference, I would have killed her at your birth and raised you myself. Just think, Elita and I would have been Mummy and Daddy to you." Julius laughed then bowed deeply. He saw that her eyes had narrowed. "Ah, yes, your traitorous little friend Elita. No doubt she is exterminated by now. I gave her to my men, as an after-work cocktail, so to speak. When they are done, she is to be staked for the sunrise. I shall feed on her after I drain the life-blood from your cowboy and his father." He snapped his fingers. "Wait, wait. Perhaps I shall turn them as well, so I can make the killing last that much longer. I will be omnipotent."

"You will have no power to turn a human. I will not give you my blood," Lizzie said.

"I will take it."

"If it doesn't come tonight?"

He stroked his chin in mock thoughtfulness. "Now that would be problematic. I suppose the timetables are somewhat nebulous for this sort of thing... I've got it! Perhaps a vigorous fuck would coax it out." He paused for effect and leered.

He swooped close and clamped her chin in his palm, wrenching her head sharply up to meet his gaze. "I have had a hundred daughters in my life. Let me be the first to tell you, after the first dozen, the charm wears off. They look the same, feel the same, fuck the same, bleed the same as any other woman I happen to need. Do not for a second imagine I harbor any shred of paternal devotion toward you."

With a shriek, she lunged to her feet, tearing herself free from his grasp. "The only thing I can't imagine is why my mother ever let you touch her."

His eyes flared briefly, a mixture of amusement and surprise. "Because she was weak. Like you." He smiled mockingly. "I can't even remember her name."

Lizzie exploded into him with a roar, her balled fists striking him in the chest and driving him back into the stone wall with such force the mountain shook. His mouth hung open as he struggled to regain his balance.

"Her name was Constance, asshole." She lashed out again, the force of her rage fracturing the bones of his cheek.

"You little bitch," he roared, throwing her off and across the narrow confines. She struck the wall and like a rubber ball, bounced back into him. He folded over, then twisted out of reach, striking a blow as he did. He stared at her, both of them breathing hard. "You have become powerful."

Grimly, she nodded.

"The time is close at hand. Give me what I want and you live, you and your cowboy. I offer my protection. In the coming age of chaos, you will be spared."

She wiped a trickle of blood from the corner of her mouth with the back of her hand. "I don't think so. I think it ends here. And I think you're scared."

He smiled. "I think you are so very, very young and quite ignorant. You cannot defeat me." He moved closer toward Lizzie, backing her into a dark corner of the pueblo ruins.

———

Tucker and Dad were letting themselves down the face of the cliff ruins slowly and methodically, hand over hand. The dogs watched them from above, whining and barking and then disappearing from view, only to return and stare longingly down. The going was torturous and the two men paused at the next level.

"It's gonna be light soon," Dad said.

Tucker was staring out into the desert, his eyes glazed with pain.

After a few more seconds and no answer, Dad said again, "Gonna be light soon."

Still no answer and he shook Tucker by the shoulder. "You okay, boy?"

Tucker started to laugh, deep heartfelt laughter that shook his frame and seemed so foreign originating from that source of pain and exhaustion.

"Tucker, you gone delirious?"

———

All those many weeks of trauma and loss now spilled out of Lizzie as they fought like no other beings from the hand of God had ever fought. Her rage influenced gravity itself, releasing its rules so that she floated here and there, always just out of reach. Julius was striking madly, rarely hitting her at all, while she inflicted tremendous damage on him.

"No," he screamed, "I deserve the power."

Her attack slackened and she settled to the ground, her body heaving from the exertion. "You deserve exactly what fate has given you, an empty existence." The adrenaline began to wane and a familiar nausea returned and with it, a weakness. Her body sagged and Julius sensed it.

His face twisted into a ferocious grin that glittered like a scimitar in the half light. Lizzie paled and backed into the wall.

"All this fun must have worn you out." He approached with difficulty. "Enough talk. Enough sermons. Enough life. Time for you to give your blood to me. All of it." He tore a rotten rung from an ancient ladder, crumbling the end into a dull point he tested

384

against his fingertip. "Crude, but it will do." He moved toward her, the stake raised.

Exhaustion gripped her muscles, but she fought it and leaped over him toward the open roof. Julius flung the weathered stake like a javelin and it soared straight toward her back.

There was a roar and a flash and the stake shattered in mid-flight, the splinters raining down around Julius. He spun in anger and in the doorway, he saw Tucker leaning on Dad for support, his Casull smoking in his hand.

"Nice shot," Dad said.

"Will you never go away?" Julius ranted, his eyes wild.

"I like to see a job through," Tucker said weakly.

"This time, I promise, you will." He lunged toward them in a near-blind rage.

"Tucker," Lizzie shouted, jumping in between them.

"Careful, darling," Tucker whispered, shakily hoisting the pistol up in an attempt to back Julius down. "A woman in your condition ought not to be jumping around so."

"What condition might that be, doomed cowboy?" Julius snarled, already imagining Tucker's sunburned throat under his hands.

"Pregnant," Tucker answered.

The word hit the air like the crack of a whip, freezing Julius a step away from the two men and Lizzie a half step behind him. The night loomed over them in silence. In the distance, the barking of the dogs carried down on soft winds. Lizzie's eyes flared.

"What?"

"You're pregnant."

"Pregnant?"

"Yeah. We're pregnant. That night in the barn, I reckon, or down in the catacombs. All this last two weeks, you've been feeling peaked, kind of nauseous, must have been morning sickness … or in your case, night sickness. And you been hungry all the time, and more'n a little cranky."

She brushed past a now-frozen Julius as if he no longer existed and took Tucker by the arm. "How could you know this?"

"That's the crazy part. Them voices told me. All of a sudden they just filled my head up and told me."

"Impossible. It is biologically impossible for an Adamite to procreate with a Vampire," Julius snapped, trying to remaster the situation. "This is ridiculous, a ploy to stall for time." He glanced out the window at the light beginning to emerge from the east. "Even dawn will not save you."

"I ain't bluffing. Use them fancy Vampire senses of yours to listen."

Julius bent his head in concentration and reached out with his mind. The voices flashed through his thoughts, the mocking laughter deafening. *A child will be born, a child will be born,*" they chanted and he covered his ears with his hands as if that might block it out. He dropped to his knees, screaming in anguish at what had come to pass.

Lizzie closed her eyes and traveled far inside herself, also in search of the voices, but what she found instead was a tiny heartbeat, muffled but steady, and for an instant she was turned inside out and the heartbeat was her own in the womb of the universe. Suns rose and set and flared throughout her as the tiny heart drove the whole vast mechanism along. In less than a second, a second that stretched from the beginning of time to the end and doubled back along the way, she too, knew the truth. There was life inside her, life that bridged the world of the living and the world of the undead. The power of the uncreation had found a vessel. It was contained in a holy grail forged of flesh and eternal love, and radiant joy spilled from her.

"You're right," she whispered to Tucker, who smiled through his pain.

"Idiots," Julius raved. "Idiot couplings of idiots to beget idiots. A chance fuck between idiots is not going to thwart my plans. "He drove his fist into his palm. "I will kill you all for the sheer pleasure of it." Foam flecked his lips and sprayed the air. "I don't care anymore. I can wait. I've waited all this time, another seven hundred years is nothing to me." He took a menacing step forward, eyes glittering and outstretched hands trembling with murderous passion.

"I guess you don't understand love very well," Lizzie said.

He spun, snarling. "Love is just a word. It isn't real. Death is real. Power is real."

Tucker cocked the pistol and Dad helped steady his aim. "Hate to disappoint you, but my boy ain't growing up without a dad."

"How do you know it's a boy?" Lizzie asked.

"I just know it is."

"I think it's a girl," she countered.

"A girl would be fine."

"If it is, I hope she don't look nothing like you," Dad said.

Julius snarled. "Shut up, all of you. None of you will live past the sunrise."

"I hear congratulations are in order," Lenny said as he hoisted himself into the room. He was tattered and bloody, and most of his hair was scorched away, but he looked very much alive, a shiny assault rifle cradled in his aims. "Never thought I'd see the day, Tucker."

"Me either," Tucker assented.

Julius backed a step away, his odds suddenly decreasing. "Your guns cannot kill me."

387

"Naw, but they can slow you down a bit."

"I could kill you," Elita said, dropping down to the sand behind him.

"Elita," Lizzie said incredulously, "how…"

She sniffed disdainfully. "Men are pretty much the same, no matter how long they have lived. All blinded by their desires. Not much of a challenge really." She pulled a cigarette from the tatters of her clothes and scratched a match to life.

"You ain't really going to smoke that around Lizzie, are you? She's pregnant, you know," said Tucker.

"Sorry, bad habit."

"You'd better get over it if you plan on being my boy's god-mother."

She smiled in spite of herself and stubbed the cigarette out. "Girl," she said under her breath.

Julius sneered, his rage barely contained. "None of you shall live. The only question is who I shall start with?"

"Start with me," Lizzie said. Her eyes burned with a terrible certainty. She left Elita by the wall and stood before him.

"Gladly," he said.

As he took a step forward, she found the light and reached inside his mind. Confused, he stepped away. The force of her will battered into his thoughts and his power, his vitality, siphoned away. He staggered. "No, impossible." Her thoughts surrounded him, hammered at his soul.

"I could turn you off like a light switch," she whispered. "Love is not a word. Love is growing inside me, and you couldn't stop it now if you tried."

Julius spun away and pushed past Tucker. "I've never been a gracious loser," he said. "I will be back. Your offspring will be mine, as will the uncreation. You cannot hide. And I dare say, many of

388

you will not be alive to witness it." He sprang through the open roof and was gone, his sinister laughter echoing behind him.

"Reckon we should have tried stopping him," Dad said directly.

"I was out of ammo," Lenny said, sitting down. "And I can't see clearly just yet. Got too close to the explosions."

Elita slid down the wall and hugged her knees. "Truth be known, there's not much fight left in me. If not for Lizzie, he would have killed us all."

"Probably," Tucker said. "I'm just glad he's gone." He looked around at the tiny hint of pink on the distant horizon. "Y'all better find some shade, gonna be morning soon." Tucker took Lizzie by the hand and gave it a squeeze. "A father," he said, shaking his head slowly. "Funny how things work out sometimes."

She smiled. "Sure is."

"I don't want to raise my boy in New York City."

"It's our girl, and I agree." She stared out at the lightening day.

"Ain't no room at my place for all of you," Dad said.

"What's poor Rex gonna think?" Tucker asked. Lizzie and Tucker looked quietly at each other and then he let go of her hand. "You ain't quite finished, are you?"

"How much time before the sun comes up?"

He looked at Lenny's wristwatch. "About an hour."

"He threatened our child."

"I know."

"I think I'm ready for my first kill."

His mouth dropped open. "But, honey, you ain't got time."

"It won't take long. I can sense him. I can sense everything." She looked at Elita who was closely following their conversation. "Do I have your blessing?"

"I will not mourn for him," said Elita, "if that's what you mean."

389

Before the words had time to settle in the air, Lizzie was gone. Moments later, a cry reverberated through the canyon. They all held their breath as it echoed, then slowly was lost to the wind that always seems to accompany first light.

EPILOGUE

"Being a father, now that's hard work," Dad said, adjusting the impromptu sling that kept his broken wrist immobilized. He and Tucker were walking through the remains of the compound, Rex and Alexandra close behind, as the sun struggled up over the horizon.

"You did a pretty good job of it."

"That's 'cause your mother made sure of it."

"How d'you think I'll do?"

"I always figured you'd be real good at it. Plus, you got a good woman to help you along."

The ground was covered with spent cartridges and a layer of ash that swirled around their feet as they walked. The ash was all that remained of those who had died the night before. The occasional limb sheltered by the shade they kicked out into the pale sunlight where it quickly dissolved. In the center of the courtyard, the crucifix that had felled Lazarus lay gleaming. Tucker picked it up and shined it on the bandages around his shoulder. The motion, since it pained him, was slow and deliberate.

"Ain't much left of him and his dreams."

"That ain't true. There's you and Lizzie. And your kid. That's enough."

"Hard to believe something good can come from all this."

"At least you got the girl."

They sat down on the steps. "Wouldn't have if it hadn't been for you."

"Glad I could help. It's just a real good thing Lenny showed up." Dad scuffed his heel in the sand. "Where is he?"

"Calling June, I imagine."

"And Sully?"

"He made it back just a little bit ago. He's in his coffin, sleeping like a baby now that Julius is gone."

"He's for sure gone?"

Tucker nodded, remembering Lizzie's half-crazed look when she had returned, her mother's pendant clutched in her hand and blood smeared down her chin.

They were silent for a while, listening to the wind.

"Love sure is a funny business," Tucker said at last. "Reckon I'm gonna head back in, check on Lizzie." He stood up. "Comin'?"

"Directly," Dad said. "The sun feels nice on my face."

"Well, c'mon, Rex." Rex watched curiously as Tucker stood and started off. He made it halfway across the courtyard, the ash drifting around his boots and already disappearing into the desert. Abruptly, Tucker turned and rejoined Dad on the steps. Rex pushed his head into his lap and Tucker petted him, smoothing his fur down.

"Maybe I will sit a spell. I always did like the sunrise," he said.

THE END

ABOUT THE AUTHORS

Clark Hays was raised on a ranch in Montana and spent his formative years branding cows, riding horses, and writing. A graduate of Montana State University, his poetry, creative fiction, and nonfiction have appeared in many journals, magazines, and newspapers. Most recently, he was nominated for a Pushcart Prize for a short story appearing in *Opium* magazine.

Kathleen McFall was born and raised in the heart of Washington, D.C. She has a master's in filmmaking from The American University and a bachelor's in geology from George Washington University. She has worked as a journalist and has published hundreds of articles about natural resources, environmental issues, energy, and health care. Previously, she was awarded a fellowship for fiction writing from Oregon Literary Arts.

WWW.MIDNIGHTINKBOOKS.COM

From the gritty streets of New York City to sacred tombs in the Middle East, it's always midnight somewhere. Join us online at any hour for fresh new voices in mystery fiction.

At midnightinkbooks.com you'll also find our author blog, new and upcoming books, events, book club questions, excerpts, mystery resources, and more.

MIDNIGHT INK ORDERING INFORMATION

 ### Order Online:
- Visit our website www.midnightinkbooks.com, select your books, and order them on our secure server.

 ### Order by Phone:
- Call toll-free within the U.S. and Canada at
  1-888-NITE-INK (1-888-648-3465)
- We accept VISA, MasterCard, and American Express

 ### Order by Mail:
Send the full price of your order (MN residents add 6.785% sales tax) in U.S. funds, plus postage & handling to:

> Midnight Ink
> 2143 Wooddale Drive
> Woodbury, MN 55125-2989

Postage & Handling:

Standard (U.S. & Canada). If your order is:
> $24.99 and under, add $4.00
> $25.00 and over, FREE STANDARD SHIPPING

AK, HI, PR: $16.00 for one book plus $2.00 for each additional book.

International Orders (airmail only):
> $16.00 for one book plus $3.00 for each additional book

Orders are processed within 12 business days. Please allow for normal shipping time.
Postage and handling rates subject to change.